FIONA MCINTOSH

and

THE VALISAR TRILOGY

"McIntosh is an imaginative world-builder, writing
fant...
careful...

Publishers Weekly

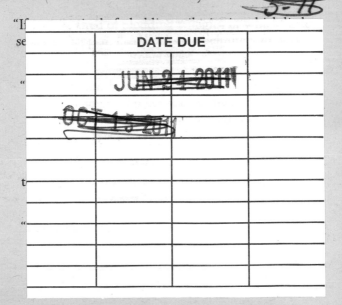

"If ... f ... holding ... is ... h ... li ...
se...

"...

	DATE DUE		
	JUN 2 1 2011		
	OCT 15 20		
t			
"			

By Fiona McIntosh

The Valisar Trilogy

ROYAL EXILE
TYRANT'S BLOOD
KING'S WRATH

The Percheron Saga

ODALISQUE
EMISSARY
GODDESS

The Quickening

MYRREN'S GIFT
BLOOD AND MEMORY
BRIDGE OF SOULS

FIONA McINTOSH

KING'S WRATH

BOOK THREE OF THE VALISAR TRILOGY

An Imprint of HarperCollinsPublishers

This book was originally published in 2010 by Voyager, an Imprint of HarperCollins Australia.

EOS
An Imprint of HarperCollins*Publishers*
10 East 53rd Street
New York, New York 10022-5299

First Eos paperback printing: December 2010

HarperCollins® and Eos® are registered trademarks of Harper-Collins Publishers.

Printed in the U.S.A.

10 9 8 7 6 5 4 3 2 1

We miss you Kipper,
our most loyal four-footed friend

Acknowledgments

➤➤━━━━━━━━━━━━━━━━━━━━━━━━━━━━━━━━━━━━◄◄

Many of you have come to know my curious style of writing to no plan and I must admit to setting out on each new novel's journey with no story in mind, a lot of optimism but also a feeling of terror. This novel rounds off a dozen adult fantasy novels, so while I assure myself not to panic—because I've done it before and my strange writing approach seems to work for me—there is always anxiety that it may not work this time! And this fear has never been greater than it was for Wrath because I had absolutely no idea where this tale was headed and as it unfolded I was regularly surprised by events, and especially at who ultimately became the villain. It was great fun to write, discovering all the twists and turns of the story, and I do hope you enjoy it.

Much of the energy for this final volume came from readers around the world—urging me to hurry and give them book three. Thank you all for your loyalty and your incredible interest in the series. My thanks to the HarperCollins team, especially the often unheralded sales force who work so hard at the coalface, but special thanks to my editor on this series, Kate Nintzel in the U.S.; to her colleague Emma Coode in Britain who, together with her team, gave us the fabulous artwork for the covers; and, of course, to Stephanie Smith in Australia for her wonderful support, supervisory commitment to this and all my series, and her constant nurturing.

I cannot end my thanks without a nod to the fantasy booksellers of the world. I am getting to meet so many of you now through my travels and you are so similar, no matter which country you hail from. You are generous, committed to the genre, great readers and your brilliant handselling is often not factored into the success of fantasy globally.

As always, I'm grateful to my loving family and friends for their encouragement and to Pip Klimentou, Marianne D'Arrigo, Sonya Caddy, Margo Burns, Michelle King, Willa Michelmore and Angela Bonnin for the Friday lattes, as well as to Mandy Macky, Judy Downs, Steve Hubbard, Phil Reed and Tony Berry.

Thanks Will and Jack, for understanding why I need quiet time . . . oh, and by the way, the recycling has to go out, the dishwasher needs emptying and your rooms need tidying! xx

Ian—always last but never least. Love and thanks. Fx

Prologue

> ⇥————————————————————————⇤

They fell swiftly, silently.

Any moment they would hit the ground and it would be over. She didn't know why he had chosen to kill her; she was his only friend. How bizarre then that she had never felt safer, even though death surely beckoned. She knew the drug had dulled her senses but she thought she heard air rushing by in a strange shrieking. And she could feel Reg's presence: the hardness of his body against hers, his long, strong arms holding her securely. Despite the disorientation, she felt wholly connected to him—down to the soft scratch of his beard against her skin.

Maybe this was right. They were lost souls anyway, neither of them able to get on easily with others. And her work at the hospital drew the wrong sort of interest; people had begun hailing her as having powers above and beyond genuine skill and talent. It was ridiculous, of course, but it was understandable given her uncanny knack for healing.

A healer. That's how she viewed herself. She was a curer of ills; she'd never said it out loud but it seemed Reg alone had understood it . . . and understood her.

And because of that she couldn't hate him for killing them both. Without him her life would be empty. Without his friendship, like a rock jutting out of the ocean that she could cling to, she would be adrift in a sea of meaningless comings and goings—even her work would feel empty, pointless.

Why was it taking so long for them to hit the ground?

What was that screaming noise, as though the very air was being torn apart around them?

Had she just heard Reg say something? Maybe *here we go, Evie*? She felt him hold her tighter still, if that were possible, tucking her head into the warmth of his neck, shielding her face from the whistle and buffet of that wind they were rushing through.

And then suddenly they were tumbling on something solid. Her fall was cushioned though; first her legs, then her back and shoulders touched inanimate objects. She had no idea what but it didn't hurt. How did that happen? She wanted to open her eyes but they were squeezed shut with fear. It sounded as though branches were snapping! *Trees? . . . How could that be?*

With no warning the breath was sucked out of her as Genevieve, the first princess of the Valisars to survive in centuries, blacked out.

And across the empire, various people felt the stirrings of a mighty magic they had never felt before.

One

Though the two men walked side by side they looked anything but companionable.

"Did you feel it?" the younger one asked.

Greven didn't want to admit it but there was no point in hiding much from Piven these days. While his mind was essentially his own, his actions were not. It didn't matter how hard he fought the bonding magic, it had him completely at its mercy. "I felt it," he said, gruff and disinterested.

"And what do you think it is?"

"Why are you concerning yourself with what I think? I just do as I'm told."

"Is this how it's going to be from now on, Greven?"

"What did you expect?"

Piven made a soft scolding sound, clicking his tongue. "And I can remember not so long ago your telling me just how much you loved me and wanted to protect me."

"I did. But my love was given freely then. And I had two hands then. And I didn't know what you were then."

"And what am I? No, don't, let me say it for you. A monster? Is that the right word?" When Greven said nothing, Piven continued, "Because I really haven't changed that much, you know. I still love you, Greven. I always have."

"You once loved your brother."

"Ah, but you haven't deserted me as my brother has. He must pay for that."

"Your sister had no choice in her desertion."

"This is true," Piven admitted, slapping at some tall grasses at the side of the Tomlyn road. "She was helpless. But she is helpless no longer, and you know as well as I she will try to destroy me now. That disturbance we just felt was likely none other than her returning home."

Greven was genuinely startled. "I felt the disturbance but hadn't given it much thought . . . of course you're right. Are you frightened?"

Piven threw him a wry glance. "No," he replied with a gentle scoff. "I have you." He pointed to where the main road forked. "We go left to the capital."

"Let's go right, Piven. Let's head south, keep you safe."

"I am safe. You are here."

"I think you are depending on me too much."

"But that's the role of the aegis. To be entirely dependable. Come on," he said, increasing his speed. "And don't claim fatigue; I know you don't even feel it. That must be amazing. No need for food or water, rest or any form of sustenance."

"Does that not strike you as a living death?"

Piven smiled openly. "Not at all. It's surely immortality. I envy you."

"Don't. Just tell me why we are going to the capital, please."

"Ah yes," Piven said, a skip in his step as though he were enjoying their awkward journey. "I was saying that I am a loyalist and indeed a royalist. My family's throne has been usurped. I intend that a Valisar will rule from that throne again."

"Then you should throw your support behind Leonel. Imagine what the pair of you could achieve together. The people would flock to the idea of the rightful heir trying to reclaim his throne."

"That is a nice thought, Greven, and I applaud your charming notion of fraternal harmony, but sadly Leo squandered his right to my support when he abandoned me to the tyrant.

"I'm afraid I can't forgive him. And besides, I'm not as sure as you of the people's support. Life doesn't seem to be so bad under Loethar. I can't imagine Denovians will happily go to war again for a family they consider long dead."

Once again Greven was struck by Piven's maturity. The boy was nearing sixteen but carried himself like a man a decade older. It was deeply unnerving, particularly as just a few anni ago Piven had been so juvenile—charming, even—in his childishness.

"In fact I would leave the whole ruling thing to Loethar," Piven continued expansively, "if he had not brutally stolen my father's crown and were I not truly Valisar. No Valisar could let theft and murder of his own go unpunished."

"Well, what about your sister? Let her rule."

Piven looked at Greven sideways. "Why would I? She is younger than me. We must do things properly, Greven," he admonished, as though explaining to a child. "If she wants to, she can fight me for the crown. Besides, we hail the Valisar kings down the ages. We have never bowed to a queen."

"There's always a first time."

"She is a child, let's not forget!" Greven gave a grim gust of a laugh. Piven ignored it. "She will have no idea of how to rule at such a tender age. Frankly, I'm intrigued to see who has been protecting her and where she has been. Definitely not in the empire—if she has been, I would have sensed her long ago. No, Greven, this is why I think my sister is a threat: she is too young at ten to be making decisions for herself and so has been returned by someone who wishes to make use of her powers. We must ask ourselves who her the puppet master is."

"Her aegis perhaps?" Greven offered, distaste flooding his mouth at the idea.

Piven shook his head. "No. Impossible. I doubt any aegis would freely offer himself. And if my sister—funny, I don't even know her name—has been living a long way from here it's unlikely that her aegis is aware of her or she of the aegis. I am guessing they are still to find each other."

Greven silently acknowledged Piven's grasp of situations. His cunning and agile mind had already thought through every scenario that could threaten him, it seemed. "Which makes her vulnerable."

"Exactly. I'm hoping to meet her long before she has that protection."

"So you plan to kill your siblings and the emperor?"

"And all who support either. A Valisar will sit the Penraven throne again. I will make my father proud."

"Are you sure of that?"

Piven laughed. "Well, we'll never know but I like to think so. My father was ruthless, Greven. You need to understand this fact. He adored his sons but he could still make some very hard decisions—he was able to leave Leo as a nemesis for Loethar and was comfortable leaving me to whatever fate dished up. He didn't get much of a chance to love his daughter but he loved her enough to get her away so that she could offer up a challenge in the future. You see, everything for my father was about the Valisar name and duty. He was a good man, there's no denying it, but in truth he was more ruthless than even Loethar."

"Whatever makes you say that?" Greven asked, astonished.

"Because if my father had been in Loethar's shoes, he would not have hesitated to have killed me. He would not have taken a chance on letting any child associated with the throne live, whether it were an invalid or adopted or both. Loethar showed mercy—and now he will pay the price for his tenderness."

"Tenderness? You are jesting, aren't you? The man has killed more Denovians than I care to think about."

"He killed his enemies, Greven; that's very normal for a conquering ruler. But if you scrutinize what he did, he didn't kill randomly. He killed opposing soldiers, and his only real targets were the royal families. He wanted no challengers. If people submitted, he did not punish or humiliate them. He didn't even segregate them . . . unless they were Vested. If anything, Loethar has been a pioneer. He has not only unified the realms and their people into one cohesive empire but he has unified two diverse cultures and succeeded rather well at it. He's actually far more impressive than my father."

"You shock me."

"Good. I'd hate to be predictable. Come on, I'm famished. I'm hoping there's a village ahead because I've tired mightily of your stale bread and dry fruit."

Greven paid no attention to his complaints. His mind had already begun to race as to how he could find and get a message to the Valisar girl.

A cold air bit at Evie's cheeks. She heard birdsong, the rustle of leaves and the sounds of what was probably a stream, she realized. And then she heard Reg's voice. "Take it slowly. Here, drink this," he urged gently.

Evie struggled to sit up, squinting open her eyes. "Reg?"

"Hush, just drink."

"Is this more of your spiked—"

"No. It is the cleanest, most beautiful water you've ever tasted. Trust me."

She gave him a mirthless smile. "I've fallen for your *trust me* line before." She sipped and did indeed taste the sweetest of waters, chilled enough to make her gasp. "Are we alive?"

"Very much so."

She coughed once, blinked hard and forced herself to open her eyes fully. "And this isn't a dream?"

He shook his head. "How do you feel?"

"Confused. Bruised."

"I wasn't trying to kill you."

"That's not how it appeared."

Reg sighed. Evie looked up to buy herself some time to think clearly. "What is this tree?"

He sighed again. "If you knew your trees," he said, with a tiny hint of admonishment in his tone, "you would probably know this as a wych elder. Here, they are known as wychwoods."

"Here?" she said, looking around, noticing the stream she'd heard not very far away and mountains in the distance behind. "Where exactly *is* here, Reg?"

He sat down opposite her and she was surprised to note that the haunted expression her friend had always possessed— the one which seemed to speak so loudly to others that he should be left alone—was gone. In fact, Reg looked almost relaxed for the first time since she'd met him.

"Here, Evie, is a place that was once known as the Denova Set. I have no idea if it still possesses that title. But if I'm not mistaken, I think this particular spot where we sit is at the base of a place called Lo's Teeth, which is east of Gormond, west of Droste, south of Cremond, north of Dregon." His smile widened mischievously. "Does that help?"

She shook her head. "You're making fun of me. Have you any idea how it feels to be me right now, wondering what the hell has just happened?"

"I'm sorry," he said sheepishly. "I haven't lied to you. The place I have described is where I believe we are. This is woodland known as Whirlow and that stream, which has a name that I can't remember right now, runs into Lake Aran, to the south."

Evie was astonished to see moisture gather in his eyes. "Reg, are those tears?" she asked. "I've never even seen you get misty."

He wiped his cheeks. "It is good to be home, Evie. Are you hurt?"

"I don't believe so. But I don't understand why not. Mind you, that query pales by comparison to my lack of under-standing as to how we're both not splattered across the pave-ment outside a city hospital right now. We leaped from a dozen stories high!"

He allowed her anger to pass, looking down, saying nothing.

Evie gave a sound like a growl. "I need an explanation, Reg, or I am going to explode or kill you . . . make a choice."

He didn't smile. "Will you stay still and silent while I tell you everything that I can?"

"Why does that sound as though I should leap up now and run screaming from you?"

He nodded. "You're right—what I have to tell you is fright-ening. But you need to hear it and you need to hear it all, or nothing will make sense to you. I need your promise that you will listen until I've told you the whole story."

Evie licked her lips. "You'd better start at *page one*!"

"Indeed. I suppose the beginning is my name, which is not Reg. My name is Corbel."

"Corbel?" she repeated, feeling anger starting to suffuse her confusion. "Not at all Reg-like!"

"My father was Regor de Vis. I borrowed from his name."

"How convenient for—"

"Be quiet. My father probably didn't survive the rage of a man called Loethar, who hailed himself the king of the barbarian horde. He came from the east." Evie saw the pain on his face as he pointed. "The barbarians were from the plains, an area known as the Likurian Steppes. Loethar was a tyrant who murdered all in his wake. From what I could gather before I left, he was killing all the royals of the Set—that was a group of independent realms with common interests—and I suspect he left my king to the last. My father was the king's right-hand man."

"What does that make you?" she said, working hard to keep all sarcasm from her tone, knowing she needed to humor her friend. She could tell that, delusion or not, this story was incredibly hard for him to speak of.

"It makes me the son of a high ranking noble and the twin brother of Gavriel de Vis."

"Twin?"

He nodded. "I was forced to leave my family."

"By whom?"

"The king."

Definitely delusional, Evie thought. Yet in her heart she couldn't really believe it. She had never known a more sane person than Reg. Should she humor him now, call him Corbel? "King?"

"King Brennus, eighth of the Valisars. We are from Penraven, which is southwest of here."

It was all getting too much to keep clear in her mind. "Reg . . . er, Corbel, if you prefer—"

"I do."

She took a steadying breath. "Corbel, why are you telling me this? What does King Bran or whatever his name is—"

Now his gaze flashed angrily at her. "His name is Brennus and I served him faithfully."

She was stung by the force in his voice. He had never taken such a tone with her before. "All right," she began again, calmly. "I want to know why I am here. What does all of what you've begun to tell me, including King *Brennus*, have to do with me?"

"Plenty," he said flatly, eyeing her with a hard gaze. "This is the land where you were born. Your real name is Genevieve. You are a Valisar. And King Brennus is your father."

She rocked back against the tree, stunned. Then in the silence that followed, which Reg clearly wasn't going to fill, she hauled herself upright. She felt momentarily dizzy but the drug was wearing off and the water had helped. "Reg, this is not going any further. In fact—"

"Look around you, Evie. Does anything look familiar? Smell familiar? Taste or sound familiar?"

She could feel pinpricks of perspiration and the hairs standing up at the back of her neck. She'd been trying to shut out all of the foreignness of where she was, hoping that as the drug wore off, so would the sense of dislocation. And while she couldn't understand how they had not been splattered across concrete, her logical mind told her that there had to be a rational explanation, no matter what insanity had taken over her friend. But it was true, nothing felt familiar. This didn't feel like scenery from a world she knew; the air was cleaner, fresher and the land around them looked virgin.

Ignoring her silence, he continued, "None of it is familiar because we are no longer where you think we are. We have traveled through time and lands."

"You're beginning to scare me, like you scared all the other people I used to defend you against."

"I never needed your defense."

"But still I gave it, because I loved you."

He flinched as though slapped. "Evie, you're going to have to trust me. Nothing you see from here on is going to be familiar to you. Hospitals don't exist here, neither does any of the technology you have taken for granted. I know you think I'm crazy but I am all you have. And I promise you that I am sane."

"Why am I here?" she demanded, her confusion mounting to the stirrings of panic.

"I just told you. You were born here. I had to return you to your home."

"Return me? So you'd already taken me from it once . . . is that what you mean?"

"Yes," he said, shocking her. "I took you from this world when you were a newborn."

"Twenty years ago?"

He shrugged. "Yes, but perhaps time passes differently in the world I took you to. How old do I appear to you?"

It was her turn to shrug. "I don't know. I suppose beneath all that terrible beard and unruly hair you are in your late thirties, early forties. Why? How old did you hope to be?"

He nodded sadly. "I was just eighteen when I was given the task of taking you to safety."

She needed to keep him talking while her mind tried to make some sense of what was going on. "So my father—the king," she said carefully, nodding at him to show that she was trying, "asked you, a young noble, to rush me away to safety from this Loethar fellow who was killing all the royals."

"Thank you for paying attention."

"So that makes me a princess."

"Yes. That's why we had to protect you."

She couldn't help herself. As much as it galled her to humor this ridiculous story any further, she was intrigued as to where he'd take the tale next. "Do I have siblings? Fellow young royals?"

"Two brothers, one of whom is adopted."

"Ah, so they were whisked off to other places, were they?"

He shook his head. "No, only you. You had to be hidden. The Valisar dynasty has never had a surviving daughter. In centuries of rule, all girls—until you—have either died in the womb or soon after birth."

She hadn't expected that and felt a fresh wave of panic. He really looked like he believed all this. "So I'm the first surviving female heir of the Valisars and they had to get me away. Why? Isn't a male heir more important, or do they do it differently in the Denova Set?" Even she could hear the sarcasm biting and hated herself as she watched those words batter against someone she loved.

"Your brother, Leonel, is the primary heir. But Leonel is not gifted in the way we suspected you could be . . . and I now know you are. We were right to take the precaution."

"Gifted?" She felt goosebumps rise on her flesh. "What are you talking about?"

"The talent that was beginning to show itself through your work as a healer will actually have been severely suppressed in the world I took you to. Here, it will presumably manifest itself far more dramatically. At least that's what I've been led to believe."

"You're losing me, Reg."

"Call me Corbel . . . please." She really did feel lost, and she assumed it showed because his expression softened. "Let me tell you everything I know and then you can make up your mind."

"About whether to stay, you mean?"

He shook his head. "There is no way back, Evie," he said gently. "Hear me out, hear it all and then decide whether you still trust me."

Her mind was reeling but she didn't feel as though she had much of a choice. Carefully, she returned to her position against the tree and nodded. "All right, Corbel de Vis, tell me everything you know."

Two

$\rightarrow\!\!\rightarrow\quad\quad\quad\quad\quad\longleftarrow\!\!\leftarrow$

Kilt Faris chewed on a piece of meat. Jewd had insisted that he eat. It had been several hours since he'd faced his nemesis and though his men had left him alone he knew that patience wouldn't last. The sickness had passed but he could still taste its acid remnants at the back of his throat. How would he ever explain his behavior to his people . . . to Jewd?

From the corner of his eye he saw Jewd and Leo nod between themselves and approach, sitting on either side of him. He knew they wanted answers.

"Where is he?" Jewd asked Leo, breaking the tense silence.

"I've asked Gavriel to get him away. He and the woman have taken Loethar higher, heading east. I'll meet up with Gavriel shortly . . . when we understand more."

Jewd nodded and they both turned to Kilt.

"Are you going to explain it?" Leo asked.

"I didn't know, if that's what you're asking," Kilt growled.

"Didn't know you were an aegis, or didn't know who your Valisar was?" Leo said firmly.

Kilt ground his teeth, flung the piece of meat down. "What was the point in admitting anything all these anni? It hasn't been relevant, wasn't relevant until now."

"Leo's just finished telling me what an aegis is. What I want to know is, did you know you were one?" Jewd demanded. His voice was quiet but his tone told Kilt that he did not want anything but a truthful response.

"Yes," he said through gritted teeth, avoiding Jewd's eyes.

"For how long?" Jewd pressed. Kilt could hear the pain in his voice.

Kilt sighed. "Does it matter?"

"To me it does, because you've been lying."

Now he did look at Jewd and saw the anguish in his friend's face, recalled promising the man just the day previous that he had no further secrets. "Jewd, please listen to me. I didn't know that Loethar was even Valisar. How could I? None of us did. I learned about the powers of the ageis at the Academy. I sensed my powers were more than just a trifling magic around the time of my mother's death, but essentially they felt like tricks for most of my life."

"I don't believe persuading people to spill their private knowledge is a circus trick, Kilt," Jewd interrupted, his voice hard. "What you've admitted to being able to do is hardly trifling. It fills me with both awe and dread. And anger—because you chose to keep it from me."

"I told you, I have not used those powers until just days ago when I went in search of Lily."

"Well, at least you admit that she means that much to you!" Leo cut in archly. "We will find her and we will get her back, Kilt, I promise you that. But right now we have to understand what we're up against here. We are not your enemy, so stop treating us as if we are. Jewd and I need to share as much as possible with you or we can't protect you."

Kilt laughed sadly. "Protect me? You have no idea what you're dealing with."

Leo was not to be dissuaded by the disdain in his friend's voice or the low threat that underpinned his words. "That's the point I'm making. We don't have any idea and so we wish to understand. I know what an aegis does, what he or she is born for. I'll be honest, I've never felt mine present." He gave a hollow grin. "But, my understanding is that as a Valisar I should feel that person and only that person who was born for me."

Kilt sighed. "That's right. The Valisars are only aware of their own aegis," he lied, grateful for Leo's obviously weak powers. "However, an aegis who comes too close would be aware of all the Valisars, which is why it's so dangerous." He felt bad for lying, but knew it was necessary. "The magic inside me recognizes you even though I am not your aegis. Your presence sickens me, Leo."

Leo looked at him, open-mouthed.

"That came out the wrong way," Kilt backtracked. "What I'm trying to say is that what you saw me experience with Loethar is, to some degree, how I feel around you."

"I make you feel ill?"

Kilt nodded. "I have worked very, very hard to overcome it. But it is always there. Your father did the same to me. The first time I saw the king from a distance my magic responded to him; that's how I knew what I was. That's why I made my home up here in the highlands, so I could avoid the towns and city, live as an outlaw, keep to myself and only have people around me I could utterly trust."

"And that's why you've been avoiding me." Kilt watched the young king throw a glance at Jewd.

"I have kept my distance, Leo, but I have *not* avoided you. Apart from your dealing with Freath, I am proud of you and what you have become. I just find it hard to be around you for long periods."

"And it's different with Loethar?" Jewd asked.

Kilt gave a snort of despair. "Wildly different. I lose control. He nearly undid me back there," he admitted. "And he knew it. If he has another attempt at me, I won't win. I was only able to resist this time because all of you came to my aid." Kilt shook his head with disgust. "Loethar's a Valisar!" he spat. "Incredible! He murdered his own brother."

"Half-brother," Leo corrected. "And he would take you to task over that. My father killed himself to prevent Loethar having the satisfaction."

Kilt shrugged. "Half-brother, full brother. Did your father know they were related, do you think?"

Leo shook his head wearily. "I don't know the answer to that. My heart says no, but Loethar seems to think my father was aware of him. My father was a man of secrets. It's possible he could have known—that might explain why he went to such lengths to have the plan in place for me should Loethar overrun the Set."

Kilt agreed. "I didn't know Brennus in the way that many did but my instincts combined with what I've learned over the anni suggest that he was perfectly capable of having this information and acting upon it."

"Why didn't he just send an army in and kill Loethar if he knew?" Jewd wondered.

Leo shook his head. "That would not be his way. My father was not a coward but confronting Loethar on his territory, with nowhere for an army to take him by surprise, no familiarity of the lay of the land or helpful knowledge of what the enemy was capable of, would have definitely made him reluctant to take that approach. And perhaps he wasn't completely sure of Loethar's birthright, so he waited for Loethar to come to him."

"Very costly," Jewd remarked.

"In hindsight, yes. Too costly," Leo admitted. He frowned and turned back to Kilt. "So in Loethar's presence you will always feel nauseous and without control?"

"In his presence I will be at his mercy. I will be made well again, of course, but only when he's bonded me."

Leo nodded and looked at Jewd, who wore a quizzical expression. "The Valisar must consume part of his aegis to trammel him."

"Consume? As in eat?" Jewd qualified, a look of dismay on his face.

Kilt nodded at the same time as Leo and Jewd looked away, disgusted, then stood. "Well, that's going to happen only over my dead body, Kilt."

Kilt smiled sadly. "I don't deserve you, Jewd."

"No, you don't," the big man replied. "You don't deserve Leo or Lily or any of the people who support you."

Kilt nodded in acknowledgment. "There's more, and you might as well know it, now that I'm being forced to bare my soul," he said. As his companions threw a worried glance at each other, he continued, "I don't know what it is but I've felt a disturbance."

"Disturbance?" they asked together.

Kilt considered how best to explain himself. "Not so long ago I suffered a sort of dizzy spell. I thought it was still part of the same response to Loethar but I've been thinking about it and it was not. I have no doubt now. It had a different signature . . . it felt different. I don't really know how to describe it and while this might sound fanciful, the only way I can pin it down is to say that it felt very clean . . . a really pure sort of magic."

"Loethar's is tainted, you mean?" Jewd tried.

Kilt shook his head. "No, not exactly. Loethar and Leo possess no magic of their own. Neither of them is empowered in the way that say I am or any Vested is. But both are Valisar and a Valisar can respond to the magic of the aegis. I should also tell you, Leo, that your Valisar magic is very weak. I'm grateful for that or I would never have been able to live around you."

"Trust me to be the weak link in the family," Leo replied quietly but savagely. "I suppose Loethar is strong?"

Kilt nodded.

"Go on," Leo said, his mouth twisted in private disgust. "What about this new feeling you've experienced? Who or what is it?"

"I don't know. I can only use the word *pure* because it feels like it has its own source, its own reason. But beyond that I don't understand it."

Each of them paused to consider this new revelation but it was Leo who broke the silence. "Well," he said, straightening, "we can't worry ourselves with what we don't know, don't understand yet. We have enough to frighten us right now. We need to make a decision about Loethar and we have to consider the next step for Lily. Whatever else is hurtling at us can wait as far as I'm concerned."

Jewd nodded. "I agree. Let's make a decision about Loethar. Do we kill him? I'll oblige if no one else has the stomach for it."

"No," Kilt said. "His death achieves little right now. We need to know more about why he's here. Why he's alone. What his intentions are."

"To bond you, clearly," Leo said.

"No, that's not right. He had no idea that his aegis was roaming the north. And if I wasn't the attraction the most obvious conclusion is you," Kilt said, stabbing a finger toward Leo. "Except he didn't even know you were alive! He wouldn't have even recognized you or known you were the missing Valisar if you'd introduced yourself under a guise. So he's here for different reasons. And he certainly didn't arrive here willingly. Why did he travel north? Why alone? We need to learn as much as we can to help Leo's chances."

"All right, but we can't let him near you," Jewd argued.

"We don't have to. I will speak with him," Leo said, his tone brooking no argument. "It is my place, anyway, to do so. His challenge is essentially at me."

Jewd frowned. "If he's the rightful heir, where does that leave you, Leo?"

"Leo is heir," Kilt growled. "His father was king. He is next in line." He looked at Leo. "The fact that your grandfather sowed wild seeds on the plains is not anyone's concern. Loethar is a bastard heir of mixed blood. Brennus married a royal; you are a blueblood. That gives you rank."

Leo didn't look convinced. "I suspect we won't get an opportunity to argue it in front of the nobles. Loethar took the crown; he has worn it for over a decade now and let's be very frank, his people are now comfortable with who is ruling. The fact that he is Valisar only improves his position, if I'm honest."

It was Kilt's turn to share a worried glance with Jewd. "Are you relinquishing your claim, Leo?"

"Absolutely not! I'm simply stating that we could argue the rights and wrongs of it until we're blue in the face. The fact is he wears the crown. Me arguing my lineage makes little difference. I must take the crown back . . . by killing him if necessary. And if that whore Davarigon giant hadn't got in my way, I might have achieved that and this conversation would be academic." He took a deep breath. "I'm going to talk to Gavriel. I've got a decade's worth of catching up to do with him."

"Don't let Loethar corner you into doing anything hot-headed," Jewd warned, "You are a king. Don't forget that. It's your calm and your inability to be taunted that will most frustrate him."

"You made a fool of him once," Kilt agreed, "hiding under his nose and then escaping so audaciously. Continue to make a fool of him by not falling prey to his baiting. That's how you'll keep the upper hand."

Leo grinned. "Thanks."

After he'd left, the two men remained quiet for a while. Finally Jewd sighed. "Were you planning to tell me or were you just going to give me the slip?"

Kilt looked up at his friend. "Why do you think I'd leave?" he asked, dismayed.

Jewd shook his head, gave a brief rueful smile. "I've told you before, I'm big, not stupid. Did you think I couldn't work it out for myself?"

Kilt looked down again. "Jewd, I don't know what to think but I know this: you are the best friend a man could have."

"I'm glad you realize that."

"I would have discussed it with you."

"Look at me when you say that. I have to know I can trust you, Kilt, or as I've told you previously, it might be easier to leave you to it."

"That's not what I want."

"Then I demand your honesty."

Kilt stood up, feeling stronger again despite his aching muscles. He sighed. "I guess I don't even need to ask if you've noticed anything about Leo."

"I've noticed. Leo is pushing for independence. He won't live for very much longer under your thumb."

Kilt nodded. "That's as it should be. He's been groomed to rule since he was on his mother's teat."

"He's still capable of poor decisions."

"Aren't we all?"

Jewd fixed Kilt with a firm stare, before he spoke very quietly. "But I suspect his next will be his least wise."

Kilt swallowed. "You're thinking what I'm thinking. Then I've got to go, get as far away from the Valisars as possible."

"Then we go together."

"Jewd—"

"We go together, Kilt. Look at the state of you. If Leo comes after you—and he will, we both agree on that—who is going to protect you?"

"Maybe it's best if I just submit and—"

Jewd had grabbed Kilt by his shirtfront before Kilt could even finish the thought. "No one is eating you, is that clear? No one is going to have you under his control! Leo has de Vis back. De Vis has always seen Leo as king and treated him as such. We can leave the two of them together and go north into Barronel via the mountains. We'll cross into Cremond perhaps; no one's going to be looking for you there. Leo will assume you'll head south in search of Lily. And we'll get to her, Kilt, but we have to ensure they lose your scent first and you have to heal too. For now we both agree Lily is safe. For now we both agree your safety is paramount."

Kilt nodded. "Take the money we've hidden and give it to the men. Tell them they should scatter. And grab the medicine. We need little else."

Three

The man struggled but, fueled by anger, got his words out. "I'm going to kill you for this, de Vis."

"Yes, well, I'll look forward to your trying. Gives me the perfect excuse of self-defense to finish you off once and for all," Gavriel replied disdainfully.

"Be quiet, Loethar!" Elka ordered. "Conserve your strength."

"Sage advice. I'll need it to kill your lover and his friend."

"He's not my lover and I suspect his friend is no friend of mine after I got in his way," she said, hefting him into a better position on her back.

"Let me down, for Gar's sake!" Loethar complained. "I'm not an invalid, simply injured."

"Do it, Elka," Gavriel said.

Elka had just about had it with both of them. She lowered Loethar, who held his groans but grimaced in pain.

"Ribs are the worst, aren't they?" he said, almost amused.

"How's your neck?" Elka asked.

"I'll survive. And the burn will be a timely reminder for when I slit my half-brother's throat."

"If I give you the chance," Gavriel said.

Loethar laughed. "Where is your great king, de Vis? Is he too frightened to face me?"

"As a matter of fact you'll likely see him sooner than you think. Elka, can I leave you with him? I have to meet with

Leo." At her nod he disappeared into the woods without so much as a backward glance.

Elka turned to regard Loethar. "He's perfectly capable of killing you, you know. I would counsel you to stop the taunting."

"And spoil my sport?"

"Well, you've been warned." He gave her look like a child, mischief in his eyes, and she couldn't help asking, "You're really Valisar?"

He nodded. "Though what good it does me I don't know."

"That sounds like regret," she commented, settling nearby.

"In a way," he admitted. "But I don't really know in what respect. I don't regret the empire. I think unifying the realms has been positive for all in the Set; I think the mix of cultures, though difficult at first, has resulted in prosperity. In the wider population people seem relatively content. So I suppose it boils down to personal regret."

"All the death perhaps?"

"Probably. Many died who didn't have to."

"None of them Valisar, of course."

"Other than the queen. I would have preferred that she had lived. I would have given her a good life wherever she chose to live out her days. But the heirs had to die. I failed there," he admitted with a humorless grin. "Leo has been the most slippery of enemies."

"He's had a lot of support from the right people, it appears."

Loethar nodded. "How true. The would-be-king in exile is surrounded by loyalty, while I, as ruler, am surrounded by treachery. Freath, my close aide, someone I considered a friend even though he was my servant, betrayed me all along." He gave a low, savage laugh. "His loyalties were always with the Valisars. I admire his extraordinary courage to live in the lion's den on their behalf. Leonel is fortunate."

"I doubt he sees it that way. His family is dead, his friends are missing, his throne has been usurped."

"You should have let him kill me."

"I believe in justice, not revenge."

"Then you are in the minority, Elka, though I respect that more than you can imagine."

"Fairness and justice are what make a people into a society. They're the cornerstone of a strong civilization."

"Indeed. But fairness and justice rarely go hand in hand. For instance, Leo feels it is fair that he should be king and yet it is not just, for I am the true heir. Kilt Faris considers it fair to do everything he can to elude me and yet his very birthright is to be my aegis. And isn't it just that I exercise that right? You see? Fairness and justice are rarely comfortable bed companions."

She smiled. "I think you are the slippery Valisar, Loethar."

Gavriel didn't have to wait too long; Leo came striding through the forest soon enough, walking like a man comfortable in his surrounds. Gavriel marveled at the figure approaching. He'd left Leo as little more than a youth, but now he walked tall and strong, with a proud chin. His hair had darkened but he still resembled his beautiful mother, while having the more powerful build of his father. Gavriel felt a spike of pride accompany the rush of relief that Leo had survived.

He stepped out from his hiding place suddenly, deliberately, but Leo didn't break stride, not at all unnerved, and Gavriel was reminded that his old friend had been living as an outlaw for more than a decade. Leo would know forest life better than most.

Leo grabbed Gavriel into a bear-hug, slapping him on the back. "I can't tell you how good it feels to see you alive," he remarked, "although my fist twitches to punch you for leaving as you did."

Gavriel grinned. "I should punch myself."

"Where is he?"

"Safe with Elka."

"Tied up?"

"No need. He's going nowhere with her around."

"I don't feel I need to apologize regarding Elka, Gav; she should never have challenged me. But at the same time any friend of yours is certainly someone I feel obliged to respect."

"I'm sure she hasn't given it another thought." Leo looked as though he wanted to say more but Gavriel was glad when the young king chose to hold his tongue. That was a relief; he didn't want to have to defend Elka against the king . . . although he would, of course. "As much as I want to sit down and learn about your life, time is our enemy. How's Faris?"

"Brighter. The sickening has passed but, like Loethar, he's quite beaten up."

"Leo, we both have good reason to hate Loethar. That grudge has to be kept separate from how we feel about his stealing the Valisar throne." Leo stared at him, but said nothing, so Gavriel pressed on. "My point is I hate him too. It wouldn't take much for my heart to get in the way of my head and order my hand to take up my sword and run him through."

"So what's stopping you?"

"My instinct is stopping me."

"Instinct, or Elka?"

Gavriel didn't rise to the bait. He fixed Leo with a hard stare, glad that he was still taller. "Elka has no loyalty to either you or Loethar."

"Is that so?"

"Why would it be otherwise? She owes neither of you anything. Her loyalty is to me. I'm sure I don't deserve it most of the time but that's how it is and her commitment to me means that she understands the need to protect you at all costs."

"Protect me? Why didn't she let me kill my enemy, then?"

"Because murdering him in that manner wouldn't have solved anything. Her actions have given you the opportunity to consider your position and make an informed decision. If killing him is your decision, you'll make it in a mood of calm, not in a blood rage. Frankly, I think you would have regretted it if you had struck him dead then. This way you get a chance to question him."

"That's what Kilt thinks."

"Then listen to him. We're all on your side, Leo. Come, we can speak alone later but first talk to him, ask him your questions."

Reluctantly, Leo followed. They found Loethar talking quietly with Elka as though they were old friends. Gavriel bristled at their familiarity but disguised it with his introduction.

"Here we are, Leo, the great and now very humbled and
hurt man who calls himself emperor simply by sitting a false
throne."

Loethar looked up and laughed. "You amuse me, de Vis.
Greetings, nephew; I was just telling Elka here how fortunate you are to have such loyalty still burning so fiercely for
you."

"From what I hear you can't claim the same," Leo said,
regarding him as though tasting something bad.

"You are right. I am surrounded by treachery at every
turn. Even my newborn daughter turned away from her father and died on me."

"A girl?" Leo exclaimed.

Loethar gave him a humorless grin. "Yes, and like all
Valisar daughters she barely survived her birth."

"Not all," Leo said. He grinned humorlessly at Loethar's
puzzled expression and squatted next to the barbarian. "You
clearly haven't spent much time around the family or you'd
know we're famed for our secrets."

"What are you talking about?" Loethar asked.

"What do you know about the Valisar Legacy?" Leo responded.

Loethar tried to shrug and grimaced in pain. "I've learned
plenty over the anni with the family library finally at my
disposal," he said. Gavriel noticed how he couldn't hide his
feelings; his expression clearly betrayed the anger he was
feeling. "I know that there is the legacy of the aegis magic
and the near enough immortal protection it offers. I know
about the so-called Enchantment that says that the females
born of the line possess the greatest of all powers . . . to coerce at will."

"Why is that so different from what some Vested can do?"
Gavriel asked.

Leo turned to him. "The magic of the Vested can be impressive, but even so, any sort of coercement of theirs is of a

low form and can probably only be sustained for short periods. The magic of the Valisars is said to be much more powerful, or so my father and grandfather told me."

"And I'm sure you are looking to gain some of that power for yourself," Loethar said and Gavriel noticed a look pass between uncle and nephew that spoke of a respect for each other's cunning. "Anyway," Loethar continued, "my heir is dead, my mother has been murdered, my wife has been banished, my brother turned traitor, my closest friend has been killed. All in all, life is hardly an orchard."

"Aludane save us! And I thought your life was complicated," Elka remarked, glancing at Gavriel.

He smirked at her as she turned back to Loethar. "I'm sorry to hear of your losses. No one should lose a mother and a daughter in such a short time."

"I'm not sorry," Leo said coldly. "The more of his kin that is gone, the better. Besides, I'm sure he and his ill-bred horde killed whole families when they came rampaging into the Set."

"You are my kin, Leo," Loethar said, with an equally wintry tone. "And you're right. I deserve no pity from anyone here."

"Nor will you get it," Gavriel remarked.

Loethar shrugged, clearly ignoring the pain it prompted this time.

Elka looked from Loethar to Gavriel. "Why don't you just kill him and be done?" she said, so sarcastically that Gavriel flinched inside. "I hardly recognize you when you act this way."

"We're here to talk," Gavriel said to Loethar, covering his dismay at Elka's attack. "Why did you come north?"

Loethar sighed. "It's complicated. In short, the death of my child and my belief that my wife murdered my mother conspired to make me want to get away from the castle. In order to do so I brought our mother's ashes to my half-brother, whom I suspected was considering rising up against me. Now I know that those suspicions were right."

"So your trip to the north was all about delivering your mother's ashes to Stracker?" Gavriel asked.

"No, that was my excuse I gave myself. My real reason for heading north was to find out who killed Freath and why," Loethar explained.

"I can put you out of your misery on that question," Leo said.

Gavriel looked at him with surprise. "You know?"

"Yes, I know. I killed him."

"*You?*" Locthar hissed. "But he was working for you!"

"He killed my mother," Leo said. "I swore a blood oath that I would kill him, so I did, once he had told us everything he knew."

Loethar let out a growl of frustration. "Freath was a traitor in my life for ten anni. All of those clever conversations, steering me onto a particular path while he went down the other." He shook his head. Then he smiled. "And still I admire him. And still I like him." He smirked. "I had convinced myself he was the most honest person in my life even when he was lying every minute. Incredible."

"I can't believe it," Gavriel said. "He protected us?"

Leo nodded. "My father asked him to pretend to be a turncoat should the time arrive. My mother asked him to help her to commit suicide, make it look as though he'd thrown her from the window in order to protect his cover while releasing her from her imprisonment and grief. Her death at his hands meant the Valisars could still have a loyalist in the enemy midst." Again he threw a bitter glance Loethar's way. "But being involved in my mother's death couldn't be forgiven. I would have killed him anyway for that alone."

"Demonstrating your immaturity and lack of capacity to rule wisely," Loethar accused, bitterness combining with a cold, controlled fury in his soft voice. "I can't begin to tell you what a tightrope Freath must have walked each day of his life on your behalf. He ingratiated himself so deeply into my life that I actually mourned him more than my own mother, my own child! And look how you rewarded him." He choked back what sounded like a sigh of deep regret.

"I wish that were the truth," Leo replied, equally cold. "It's my impression that Freath admired you more than you can know. He was torn, I think. His loyalties were to my father and myself, also to Piven. But he had an abiding respect for you . . . more's the pity."

"I thank you for sharing that," Loethar said quietly.

Gavriel's head was in turmoil. Freath, never a traitor! "Well, now you have the answer you came looking for. I think we should just throw you back at your dog of a brother. You can kill each other."

Loethar smirked. "If you really thought that, you wouldn't have interfered in the forest."

"It wasn't my idea, believe me," Gavriel growled.

Gone was the sorrow in Loethar's eyes. Suddenly he was all hardness and ruthless control again. "Then let's get this done, shall we? My sympathies are with Elka. Like her, I tire of your empty threats. If you mean to kill me, do it now and be done with it. Leo, here's your chance to be the brave Valisar. Run through the pretender—if you truly believe I am just that."

Gavriel saw Leo stiffen and knew he had to keep his own anger in check as an example to the young king. "Leo, a word," he said, gritting his teeth. Mercifully, Leo stood, turning his back on Loethar. Gavriel glanced at Elka. "Shut him up," he said, loading his voice with disdain. Then he followed Leo to a quiet spot far from where they could be seen, let alone heard.

"Don't say it," Leo warned.

"As your friend, as your Legate, my king, I must say it."

Leo scowled but remained quiet.

"It would be a mistake to kill him. This wedge now driven between him and Stracker is playing precisely into your favor."

"How so?"

"My father taught us that there is always more than one way to regard a situation, more than one way to treat an enemy. Loethar is our prisoner. We might be able to make use of him. Let's at least consider it. Think on it. Killing him solves nothing. Using him might give us options."

Leo nodded, considering the advice. He paced around, looking up into an overcast sky, and Gavriel was again struck that such a young man had such a weight of responsibility on his shoulders.

"Gavriel, I know you haven't been around the region for a decade. Me too, I've lived on the fringe of life. But I don't think either of us will ever forget his cunning or just how wily he is."

"I accept that," Gavriel replied, frowning. "What's your point?"

"My point is that he will find a way to turn on me. If I give him so much as a finger width of movement, he'll make it work for him. He is far cleverer than most give him credit for."

"It seems Freath had his measure," Gavriel murmured. "Damn it, Leo, was it necessary to kill him?"

"Freath. I will not be allowed to forget that decision by anyone, will I?" Gavriel shrugged and Leo shook his head. "You are not the first to criticize. Kilt has never forgiven me my rash fury of that day. But I defy you to have faced Freath in the same ignorant situation."

Gavriel glared angrily at the king. "Leo, I've had to save the life of the man who brutally slaughtered my defenseless father before me. Do you forget how my father died? His head hacked from top to shoulder, his horse dragging him behind it while Loethar howled his glee? I've had to keep that monster company, keep him protected. I did it for you alone. Don't talk to me about losing control."

Leo had the grace to look admonished. "Forgive me. I haven't forgotten what you've been through on my behalf. But I am perhaps at the mercy of the brutal images of my boyhood. I still have nightmares of my baby brother dragging around the gore from our freshly decapitated father as my mother watched on in shocked horror."

Gavriel held both hands up in defense. "Look, this is all history and we can't re-make it. Our parents are dead, may Gar rest their souls. And Freath is gone. There is no point in our re-hashing the rights and wrongs of it. But killing Loethar doesn't solve the problem at hand. Do you agree that alongside his half-brother he is the lesser of the two evils?" Leo gave him a pained look. "I know, Leo, I know. They are both killers. But Loethar has a modicum of control. He seems to kill only with specific reason. In fact, everything he does, everything he says is considered. I'm not condoning his usurping of the throne or the manner in which it was done, I'm simply saying that Stracker has no control, no subtlety . . . *he has no conscience*! If you kill Loethar, Stracker will take easy command of the throne and army. Imagine what will happen then."

Leo walked away and Gavriel gave him some time to let his points sink in. At last Leo turned back, a sly look on his face. "We will not kill him," he said. "But I'm not sure you'll get him to agree not to kill me. Face it, Gav, he's been hunting me for too many anni. The first chance he gets—all we have to do is slip up once—and he'll take that chance and slide a blade into me, or choke me, or poison me."

"I agree that he cannot be trusted. But it's my task to protect you. That's my problem, not yours."

Leo smiled and Gavriel didn't like the cunning in his face. "It doesn't need to be your problem. I am Valisar, so I too have an aegis."

Gavriel took a breath, frowning. "All right, but where does one start hunting down—"

"There is no need to hunt down mine, not if one I can take is right before us."

Gavriel stared at Leo uncomprehendingly and then understanding hit him like a thunder crack. "You wouldn't!"

"Why not?"

"Faris is . . ."

"An aegis?"

"I was going to say your friend. A loyal friend."

"Yes, and now he can demonstrate the ultimate form of that loyalty; he can become my champion. Gav, don't you see, he can offer me the most superior form of protection against Loethar, against anyone!" Gavriel heard glee in his king's voice. "My enemies can try anything they like against me and it will have no effect. I would only be able to die for natural reasons." Leo's eyes were sparkling.

"You could do that? You can see yourself claiming him? Maiming him?"

"Oh come on, Gav, don't be squeamish! We're talking about my life now. Kilt wouldn't have to be hurt that badly."

"And you'd eat part of him?"

Leo bristled with anger. "I will do whatever I have to in order to reclaim my throne." He pulled open his shirt. "Remember this? We made this scar together. And we took an oath together. It wasn't the promise of a child. That was the promise of a king. I have been in exile for most of my life. Need I remind you how many lives were given to keep mine safe for this very reason, your own father's included?"

"I don't need reminding," Gavriel replied sharply.

"Then don't fight me on this. It is the right solution."

"It's the right solution if Kilt agrees but I can't imagine he will."

"He gave his word to my father that he would protect me. Now this is the only way that Kilt can keep that promise."

"He hasn't done a bad job so far."

Leo opened his mouth to respond, then closed it again, looking frustrated. He appeared to take a steadying breath. His voice was hard when he spoke again. "I'm going to trammel him, Gav, and I'll probably need your help."

"I'm not sure I'd—"

"I'm not asking. I'm telling you that I require your help."

It was Gavriel's turn to fall silent. As he regarded Leo he realized his father must have been put into an identically difficult position time and again with Brennus. And Regor de Vis had never failed his king. He nodded. "As you wish, your majesty."

"Good. Jewd will be the problem rather than Kilt. You may need to disable him, but he is not to be harmed permanently."

Gavriel didn't reply.

"We may also need Elka's help."

"That will be her decision."

"Well, she's hardly going to do it for me, Gav. I'm hoping that you will persuade her."

"I can try, but I'll tell you now she answers to no one."

Leo gave him a glance and Gavriel wasn't sure whether to read pity or disdain in it. Either way, it was condescending and he was shocked at how hurt he felt.

"When do you want to do this?" he demanded, making sure his voice sounded anything but servile.

"Immediately. Loethar must not get wind of what we're planning. We will have to tie him up or drug him."

"I saw the look he gave you, Leo. I think you're underestimating Loethar if you don't already think his mind has taken him there."

And Gavriel knew he was right when Leo turned away, unable to meet his gaze.

Four

The youngster caught up. "You walk fast."

"Sorry," the man said, his voice slightly hoarse.

"How do you feel?"

"Powerful," he replied and they both laughed.

"I would consider it far more powerful to be a bird."

"More freedom perhaps, but not more power. Look how I can swing my arms, notice my long stride, and listen to this." He began to sing.

Roddy laughed delightedly and the newly formed man called Ravan stopped singing and swung the boy around in a moment of unfettered pleasure. "I like your laugh, Roddy."

"I like your voice," the boy replied as he was set back down.

"Anything's better than that dreadful caw I used to have."

"You were a most handsome bird."

"Now I'm an even more handsome man."

"That you are. Can your long stride get us all the way to where we need to be?"

"Easily. It's not so far."

"Further on foot than as the crow flies, though," Roddy said and they both chuckled. "What do you think our real task is?"

Ravan had been thinking about this ever since he had seen Sergius speaking to him from the flames. "Our role is to help the princess."

"But how?"

"I don't know yet, Roddy. We have both been given powers and we have to work out not only what but how to use them."

"How will we know her?"

"I don't know the answer to that. But we have to push on and hope we'll discover all that we need to know."

"Do you remember what Sergius said when he was dying?"

Ravan smiled. "He spoke about several things."

"The bit about telling people about Piven."

Ravan paused again, frowning as he thought back over the conversation with the dying Sergius. "He did say that, you're right. That's very sharp of you, Roddy. I had overlooked it."

"Well, I was just wondering who we had to tell and where they may be."

"I think I know exactly who he meant."

"You do?"

"I suspect he meant anyone who is loyal to the Valisars."

"Who might that be?"

"That would be Leonel and his supporters."

"The prince? But they say he died in the wars."

Ravan let Roddy down off his broad shoulders and squatted so that his friend did not have to stare up at him. "Leonel did not die in the wars. He survived, escaped Loethar's clutches, and fled into the forests north of here. He has grown up, tall and strong with a fierce desire to be king in more than name."

Roddy's eyes shone. "Really?"

Ravan nodded. "I think we need to find him and let him know that his sister returns and that his brother is now his enemy."

"Will he believe us?"

"He has to. We must make sure he does."

"How long will it take us to reach the forest?"

Ravan frowned. "Too long. We're pretty far west still, so we need to swing east now if we want to make it into the Davarigon region of Droste."

Roddy smiled. "Then we'd better run!"

"We could never keep pace with each other. My legs are too long."

The boy regarded him seriously. "When you were changing, just before the beautiful serpent woman arrived, I thought I saw something."

"Oh yes, what was that?"

Roddy bit his lip and squeezed his eyes shut as he made himself remember. "It was like a dream. I could see you running."

"Running, eh? Perhaps because I was about to be given the legs of a man."

"No, it was as though I was being shown something. I see things sometimes. I keep them to myself because they can be bad. There was a time when I had a vision of the crops failing. Another time I saw that the Robbun family's only son would die of the shaking fever—and that was a whole anni before, when he was healthy."

"I see. Those aren't nice visions to have."

Roddy nodded. "My mother told me to keep them to myself. So when I saw the fire in my mind—the one that I told you about, that brought me here?" Ravan nodded. "Well, I didn't tell anyone that it would happen but every day I waited for it. And one day it came and I was ready." He pulled a rueful face. "I didn't know I'd have to try and save Plod, of course." At Ravan's frown, Roddy grinned. "My cat."

"Ah. Brave."

"Not really. He was a good friend to me."

"Did you see Piven in your vision?"

Roddy shook his head. "No, but I knew I would be hurt badly but survive. I trust my visions. They are never wrong."

"And so you've had a vision about me?"

"I think you have the power to move as freely and easily as you did when you were a bird," Roddy replied gravely.

"Fly?"

Roddy exploded into laughter. "No. You don't have wings any more!"

"Then how?"

"On those legs you are so proud of. I think they will carry you much faster than you can imagine."

"Really?"

Roddy nodded. "Let's try."

"All right," Ravan said, bemused. "Stand back!" he said

dramatically, making Roddy grin. "Here goes." He ran and was out of Roddy's sight within moments, but returned at immense speed, dust swirling in his wake.

"Strike me!" Ravan declared. "I'm glad you shared your vision!"

Roddy laughed loudly. "You were gone from sight within a blink. Have you any idea how fast you are?"

Ravan shook his head with wonder. "I see everything ahead in perfect clarity but everything else is a blur rushing by. I can feel the wind created by my speed. I know it's fast."

"I think we can get to the forest rather quickly if you can manage me on your back."

"Manage? This incarnation has given me the strength of two men, I'm sure. Come on, Roddy, we have a journey to make, into the hills above the Deloran Forest."

Loethar looked at Elka and gave her a wry smile.

"And what am I supposed to read into that expression?" she asked.

"I thought you'd like to know what your two friends are discussing," he replied.

"Oh, so your Valisar powers permit you to read minds or overhear from long distance, do they?"

He laughed. "I do like you, Elka. De Vis is a lucky man."

"A short one."

He laughed deeper, genuinely amused. "I wish I had some of the famed Valisar magic. I have none. My only power will be borrowed if I can reach it."

"But why?"

He sighed. "You know, I've been beginning to ask myself the same question. I'm asking myself why about a lot lately. At least Denovians are happier under my rule."

"If that were true I could only be impressed."

"But it is true," he pressed.

"No, Loethar. The Denovians were not given any choice. You might think your way has been better for them—and you could be right—but harmony is really only achieved when there is free choice."

"Are all Davarigons so philosophical?"

"I'm afraid so. It's why we keep to ourselves."

"In case you bore people."

It was her turn to laugh. "You know, for a bloodthirsty tyrant you are also reasonable company."

He bowed his head in a mock salute. "So are you interested in what I was going to share with you?"

"I don't suppose saying no will shut you up?"

"No. Besides, I want to dazzle you with my insight. I'd like to show just how easy my nephew is to read and how blinded by loyalty your friend de Vis is." He saw her bristle. "Forgive me. While I'm happy to taunt them, I bear you absolutely no ill will. You have been more than fair and extremely generous. I see that I hit a sore point with my barb."

She shrugged. "If I had my way I would already be back in the mountains."

"With or without him?"

She nodded.

"Ah, and your head and heart are sore at this."

"On the surface we are ill-suited, I know. But we are a good match. Regor . . . or Gavriel, as I must now call him, has a blind faith in the Valisars."

"It is to be admired."

"I do admire it. But it brings only sorrow to my life."

Loethar just nodded, watching her.

Elka gave a sad smile. "What are they discussing?"

"Did you understand what they were talking about regarding the aegis for each Valisar?"

"I followed it. It's a horrifying concept but the more I learn about the family, the less surprised I am. Would you really bind a man to you in such a vile manner, committing him to a living death?"

"Faris would be alive, Elka."

"To be alive is to have free will."

He nodded. "Ah, back to that. But life is rarely fair or neat."

"I agree. But you two would be bound together in hate. Imagine spending the rest of your life under the protection of someone who hates you."

He shrugged. "My whole life has been spent like that."

"I'm sad for you, Loethar. I wonder what sort of man you'd have been had you been born into the palace as the true Valisar son and heir."

"Quite different. Anger and the drive for revenge against the family that disowned me has sadly shaped me."

"You are a good ruler."

"I know."

"Even Gavriel admits it."

"But against all of his good sense, all his instincts and admiration for you and your sense of what is right, he will follow Leo down a dark path."

"Dark path?" She frowned. "What does that mean?"

"Right now, if I'm not mistaken, Leo is sharing with de Vis his plan to trammel Faris."

"What?" Elka's expression darkened.

"I'd lay my life on it."

She was silent a moment, considering. "He can't, though," she finally replied, her brow knitting deeper. "Isn't Faris your aegis?"

"He can. Any aegis is available to any Valisar if we recognize him or her. It's just that the aegis can hide relatively successfully if he doesn't run into his own Valisar. Faris did. And now he's a marked man for either Leo or myself. Your friend de Vis will be drawn into the subterfuge, and once Leo trammels Faris he will kill me."

"I won't permit that to—"

"You will have no say. You will also have no weapons or even ability against an aegis. Leo will command Faris. And Faris will use magic against anyone who so much as stands up to Leo. He will be invincible against any sort of threat."

She looked at him, aghast. "Would you have done the same?"

"I am Valisar," he replied, vaguely embarrassed.

She gave a low, animal-like growl of fury. "That sort of power should not be in anyone's lap."

"Well, Leo will probably argue that it's to protect the people, return the true heir to the throne, get rid of the tyrant . . . he'll have many compelling arguments. Power corrupts."

"Gavriel won't agree to this."

"You've just finished telling me that Gavriel has blind faith in his role to protect Leo . . . the true king."

Elka bit her lip. "What do we do?"

"Warn Faris, perhaps, although if he's as smart and cunning as he's been all of these anni I suspect he might have worked it out for himself."

Elka looked at him. Loethar didn't need to ask, could see the comprehension revealing itself in her astonished expression. "You want me to let you go?"

"I am happy to remain your prisoner but at least put some distance between Leo and myself. Just give us some time to work out how best to handle this. I know you need time to let it all sink in."

"You want me to desert Gavriel and the king we've come back for, in order to protect the very man they have wanted to kill for the last decade?"

Loethar took a long breath. "When you put it like that it does seem rather a lot to ask. But yes, that is what I am asking of you."

Elka walked away, turning her back on him.

"There's not much time."

"Be quiet!" she ordered and he obediently fell silent. Moments later she turned back and hauled him to his feet.

"Well?" he asked.

"Just get up and get moving," she instructed. "I'm going to hide you, and then I'm going to find out exactly what Gavriel and his king are plotting."

"Thank you, Elka."

"Shut up, Loethar. Have you any idea what a betrayal this is of Gavriel?"

"It's the right decision until you can be sure that theirs is best. If you do, then I'll accept death. So you hold my life in your hands."

"Can you move?"

"Not easily but yes, of course. I can ignore any amount of pain if it means survival."

"I will kill you myself if you try anything. Now grit your teeth and move!"

He did just that, setting his jaw, ignoring the pain jarring throughout his body, forever thankful that his legs could still work freely. And together, he and Elka headed deep into the higher part of the forest.

Gavriel spun around twice, confused and then shocked. "She's gone," he said.

Leo let out a howl of anguish. "I knew it! I knew the Davarigon bitch couldn't be trusted!"

Gavriel loomed before him. "Be careful, Leo. Be very careful. I'm sure Elka has an explanation for this."

"Explanation? *Explanation?* How about treachery? Or betrayal? That has a nice ring. Was it just my imagination or did you notice how friendly the two of them were? She protected his life with her own not so long ago. Now she's taken him somewhere."

"You don't know that!"

"Open your eyes, for Gar's sake, Gav! She's gone. And so is he. It doesn't matter how it came about. It makes no difference whether he charmed her or overwhelmed her or simply persuaded her with reason, but she must be helping him. Or at least one of them would be here where we left them not so long ago."

"But why? Give me a reason why she would do this?"

Leo shook his head. "What does it matter?"

"It matters. Elka does nothing without rationale. She thinks everything through. I think the last truly spontaneous act that woman made was interfering in my life and wresting me back from those barbarian soldiers."

"Well, here's her latest rash act. She's chosen the emperor over you."

"That's ridiculous. Elka and I . . ."

"What?" Leo demanded, his tone full of derision.

Gavriel paused and ran his hand through his hair. "Well, we've been close friends for a decade. She hardly knows him. And she's disgusted by the death he's wreaked on the Set."

"And now she's met him and he's convinced her to get him away from us. Now more than ever I need the protection of an aegis. Until now I've had the disguise of anonymity, the cover of Loethar's belief that I was killed a long time ago. That is all shattered now. You have to help me. We have to get Faris trammeled."

"I have to go after her. Make her see reason, understand why she did this. She could have been startled. Maybe she saw other enemies and got him away for all the right reasons?" Gavriel tried.

"Then where are these intruders? We'd see some evidence. And who is going to be traveling this high up, this deep into the forest, by chance?"

Gavriel shook his head. "I just want to know why."

"First we must return to Faris. I'm now so vulnerable we can't waste another moment on recriminations. Let's get the protection we need and then worry about Loethar. He's injured. He can't get that far, even on her back," Leo said with immense disgust. Turning, he headed back through the woods toward where they'd left Kilt.

Gavriel followed, his mind in a daze of confusion.

Five

He glanced over at her. "Are you all right?"

She gave a tight, nervous smile. "Yes. Just a bit overwhelmed, I suppose."

"Just move as though you mean it, Lily," Kirin counseled. "Freath told me this many times over the last ten anni. Half the battle with any form of guise is confidence. *Talk like you mean it, walk like you mean it,* is what he used to say. If we can convince the first few people we meet, you'll blend into the palace with ease. I have rooms well away from any of the people you need to fear."

She nodded. "I trust you, Kirin."

"I'm glad. Just act the role, Lily; no one's got any reason to disbelieve it. We've gone over our story so many times I almost believe it."

"Well, we're not lying, we are married," she said as she held up her hand. They both looked at the ring on her finger. Lily's expression was a study in disbelief.

Kirin made his voice as gentle as he could. "Come on, Mrs. Felt, let me show off what a beautiful wife I've caught on my travels."

"After you, Master Felt," she said, nodding.

Kirin led the way toward the great palace gates, slowing his horse as the guards stepped out. He recognized three of them.

"You're back," said a young man whose name, Kirin recalled, was Jert. "People have been worried about you."

"Worried?" Kirin frowned. "Why? Surely Master Freath told everyone I was on a sabbatical?"

"Erm, well, we've had bad news from the north," Jert said, pointing him through the gates.

Kirin's anxiety deepened. "What kind of bad news?" he asked as he got off his horse to lead it through.

The young man shook his head. "We're not sure what it means—not much detail filters down to us. But the news this morning is that General Stracker is headed back to Bright-helmstone today . . . alone. He should be here shortly. The runner came by almost exactly on the last bell."

"Alone? Without whom?" Kirin asked, shaking his head, confused as another familiar soldier joined them, an older man. "Hello, Kain."

"Master Kirin. Good to see you back safe and sound."

Kirin found a grin. "I've been a little busy finding myself a wife," he said, gesturing to Lily as he handed over his reins to a young stableboy.

His two companions laughed and Kirin snuck a glance at Lily. She was smiling, but he could tell she was uncomfortable with the men's attention. Clearing his throat, he said hastily, "I suppose I should have sent word but I presumed Freath would advise all who needed to know. Anyway, who did you expect should be accompanying the general?"

"The emperor, Master Kirin," Jert replied. "Loethar went north in search of his brother after their mother died."

Kirin paused, privately delighted at this news. "Gar's breath!" he forced out, making sure he sounded shocked and appropriately sorrowful. "She seemed in good health when I left."

"She was," the older man said, an edge of sarcasm in his voice. "And while nothing's being said, we all think that's why the empress has been banished."

"Banished?" Kirin repeated, definitely surprised by this news and even more delighted. "Why?"

Kain winked. "It's not for me to say. Let's just agree that the emperor didn't trust her story that his mother died of natural causes." He tapped his nose as though they were speaking in confidence.

Kirin felt his mouth drop open. Finally he said, "I've only been gone a short while. Any more death or drama to speak of?" He said it lightly, as a means of extricating himself and Lily, expecting the guards would shake their heads and he could move on, but the soldier called Kain grew serious.

"It sounds like you haven't heard about Master Freath?"

Kirin felt the hair rise on the back of his neck. "Freath? No. What's wrong with him? I was at his side just a few days ago."

Kain nodded. "Yes, I thought so. I presume that's why the general is keen to speak to you."

"What? Why?"

Kain shrugged. "To ask you who might have killed Freath."

"Killed . . . pardon?" Kirin took a breath. "Freath is dead?" he murmured, the final word catching in his throat.

"Already buried, I believe."

"But why . . . who? . . ." Kirin trailed off, feeling sick and frightened. "And the general thinks I had something to do with it?" he continued, his throat feeling as though it were closing.

The man nodded. "Well, I think the emperor and our general believe that you might have some information that could help," he said carefully.

Kirin couldn't speak for a few moments. Finally he stuttered, "Forgive me, this news is a shock."

"I know you and he were close. Anyway, I shall let General Stracker know you are returned. He will want to speak with you immediately."

"Excuse me, Kain. I . . . I need to . . ." He didn't finish his sentence. Grabbing Lily's arm, he urged her away from the guards. "We have to get away from here," he growled beneath his breath.

"What?"

"Don't react. Just walk. Smile at me. I said smile." She found one. "Good, well done. Now put your hand against my chest as though you're concerned for me."

She did as she was asked. "Believe me, I am concerned for you. What happens now?"

He turned to her and swallowed. "Freath's dead. I don't know what to do. He was our protection."

Lily looked ahead, and he could tell her head was swimming with the same anxieties as his own.

"We're going to get some money and then we're gone. All right?"

She nodded, looking frightened. "Are we in immediate danger here?"

"Yes, we could be."

"Oh, Kirin—"

"You have to trust me now. I won't let anything happen to you, Lily."

She didn't look convinced. "You said I was a liability from the moment I opened my mouth and claimed to be your wife."

"None of this is your fault. And you are my wife, don't forget that."

She nodded, none of the fear leaving her expression.

"I need you to force yourself to be calm and to just pretend. We will get through this."

People nodded and smiled at them, some even stopped to pass a few words with Kirin, and Lily felt herself in a whirl of activity and congratulations as her husband put aside his fears and feigned precisely the right blend of charm and sorrow. Yes, he'd just received the terrible news of Freath, yes, they'd only just arrived back into the capital to hear the dire revelation, wasn't it dreadful about Dara Negev—whoever she is, Lily thought—and this was his new wife. She found herself being admired, eyed up and down, even hugged by a very jolly woman, and all the time Kirin was dragging her gently forward. They walked down corridors, up two flights of stairs, across landings, and then up another spiraling staircase. The palace became quieter and quieter until Kirin stood before a door. From around his neck he pulled a thong. And the key that hung from it opened the door, the timber creaking as he pushed it open.

"Here we are," he said, throwing her a sad glance. "Welcome to my home of the last ten anni."

* * *

The general threw the reins of his horse at the approaching stableman, barely acknowledging the soldiers around him who stood straighter and touched a hand to one cheek in a sign of recognition of the tribes.

Stracker's tatua was drawn back by a snarl. *How had Loethar got away?* He'd ridden ahead of his henchmen, too disgusted to travel with them or even look at them right now. *Fires of Aludane! The man had too many lives!* Now he had no ally, only enemies.

Stracker strode through the halls and corridors of Brighthelmstone, startling palace workers, making for the wing reserved strictly for the emperor. His towering, threatening presence brooked no argument and he was permitted to barge into his brother's chambers unchallenged. Once in Loethar's salon, he slammed the door shut, yelling that he was to be left undisturbed unless information was forthcoming. Then, standing by one of the tall windows where he had so often seen his brother position himself as he pondered an issue, Stracker now adopted a similar position and brooded.

He had never been the clever son but it angered him that his family constantly underrated his ability, ever since Loethar had beaten him—more than beaten . . . humiliated him—on the day when the tribe fought for leadership. Yes, Loethar had been a magnificent warrior in his day, although Stracker wondered how fast those lightning quick skills might be today. He had certainly capitulated with ease back in the forest; hadn't even offered the slightest resistance.

Instead, his brother had spoken about honor and duty. Stracker gave a choked sound of anger as he stared out toward the forest fringe. Loethar had become so naturalized as a Denovian that not only did he no longer look like he was Steppesborn, he didn't even seem to think like a tribesman any more. His brother had become more and more a stranger to him until now their intentions, their whole outlooks, seemed to be on opposite ends.

Once again Stracker wished he had been able to wheedle out of his mother which of the tribal lords had fathered Loether. Stracker had tried many times but it was one subject she had been entirely closed to. Being her first born he would have thought she'd one day share this detail with him but she took that secret to her death. He wondered if Loethar knew.

But where was he now? he screamed in his mind. *And who was protecting him?* He had never seen who hurled the stone that struck his temple. He touched the spot now and felt the tenderness, pain shooting across his head. It made him livid to think that anyone would dare take a shot at him. He would find that person and tear him limb from limb with his bare hands.

A knock at the door interrupted his angry thoughts.

"What?" he roared.

The door opened slowly, tentatively, and a young messenger peered in.

"You'd want to have some news to risk interrupting me," Stracker snarled.

The young man cleared his throat. He didn't step inside any further and he didn't close the door behind him. "General Stracker, you asked me to find out if there was any news regarding Kirin Felt. General, Master Felt arrived today."

"What?" Stracker roared and took a pace forward.

The youngster quailed, instantly fell into Steppes language in his fear, and began to gabble. "He is in Brighthelmstone. According to the men at the gates, he has a new wife. They . . . they arrived during the last bell, not that long before you did."

"Find them! I wish to speak with them immediately."

"I thought you would say that, general, and I have already organized an escort. I sensed this man is important to you."

Stracker was surprised. The boy showed intuition. The useful kind. "Very good. What is your name?"

"Leak, general."

"I will remember you, Leak. Go fetch Kirin Felt and bring his wife also. Do not brook any argument," he said, returning to the Denovian language that Loethar had always insisted upon. "And one more thing: I want you to fetch someone else for me, too."

As soon as he was inside the deceptively large chamber, Kirin appeared to crumple in on himself. All the bravado and courage deserted him and he sat on the bed staring at the straw on the floor.

Lily waited, unsure at first. Then she sat alongside him and took his hand. Cradling it between her palms, she rubbed it softly. "I'm so sorry about Freath," she began gently.

He shook his head. "How can it be? I should have stayed with him. Perhaps I could have—"

"Kirin," she cut in, determined to stop the wave of recrimination that she sensed was coming, "no amount of blaming yourself can convince me that Freath didn't know he was living on borrowed time."

He turned to stare at her with damp eyes. "What do you mean?"

Lily raised his hand and kissed it softly, briefly. "From everything you've told me about courageous Freath, he has been risking his life since before you even came to the palace. He had committed himself to his double life, knew the risks, accepted the consequences. In a way, he'd already given his life to the Valisars."

Kirin looked broken. "He often said that. He would tell me that death was not something he feared because death walked alongside him each day."

Lily nodded. "He truly was a brave and loyal man. Leonel owes him so much."

"He was on his way to meet with the king. I just don't see how things could have gone wrong."

"I imagine we'll hear the details soon enough. For now you must accept that nothing you do can bring him back. You have to concentrate on protecting your life . . . and mine."

He gazed at her for a moment, unblinking, and then nodded. "You're right. We haven't time to spare for grieving. We have to get away from here. That's the main task."

"What are you planning? Where shall we go?"

"Where we go is the least of our problems. Right now we just need to get as far from General Stracker as possible. The man is mad and has always hated us Vested. With Freath I enjoyed a certain amount of protection simply because he was so close to Loethar. But his death will signal a change, especially with the emperor not even in the palace. Loethar might have tolerated Freath's association with me but I doubt very much if he'll lose any sleep over hearing that I met with an accidental death on the end of one of Stracker's swords." He gave a grim smile. "And even if he doesn't kill me he's almost certainly going to pack me off to wherever the hell they were taking all those other Vested."

"Right," Lily said, nodding, desperate to be optimistic in her trust of Kirin. "What can I do?"

He began opening drawers. "Pack whatever you think we might need. Keep it light. There's some medicines in that cabinet over there," he said, pointing.

Lily made a scoffing sound. "We don't need those. I am a walking medicine cabinet, please trust that."

He nodded. "Fine. Help me with this floorboard then." Quickly he inserted a thin letter opener into a crack between two boards, raising one of them slightly.

She squatted opposite him. "Is this where you keep your money?"

"I'm afraid so. Not very creative, am I?"

She smiled and pulled on the lifted board. It sighed and then with a soft creak gave way. Beneath it was a sack. Kirin lifted it out and opened it for her to look inside.

Lily raised a shocked gaze to him. "Kirin, that's a small fortune in coin."

He shrugged. "I've never had need for money but Freath insisted on my receiving a stipend from the Crown. I'm not sure whether Loethar or Stracker even knew about it. We'll split it up between us, just in case we get separated or robbed. It's too noisy for one person to carry anyway."

Lily nodded, still amazed at the amount of money before her. They busied themselves stashing the coin in pockets and little pouches that Kirin produced, stringing the pouches around each of their necks and two each from their waists.

"There," Kirin said at last, satisfied. "Whatever we now need we can buy."

"Then let's go. What's the plan?"

He bit his lip. "It's too risky to try and organize horses.

We'll have to leave on foot and worry about transport later. We can leave by one of the side gates. I think it's best if we head down to the chapel. It's probably the quietest area of the palace complex and at this time will likely be deserted. There's—"

A loud banging on the door interrupted him. Both Lily and Kirin froze. "Master Kirin?" a voice inquired.

Lily melted into his side as Kirin put a protective arm around her. He nodded encouragement when she stared at him, terrified, and then called out, "Who is it?"

"It's Leak, Master Kirin, General Stracker's messenger."

She felt Kirin straighten and knew her own body had stiffened at the mention of the barbarian.

"Don't panic, Lily," he whispered. "We just have to continue playing our role."

She nodded, swallowing. Her father had always cautioned that there was no good to be had in the cities. She'd been aware that he had always avoided any contact with the capital in particular; even at festival time when it seemed as though everyone except themselves would travel to Brighthelmstone to enjoy all the merrymaking, she and her father had remained deep in the woodland. When she was younger, Lily had resented their isolation.

But now, sensing Kirin's fear, knowing that General Stracker was a thug, she realized that life in the woods with her father, and more recently with Kilt, had been so wise. How had Kirin and Freath lived with such constant anguish all these anni?

"Just a moment," Kirin called out and he looked her way. They had no choice. She nodded.

Kirin opened the door. "Yes, what is it, Leak?"

"General Stracker wishes to see you immediately, Master Kirin."

"Immediately?" Kirin repeated. "I thought the general was away."

"He returned a short while ago, Master Kirin."

"I see. And why the urgency? I have only just returned from a long journey myself. My wife and I are weary, keen to—"

"I'm sorry, Master Kirin. I was simply asked to fetch you. I have a soldier escort waiting."

Lily felt her throat go dry as she watched from behind as Kirin peered into the hallway.

"Since when do we use armed escorts around the palace?" he demanded, his voice even tighter. "What is going on?"

Lily stepped up to her husband and linked arms; she had to convey to him that she would be brave and he must do whatever he had to in order to keep up the front they had constructed. As frightened as she was, and she knew Kirin must be, it sounded as though facing the general was his only option now. Escape would have to wait.

"Forgive me, Master Kirin. I am just doing as bid by the general. Can you please come with us now." The messenger's voice was polite but even Lily could hear his waning tolerance.

"Let me just settle my wife, please. This is most inconvenient and—"

"Er, the general has requested your wife's presence too."

Lily's heart skipped. "Now look here, Leak," Kirin tried, "this really is—"

"General's orders," a new voice growled.

Lily didn't think Kirin had even seen the soldier approach. His bulk filled the doorway without warning as the man stared down at them with an unswerving gaze.

There was nothing her husband could say. "Right. Just give me a moment." He closed the door and turned to Lily, his mind clearly scrambling.

"Listen, Kirin," she whispered. "You have nothing to fear. You had nothing to do with Freath's death. Your conscience is clear and they will see that as they question you."

"But, Lily, I am a traitor. Perhaps they'll see that too," he whispered back, sounding helpless.

"You've hidden it for a decade. Keep hiding it. Come on. How do I look?" she asked, pushing back her hair and pinching at her cheeks.

"Beautiful," he replied, taking her hand and kissing her cheek. "Let's go face the barbarian beast."

"I sense you would prefer to face Loethar."

"Not really. Stracker is just a thug. Loethar is far more dangerous because he's clever and cunning."

"So there's hope, then," she quipped and felt a surge of helpless affection for Kirin's lopsided smile when it came.

Kirin hesitated. "Why are we being taken to the emperor's salon if we are to see General Stracker?"

"The general has summoned you from these rooms," Leak explained.

Kirin glanced at Lily. She looked so pale. He hated himself for bringing her here suddenly. He had endangered her life in order to secure his cover. Glancing at the two guards who flanked him, he caught Lily's attention and gave her a soft sad smile of encouragement. And as the messenger knocked on the door, he promised himself that come what may he would get Lily out of the palace to safety . . . even if it killed him.

"Enter!" boomed the familiar voice.

"Kirin and Mistress Felt to see you, general," Leak said, entering first.

Kirin duly trooped in, resisting the urge to quail before Stracker's overwhelming bulk. The general eyed them both smugly and with what Kirin sensed was malicious intent.

"Welcome back, Felt. You've had us all worried." He looked over their heads to the soldiers and a slight inclination told them they were dismissed. "You too may leave, Leak."

Kirin waited while the three others left. When the door closed he swallowed. He thought about Freath and how he no longer had the man's cunning to rely upon; now it was down to him to find a way to extricate them from Stracker.

Stracker seemed to be waiting for a response. Kirin frowned and shrugged. "I don't know why, General Stracker. There was no need for anyone to worry. Master Freath gave me permission to leave Francham."

"Freath is dead."

Kirin blinked. "I still can't believe it. I've known the news barely minutes. It seems unthinkable."

"And yet it's true. His body was brought back just days ago. He lay in the morgue while my brother came to terms with it." He turned, walked back toward the window and seemed to ponder this thought. Kirin glanced at Lily, trying to reassure her. She looked petrified. "He was murdered, you see." He swung back and gave Kirin a hard look.

A silence lengthened as they stared at one another.

Kirin swallowed as the horror of what he'd just heard sank in. "Murdered?" he finally repeated. "Kain at the gate mentioned he'd been killed. I assumed it was an accident."

"No accident," the general said harshly. "Stuck in the gut like a pig."

"When?"

The general smiled maliciously. "The same night you disappeared. Coincidence, eh?"

Kirin felt his throat go dry. He swallowed again. "And you think I had something to do with it, general? That I might have organized the slaughter of the man I have kept company for the past decade, with whom I have been friends for all of that time, my superior?"

Stracker shrugged. "We've been waiting to hear your side of it, certainly."

"I did not kill Freath. I did not know of any plot to kill him and I have no knowledge whatsoever of anyone who would wish him harm."

"Apart from any number of people he has offended at the palace, starting with me," Stracker continued acidly.

"No one knew of our arrival in Francham. He hadn't even met anyone official for anyone to be forewarned."

"Well, you knew. And then you conveniently disappeared."

"I left Freath, at his behest and with his best wishes, to visit my old home. There was nothing untoward about my departure. We planned to see each other back at Brighthelmstone on this day, as arranged," Kirin lied.

"And he had no other meeting arranged in the north other than with the local mayor?"

Kirin frowned. "None whatsoever," he said indignantly, hoping his lie sounded convincing. "Certainly none that I was privy to."

Stracker's glance slid across to Lily. Kirin could feel her flinch beside him.

"This is my wife, Lily."

Stracker's tatua stretched and a ghastly, malevolent smile spread over his face. "Mrs. Felt. How beautiful you are."

Lily bit her lip. "General Stracker," she said, curtseying.

"You can't have known Master Felt terribly long."

"Actually, general," she said, nervously smiling, glancing at Kirin, "I've known him since childhood. We . . . er . . . we both grew up on Medhaven."

"Is that so?"

She nodded. Kirin felt his gut twist. "We were childhood sweethearts. I thought I'd lost Kirin for good," she said, giving Kirin a sweet side smile. "But then he came back. No warning," she said archly and Kirin loved her all the more for trying so hard when he knew how frightened she was. "He just arrived back on the island. 'Hello, Lily,' he said, as if we'd only parted a few days previous." She gave a soft laugh. "I'm embarrassed to say my heart leaped. I thought I was over him, particularly as I was seriously considering Link Chervil's proposal of marriage."

"Link Chervil?" Kirin repeated in mock astonishment. "What an oaf."

"Link's doing very well, if you don't mind."

"What does Link do for a living?" Stracker asked and Kirin knew he wasn't in the least bit interested. This was a test.

"Link is a—"

"I asked your wife, Master Felt. Mrs. Felt?"

Lily hesitated, but tried to cover her nervousness with a small smile. "Why, Link is a miller."

Kirin died inside.

Six

Loethar was breathing hard. "Elka, stop," he croaked.

She turned around and came back to him. "Are you in pain?"

He shook his head, unable to talk, as he sucked in air. "Can't breathe."

"Does your head ache?"

"As though it may explode."

She nodded. "Sit down." He needed no further encouragement, and dropped immediately to the ground. "I think you've got what we call 'mountain sickness.' It's the air up this high. It does affect some people this way if they're not used to moving around at such a height."

"I'm a tribal man from the plains," he said, trying to grin but it quickly turned into a grimace. "All right, now I'm hurting. Everything hurts."

"So much for the barbarian warlord."

"I was never either of those things," he complained. "That's a title the Set royals gave me. I'm a king in my own right, of the Steppes even before I took over the empire."

"Forgive me."

He waved a tired hand. "Is this going to get any easier?"

She shook her head. "Only with many moons of practice. So, first things first. Watch how I'm breathing." She began to take very quick but deep breaths. "This will fill your chest with air faster than trying to breathe normally at this height."

"Like this?" he asked, trying to mimic her.

"Good. A breath every five counts if you can and as deep as you can achieve. And drink. You have to take on more water than normal. Believe me, it will really help."

He immediately swigged from the water sack she handed him.

"Keep sipping. It's important," Elka urged. "Now," she said, sounding distracted as she scanned the landscape, "what we have to do is get you lower."

"Lower?"

"You can't stay this high. Your sickness will only get worse before it gets better. And we don't have time to spend getting you used to this height. We'll have to descend. The problem is I suspect Leo knows his way around those lower levels."

"Let's face it, Elka, after living around you I suspect de Vis knows how to handle the higher levels, too. We're trapped."

"Yes, but Gavriel doesn't know the geography of the higher altitudes as the king must of the lower forest. Besides, we can outwit Gavriel, I know how he thinks. But not the king."

"Don't call him that."

"Why? Does it offend you?"

"Yes, damn you. I am the true King."

"And just look at you." She laughed but not unkindly.

Loethar found himself smiling bleakly. "I'm a picture of power, right?"

She helped haul him back to his feet. "Come on, my lord. You can fight it out for the title another time."

"Why are you helping me?"

"Frankly, I don't know. Behind me is the man I love. And even if I find his loyalty to Leo pig-headed, I couldn't tell you why I've chosen to betray Gavriel and side with the enemy! The problem, I suppose, is that I expected so much more of Leo."

"No, the problem, my beautiful mountain goat, is that you didn't expect to like me as much as you do. You'd anticipated some sort of thuggish monster and what you've found during our journey into the forest is the opposite. Handsome too." He gave her a smile.

"Lo save me. Are all the Valisars this arrogant?" She pushed him forward and they traveled in silence until he needed to stop again.

She watched him settle himself against a tree. Her brow knitted together. "Do you hate him?"

"Who, Leonel?" She nodded and he paused while he considered her question. "In a way, like you, now that I've met him I've changed my opinion. I wanted him dead like his father. But now that I see him, I see a young man desperately trying to fulfill what his father had been force feeding him, insisting he achieve since he was born. These last few hours I've put myself into Leo's position and I would be lying if I didn't admit that I would have acted no differently. So I don't hate him. I pity him. He is compelled—as I am—to claim what he believes his."

"But now neither of you have it. Your brute of a brother does."

"He's my half-brother. We shared a womb, that is all. I wouldn't hesitate to kill him, nor he me—as you witnessed."

"I was surprised that you didn't fight back."

"Perhaps it was a mistake. He is fearless but he is a lout, never did bother to learn the art of war or how to fight with skill rather than brute force." He gave a small sigh. "I didn't even bother to arm myself properly. I anticipated a fight, but I should have anticipated the ambush. Somehow I wanted to believe our family had been raised to fight fairly. I am not his enemy. I never was. But he hates me and," he shrugged, "I am not overly fond of him."

"You seemed ready to die." She shook her head. "I mean, you appeared to accept your fate."

He nodded. "It was a strange moment. It felt fitting at the time. I think I'd become disillusioned. My mother should not have died—certainly not the way she did. I have never loved my wife. I have never loved a woman." Elka looked astonished. "It's true. This sounds arrogant but it's genuinely the reason: I've never found anyone who matched me. Valya is beautiful but I am not a man who chases outward beauty. I love things only if they appeal to me on all levels. Valya is cold, calculating. She is driven by a poisonous bitterness that dates back well before she ever knew of my existence. The tragedy is that Valya, I believe, does love me . . . and in the right way." He shook his head with regret. "She is a stunning woman but her looks are constantly compromised by a grasping, shallow, vain, and cruel personality. She actually enjoys watching people suffer. I suppose many would level the same accusation my way," he said, when he saw the look of astonishment flit across Elka's face. "But when I punish people my only satisfaction is knowing that I am right. I don't torture for the sake of it."

"You just leave that to your brother," she finished dryly.

"My *half-brother* can be useful if he's channeled the right way. Until now my mother and I have been the only people who can really exert control over him. Her death changes everything—from the way he views me to his believing he answers to no one any longer. And that's dangerous. He's happiest when there's chaos, bloodshed, disruption."

"And people he can hurt," she remarked.

"Indeed."

"From what I hear, you seemed pretty happy with yourself during the overthrow."

His brow furrowed. "War is different, Elka. War is not polite or pretty. But there should always be a decency to it, for want of a better word. If people surrender, it should be accepted without further death. I only ever held the royals of each realm responsible. Their heads were all I was after. The Set kingdoms were so smug and impressed with themselves. We got word that they were laughing at the thought of a Steppes invasion. Not one of the kings ever for a moment thought a horde of tribal warriors from the plains was a match for even one of their fighting units. So we had to desecrate the armies, completely crush their sense of superiority. That was the only way to force quick surrenders before the civilians began to suffer."

"Spoken like a true king," Elka said lightly.

"I am Valisar," Loethar replied. "Even if my father refused to acknowledge me." He gave a harsh laugh. "You know, my mother was just a night of diversion. A warm and willing body to forget about the minute he mounted his horse the next morning. But she never forgot him; I suspect she loved him more than she cared to admit." At Elka's look of wonder, he shrugged. "She was young, impressionable and no doubt vulnerable. An older, very important man wanted her. Why wouldn't she fall for him?"

"Forgive me, but can I ask how it comes about that a woman with a child, already married, is able to lie down with a stranger . . . a foreigner?"

Loethar sighed. "I know it seems hard to imagine in this day and age but nearly forty anni ago there were strange customs. The Steppes people were quite used to seeing trade caravans going into or out of the Set. I think my mother and Stracker's father were having difficulties. I don't really know what occurred—she refused to talk about it with me—but whether she spent that time with the Valisar royal simply to spite him or there were other circumstances, I'll never know. The fact is Stracker's father treated me as his own son. I will always respect and admire him for that. He was a good man."

Elka shook her head in quiet disbelief. "Did your mother know her lover was the king at the time?"

"I honestly don't know. Perhaps."

"But his scorn hurt her," Elka mused.

"That's right. When he didn't come back for her or show the slightest care about the child she was carrying she wanted to make him pay for using her. And by then she did know his position and I suspect it offended her to realize she was carrying a royal child in her belly that no one wanted to acknowledge."

"How was he supposed to know she was pregnant?"

"I gather she sent word somehow."

"Did she really believe he would look after her?"

He nodded. "I think she did," he said softly. "She was a beautiful woman in her youth and she came from an old, very proud line. I imagine she convinced herself that a marriage between a Steppes woman and a Valisar king could work."

Elka shook her head. "And you?"

"Me?"

"Do you think marriages between different cultures can work?"

"I do. I'm proving it. We have mixed marriages all over the empire. It's just a matter of breaking down old attitudes."

"So in your eyes, Gavriel and I aren't such a ridiculous match?"

She said it lightly, but Loethar took her seriously. "You are a bad match, you two. He doesn't love you romantically, Elka. He loves you as his best friend."

He watched the amusement and the interest in their conversation in her eyes wilt and found a grin for her. "So, marry me instead, Elka. I think we'd make a fine couple and a great example to the rest of the empire."

"You're married already, and a father."

"I despise my wife and we are estranged. My daughter is dead. Truly, what a ruin I am." He kept his tone dry, afraid of sounding self-pitying.

"I'm really very sorry about your daughter," Elka said quietly.

Loethar was surprised to feel his throat close up. He swallowed hard and nodded, trying to keep his emotions in check.

"Forgive me, I don't mean to upset you."

"You're not, Elka," he said softly. "You're a comfort. I haven't yet grieved for my daughter. I needed a son for political reasons and it was a disappointment that a daughter was born. And then to hear that she was sickly and likely to succumb . . . I walked away. I had just lost my mother and Freath; I couldn't bear to look upon my daughter and love her if I was only going to lose her. But I regret that decision now." He shrugged. "Here, beneath the sky, away from all that and with a clearer view of life, I wish I could hold her, tell her that I love her and am proud to be her father." His throat felt tight again, and he cleared it. "My true father didn't love me and I just gave the same hurt to my daughter."

Elka looked shaken. "I'm so sorry."

He gave her a searching glance then shook his head hopelessly. "Don't be. I deserve to suffer."

She smiled quizzically. "You're a very complicated man, Loethar. Lucky for you life is a lot less complex in the mountains." She sighed. "Come on, let's find somewhere safe but lower. You'll feel better almost immediately once we descend but you'll still need to rest."

"Excellent news. Now you'll have to forgive me, Elka, because right now I have to—"

He didn't finish what he was going to say. Instead, he turned quickly, and violently retched.

She sighed. "Men are so weak," she muttered, and won a growl from her companion.

Back at the camp the men had gathered around Leo. It had taken him a long time to assemble them, but he was determined to gauge their reaction as a group, hoping one would give away the truth if they knew what their leader was up to. And he had to be careful about it, for each of these men, he was sure, remained intensely loyal to the outlaw.

"None of you have any idea where Kilt has gone?" he asked, masking the disbelief in his voice, turning it into concern. "I was with him only a short time ago, just before he sent me to speak with Loethar. I need to know what he wants us to do. I have to report to him."

"We haven't even seen Kilt or Jewd for hours," Tern replied.

Leo held his tongue with difficulty. Tern was doing a good job at disguising the stiffness in his tone but Leo had spent many anni learning how to see past the obvious. "Well, I'm sure they'll let us know soon enough what they're up to," he finally said, deciding it was better to appear confused in return for remaining close to the only family he'd known in a decade. "What now?"

"We're moving camp," Tern replied. "It's no longer safe here."

"Really? We weren't followed," Gavriel said.

Tern shook his head. "Kilt never takes chances. In fact, we're splitting up."

"What?" Leo, who had been sitting down, trying to remain casual, jumped to his feet. "Who ordered that?"

The men around him began to mutter between themselves.

"No one did, majesty," Tern said and Leo noted with satisfaction Tern's use of his title. "This is what we do if we feel in any way threatened. It's a precaution. We will re-group."

"When?"

Tern shrugged. "Whenever. You know how it is. We always seem to find one another."

"What should I do?"

"You are welcome to come with me, majesty. I would consider it an honor."

Leo had to think. He glanced at Gavriel. So long apart hadn't changed that bond they'd shared through his childhood. He could see that Gavriel didn't believe a word of what was being said here.

"No, thank you. I might wait here in case Kilt returns. I have things to tell him. He would expect it of me, I think. I've made too many mistakes recently and I don't want to disappoint him again."

Tern nodded unhappily. "As you wish, highness. De Vis, can I leave you to protect the king?"

"It's what I was born to do apparently," Gavriel replied. He said it lazily but Leo could hear the barb in it.

"We'll carry on then," Tern said, and motioned to the men to continue their plans for dispersal.

As they moved away, Gavriel arrived alongside Leo. "They're lying."

"I know."

"Why?"

"Kilt got to them." Leo's face twisted in anger. "He knows what we were planning."

"How?"

"I think you've forgotten just how sharp Kilt is. He and Loethar are well suited for their cunning minds." He grimaced. "All the more reason we can't let them meet."

"Leo, you have to trust me when I say that Elka will not permit Loethar to do this . . . this . . ."

"Trammeling," Leo offered.

"Exactly. And even if she did entertain such an idea, it wouldn't be without my sanction."

"I hope your confidence is borne out, my friend. Otherwise Loethar will be invincible and you might as well run me through with that blade of yours now."

"So what do you suggest we do now?"

Leo shook his head with disgust. "I'm torn as to whether to hunt down Kilt, who I need for protection, or Loethar, to ensure my safety."

"Do you want to hear what I think?"

"I know your idea will be to pursue neither of them."

Gavriel waited.

"All right, let's hear it, Gav," Leo sighed.

"Loethar isn't your primary threat any longer. Right now he's too injured. And no matter how you like to color it, he is my prisoner."

"Yours?" Leo said, surprised, unable to mask the scorn in his voice.

Gavriel nodded, irritatingly calm. "Elka will do what I say."

Leo wanted to say something cutting but was all too aware that apart from Gavriel de Vis he had no one. "You said Loethar is no longer my biggest threat. So who is?"

"His half-brother, Stracker."

"Stracker doesn't even know I exist."

"That's a fair point. But he doesn't need to know you exist to be your problem. As we stand here, Leo, Stracker is, I imagine, laying claim to the empire. And because, according to Steppes law, any man of any tribe can fight for kingship when the king dies, Stracker won't claim Loethar to be dead. Instead, he'll say he's lost or was grabbed by renegades, so he can continue to sit the throne without having to fight for it. As long as Loethar lives, we have time to plan properly. The empire won't be embroiled in war or a struggle for rulership. We can move around freely. No one outside of this forest knows either of us is alive; neither of us is recognizable either."

"All right. But what is your actual plan?"

"To remain here for the time being. I have no plan. I think we need to take some time to think everything through properly. No rash decisions."

"But what about Kilt? I need him."

"Faris has kept you safe and alive for a decade without your having to eat him!"

"And I intend that he will continue to do so."

Gavriel looked pained. "I'm sorry, Leo, but I won't be a party to such a move."

"Your father never refused his king."

"My father was never asked to participate in such a debased practice."

"You can't know that."

"No, that's true. But I do know my father . . ." Gavriel hesitated but said no more and Leo knew his old friend wanted to add: *which is more than you can say about your own*.

"Well, you've made your position clear."

Gavriel's eyes narrowed. "All I'm saying is wait. Don't do anything rash. I am prepared to agree that if as a last measure all I have standing between you and Loethar's blade is Kilt Faris, I won't permit your death."

Leo felt a thrill of relief. So they weren't really on opposite sides. Gavriel just needed time to adjust. He could bide his time. Plus they were safer up here in the forests than anywhere else. He was sure Kilt wasn't coming back to the camp and Loethar wouldn't dare. "All right. We'll remain here and consider our position."

Gavriel nodded. "Very good, Leo," and from the tone of his voice Leo knew his old friend meant it from the heart. "I'm starving. Do we have any food in this place?"

Elka returned to where she'd left him. "No signs of anyone. I think we'll be all right here for the time being," she said, looking up into the tall tree beneath which Loethar was slumped.

"How are you feeling now?"

"I might not look it but I feel entirely different."

She nodded. "Recovery is surprisingly fast if we get a rapid enough descent in time. We did the right thing for you. Now I have to think about all your other problems. Did you keep drinking?"

He nodded. "Lucky we found that mountain stream. My nephew would have given me nothing."

"Neither would your aegis, remember. Leonel was simply following orders."

"Orders." Loethar grimaced. "He's a king apparently. He's Valisar. He should be giving orders, not taking them."

She sighed. "Frankly, I'm tired of the Valisars."

"They're so unnecessary now, aren't they?" he asked in an ironic tone.

She joined in, smiling. "Too pre-empire for my taste!"

Loethar gave a big belly laugh. "I'm glad I'm with you, Elka, and not that sour de Vis. He doesn't deserve you."

"Gavriel's a good man. Worth far more than you credit him. The very fact that he's not hunting you down—and believe me, he is now a frighteningly good tracker—means that he's somehow controlling Leo's desire to bond you."

The emperor's face grew serious. "Why would he do that, do you think? He hates me, wants to kill me."

Elka sat down beside him and took a swig from the water sack. "With good reason. But you've seen for yourself that he's not nearly so one-eyed as Leo clearly is. Your nephew . . ." She shook her head. "I still can hardly believe you're doing this to each other. You are family."

"I learned the hard way that the Valisar family is one-eyed, particularly if you're the one on the throne," he said, bitterness lacing his tone.

She nodded. "Anyway, I suspect your nephew is being driven by a different hunger. He wants revenge and he's also got the Valisars' problem of believing nothing and no one matters but them. You laid waste to the royals of the Set. Don't blame Leo for wanting to punish you. But I think Gavriel sees beyond his own youthful craving to make you pay for the savage, cowardly death that you gave his father. Gavriel's older, wiser, and doesn't have the all too proud, too self-absorbed, too-royal Valisar blood pounding through his veins. And he can see that times have changed—that there's peace and prosperity now."

"So now I have to rely on my enemy?"

She laughed. "Yes, Loethar. I think you do. And until I hear from him you remain my prisoner."

"If I give you my word that I will not harm you and won't

try to escape, will you agree to unbind me so I don't feel like an animal? Perhaps I can actually be of some help."

She considered this, staring at him. He returned the gaze steadily. Finally, Elka nodded. "Gavriel will kill me but I'm going to trust you, Loethar. I do believe you are a man of your word."

"Indeed. I am Valisar, after all."

She snorted with derision. "That has no effect on me."

"Then I give you my promise as a man who owes you the debt of his life."

"Now that means something to me." Producing a blade from the sheath at her hip, she cut his bonds. "Are you ready to travel? We might as well keep moving while you have some strength."

"I'll move until I drop. Where are we going?"

"Home. I can keep you safe in the mountains."

"Indulge me, Elka."

"You have a better plan," she said. "Yes, of course you do."

He shrugged, though it obviously hurt him to do so. "Will you hear it before you dismiss it? I will not risk your life, that I promise. And we will go to the mountains directly after."

She stared at him for a few moments, weighing him up. "Tell me on our way to Francham. Wherever we're going we'll need horses and medicine. Let's go."

Seven

➤➤ ━━━━━━━━━━━━━━━━━━━━━━━━━━━━━━━ ◆◆

Roddy clung to Ravan gleefully, his breath whipped away by the speed at which they were running. They were already approaching the forest and he knew they would be into the trees in a few heartbeats. Ravan began to slow. He didn't even sound breathless when he spoke.

"We are close now. I'll set you down in a moment." He turned his head and Roddy could see his friend was smiling. "You can catch your breath."

"How about you?"

"I feel perfectly normal. Not even slightly hard of breath." Ravan laughed. "Onward we go!"

Gavriel and Leo were sitting in a comfortable silence. Dusk had closed on the forest and though the birds had fallen quiet the crickets were just beginning to exercise their legs. Leo had found a decent spread of cold food. Neither of them considered it a good idea to light a fire just in case any of Stracker's warriors were still straggling in and around the region.

They had talked for hours about Gavriel's life in the mountains and Leo's growing up in the forest. Inevitably the conversation had run to talk of the old days, of them trapped in the ingress of the palace and life on the run. Now they'd fallen into a comfortable silence, enjoying the summer's mild evening.

And so it was with some shock that Gavriel heard the

sound just when he had announced he would be turning in for the night. "Someone's approaching," he said, leaping to his feet and reaching for his bow.

"I heard. It's not one of the men," Leo replied, quietly picking up his own weapon, belching as he did so.

"Are you all right?"

"I feel a bit ill. I'll get over it. I probably just miss Lily's food."

They instinctively separated and began widening their distance from each other, circling closer to the person they could hear approaching. Gavriel nodded at Leo and ducked behind a large tree, his arrow already nocked. He could still see into the clearing but he'd be invisible to anyone who wasn't aware he was there.

"Who comes?" Leo demanded.

"Friends," came the response. It sounded like a child's voice.

Behind the tree Gavriel frowned and although he didn't step out, he did release the tension on his bow. Finding this camp was hard enough for a tracker so whoever was coming was either very determined or knew the way in.

"Stop!" he heard Leo say. "Name yourselves."

Gavriel peeped around the tree trunk and could just vaguely make out two shapes, a tall person—a man—and then a shorter figure next to him. A boy?

"I am called Roddy and this is Ravan," said the younger one.

Leo nodded. "You call yourselves friends but I don't know you."

"You know Ravan."

"Does Ravan not have a voice?" Leo asked.

"Yes," the man replied. "He does."

"I don't recognize it. I don't recognize either of you. Step into the light or I will order the men who have you encircled to fill you with arrows. We don't take kindly to strangers here."

"Please," Roddy said, and Gavriel could hear fear in his voice. "We come alone. There's just the two of us. And Ravan will explain. You are King Leonel, aren't you?"

Gavriel let go of all tension on the bow and stepped around from the tree fully. He noticed that the man called Ravan saw his movement immediately. *Sharp eyes*, he thought.

"You should be careful what you claim," Leo said but Gavriel could hear the shock in it. He saw the king rub his eyes. "Come into the light of the lantern."

Gavriel circled behind the pair as they approached Leo. The man registered his presence again, turning once and nodding. Gavriel was impressed by both his keen sense of his surrounds and his composure. He was impressive: tall, strong-looking and with a set of his jaw that looked as though he was used to making his own decisions. His hair was dark, loose to his shoulders and even in this low light seemed to gleam. And though he was clean-shaven and dressed in simple black garb Gavriel's sense of him was that he was anything but uncomplicated. Even silent his presence was commanding and vaguely reminiscent of someone. He couldn't place who or why. He frowned again, deeper this time.

"How did you find this camp?" he asked.

"Ravan knows the way," the boy answered.

"Who are you, Ravan?" Leo asked. Though his tone was pointed, Gavriel thought he looked a little distracted. Was Leo sweating?

Gavriel came around to face the strangers, his weapon by his side.

The man bowed. It was elegant, at the same time humble. His companion followed, far clumsier in his execution. The boy looked unsteady as though slightly drunk.

"My name is Ravan," the man began, "but I am known to you under another name. One that will shock. I would ask for your indulgence to hear out our tale." He glanced at the boy, who nodded vaguely.

Gavriel's eyes narrowed. The man was deferring to the boy?

Leo did not miss the glance either. "Do you take your orders from a child, Ravan?"

The man smiled but there was no conceit in it. "Roddy has a better grasp on the world of men for the time being. He and I are close traveling companions. And we are friends. I trust his judgment."

"Over and above your own? How odd."

Ravan gave a shrug. "We share our thoughts."

"Stranger and stranger," Gavriel remarked. "Let me search them first," he said to Leo.

Leo nodded, looking pale in the torchlight.

Both raised their arms without having to be asked. Gavriel could see neither had a weapon but he went through the motions to ensure they had nothing concealed about them. He shook his head at Leo.

"Join us in the light," Leo said. "I'm afraid you are mistaken about King Leonel. He is not—"

"Please, your majesty," Ravan said, his voice even, with not a hint of disdain in it. "I recognize you. I have known you since you were a boy."

Leo had been settling himself on a log but jumped to his feet. "You will have to explain that. I do not recognize you."

"It does need some explanation—this is true. May I politely ask for some food and water for the boy, please?" He looked at Roddy and frowned. "He has made a long journey to meet you."

Leo glanced at Gavriel, who felt obliged to assemble some cheese, nuts and berries from their meager rations. He set them down with a fresh pitcher of water. "Help yourself," he said to Roddy.

"Thank you," the boy said and began picking at the food. Gavriel didn't think the youngster looked well at all.

"Yourself?" Leo offered.

Ravan shook his head. "Thank you. You may remember me as Vyk," he began without further preamble.

"The only Vyk I knew was a bird, I'm afraid," Leo said, shaking his head. "I have excellent recall of faces and names, even from my childhood but—"

Ravan nodded. "What sort of bird was the Vyk that you knew?"

"Well, not that it's relevant but he was a . . ." Leo stopped.

Gavriel also paused in the action of lowering himself to one of the logs. The shock spread through him like fast moving molten. "You jest," he said, the words tumbling out before he could think them through.

Ravan's gaze hadn't left the king. "I followed you through the forest. De Vis here would have killed me if not for your compassion."

Gavriel blanched and Leo's slack expression told him the king was equally in denial.

Ravan continued, "Forgive me, I know this sounds incredible but I can prove everything I say. I led the girl called Lily to you. She helped you," he said, turning to Gavriel, "with the wound you received from the two poachers. She took you back to her father's hut. He was a simple healer, a forest dweller called Greven, and they kept you overnight. If I'm not mistaken, your majesty, you spent that night in a crawlspace hollowed below the hut. They were terrified when they found out that you were Prince Leonel, on the run from Loethar. I—"

"Wait!" Leo stopped him. "You want us to believe that you are the big black raven that Loethar brought to the palace, that everyone despised?"

"I'm disappointed that I was so loathed. I was a good friend and companion to Loethar."

"But you're a bird!" Leo exclaimed, helpless confusion in his expression, his tone, even his open-armed stance.

"He was one, majesty. Now he's a man, made in the image of King Cormoron, First of the Valisars," Roddy said, a proud edge to his tone. Gavriel could see that Leo was speechless at the mention of King Cormoron. He waited a moment or two longer and then cleared his throat when he saw that Leo was not forthcoming.

"Well, that's a great story. Why don't we start at the very beginning, though. You want us to accept this is Vyk, the raven, now a man?"

Roddy nodded with a wince. "Yes. I'm sorry, who are you?"

Ravan smiled again. "Roddy, this is Gavriel de Vis, champion and Legate I believe to King Leonel."

Silence followed the introduction, everyone looking to Leo.

"I have only questions. You will need to answer them all to my satisfaction or you—"

"Please," Ravan said gently. "Feel free, your majesty. We have come to see you. Roddy, eat, or you will collapse from hunger."

"Why don't you need to eat?" Leo began.

"Because I suppose I am not real. I was a bird. I now have to wonder if that was real too." Ravan shrugged. "Now I am made in the image of a man. You don't look well, majesty."

Gavriel noticed even in the low torchlight that Leo's pallor was worsening. "Leo?"

"Don't worry about me. I've eaten something upsetting. Who made you this way?"

"The serpent."

"Cyrena?"

Ravan nodded. "She came to us."

"Roddy, who are you?"

Roddy had a full mouth. He swallowed awkwardly. "Your majesty, I am no one. I come from a village in the south." There was a big fire there not long ago and my cat was trapped in the barn. I tried to save him but I got confused and then I felt the heat and my clothes went up in flames and I could no longer breathe. I know a man ran into the flames to save me but to be honest I only learned that afterward. I don't remember much of that time except that when I woke up I was whole again."

"How did you meet up with Ravan?"

Gavriel could see that Roddy was trying his utmost to answer clearly and concisely. "I met him," he frowned. "Well, I first saw him in a small woodland on the edge of our village but we first spoke at the cliff edge after the death of Sergius."

Gavriel sighed with confusion. "All right, let's go back to the fire. I'm curious, Roddy, as to how you escaped death if you ran into a burning barn."

"I told you I was healed."

"Healed of burns?" Gavriel asked archly.

The boy nodded. "So was poor Clovis."

"Clovis?" Leo wondered.

"He was the man who ran into the barn after me. I have to lie down."

"We have traveled a long way," Ravan said. "Sleep, Roddy. I will explain everything. I haven't mentioned this to Roddy but Clovis was also at the palace," Ravan remarked, surprising Gavriel. "He was one of two Vested chosen by Freath as part of a bargain made between Freath and Loethar. Clovis wasn't very powerful." Ravan shrugged. "My understanding is that he could predict rough weather on the seas or which provisions to stock up on, that sort of thing. But he couldn't wield his magic against anyone, not like I suspect Kirin Felt could."

"Felt?" Leo narrowed his eyes. "Wait a moment. Felt! Isn't that the man Lily has gone away with? I'm pretty sure that's the name Tern used. Lily was meant just to keep him under observation but she ended up pretending to be his wife so she could stay close." His eyes narrowed. "Tell me, how empowered is this Kirin Felt?"

"I really couldn't say," Ravan answered. "He hid his ability from Loethar and Stracker."

"Ah, now we have it," Leo said. He still looked pale, but he stood to pace. "I wonder just how powerful he is." He swung around to face Ravan. "Do you know what an aegis is?"

Gavriel felt a spike of uncertainty run through him. Where was Leo going with this? He was getting too obsessed with the idea of his ageis for Gavriel's comfort.

But before he could say anything, Roddy seemed to crumple beside Ravan. "My apology, I must be excused."

"Are you feeling faint, Roddy?" Ravan asked.

"Come with me," Roddy choked out. "I don't feel well."

Ravan looked to Leo, who shrugged his permission. The two newcomers walked away; Roddy seeming to be doubled up, as though preparing to retch, Ravan was rubbing the boy's back.

Gavriel frowned after them.

"Don't worry, they're not going anywhere," Leo remarked. "Do you trust their story?"

"It's almost too remarkable not to. Why would anyone lie about something like being a bird? And he knows too much not to be that awful raven."

Leo gave a helpless gesture with his hand. "I'm glad we didn't kill him. He might be helpful to us. He certainly seems keen to tell us all that he knows. Look, they're coming back."

Gavriel nodded absently, watching the pair approach again, Roddy still clearing his throat. "Better?" he asked Roddy.

The boy didn't answer. He looked pale, weary.

"You were telling us about Felt," Leo continued. "I think he may be an aegis. Do you know what that is?"

"The legendary champion of the Valisars," Ravan responded. "One born secretly for each child, who must be found and bonded. You want to find and bond Kirin Felt?" Ravan asked, surprised.

"Exactly! I need protection now, more than ever. An aegis offers the only true protection I can count on."

Gavriel felt his stomach drop.

"No offense to you, Gav," Leo said over his shoulder without looking at him.

"None taken," Gavriel lied.

"I think we should go after Felt," Leo threw at Gavriel, "especially now that Faris is onto us."

Gavriel blinked in confusion but Leo wasn't waiting for an answer; he had suddenly swiveled around and levelled his sword at Ravan. The man and boy stood, both looking daunted but not, Gavriel noted, especially surprised.

Leo noted it too.

"You know my next question," he accused.

"And let me answer it, highness," Ravan replied carefully. "I am not an aegis and Roddy—"

"How can I be sure?"

Ravan thought about this. The boy looked terrified, ready to flee. "You can't. But I doubt very much that we'd have risked walking into your midst."

Leo regarded Ravan without speaking. In the silence, Roddy sank to the ground, holding his head between his knees.

Gavriel held his breath but his old friend finally lowered the sword. "You're right," Leo admitted and rubbed at his head. He looked ill too. "You wouldn't have risked it. But we now know we have Faris and potentially Felt. Felt won't know we're coming so he's the better option."

Gavriel's already diminishing tolerance gave up. "Leo, this is—"

The king raised his hand. "So why *did* you come here?" he suddenly challenged the pair before him.

Ravan glanced down at Roddy. Again Gavriel sensed, rather than understood, the slight tension between the pair. The man was, he was sure, deferring to the child. "In a way, your majesty, it does involve the question of an aegis."

"What?" Gavriel and Leo said together, both astonished.

Ravan took a moment to gather his thoughts. "Actually, it's Roddy who should tell this." He glanced again at the child and nodded. "He was there from the beginning. But he doesn't look to be in any shape to talk right now."

"What's wrong with him?" Leo demanded.

"He's been through a great deal. I suppose he's tired, relieved, frightened. Perhaps I should tell you what I know."

"Go ahead," Leo suggested.

Ravan nodded. "After Clovis and Roddy were saved from the fire, returned from death, both Roddy and I witnessed a man being bonded. That's one of the reasons that Clovis is dead."

Leo sat down again. Gavriel remained standing but stepped a little closer, not sure where Ravan was going.

"The man who was bonded is called Greven," Ravan continued.

"Wait! Was this man a leper?" Leo interrupted.

Ravan nodded. "It is the same Greven you know, even though he no longer shows any sign of his sickness. The leprosy was the sign, you see."

"I can't believe it," Leo finally said, his voice tight. "We were with him in the forest. Lily doesn't know, I'm sure of it."

"More to the point," Gavriel continued, suddenly feeling chilled, "who bonded him?"

Leo's eyes blazed with a new fire. "Indeed, that is the most important question. If not me or Loethar, who?"

"Loethar?" Ravan replied, taken aback.

"Is Valisar," Leo answered, the words coming out as though they were dirty in his mouth.

Ravan said nothing but Gavriel could all but see the wheels turning in the strange man's mind. The silence lengthened between them and finally Ravan nodded, as though accepting the logic of the incredible claim. "There is another Valisar on the loose, you could say, your majesty," Ravan began quietly. "In my former guise I kept an eye on him these last ten anni."

Gavriel watched Leo's expression droop. In the lamplight he looked even more gray. It took no more than a heartbeat for him to work it out, far quicker than Gavriel could. "Piven?" Leo whispered and Gavriel felt like a blade had been stuck in his gut. Surely not?

But Ravan nodded.

"You're sure," Leo insisted, his voice hoarse. "He's mute, he's lost in his mind, he's . . ."

"He is whole, your majesty," Ravan insisted. "You must forget the little boy you knew. He is now a strapping youth with anger in his soul. According to Roddy, he had both Clovis and Sergius killed."

At the mention of the second name Gavriel saw Ravan's composure slip for the first time.

"Sergius?" Gavriel asked. "Should we know him?"

"Perhaps not, my lord," Ravan replied. "But Sergius was not only my friend, he was also the most loyal of servants to the Crown. He was dedicated to the cause of the Valisars."

"And yet I don't even know his name," Leo challenged.

"You would have, had he survived. He lived as a hermit on the western coast but he was known to both your fathers. He was a wielder of magic. He made me."

"Made you?" Gavriel exclaimed. "What? So your presence in the palace was contrived?"

The man shook his head. "I am yet to discover what my role is. I was Loethar's companion and I loved him. I knew nothing else. But I loved Sergius more. He was my true friend and he gave me to Loethar. I reported back to Sergius on the palace intrigues."

"You were a spy?" Leo asked, incredulous.

"Of sorts, yes. With Valisar interests at heart. I didn't know Loethar was Valisar, of course."

"Incredible!" Gavriel remarked. "You were Freath in bird form."

The set of Leo's mouth told him the king didn't appreciate the mention of the old manservant. "Piven . . ." he murmured. "Piven was supposed to be an orphan that my parents took pity on. It was true they doted upon him but—"

"Another purposeful secret, no doubt," Gavriel interrupted bitterly.

"They doted on him, your majesty, because he was their true son, as you were. The Legate is right. Piven's lack of genuine royal status as far as the barbarians were concerned is what saved him—that and Loethar's genuine fondness for the boy."

"Are you serious?"

"About what, highness? Piven's legality or Loethar's fondness?" He shrugged. "Loethar liked Piven but if he'd known his true heritage, he would have been put to the sword, I can assure you of that. And Piven *is* Valisar. Don't doubt it. He has successfully trammeled Greven. He hacked off Greven's hand, cooked it and ate some and instantly Greven fell under his control."

Gavriel listened in silent revulsion. But while Leo's mouth twisted at the mention of the brutality, Gavriel could see the king's fascination had only deepened.

"And you know it worked?"

Ravan shrugged. "All too well. Greven is being commanded against his will. He slaughtered Clovis, who was unarmed, and he threw Sergius off a cliff."

"But Greven is an old man," Gavriel said, desperate to discredit the tale.

Ravan shook his head. "The Valisar Legacy has made him incredibly strong. Piven is untouchable, and his arrogance and confidence continue to heighten."

"Where is he?"

"We dared not give chase. We needed to find you, your highness, to warn you that he wants to kill you."

"Why?" Leo looked aghast. "I'm his brother. We are both Valisar."

"He hates you for leaving him at the palace."

"Leaving him?" Leo sounded shocked. "I . . . but I had no choice."

"He doesn't care," Ravan said. "He is suffused by a madness—revenge. He plans to kill both you and Loethar."

"Where do you think he'll go first?" Gavriel asked. "Does he know where Leo is?"

Ravan shook his head. "I don't believe so, although I'm guessing, my lord. The palace, I imagine, will lure him. He intends to rule."

Gavriel sighed. "Well," he said into the tense silence, "he's not going to find us here tonight. I don't know about everyone else but I need to sleep and ponder all of today's events. You are both welcome to stay here—in safety—and tomorrow morning we can discuss the best course of action. Is that all right, your majesty?"

Leo's lips thinned but he nodded. "Fine. I suppose we can't achieve much right now anyway. And I do feel strangely exhausted. Too much to think about probably."

"Well, you get some rest. I'll take first watch."

Leo stood and stretched. "There are things I want to think over. I will want to speak with you at first light, Ravan. You and the boy."

"I'm up with the birds, highness," Ravan quipped, but no one smiled.

Eight

➤➤➤ ———————— ◆◆◆

Ravan and Roddy appreciated the blankets that Gavriel found for them but they preferred to sleep in the open, well away from the awning of timber that the king had retired beneath. The night had become so still that only an owl hooting somewhere deep in the distance was a giveaway that another living creature was awake.

"I'm too frightened to sleep," Roddy admitted in the tiniest of whispers.

"He won't come after you tonight. I promise. Besides, I won't let anyone touch you."

"Does he suspect?"

"I don't know. He clearly wasn't feeling entirely well but he also wasn't registering the presence of your magic. If you could hurl fireballs, or possessed the strength of ten men, or even if you could run as fast as I you might be more tempting. Being Vested doesn't mean that you are an aegis, Roddy. What's more, if you were one, surely the king would have known it immediately."

"Don't forget Greven lived alongside Piven all that time. And this Kilt Faris they speak about had been living with the king for many anni, hadn't he?"

"Yes."

"So obviously with real strength of will it can be overcome. It was awful. I thought I was being sucked into a dark hole. I was fighting it from the moment we stepped within range of the king. Ravan . . . I think we have to accept I am an aegis. I wanted to be near him and yet I wanted to escape."

He paused for a long time, and then said, "It's like when I followed Piven even when I didn't want to. I had no control."

"All right, even if I accept that, every aegis is marked. Greven by his leprosy for instance."

Roddy sighed. "And me by my tremor."

"You said it was a palsy, that your father had it, that so did his brother."

"I lied, Ravan. I was frightened. I don't even know my father. My mother refused to speak of him. The tremor belongs to me alone—it's my mark."

They lay in silence, staring up at the stars, neither daring to speak. Ravan was the first to break the silence, his voice barely above a murmur. "In light of that, Cyrena's instructions make sense now."

"Yes. There is someone else who needs me."

Ravan felt the sorrow bite deep. "You don't have to do anything, Roddy."

"I'm afraid I do. Piven is too dangerous."

"Well, his brother isn't exactly what I'd imagined. I rank them both almost equal in how much I don't want to be near them."

"I know. I don't like the hungry way he looks at me. At least it seems he's unaware of it. Perhaps he has to come face to face with his true aegis—the one born for him—to really feel the magical connection."

Ravan sighed. "I suppose we have to forgive Leonel. His life has been shaped by events out of his control. But that doesn't mean we have to give in to him. Sergius is who I trust and he told me to trust Cyrena."

"And she told us to head for Lo's Teeth. Piven knows about her, by the way. He is frightened of her. Why?"

"I suspect he fears her magic."

"Now I understand why you told me not to say anything about Cyrena's message to us. You chose a good moment to step away."

"I didn't think he'd let us go if he knew we were heading

in a different direction. Now I know he won't let us go at all. He wants an aegis badly enough to eat me this very night."

"We should not stay here another moment," Ravan said. "Quietly now. We leave. They can't possibly keep up."

"The Legate suspected something," Roddy warned.

"That's right, I did," hissed a new voice. "And now I know the truth."

Ravan flinched as out of the dark, able to touch them if he wanted, melted Gavriel de Vis with his bow pulled taut and an arrow pointed directly at Ravan.

"You're good, Ravan, but I think I'm better. I've had years of training with the Davarigons, after all. Perhaps your bird senses are dulled now that you are a man?"

"Are you going to kill us?" Ravan demanded, his voice even.

"No. Fool that I am, I'm protecting you. Get up and leave."

"Leave?"

"That's what I said. Hurry up, both of you."

"Why?" Roddy whispered, silently leaping to his feet next to Raven, staring between the two men.

"Because I don't like where the king's thoughts are heading. He may have none of its famed magic but the Valisar blood runs thick through his veins. He's become as driven and ruthless as his father, his uncle, and even his brother, it seems. So go. Save yourself, Roddy."

"But what about—?"

"Just go. I shall deal with the king's wrath."

"How much did you hear?" Ravan asked.

"Enough."

Ravan looked back at their conspirator in the soft moonlight. He raced back over his conversation with Roddy and realized they'd never mentioned the princess by name or title, and they'd not said Corbel's name either. Perhaps Gavriel thought the *she* they'd been talking about was Cyrena. It was better to keep him confused.

"Where will you go?" Gavriel asked.

"We came here purely to warn Leo of his new enemy." Ravan shrugged again. "I am following my instincts, my lord, as instructed. We were told to head for the mountains so Lo's Teeth is where we shall head."

Gavriel nodded. "Look to the Davarigons, they will help. If you mention my name, or that of a woman called Elka, you will be treated as friends. In the meantime I promise the king will have no attempt at you, Roddy, certainly not under my guard. How you choose to use your magic is your business. I will not stand by and watch it stolen from you. My father would turn in his tomb . . . if he had one." His voice was so deeply tinged with sorrow that Ravan stepped forward, his hand held out.

"Forgive us, my lord, for putting you in this position. We felt it was important that the king know about Piven but . . ."

"You did the right thing. Now we are forewarned. So flee. He sleeps now but should he awake I will slow him down."

Roddy grinned and hugged Gavriel, surprising the Legate. "Thank you, my lord. Thank you. And don't worry about us. You couldn't catch us even if you wanted to."

Gavriel, still crookedly smiling from the youngster's affection, gave a bemused frown. "What do you mean?"

"Watch," Roddy whispered and clambered onto Ravan's back.

Ravan nodded at Gavriel and some unspoken message traveled between them—a mixture of respect and thanks, with a promise to meet again.

"I will look out for you, my lord. You have my loyalty, even if King Leonel does not." He took one quick step, then another, and then they were gone.

Elka had found a deep ditch, a hollow that an old stream had cut into over many anni, before Francham had redirected water as the town had grown.

"Here?" he had asked, unable to mask his surprise.

"No one will see you."

"And you trust me?"

"If I take you into Francham and you're recognized, we're in instant trouble."

"Oh I agree, and you're so inconspicuous of course." It was not said unkindly—in fact, it sounded almost affectionate.

He was charming her! What a rogue. Even so, he didn't have to try hard. He was good company; she appreciated his sharp intelligence and had grown to understand that he had a grasp of fair play as well as a sense of nobility about him, which was attractive. She really couldn't help liking the man, which surprised her; when she had argued to save his life she had definitely not expected to enjoy him.

In fact, since they'd fled the camp, she'd begun to accept that the people who were so embracing of the emperor were not wrong about Loethar. Yes, he came from the Steppes and had brutally wrested rule from the rightful kings of the realms. And yes, his methods had been savage. But the fact that he'd stopped all animosity as soon as he believed he had control had impressed her. The ugly overthrow had, by all accounts filtering back into the mountains, been stupendously balanced by the last decade of dignified rule.

"Here's my problem, Loethar," she had said as they struggled to slowly descend into Francham via difficult terrain, far from what she believed might be an area that Faris's people would scour. "Everything I've come to believe about you is suddenly challenged."

He had not replied immediately, his silence compelling her to explain her remark.

"As you know we Davarigons keep to ourselves but news obviously finds its way through. Initially we heard such terrible stories that you became almost larger than life itself."

"The rampaging monster from the east who eats babies," he finished for her.

"No, who eats kings!"

He had had the grace not to smile but she sensed he wanted to. "The stories were true."

"What was in your head? The person I accompany now does not match up with that madman. I walk with a sane, insightful . . ."

"Handsome?" he offered.

She ignored the comment. "I was going to say *calm* individual, who shows no sign of the cruelty he was famed for."

He nodded. "The notion of imbibing the magic by drinking the blood of the Valisar king and eating his flesh had haunted me since childhood, since my mother had first whispered the truth of my lineage."

"What in Lo's name would possess her to do that?"

"Anger. She was a woman used and scorned by King Darros. She raised me to have a burning hate for the Valisars. She insisted I was not a Steppes child. She said I looked different, I was royal, I was from the west. Over and over she taught me that one day I would fight to rule my people, that I would lead an army toward the sunset and take revenge against the throne that ignored my existence."

"And you think King Brennus knew about you?"

"I know he knew," Loethar had growled. "If he'd only tried to reach out to me, recognize me, I think we might have behaved as brothers and I would have accepted that it was no fault of his that he wore the crown of Penraven."

"Why didn't you extend that generosity to Leo? It is not his fault that he is the son of Brennus, born a prince and raised to be king."

Loethar had regarded her with a rueful gaze. "Because I was a man obsessed ten anni ago. I wanted to punish Penraven for ignoring me. I wanted all the Set to know that it was Penraven's arrogance that had brought such destruction to their lands."

"And now you feel differently?"

He had sighed. "The obsession has passed. Now I'm more than just an angry, headstrong leader; I've become a good ruler with the respect of the people of this empire. I can make our empire the most powerful region of our world."

"And Leo cannot?"

"Leo is where I was ten anni ago. He's angry, confused, capable of trying anything to get his hands on that crown because he believes it is his right. That's how I felt. Except in contrast to me Leo is still a very young man and his youth makes his outlook even more narrow, even more desperate than mine was. I'd already ruled a nation. Leo has been answerable to Faris for all this time."

"Not any more, I'd guess."

"You're probably right." Loethar had paused, and then said, "You know, Faris has been my nemesis for this last decade. He hasn't been able to outwit me for so long by being a dolt. He's cunning, wise, patient . . . I have no doubt that it's because of him that Leo has had the time to grow up and feel safe, begin to believe in himself as a king. Faris has given him a great gift."

"And now Leo wants to take Faris's life."

"So do I."

"You know I won't permit you to trammel anyone."

"Not yet."

"Never."

"Never say never, Elka. Who knows what decisions lie ahead?" he had said, and smiled at her without guile. She had sensed sadness behind his charm, though, as if he knew something she didn't.

So, having left Loethar in hiding, she now found herself entering Francham. It was still early and Francham tended to be busiest by night. The smell of baking bread was fresh in the air, though, and too seductive to resist. She followed her nose to the baker, who turned at her early entrance into his shop, just hauling a steaming loaf from his oven.

"Lo, but that smells good," she said, smiling.

"Stars save me, woman, but you're big," he commented. "I nearly dropped the damn bread."

Elka didn't take offense. "Let me buy it then, if it has my name on it."

He grinned, reaching for a cloth to wipe at his damp forehead, leaving a trail through the flour that had gathered in a light dusting across his face. Nearby his wife and a youth, perhaps his son, were banging and kneading dough. Behind them she could see two neat rows of small loaves, uniform in size and appearance.

"I won't give you this one. It's too hot and you look like you might want to eat it straight away."

"You're right. You'd better give me another small loaf too for later." She dug in her pocket for a couple of coins.

"What brings you here from Davarigon?" he said, turning to sort through some money on a plate to find change for her.

"Nothing important. I felt like a journey."

"Are you traveling alone?"

She shook her head and then decided to add some detail just in case. "I'm joining a trading caravan later today."

"Oh yes, headed where?"

"They're going south, I'm told, heading in an easterly direction to Camlet, and then into Vorgaven if I feel like staying with them."

"I've always promised myself I'd go to Vorgaven one day," he said, handing back coins. "I hear Port Merivale is a lively spot."

She gave a soft laugh. "I would have thought Francham was lively enough."

"Have a drink for me if you make it there," he said, giving her a wink.

"I'll do that," she said, ripping off a small knuckle of the bread, enjoying the crack of its crust and the warmth that it was still protecting. "Mmm, delicious," she said, chewing off a piece as she turned to leave.

"Best in the empire," the youth remarked and she smiled, noting that he blushed.

"Oh, by the way, who is a good healer in the town?" When the baker frowned, she rubbed her belly. "Women's troubles." She glanced hopefully at the wife.

The wife nodded. "There's Physic Alpert on main street, although he's hard to see. There's always a queue."

"Physic Orlem over the town square, by the statue," their son offered.

Elka nodded.

"Wait," the baker said. "There's also Janus. He lives on the eastern fringe of town, in a small hut behind the trees that line the roadside." Elka noticed the scowl that his wife threw at her husband. "Granted, he's not very popular, but he's always available. Keeps himself to himself." He returned his wife's glare with a helpless shrug. "He could use some business."

The wife turned to Elka. "Just get there early if you decide on him."

"Thank you," Elka said, slightly bemused, and lifted a hand in farewell. Again the youth blushed. She smiled to herself as she left the shop. Were Davarigons still really that daunting?

They'd been traveling into and out of Penraven, moving freely around the empire, for several anni now.

She shook her head and moved off toward the eastern side of the town. This Janus fellow sounded exactly like the sort of person she needed.

She found the hut with little difficulty, but no one answered when she banged on the door. She banged louder to no avail, then looked around for signs of life. Walking quietly around the small property, she found a few chickens who scattered at the sight of her and an old black and white dog curled up in a small patch of early morning sun. It opened the one eye it had and regarded her warily but its quietly thumping tail told her it was not frightened.

"Hello there, old fellow," she said softly and let the animal smell her hand as she crouched down. Its tail beat harder. "Where's your master, eh?"

It yawned and whether it understood or not, it looked toward the back door. She nodded. "Inside?" The dog stretched and let her stroke its belly. "Let's go find him."

She tapped on the back door but again received no answer. She glanced at the dog, who had now hauled himself to his feet and stood beside her, grinning as some dogs do and wagging its tail. She winked at him and opened the back door. "Hello? Anyone home?"

No answer.

The dog pushed past her and she followed it inside, right up to the prone form of what was presumably Physic Janus, snoring in a huge chair. She glanced around, taking in the well-made furniture, but she also noticed dust and grime, the pervading smell of decay and decline and old pots and pans that hadn't seen a clean in far too long.

She returned her attention to the snoring man. The dog pushed its snout into his hand and then licked it. From somewhere in the depths of sleep the man recognized the familiar sensation and began to rouse himself.

"Hello, Badger boy," he murmured.

"Physic Janus," she said loudly.

His eyes snapped open. "Lo come down and take me," he slurred. "It's a giant."

"Good morning," Elka replied, stepping back from the waft of fumes that hit her as he tried to sit up.

She waited while he collected himself. He cleared his throat a few times and tried his best to straighten his straggly gray hair. The doctor stroked the dog's head and gave a small smile before he stood unsteadily and regarded her through a bleary gaze. He was of medium height, with sunken eyes and a sallow complexion. And he smelled of old liquor and even older food. "Should I know you, giant?"

"Call me Elka. I was given your name only this morning."

He smiled a loopy smile and then belched, politely covering his mouth. "By whom?"

"The baker."

"Ah, Jenfrey. Nice man. Wife's a bit sour. Probably her gout."

Elka looked surprised. "I didn't think you were her doctor."

"I'm not. But I'd stake my next bottle of Rough on it. Not her first attack I'd suspect but definitely affecting her gait. She'll need that big toe amputated if she's not careful."

Elka frowned. "How much Rough have you had this morning, Physic Janus?"

He gave a gust of laughter. "Is it morning? Ah yes."

"So the drinking began last night?"

"The drinking began several anni ago, Olka."

"Elka," she corrected. "How long will it take you to sober up?"

"I hate to be sober."

"I am prepared to pay for you to be sober. I need help with some injuries."

"You look all right to me. What's wrong?"

"Nothing with me. Your help is required for a friend." *Friend?* When had she come to think of Loethar as her friend? And yet the word felt right in her mind.

"My doctoring skills are not what they used to be." He laughed ironically at what Elka supposed was an understatement as he pulled at the dog's ears.

Badger was enjoying the attention, but Elka was losing

patience. "What I need most, apart from your ministrations, is your discretion."

She had his attention now. "Well, well. A beautiful, big-bosomed giantess with a secret. How intriguing."

She raised an eyebrow at his familiarity.

"Can I count on your tongue not loosening?"

"Who am I to tell? Few people notice me these days." He gestured to the stand of trees through the window that hid his hut. "You can see where I choose to live. I'm hardly a sociable sort."

"Do we have a deal?"

"Do we have a patient?" he inquired archly, making a show of peering around her large frame.

"He is not here. I will take you to him."

His gaze narrowed as he considered her. "All right. Because you're the first visitor I've had stand in my house in many a moon—and especially because you have magnificent breasts—I'm going to attempt to clean myself up. Why don't you make us a pot of dinch? Do they have that where you come from?"

She sneered, to cover her astonishment at his directness. "Do you have any dinch or a clean pot to make it in?"

He nodded to a small sideboard. "I'll bring out the good stuff. Look in that weaven cupboard."

She nodded and as he turned to leave her he said over his shoulder, "I'll need it strong."

Elka busied herself preparing the dinch and was surprised by how quickly he returned. "I thought you'd need all day," she said, not even trying to disguise the sarcasm.

Janus was in a fresh robe. "My last clean one," he said, as if reading her thoughts. "I was surprised to find it, to be honest."

"You should burn the other one," Elka remarked.

He nodded. "Dinch?"

"I'll pour it," she said, picking up a cloth to handle the pot. "Aren't you frightened a spark will set off a fire while you're out cold?"

"Hasn't happened yet and it may do me a favor."

She frowned as she poured the brew into the two beautiful, fragile cups she had found in the cupboard. "What about Badger?"

"He'll survive, won't you, boy?" Janus said, rubbing the dog's head. "He's not mine, to tell the truth. He just likes it here. If there's no food in the offing, he goes off elsewhere. I have no idea who else feeds him but as you can see, he does just fine." He took a sip from the cup she pushed toward him and sighed. "Well, it's not a perfect Penraven brew, but it's not bad at all. Thank you."

She gave him a soft glare. "How do you feel?"

"Well, I know I'm not sober."

"You act as if you are."

"I'm a doctor. I should know. Anyway, I'm certainly lucid enough, so tell me about this patient of yours . . . the friend in need."

"He's on the other side of Francham."

"That's no answer."

"It's all you're getting."

"I see. So he must be someone either very important or someone that others might be looking for."

"Or both," she offered tartly.

"Indeed. In fact, I would guess at both. But he's not Davarigon?"

She shook her head. "How much will you charge to come help him?"

"That depends on what is required."

"Are you a surgeon?"

His eyes flashed wide. "He's that injured?"

"Give me an amount, Janus. One that ensures your lips stay firmly shut."

He sipped his tea, blowing on it between sips. Finally, he said, "I'll do it for free if you'll show me your giant's ti—"

"Forget it!" she bellowed. "You're a waste of my time."

"Forgive me, Elka. That was outrageously impolite of me."

"You cover your mouth when you belch, you drink from fine porcelain and yet you live like a slob and your mind is even filthier. What kind of contradiction are you?"

He nodded. "I deserve that. Again I ask for your forgiveness."

She gave him a look of disbelief mixed with disdain. "I don't understand you."

"Now you know why I am considered worthless in this town."

"What happened?"

He sighed, drained his cup. "I'll have another please." As she poured, he looked down. "Have you heard of the sickness called 'sullied tongue?'"

She shook her head, frowning. "It sounds like a jest."

He nodded thoughtfully. "It is certainly an affliction that the gods had some fun with."

Elka caught on. "You have this problem?"

"You're fast. Yes. I am openly rude to people I least want to offend. I have no control over what I say at times, or any warning."

"I've never heard of this disease before."

"Oh, I've met two other cases. One of them was the son of a prosperous merchant turned into a seeming lunatic who wandered from town to town as a beggar. The other was a teacher whose career was cut short by the onset of this disease as he hit his third decade. It seems to afflict men."

"And it happens constantly?"

He nodded. "I can behave perfectly acceptably most of the time. My affliction is actually rather mild. And yet it is offensive enough to have singled me out for ex-communication. I think the baker takes pity on me because his father and mine were friends. We didn't exactly grow up together but he knows my outspoken words are never intentional. Again, I apologize for what I said. Being drunk keeps me lucid and my tongue clean. Ironic, eh?" He paused. "Your giant arse must be stunning naked."

She swung around and gave him a look of total disbelief. He shrugged, his expression one of mortification. "I will be apologizing constantly if you seriously want to go ahead with your proposition."

Elka laughed. "I've got broad shoulders, I'm sure I won't wilt. How much?"

"How long will it take?"

She looked doubtful. "I can't say for sure. A day?"

"Two gold trents," he said sharply.

"That's robbery."

"I'm an opportunist, can't you tell?"

Elka nodded. Loethar needed help sooner rather than later. "All right. We'll leave now. You're sure Badger will be all right without you?"

"Lo, woman! You care more about the dog than me."

"The dog hasn't tried to steal from me."

"I would like to rub your breas—"

"Let's go, Janus!" she said briskly, cutting him off before he disgraced himself again.

Nine

➤➤ ———————————————— ◀◀

Gavriel had deliberately not woken Leo to take over watch but the king had roused himself before dawn and he'd had to come clean with the news.

"You did what?" the king replied, a cup of water halfway to his mouth. Leo had heard it the first time, Gavriel knew, but he was making Gavriel repeat it in order to give himself time to digest the repercussions. He'd seen Brennus take an identical approach when his ire was up.

"I told them to go."

"Why would you do that, Gav?"

Gavriel hesitated.

"Speak plainly," Leo urged, his voice horribly cold but calm.

Gavriel scratched his head. "Well, they were scared of you. Ravan is no enemy of yours and—"

"That's rich, coming from the person who wanted to butcher the bird at the first opportunity," Leo cut in quietly.

"You've shown me the error of my ways," Gavriel replied equally quietly. "If not for your reluctance to kill we would not now have a new ally."

"Do you really believe he's our ally, even after he ran away from us?"

"I do. Especially now that we have permitted him to go on with his journey . . . whatever it is."

"Not we, Gav. You. You made that decision, against the

wishes of your king. I wonder if your father ever defied mine?"

"We shall never know," Gavriel said, keeping his tone even, not at all appreciating the way Leo kept comparing him to his father. "But I do know this: I didn't like the way you looked at that boy, Leo. You don't need to resort to acts of barbarism to prove your worth as a king. You are Valisar. No one can take that from you."

If Leo felt any offense it certainly didn't show. "But my throne has been taken from me. And now I learn that perhaps even the crown isn't mine, that the barbarian warlord is also Valisar and every bit as entitled to wear it as I am. I can't be sure but I imagine Loethar—my own blood—would still kill me if he could, and now I discover I have a blood brother who also wants to kill me. And I have access to protection from death, but you, my loyal Legate and champion, is steadfastly denying me that protection." Leo shook his head, then took a deep breath and stood. "I don't need you any more, Gavriel. Your stupid Davarigon bitch has defied me and now you have blatantly defied my orders, believing you know better. My father would have had your father cleaved in two for less." He laughed once, bitterly, not even ashamed for such a barb. "Except your father was loyal in a way you clearly cannot be. He always did what my father asked of him."

"Yes," Gavriel said coldly. It was taking all of his will not to strike Leo for the way he spoke about Elka or jested at his father's fate. Only the thought that Regor de Vis would turn in his grave if he knew his son had behaved so ignobly stayed his hand. "Perhaps my father would be alive today if he hadn't. And my twin brother might be living alongside me too, and I wouldn't have lost a decade of my life. The de Vis family has served yours faithfully, Leo, but it seems our role is to just keep on giving while you Valisars keep on taking. You're a king, damn you. Act it! Stop bleating about who has done what to you and why your life is so full of woe. You've done nothing but cringe in the forest, Leo. Do you even really want to be king?"

Leo had fallen ominously quiet, staring at Gavriel with an undisguised rage. "You know I do," he growled.

"Then take the crown! Stop hiding, stop blaming other people for everything that's happened, and take responsibility for yourself. You don't have to chop the hand off a child and eat it to protect yourself. Your father didn't!"

"My father was not at war."

"Neither are you."

"You heard what they said. Piven is hunting me."

"And Loethar has been hunting you for ten anni and didn't find you because you were cunning and you were patient . . . and because you had allies like Faris and Freath. But you killed Freath because of some obsessively misplaced sense of duty that your mother would turn in her grave to learn of and you've driven away Faris because he rightly believes you want to maim him and turn him into a jabbering puppet. I would run too, Leo. I don't blame Faris one bit. And I'll be damned if I was going to let you hurt a ten-anni-old in the vain hope that he might make you invincible. The child may have been Vested but that doesn't mean he was an aegis."

"We didn't know that he wasn't," Leo hissed.

"That's true. But I'll sleep more soundly knowing we didn't hack him to bits only to learn he wasn't. This is turning into a madness!"

"You don't seem to think Loethar was mad."

"I am not loyal to Loethar. What I think of him is irrelevant. What I think of you affects me profoundly."

"Well, Gav, I think you'll have to get used to the notion that in order for me to claim my throne I need the same protection my rivals have. I suspect Loethar will have his aegis soon enough—despite what you think about the Davarigon's intentions—and we already know that Piven has his. Are you happy to have me that vulnerable?"

Gavriel took a deep breath. Then he said quietly, "Leo, you were born vulnerable! You were Crown Prince. History attests that there is always going to be someone who wants that crown. You wanted yours handed down on a golden plate. Well, that didn't happen. Another Valisar wanted it. Crowns are won and crowns are fought for, Leo. My father died trying to protect it for his king. Your father died trying to give you a chance to claim it. So claim it! Fight for it. And don't give me that petulant story that no one's fighting fair. Life isn't fair! Lo knows I've learned that the hard way. Neither of us has lived a fair life but it's no use you bleating about it. But what you are suggesting is morally reprehensible. Stealing a child's life—or anyone else's, for that matter—cannot be justified by your wanting the crown. Killing to defend one-self or in war is one thing; killing in cold blood because you want something that another has is just plain murder."

"I wasn't planning to kill anyone."

"Tell Roddy that—it would be living death and you know it."

Leo walked away and Gavriel waited. He watched the king he had loved, the friend he would have given his life to protect, turn and face him with a set to his jaw that Gavriel recognized with dismay. He had lost the argument.

"I need the protection that is my birthright. If Cyrena thought that trammeling was wrong she would not have made it possible when Cormoron first walked this land. This, right now, is probably why such a magic as the aegis was given to our family, to ensure that one of the four of us would hold the crown."

Gavriel felt his throat close. "What are you talking about?"

"That's right, you didn't know about my sister, did you, Gav?" Leo didn't wait for Gavriel to answer. "Oh yes, my father made provision for her. I don't know how or where. All I know is that her death was a sham for the sake of Loethar's horde."

"But she'd be only ten," Gavriel argued. Suddenly Ravan's and Roddy's curious conversation began to make sense. They must have known about the princess—that's who they'd been talking about. They were traveling to the mountains for her! And if she was there, perhaps Corbel was with her. His heart leaped with excitement but an inner voice told him not to share any of this with Leo, who was still talking.

". . . nevertheless is still an heir and who knows how em-powered she might be? She might be the most powerful of all. And as long as I have nothing to protect me, I am the least able to contest that crown and yet I believe in my heart that I am the right sovereign. I am the eldest child of Brennus. I am Leonel,

Ninth of the Valisars. It is not my fault or my concern that my grandfather laid his seed in the stony ground of the Likurian Steppes or that his crown passed to his younger son, my father. The way the line has gone is not my doing. But I am the result. I am the king. I believe this with all of my heart."

"So do I, Leo."

"Then fight for me, not against me!"

"I will not fight for you if it means butchering another person in cold blood. You don't need me to do that."

And now Leo turned his suddenly cold blue eyes on his long-time friend. "I don't need you at all, Gavriel de Vis."

Gavriel stared at him in disbelief. It felt like an eternity passed between them. He felt short of breath and as though his heart was beating erratically.

"So be it," he finally said. "I will take my leave."

Leo smirked. "Make good distance. Next time I see you, I will kill you, Gavriel de Vis."

"I know you will try," Gavriel said. He picked up his weapons and bowed. "Your majesty," he said solemnly before he turned and walked away, not once looking back. He did not want his king to see his tears.

They found Loethar where she'd left him; she really wouldn't have been surprised to find him gone but her heart leaped to see him watchful but nevertheless patiently awaiting her return. He seemed to guess her thoughts.

"I made a promise," he said with a resigned smile. She grinned. "And you must be one of the horses she went off to purchase," he said to Janus, who frowned and cast a glance at Elka.

"This is Physic Janus."

"Forgive me, Janus. As you can see I'm bored and resorting to childish humor."

Janus hadn't stopped frowning. "You know my name, may I know yours?" Loethar glanced at Elka inquiringly. In the hesitant pause, Janus followed his line of sight back to the giantess. "You're being very mysterious, Elka."

"I have to be," she said to him before looking back at Loethar. "I think we can trust him."

Loethar shrugged and winced. "This is your idea."

She sighed. "Janus, you don't recognize him?"

Janus regarded his patient. "He looks like a horse's arse. Sorry."

Loethar blinked and when Elka gave a small chuckle he turned his gaze back to her in a soft glare of astonishment.

"I'll explain," she said, enjoying his confusion. "Janus has a problem."

"I'll say," Loethar replied. "You called me handsome just hours earlier."

"I didn't call you handsome. You did," she corrected. "Janus has an affliction that compels him to say outrageous remarks. It doesn't prevent him from being a good physic."

"And you know this how?" Janus asked, smiling softly at her.

"I know," she replied, turning to the physic. "I trust you with our emperor."

"Emp—?" Janus's head swung back, his expression shocked, as he looked at Loethar. "No, it can't be."

"I'm embarrassed and disappointed to say it is," Loethar replied. "I am Elka's prisoner."

"She has wonderful breasts," Janus said. "Forgive me," he added, looking instantly contrite.

"She does. You're forgiven," Loethar said.

"Right, gentlemen," Elka said, her tone chilly. "Shall we focus on the task at hand?"

"I'd like to focus on your arse," Janus remarked, looking at her with an expression of fresh mortification.

Loethar laughed openly. "Marvelous!"

"Janus, I'll find a way to close your mouth even if I have to stitch your lips together," Elka said sweetly.

Janus pointed at her, his expression a mixture of remorse and defiance. "It comes on especially strong when I'm nervous and sober. You were warned."

She nodded. "That's true, and I will bear the repercussions of my own decision. Can't you try and concentrate on something else? Like your patient?"

"This is not a good place to be doing an examination," Janus remarked, looking around. "My hut—"

"Is too dangerous," Elka finished. "I'll carry Loethar slightly higher up into those trees for coverage. We can't go any higher, though. He has been suffering from the sickness of height and is barely recovered from one bout."

The doctor nodded. "I suffer the same myself."

"All right then. Let's get to those trees."

Later, with the doctor finally sitting back on the ground and after much peering and prodding by him and cursing by Loethar, Janus took a deep breath. "All right. We have bones to set, cuts to stitch and bruises that can use some unguent."

"Do you need my help?"

"Not really. You're a distraction for my foul mouth." She couldn't help but smile. "And it's hard enough concentrating when I know who I'm working on. How has it come about that I am repairing our emperor?"

Elka smiled. "It's a long story," she said, just as Loethar said the same thing. She threw an amused glance at him, which he returned.

"Well, you can tell me all about it in between more curses because what I'm about to do is not going to be without discomfort," Janus said to Loethar.

"I understand."

Janus glanced at Elka. "Just light me a fire and get some water on to boil. I shall take it from there. I want to feel your tits on my—"

And to the roar of Loethar's amusement, Elka stomped away to find kindling.

Ten

◆━━━━━━━━━━━━━━━━━━━━━◆

They'd been heading north since they began walking. It was getting cooler the higher they went but it was still relatively mild—enough that Evie had rolled up her cloak and tied it to hang at her side. She felt ridiculous in this garb but the more she looked around at this landscape, the more foreign it all felt. The growing pit in her stomach had begun to assure her that she was nowhere close to anything familiar.

Corbel, as he now insisted she call him, looked anything but awkward. In fact, he seemed to stand even taller than she recalled and was that a slight swagger in his walk? Where was the withdrawn, closed individual she had loved all these anni? Now there was a glint in his eyes and a smile playing constantly at the corner of his lips. He was happy, Evie realized, and almost childish in his excitement, pointing out this plant or that landscape, none of it of any interest to her.

She was still trying to come to terms with the alienation she was feeling, not to mention the anger at him as much as fear. And yet instead of explaining he insisted they walk.

"Reg!"

"Corbel," he replied.

She took a breath to ensure her words came out calmly. "Corbel, where exactly are we going? And why exactly am I here?"

"I've tried to explain—"

"Except you've explained nothing," she huffed, catching up with him. "Slow down. I can't walk as fast as you."

He halved his long stride with obvious effort. "I wish there could have been a better way to ease you back into your world."

"My world?" she hurled at him, her voice full of accusation. "My world is the city I belong in, where I'm a healer and everything makes sense."

Corbel stopped. "Nothing made sense! Nothing. And you know it. You were the misfit there. You said it often enough. The world you belong to, Evie, is here. It was called Denova and your place of belonging is Penraven. And yes, you are still a healer."

"Have you any idea how this feels?" she begged.

He gazed at her for several moments and she saw only pain in his expression. Finally, he nodded. "I do. I have lived with that confusion and despair every minute of the last twenty anni, looking after you in a strange land."

She hadn't expected that. She bit back on the ready retort as she considered his words . . . "I . . . I haven't considered it from that point of view. I'm trying to wrap my mind around the notion that this is where you come from. Rationality and science is my life. Magic has no place."

"Really?" he asked. "Search your heart, Evie, and perhaps you can privately call yourself a liar. I won't."

She glared at him. "That's a ridiculous accusation."

"Is it?" He shrugged. "You can't keep pretending what you did every day to save lives was science. Both of us know that's a lie. Perhaps you couldn't explain the strange skill you have to heal people, but I can assure you, Evie, it wasn't all scientific training. I'm taking you to a place where you can ask all the questions you need and you will get a far better insight than I can provide."

"Where? To the man you call Sergius?"

He shook his head. "He told me never to look for him should I ever bring you back. He made me promise that when I came back I would first take you to meet someone called the Qirin."

Her mistrust deepened. "Who and what is the Qirin?"

Corbel shrugged. "I don't know. But I suppose we shall soon find out."

"Corbel, I'm tired."

"It's not far and I promise you a roof over your head tonight, perhaps even a bath."

She felt deeply weary. "I admit that is a seductive promise."

He began walking again. "There," he said, as she clambered up beside him.

Her gaze narrowed as she focused on the buildings in the distance, nestling among an almost perfect crescent of rocky outcrops. "It's beautiful."

"The mountains in the background are called Lo's Teeth."

"They look daunting."

"They are. I've never been further north than this region. But people called the Davarigons do live in the mountains."

She shook her head in wonder. "Mountain dwellers?" She shook her head again. "I can't—"

"I know, Evie. I really do understand how hard this is. Please don't cry."

She bit her trembling lip. "I'm sorry. This is all so impossible to calculate."

"Don't calculate. Analyze none of it. Nothing will make sense. If you can accept that it's not worth wasting the energy trying to understand but instead just try to blend in as best you can, I promise you that you will adapt."

"Yes, but what if I don't want to?" she snapped.

Corbel sighed silently but she saw his frustration. "Evie, I don't want to keep saying this because it sounds as though I'm the villain here, but you have no choice. I can't say it any plainer. Your pathway was mapped out a long time ago. Your father chose it. He also chose mine, to protect you until you could return to the land of your birth."

She nodded, swallowed a soft sob of her own frustration and confusion. His voice was so tender. She had never questioned his friendship or his honesty. Evie lifted her chin and made a silent promise that she would trust Corbel de Vis until this nightmare ended. She had to believe it would, even though this place he called Denova certainly looked and felt real enough.

Evie sniffed. "So what is this place you're taking me toward?"

The anxiety in her friend's eyes lessened and she saw a sense of relief relax his expression. He had obviously thought she was going to crack. Grinning crookedly, he said, "A convent. There you will have your bath and I hope there is where you will find some answers. A word of warning," he cautioned. "If we're going to blend in, we both need to leave our most recent lives behind. Forget the hospital, Evie, forget everything you know. In order for you to survive, I need you to trust me and do your utmost to avoid all mention of what has gone before for you. Today is the first day of your life."

"To survive? That sounds scary."

He nodded. "We should be scared. There are people who wish you dead."

She looked at him, aghast. "And still you brought me here?"

Corbel looked back at her sadly. "I take some comfort that you're at least acknowledging that you are here. But I don't know how to answer your question. I had no choice. I am the son of Regor de Vis and my duty is to the Crown of Penraven, and to the Valisars."

"And what about me?"

He gave a sad smile. "I'm fulfilling my duty, Evie. You *are* a Valisar."

"So I'm just a duty now. A chore to be done?" She watched his eyes flash with pain but for once she felt no guilt; her confusion demanded more answers.

"Don't ever think that," he hurried to say. "I have loved you as . . ." He appeared flummoxed. "I care about you as if you were the most precious thing in the world."

She nodded, hating to see her favorite person looking so tongue-tied. Reg had never been anything but a rock in her life. If she were honest she couldn't imagine her life without him in it. "I love you too," she said without hesitation, surprised when he glanced at her with strange sorrow.

"You say it so easily," he replied, looking away.

"Because I mean it. I only hesitate if I'm telling a lie."

"I know," he said softly. Clearing his throat, he continued more curtly, "If I'm going to keep you safe, you must listen to what I say and follow my lead in all things. There is no technology here. None at all. But there is magic, as you've discovered for yourself. I know it all sounds like a confusing dream but I stress again, this is your new reality. You must . . ."

"Acclimatize?"

"Yes, but don't use words like that again."

Evie sighed. "Reg . . . I'm tired of arguing with you. All right, I'll try to speak 'plain Denovian.'"

He found a smile. "It's in your soul. Hunt it down. You know how to do this."

She looked at the impressive stone building as they slowed on their approach and shook her head.

Just as she fell into step alongside Reg, vowing to try very hard to acclimatize as her friend needed, three men rounded the bend in the path they had been following.

"Aye, aye, what have we here?" the eldest of the trio asked.

"Morning," Corbel said, surprising Evie at how cheerful he could sound. "All well with you?"

"Now it is," the youngest said. He had a black tooth at the front of his mouth and a smile that suggested he was a few strides short of a span.

Evie felt a tremor of alarm.

Corbel sensed the danger immediately. Years of training in his youth alongside his father and then two decades on the streets of a city in the other world had taught him plenty about people. And he'd learned that one could tell a great deal about a man long before he spoke. And Corbel was reading only the most dangerous of language from the silent newcomer whose gaze had yet to alight on him; so far his eyes were only for Evie.

"Morning," Corbel repeated, deliberately slowing, loading his tone with lightness and cheer but all the while using the time to gauge what he was up against.

The black-toothed one was gormless enough not to trouble Corbel. The elder one who spoke first looked wiry and strong but he was small, with a limp, and carried only a dagger at his belt. It was the middle fellow who troubled Corbel the most.

Silent, powerfully built and clearly with mischief on his mind, he wore a sword on his hip and moved like a fighter.

Evie had paused, he noticed, presumably sensing the man's interest. He stepped slightly ahead of her to shield her.

"Tasty lady," said Blacktooth, leering around him at Evie before grinning stupidly at his companions.

Corbel raised a hand. "We want no trouble here."

"Forgive our Clem, he has no manners at all," the dangerous one said.

The man's voice was mellow, almost silky, but Corbel wasn't fooled. "We don't want trouble either."

"None from her, anyway," Clem said and now the older man grinned.

"This is a lonely track for travelers," the dangerous man continued.

"Yes it is," Corbel admitted. "But we are taking the shortest route to the convent." He shrugged, noting as he did so that the man's hand was resting easily on the pommel of his sword. "How about yourselves?"

"On our way to Francham."

"Francham? You have a long walk ahead," Corbel remarked, taking note that it wasn't the old man's leg that was injured; it was his hips, if he wasn't mistaken. "No horses?"

"Lost them," Blacktooth chimed in, chortling. That won a glare from their leader.

"Lost them?" Corbel repeated, using the time to take in his immediate surrounds.

The leader sighed. "An unwise gamble."

Corbel gave a soft shrug as though he understood it was none of his business. "Well, we must continue. Come, my love."

"Is this your wife?" the man asked.

"Er, yes. We are newly wed."

"On our way to pay a tithe to the convent," Evie piped up, surprising everyone, most of all Corbel. "My father insisted," she added with a shy smile. "Well," she said, "nice to meet you. Safe travels." She took a step forward.

"Now what is a pretty young thing like you doing marrying a rough-looking older man, I wonder?"

Corbel stepped between Evie and the stranger, all of his senses on high alert. The older man was reaching for his dagger and the younger one had only dopey amusement in his eyes, as though he'd witnessed similar scenes previously.

"I thought you wanted no trouble," the stranger remarked, still appearing loose limbed and relaxed.

"I still want no trouble," Corbel replied, a new hint of warning in his tone.

"Then why this confrontation?"

"Stranger, my wife and I just want to continue to the convent. We have no money worth stealing."

"Other than the tithe," the man corrected.

"Other than the tithe," Corbel repeated, "which I fully intend to pay to the convent and not to bandits."

The man and his elder companion feigned shock. "Did you hear that, Barro?" the older man said. "He reckons we're thieves."

"I heard it," the dangerous one drawled, and blinked slowly.

Corbel tensed and pushed Evie back. "Corbel!" she murmured, anxious, as the ring of a sword being lifted from its scabbard sounded harshly in the peace of the countryside.

"Hush, now, Evie," he said, keeping his voice low and calm. "These men intend us harm."

"It didn't have to be like this," the stranger said. "I just want your money but Clem here will probably settle for a grope between your wife's legs."

Evie made a gagging sound of revulsion. "Go fu—"

"Evie! Hush," Corbel cautioned, not once taking his eyes from the sword that was now being weighted in his opponent's hand.

"What a pity it had to come to this," the man remarked casually. His companions sniggered.

"I have no time for thieves," Corbel warned.

"Even when they are carrying weapons and you have none?" the man asked, surprised.

"Even then," Corbel replied.

"Corb—"

"I said quiet, Evie. There is no further need for us to be

civil," he cautioned, silently measuring the distance between himself and the old fellow.

"Actually, I prefer civility when I'm working. There's really no need for harm," the leader assured. "I simply want your purse. What my companions require is their own business."

The old man laughed and grabbed his crotch. This sent the youngest one into peals of shared laughter, his mouth wide open and showing more ruined teeth.

"My wife is not for your companions' sport and my purse is my own."

The man sighed. "Don't make me take it from you. It might cost you more than money."

"Don't make me have to stop you," Corbel said, his voice very quiet. His calm made the stranger hesitate momentarily, but his companions hardly registered the change.

"Let's cut off his bollocks, Barro," Blacktooth said, saliva forming at the corners of his mouth. "Then he can't fuck his wife again."

"We'll have to do it for him," the older one tittered.

"You'll have to forgive my fellow travelers, sir. As you can tell, they have no refinement."

"I forgive them nothing," Corbel said, his voice so cold it was now brittle.

The man shifted his gaze back to Evie. "Your husband is courageous, madam. And he speaks like a noble. I think I understand your attraction to him."

Corbel was glad to note that Evie remained silent. The man smiled, shifted his weight, and Corbel didn't wait for him to make the first move. Instead, he bent sideways and kicked out suddenly with his leg, smashing his foot into the old man's hip. The sound of a bone breaking in the old man's skeleton was chilling and both Evie and the victim shrieked in tandem. But Corbel heeded neither. He had already regained his balance and crouched, spinning low and kicking Blacktooth's legs out from under him. He was vaguely aware of the old fellow writhing on the ground and very aware of Barro raising his sword to strike.

In a fluid move that was already in motion while he was

spinning, Corbel retrieved the hidden blades stored vertically along the sides of his ribs. One quickly found its way into Blacktooth's throat, and the young man began gurgling helplessly as Corbel straightened and leaped away from Barro's sword in the space of the blink of an eye.

Turning back, both he and Barro looked at the dying youngster and his companion, who was on the ground next to him, screaming and covered in Blacktooth's blood.

"That wasn't very sporting of you," Barro remarked. "Although perhaps I should offer some gratitude. I was desperately tired of them both."

"I've simply made the fight a bit fairer," Corbel remarked. They both smiled. And began circling each other.

Evie watched in horrified disbelief. There was a sense of the unreal—as though she were participating in a piece of medieval theater. Except it was all sickeningly real. The screams were genuine, the blood was real, the knives and sword were not toys and this was not make believe. Corbel de Vis and the man known as Barro were engaged in what she sensed was going to be a fight to the death.

She stared at Corbel circling the man, a cold and calculating expression on his face that she had never seen before. She thought she had known Reg so well, but though the man who now accompanied her looked like Reg and talked like Reg that icy smile was chillingly unfamiliar. Reg meant to kill Barro, she was sure, because he had threatened her safety.

In fact, only now, as Barro began to laugh, did she realize she hadn't taken a breath since the youth called Clem had fallen.

Clem! She looked again at the two figures on the ground. And finally her instincts kicked in and she moved into action.

"You fight like a soldier. I'm impressed."

"Then engage me, or I'll think you're scared of me."

"Engage?" Barro grinned, prodding at Corbel. "You speak like you're from the old world."

"Perhaps I am," Corbel replied.

"Stop this!" Evie cried.

"Too late, madam. I think your husband is determined to fight for your honor . . . not that I had any intention of threatening it."

"But your accomplices did," Corbel snarled. "And you will share the punishment."

Barro laughed again. "You have a single dagger, my friend. You'd better ask your wife to look away. I'll tell you what," Barro said, feinting with the sword and failing to lure Corbel into his trap. "I'll marry your widow and treat her well when this is done. I can't be more fair, can I?"

"I'll tell you what," Corbel replied. "As you have no wife to mourn you with flowers, I'll bury you in this deserted landscape and piss on your grave so the weeds can at least grow over you."

Barro appeared to enjoy his threat, laughing loudly. "I think I'll regret killing you."

"No more talking, Barro. Fight, or die as you stand."

"As you won't share your name, soldier, I'll ask your wife for it later."

Corbel was aware of Evie's movement but his focus was now entirely on his opponent. He knew his dagger looked like a pointless weapon against the long sword but wielded with skill it could triumph. Barro's sword was heavy—deadly, for sure, but cumbersome by comparison. Corbel would just need speed. And cunning.

Barro stabbed and though Corbel leaped backward the blade caught him high on the arm. He felt the telltale sting but had no time to even check how deep the wound was, for Barro continued advancing without pause.

He thought he heard Evie yell but then everything dulled to the roar of his blood pounding. Nothing mattered but the man before him. He could smell Barro's sweat and noticed, for the first time, that Barro carried an injury. While the man was right-handed, he favored that right side. It must be his shoulder. And now that Corbel concentrated on it, still ducking and weaving and knowing he was entertaining Barro by permitting him to slash at him—taking the punishment but mercifully unable to register any pain for now—he saw that the man's fighting arm was lowering. The sword was heavy, Barro's fighting side was injured, and he had to keep adjusting and straightening his stance.

Corbel took a deep breath. He needed to unbalance Barro. His opponent's natural inclination to re-align himself might do the rest and give Corbel the opening he needed. On the rim of his mind he could hear Evie still yelling, but he had to ignore it.

In that moment he felt a deep pain, one that made him want to retch and dragged him from the special place in his mind, back outside to where the smell of blood hung in the air.

"No, please, Barro, please . . ." he could hear Evie screaming.

Corbel had taken all the punishment that he knew his body could withstand. But wearing Barro out was working; the strength in the man's arm had so dissipated that he looked lopsided now, as he struggled to rebalance himself. He lifted the sword one more time, and, oddly, Corbel heard his brother's voice in his head: *Now, Corb, now!*

Without thinking, Corbel launched himself forward, dagger extended. He glimpsed a look of bemused surprise on Barro's face before he hit the man in the belly and then toppled with him. Regaining himself quickly, he straddled the soldier and, to a howl of protest from Evie, he plunged the dagger with great force into the man's chest, just beneath the ribcage, feeling the satisfying give of flesh and the sudden sigh of breath.

It was over. Barro stared at Corbel with confusion and then looked down at his own chest. "You got me," he murmured. "Damn you," he said, with what sounded to Corbel like a hint of respect.

"Corbel . . ." Evie sounded ragged. "Corbel!" Then suddenly she was upon him, shoving him off Barro, whose head had lolled back.

"No!" she screamed.

"Evie," Corbel murmured, a tremor claiming him now as

his mind began to accept that the immediate danger was over and his body began to register his wounds.

"Shut up!" she yelled into his face. "Just shut up, you fucking murderer!"

Corbel rocked back into the dirt on the ground, lost for words. Murderer? No. The fight had been fair. Unbalanced perhaps, but fair. He watched, disbelieving, as Evie replaced him on top of Barro and lay her hands on him.

Exercising the enormous control she had trained herself to wield when performing surgery, Evie wrestled all her nervous energy back under her own control and focused her mind on Barro.

She was surprised by how quickly she found her calm but she was genuinely shocked at the new and strange sensation that felt like electricity running through her as she went to work on her patient. She had no time to ponder what it meant, though. All that mattered right now was seeing if she could save Barro. It didn't matter that he had attacked them. She was a doctor. She had taken an oath to preserve life.

Corbel was breathing hard, watching Evie, hardly daring to believe that she was offering ministrations to their enemy. The man had done his utmost to kill him and yet here she was snarling at him, accusing *him* of murder, swearing at *him*. His offense deepened when he realized that she wasn't even going to turn her attention away from Barro for a second to check on his injuries.

He angrily shifted his gaze to the other two bandits. Blacktooth looked to be dead, lying in a surprisingly large pool of blood. The old man was groaning, also prone; Corbel had probably dislocated or re-broken that hip. He didn't care.

"Finish it!" Barro growled at him. "Soldier to soldier."

"Don't compare us," Corbel replied. "Suffer on. I—"

"Quiet! Both of you, just shut up!" Evie yelled. "I need to concentrate."

He heard Barro sigh but it didn't sound like the sigh of

someone accepting a rebuke so much as the sound of someone resigning. Corbel had heard it before. And he was sure
Evie had. Barro sighed once again, accepting his death.

"No, please, no! Hang on. Stay alive, Barro. For me."

"Evie. Let him die," Corbel urged. "I hope you're not
thinking of—"

She turned on him, though her hands never left Barro's
major wound. "Don't you dare!" she raged, her voice barely
under control. He had seen her annoyed before, he'd even
seen her angry but he had never seen this; this hot rage, and
the temper directed at him! Corbel bit back on his next words
and staggered slightly, shocked by the snarl on her mouth,
the contempt of her tone. He was sure he could see disgust in
her gaze. "Don't you dare tell me what to do, de Viz, or whatever the hell your bastard name is!"

It felt worse than a shock slap, worse even than a punch in
the belly. Corbel felt his very world tilt. "It's de Vis," he corrected, unable to think of anything else to say. He heard his
own voice sound soft and shocked.

But she didn't care, it seemed. "Go to hell!" she spat at
him before returning her attention to Barro.

"Evie," he began.

"Don't," she warned. "Don't say anything more."

He didn't. He left Evie to her ministrations. He carelessly
hauled Blacktooth's body away and left it behind some rocks.
Then he busied himself, studiously ignoring the old man
prone nearby, pushing soil around with his boots to disguise
the pool of blood that had begun to dry into the ground. Satisfied that the worst of it was covered, he glared at the injured
man.

"I won't be helping you," he snarled.

"Just something for the pain—arack perhaps?"

Corbel shook his head.

Evie silently moved in front of Corbel and knelt down
beside the wheezing old man, laying her hands on him. Corbel was desperate to speak but bit back on his words, this
time looking away in despair. Her defiance might get them
both killed.

He looked back over at Barro and saw what he most

dreaded. The man was sitting up, holding his head. "What just happened?" Barro asked, touching his chest, his belly, looking down at his body with incredulity.

Corbel walked over to him but said nothing.

"You killed me. I died. I'm sure of it. I felt the life leave me."

"Seems you imagined it," Corbel muttered.

Barro's crazed eyes searched his own. "You killed me, damn it!"

Corbel put his hands up defensively. "All right. Hush." His mind was racing. How could he keep this situation under control?

Barro's confusion deepened, his brow almost hooding his eyes. "All right? *All right?*" he demanded. "You mean you agree?"

Corbel sighed. "I clearly didn't kill you," he said, his exasperation spilling.

"It's done," Evie said, sounding suddenly drained. "I've put him to sleep. We need to talk," she said, her voice hard, eyeing them both.

Barro shook his head. "I don't understand any of this."

Evie glared at Corbel. "Are you going to explain?"

He shook his head slightly. "You're the one taking control. Why don't you throw us straight into deeper danger? Your father—" he began but was cut off by Evie.

"My father, whoever he was, was a cowardly dog. If I'm to believe what you've been telling me then what on earth was in his head to think he was doing me a favor sending me off with you in the manner he did, all the secrecy, and the risk of such dislocation?"

"He kept you alive," Corbel said.

"For what? Ask yourself. What do you think we can achieve in terms of the grand fight you seem to believe we are up against?"

Before Corbel could think of how to answer her, Barro began to get to his feet and Evie snapped her head around to glare at him. "And I'd suggest you remain still for a while longer."

"Who are you both?" the bandit asked, sounding deeply

bewildered. "I thought I heard the name de Vis being bandied around. But perhaps that's just part of my present madness because I am sure I am dead."

Corbel felt momentarily sorry for the man. He walked over and helped Barro to his feet. "Slowly," he said. "Listen to her regarding your health. She knows what she's talking about."

Barro's fist bunched Corbel's shirt. "Answer me, damn you. I should be dead, right? Gar knows I felt the keen pain of your sword entering my flesh."

"Listen to me, Barro," Evie said, her tone plain. Gone was her polite bedside manner. "You're going to have to accept something that seems impossible. You are walking proof that magic happens. Get past it!"

Corbel threw her a glance of gratitude. He'd feared for a moment that she was going to launch into a discussion about medicine and physiology. But she ignored his gaze, continuing to stare hard at Barro. "Do you believe in magic, Barro?"

The man looked between them both but Corbel refused to look at him. This was too difficult. Besides, it wasn't right. It was opening them up to a raft of new problems.

"I believe only in what I see," Barro answered carefully.

Corbel watched Evie's eyes flare. "Excellent," she said, all brisk efficiency. "Then you believe yourself healed?"

"I have no choice, do I? But I want to understand how it comes that I am whole."

"I'll explain again. I used magic on you," she said matter of factly. "I healed you."

"But that's impossible," he began, again flicking his glance between the two of them. "Prove it. Heal the boy," he said to Evie.

"I don't have to prove it to you. I have already shown you by the fact that you are not bleeding out into the soil. I'm sorry to say that it's too late for him. He is already dead."

Barro laughed. "And you can't bring back the dead?" he said, his voice ringing with sarcasm.

"No," she replied gravely. "That's something I can't do. I have to be with the dying person, lay my hands on him before he gives up his last breath."

Barro swung his attention fully onto Corbel. "What is this madness?"

Corbel shrugged. There was no point in denying it. "She speaks the truth."

The two men held each other's gaze for a few moments as they sized each other up. Finally, Barro raked a hand through his hair. "I will need time to ponder this situation."

"I know the feeling," Evie said, moving back to the old man to check on him.

"And you?" Barro continued, pointing at Corbel. "I heard the name de Vis. Is this another jest?"

"No jest," Corbel said, no longer attempting to keep up the pretense. "Why is it important to you?"

"I've only ever seen one other man fight like you do. He carried the name of Regor de Vis," Barro said. "A man I loved and respected."

Hearing his father's name tore at Corbel's heartstrings. "Then why do you shame him by your monstrous actions? Regor de Vis was a man of honor, not a thief and cutthroat."

"How are you related to Regor de Vis?" Barro demanded.

"Who said I was?"

"The fire in your eyes, the tremble in your voice. You speak of him and I hear the awe. Besides, didn't you just admit to her to the name?"

There was a silence, which Corbel refused to fill and Barro seemed equally determined to hold.

"This is his son, Corbel de Vis," Evie said suddenly, wearily.

Barro seemed to be even more shocked by this revelation than his coming back from the dead. He visibly paled before Corbel.

"Well, say something," Evie urged, sounding exasperated as she looked between them both.

"You can't be," Barro exclaimed.

Corbel scowled. "Get used to the idea."

"Why can't he?" Evie asked.

Barro frowned. "I . . . well . . ." He shook his head as though clearing it of a fog. "My general was slaughtered ten anni ago. His fine sons had not yet completed their second decade. You look too old."

"How do you know either of the sons of Regor de Vis?" Corbel demanded.

Barro was still looking stunned. "I never met either of his sons but like all the soldiers of the Penraven army we saw them from a distance, watched them grow up from that distance. Prove you are who you claim!" he suddenly demanded.

"Not to you, I won't," Corbel said disdainfully, "not to anyone but a royal."

The man actually laughed. He turned to Evie. "Your friend is deluded. Now I know he is not who he claims to be. There are no *royals* left. I'm sure the emperor will be as amused as I am to meet him."

"As he will you when you try and explain that I killed you. You'll be thrown into the madhouse," Corbel snarled. "Are you coming, Evie?"

"The emperor and I share no friendship. I remain loyal to the Valisar Crown, even though the Valisars are long gone. Why do you think I find myself roaming Penraven like a soul lost?"

Corbel swung back to face the man. "Loyal? By being a cutthroat? King Brennus would turn in his tomb. As for my father—"

"If you are who you say then you should know that I loved your father. I would have gladly followed the Legate into death and never questioned the order." Barro looked down. "I'm not proud of where I find myself. After the death of the royals, your father, those of us who were loyal to Valisar lost our way. I'll hand it to Loethar; he didn't slaughter us as I'd anticipated. Sometimes I wish he had. I didn't cope well under the new regime, not after watching how the Legate was treated, how the royal family was destroyed. We heard the king was butchered, the queen murdered by her own aide . . ." His voice trailed off. He shook his head, seemingly trying to rein in an old emotion. "There was nothing else for people like me. I had no place in the new empire. I was a soldier. I knew nothing else but I refused to take orders from Stracker."

"So you decided to steal from honest Penravens," Corbel finished, winning a glare from Evie.

"I had no trade. I couldn't offer my services as a merce-nary. I did odd jobs. I slowly slid from proud Valisar lieuten-ant to a pathetic cutpurse. You should have let me die. You would have done me a favor in ending my miserable life." Suddenly, unexpectedly, he rounded on Evie. "You should have let me die, you witch!"

Corbel leaped at Barro, pummeling him. "You bastard!"

Evie flung herself at both of them and wrenched Corbel away with a string of colorful insults. They all stood, breath-ing hard. Finally, Evie spoke. "I saved your ungrateful arse because I could and I didn't think you deserved to die. Corbel's got a strange fire in his belly that you haplessly stoked. That's why I saved you."

"For a lady, you have a foul mouth," Barro muttered.

"Really?" she said, a hand moving to her hip. "And for a soldier meant to defend a Valisar you have a strange way of showing your loyalty."

Barro's face creased in yet another wave of confusion. "What's that supposed to mean?"

"Evie," Corbel said softly. "Please."

Barro looked between them. "What do you mean?" he re-peated, angry now, urgent even. "The Valisars are dead and gone. I would give my life for any one of them."

"You almost did," Evie snapped.

"What?" Barro looked frantically at Corbel. "What is she talking about?"

"Nothing. She's raving. Come on, Evie, let's go."

Evie addressed Barro with thin lips despite her suddenly overly polite air. "You might feel a bit shaky for a few hours so don't do anything too strenuous. Drink fluid. Your com-panion will sleep for a while. When he wakes I suspect he will remember little of what occurred."

Corbel frowned at her. She shrugged. "It's a trick I used to use to help patients forget the horror of an accident or the pain of an injury. I thought it was just a mind game I played with them but I realize now it's something real I can do. I used it on the old man because I suspect his lips are looser than Clem's."

Barro put a hand up. "Please," he said, his voice pleading.

"Help me make sense of what's just happened. Are you really Corbel de Vis?"

A fresh silence lengthened as Corbel took Barro's measure. His skills definitely singled him out as an army man. And he was proud, eloquent. Perhaps he was loyal. Perhaps he did deserve better. "I am."

Barro did a sort of skip. He began to laugh and then he clapped his hands. "How have you escaped his notice?"

Corbel didn't need it clarified who "he" referred to. "It's a very long story."

"I would hear it if you'll share it." But before Corbel could respond, Barro bowed deeply and unexpectedly before him. "De Vis, I pledge my life, my service, to you."

Corbel was speechless for a few moments. "You owe me no fealty."

"I owed your father. And I lost my way, as I've explained. You have not, it seems. Let me walk with you, de Vis, let me serve whomever you serve. Here." He crossed his arms across his breast in the Penraven way. "You have my loyalty. Until my blood is spilled and I am dead . . . again, I am your servant. It's time to regain my sense of worth."

Watching the man sign, as he had watched so many sign before his father, Corbel was touched . . . far more deeply than he was ready for. He suddenly felt choked by strong emotion.

"Accept me, de Vis," Barro urged. "I will help protect you and your wife."

Corbel hesitated. An extra pair of eyes, an extra sword. They needed all the help they could win. And it did seem that Barro was in earnest. Amazing what death could bring on, he thought cheerlessly.

"She is not my wife but she does need protection."

He noticed relief flare in Evie's eyes and Barro, who seemed to have been holding his breath, let it out with a sigh. "Thank you."

"I will kill you sooner than wait for explanations should I ever believe that you are insincere."

"And you have my permission to kill me . . . again . . . should I prove myself below my word." Barro held out a hand, and Corbel took it.

"Will you tell me your story?" Barro asked, intensifying his grip. "I have to understand everything, especially you," he said, glancing at Evie.

Corbel nodded. "I hope I can trust you with it. Walk with us. We are going to the convent."

"What about your friends over here?" Evie asked.

"The old man is nothing to me. You have made him safe and he is whole. Presumably he will wake and remember nothing. And the boy was a halfwit. He had no family, no friends, no way of caring for himself. He's better off where he is."

"That's harsh," Evie protested.

Barro shrugged. "That's his lot."

Corbel felt a pang of sympathy for her. She had not been raised in this way of life; she had little concept about how cheap life could be.

"If the old man finds the body and remembers," Barro continued, "he'll just be glad to have got away with his own life. I imagine he'll wake up and walk away. He's a drifter, an opportunist. He'll fall in with the next halfwit he can persuade into some scam alongside him."

Evie gently touched Corbel's arm. "Let me heal those injuries."

He shook his head. "I can stitch myself once I reach the convent."

Her eyes narrowed in fresh irritation. "How do you think you will look when you present yourself to the nuns bleeding from these wounds?"

Corbel hadn't considered this. Her logic was correct. He nodded unhappily and tried not to react to her touch when she guided him to sit against a big boulder so she could concentrate. He noted Barro watching in awed fascination and chose instead to close his eyes, lean his head back as he felt his beloved's hands placed against his chest. She was leaning near enough that he could feel her breath against his face; close enough to kiss. He ground his jaw, turned his head away and hoped she wouldn't sense his despair but it seemed Evie was too entranced by her ministrations to notice his discomfort and he was glad of the distraction of the strange ice-like sensation that spread through him as though moving within his veins, the magic swimming with his blood to all parts of his body and healing as it went.

Finally her hands lifted and he felt their removal as a private grief. He missed them already but wasn't prepared to feel them touch his face. He flinched.

"Sorry," she said gently. "How do you feel?"

"Grateful," he replied. "Thank you."

Evie sighed and he couldn't bear her looking so deeply into his eyes. "I hope it didn't hurt."

"Worrying about you hurts more," he said, trying to be flippant, but his voice caught.

She leaned forward and kissed his cheek, slow and deliberate. "No more fighting. I should be honored, I suppose, that you'd risk your life, but don't do that again for me. I couldn't bear to lose you."

Corbel swallowed. If only she knew how unbearable this closeness was for him. He nodded perfunctorily. "Help me up, Barro. We need to get going. But Evie's right, we should wear our jackets to hide the bloodstains."

The big man offered a hand and heaved him up easily. They turned away from the bodies and continued toward the convent.

"So, my lady," Barro began. "You have my name. May I know yours?"

"I am called Evie." She looked to Corbel and Corbel haltingly began to tell their tale.

The small opening revealed a pair of rheumy eyes. "Yes?"

"Visitors to speak with the Mother, please," Corbel began.

"She is not seeing anyone today. Make an appointment for next moon."

"Er, please, sister. We are so weary. We have come from a long way. Please tell her that a man by the name of . . ." He hesitated. "Please say that an old friend called Regor awaits her patiently. It is important, sister. I am a former noble. That alone should open the door."

"Pushy . . . and arrogant!" she remarked as though tasting something sour.

The opening closed abruptly and he flinched.

"That went well," Evie commented.

He bit his lip. "I have this immense charm with women, as you can tell."

She burst into laughter. It was the first reason she'd had to smile in what felt an age.

Barro had been silent for a long time. She noticed he'd begun regarding her with awe, stealing furtive looks as though he had to keep mentally pinching himself that she was real. So she was surprised when he spoke up. "It's nice to hear you laugh, your majesty."

"It certainly feels good," she admitted. "Barro, Corbel has asked you to stop addressing me in that way."

He adopted a contrite expression. "I promise it will not happen again, although you understand, my lady, that I am still in a state of utter disbelief."

"I do understand but according to Corbel your disbelief—if you don't rein it in—could get us killed." He nodded somberly, no doubt more aware than she could ever be how true her statement was. "Now how exactly should I behave here if I'm supposed to be royal?"

"Humble," Corbel replied. "Only Sergius knows of your existence and he won't know you have returned. I don't even know if he is alive, although it was his magic that brought us back."

Evie blew out her cheeks. All the anger she'd previously felt had diffused. She wanted to speak with Corbel in quiet. He had said so little to her directly in the last few hours. She knew he would have been hurt by her earlier attitude toward him, but how was she supposed to react to witnessing such savagery and death? She still saw the young man's face, slack and lifeless, in her mind's eye. He hadn't had to die. "I am so confused."

"You are?" Barro queried with an edge of sharp sarcasm.

They had waited several long minutes, talking quietly. But at last the door was unbolted, interrupting their conversation. It swung open with a loud sigh, as though unused to the movement. Before them stood a woman of senior anni and behind her, scowling at the gate was another, a bit younger, and likely the sour-sounding sister who had tried to turn them away.

The elder smiled.

"Are you the Abbess?" Corbel asked.

"I am. Call me Mother. It wasn't so long ago that I welcomed another Regor."

Corbel hesitated, surprised.

She noticed his reaction. "A relative, perhaps? Though you'd have to be close to share the same birthname."

"It . . . it's a family name. I don't use it often."

"Just to open doors?" Her eyes twinkled in amusement. "Regor?" She tasted the name on her lips. "Such a steadfast, proud name of the former Denova."

Former Denova. If they had shocked Barro with their story, he'd certainly surprised Corbel with a few of his own. Corbel felt he was now as well informed as he could be about the new empire and its politics. But he was on such unsafe ground now not really knowing who might be a potential ally . . . or enemy.

"Are we allowed to say that now?" he said with a wink.

The wrinkles around her eyes creased as her smile deepened. "I shouldn't have mentioned it. We're all accustomed to saying empire now. Come in, my dear," she said to Evie, eyes sparkling. "And welcome," she said to Barro. "Follow me; you all look starved."

They glanced at each other and fell in behind her. "Thank you," Corbel said.

"We'll talk in a moment," she said over her shoulder. "Go in there. Be comfortable. I am going to send for some food for you. I hope a plate of soup will suffice?"

"Soup, porridge, anything, Mother. We are grateful," Evie said carefully. Corbel gave a smile of gratitude her way.

The woman rang a bell and as they settled themselves into a room, sparsely furnished but brightened with fresh flowers and pretty tapestries. They heard her giving a request for food to a young nun, who quickly hurried away. The Mother returned to the room beaming. "There, now we can fatten you all up a bit. Where are you headed?"

Corbel had already decided he would need to be honest with her, sensing that she would see through any guile with those bright eyes of hers. "We are going higher into the mountains."

"Good gracious, without transport or supplies? Why? It might be early summertide but it's still dangerously cold up there. Most people visit us on their way out, when they are grateful to see civilization again. In fact, the other man called Regor was here just a few weeks back, in exactly that situation. He came down from the mountains with a Davarigon."

"And?" Corbel asked, hoping he sounded offhand and casually interested.

She frowned. "I didn't discover much more. He was traveling with a woman I like—I know her family and I trust her. They were good friends and I had no reason to fear him. He seemed rather confused about his past."

"In what way confused?"

"He had lost his memory. Elka believed that bringing him to meet the Qirin might help."

"Did it?"

She nodded, but smiled sadly. "I think Elka loved the man she brought here."

"I don't understand," Corbel said, frowning.

Evie nodded. "The man who left here was different. Is that what you mean, Mother?"

"Female instincts," the Abbess acknowledged with a smile at Evie. "You see, Evie understands. Yes, the man who left here was changed. They both knew it might happen and they took the risk."

"Did he love her before?" Evie asked.

The Abbess's expression clouded. "I cannot say. They were close friends. Had been companions for a long time from what I gather and he had been living in the mountains with her people for anni. What he discovered I suspected changed his outlook sufficiently that it meant his whole way of life might change." She turned to Corbel. "Does this sound like someone you might know from your own family?" He hesitated. "Surely you know if you have family in these parts?" Both women watched the color drain from Corbel's face.

"My friend has been away a long time, Mother," Barro said, rescuing him, his eyes urging Corbel to take up the thread.

"Yes," Corbel admitted. "I've been traveling to different lands," he said carefully.

"Did you get as far east as Percheron? Now there's a place I'd love to see, especially as our own queen came from that region."

"To be accurate, she came from Galinsea," Corbel corrected.

"That's right, she did," the Abbess acknowledged. "She was so beautiful. I saw her only once. Did you ever see the royal family? So handsome. I know we're not supposed to talk about them here but it's history now."

Corbel cleared his throat, threw a glance Evie's way.

"What is it?" the Abbess asked, and Corbel realized she missed little.

He searched for a way of covering their self-consciousness. "Evie here has some Galinsean blood running in her veins," he said.

He wished he hadn't. It only led to more tension. "Really? I thought all Galinseans were golden-haired."

Evie looked up and calmly spoke. "I take my coloring from my father," she said, startling Corbel. "I never knew him. He was a great traveler though, I'm told, and must have visited Galinsea and met my mother."

"What did this Regor look like?" Corbel asked, desperate to steer the conversation elsewhere.

"Well, he had your build but the similarities end there . . . although to be honest it's hard to tell," she said with a smile.

Corbel scratched at his unruly beard. "I know. I hope you'll indulge me with a bath, Mother. We will gladly pay," he said, thinking of the money given to him by the King that he had buried in a park near the hospital for all those anni and had to dig up just before they left. "I hope you take the same coin," he commented absently.

The Abbess frowned. "What do you mean?"

He felt color at his cheeks. That had been a mistake. His hesitation was about to undo him, he was sure, when Barro suddenly joined the conversation.

"Oh, my cousin has been away many anni. Wait until my mother catches up with you, Regor! I suppose you've been dealing with different coin in strange parts. Let me guess: you only have money from the days of Brennus."

Corbel swallowed. "Er, yes. Ridiculous, isn't it?"

The Abbess blinked. "You have been away a long time. We haven't used that currency for six anni. Nevertheless, it is still accepted, particularly here in the north."

Barro warmed to his theme. "And you can always exchange the coin at Woodingdene at the imperial mint."

"But for now," the Abbess smiled, its warmth touching her eyes and making Corbel feel safe, "you have nothing to worry about. Our food and our water are free."

Corbel's relief was huge when they heard a knock at the door.

"Refreshment," she said happily. She looked at the door. "Come."

A woman entered carrying a tray. The hood of her habit was up so they could not see her face. She set the food down between them. The tasty aroma of a steaming, meaty soup made Corbel's belly softly grind. Warm buns and oil to dip them in was provided, along with a soft herb paste he hadn't tasted in a decade.

"I hope you like beef and colac?" the Abbess inquired.

Evie glanced at Corbel. "Er, yes, delicious, thank you."

"Help yourself to the sherret. I wasn't sure if you preferred it with or without," she added, smiling at Evie.

"Without would be an insult to the fine soup of the region," Barro said, waving a hand widely and smiling somewhat wolfishly at the Abbess. Corbel inwardly smiled at Barro's passing a disguised message to Evie.

"May I?" murmured the newcomer. Corbel watched the nun dollop a small scoop of the dark green paste into the stew and give the gravy a stir. Then she stepped back, gesturing for them to taste. Corbel's first mouthful transported him back many anni. The nutty taste of the sherret paste mingled perfectly with the beefy richness of the meat stew, the slightly bitter crunch of the colac and the bright tang of citrus from a squeeze of lemon.

"Delicious!" he said, meaning it.

"This is so good that if we were in an inn I would feel obliged to leap up and give you a kiss, Mother."

Corbel looked over at Barro quizzically and yet unable to hide the amusement that creased across his face as the Abbess gave Barro a searching glance.

"I suppose I should feel deeply complimented," she finally said.

"Indeed you should, for I reserve my kisses for only the most beautiful women."

The Abbess shook a finger at him but she was smiling. "Lo knows just how to deal with helpless flirts, young man. And you are a guest in his house."

Barro held up his hands in mock defense.

"Mmm, this is good," Evie added, giving a grateful look toward the Mother and a grin to Corbel. "Thank you," she said, turning toward the woman who served them.

"Eat, eat," the Mother said. "Let me pour you some water," and she busied herself fetching the pitcher of cold water that was already in the room and pouring each of them a cup. "The convent's well provides the sweetest water," she said and watched as they ate and drank with vigor. "And while you eat, let me introduce someone to you. I would like you to meet Valya, our empress."

Corbel dropped the knuckle of bread he was holding into the soup, his mouth open in astonishment as the woman who had served him pulled back the hood of her robe.

Janus took advantage of Loethar's unconscious state.

"Well, that won a strong reaction," Elka said, concerned.

"It's good fun hurting the barbarian."

"Is that your illness speaking?"

"No, it's all me. This is the man who slaughtered hundreds of innocents." When she raised her eyebrows doubtfully he added, "You are aware of the poem that begins 'And the Set ran awash with its children's blood?'"

Elka pinched her lips together. "Yes, I am aware of it," she answered tersely. "But isn't it true that Loethar only attacked soldiers who attacked his army?"

"His army attacked our soldiers first," Janus replied, looking incredulous. "They were the invaders."

She ignored his remark and his expression. "I wasn't aware that he allowed any of his people to kill randomly."

"What about the boys murdered across Penraven?" he demanded. She looked at him in query. He rolled his eyes and explained. "They say he would have killed every boy within a certain age group to be sure he had finished off the Valisar heir."

"Janus, I'm not disputing that the man is capable of stunning ruthlessness but I would argue that any ruler is capable of the same, given the right circumstances." She watched him stitch Loethar's skin angrily. "Brennus might have done the same to save his people, his family."

"I can't say," the physic said, shrugging. "The fact is, this man did do that and did kill a lot of our sons."

"It was war."

"That *he* brought to the Set," Janus said, his voice gruff.

"Granted," she replied, feeling torn. She stared at Loethar, vulnerable, near naked, totally at the mercy of Janus, she herself his only protection. "I'm sorry, Janus. I know this must be hard for you."

He sighed. "No. When I'm working on a patient, everyone is equal. I could easily take this man's life but I won't, be assured. I'll leave Lo to make that decision."

"Thank you," she said as Loethar groaned. "You know, when your ire is up, or you're very focused on work, your ailment leaves you alone."

He nodded as though he'd heard that remark before. "Here," Janus said, offering her a tiny, silver cup. "Get this down him. He must sleep. He will heal faster if his body is at rest."

"It is too dangerous here," she warned.

"If that's the case you should carry him to higher ground and hide him. But he needs a day of being still." She nodded. "And during that time you will tell me how it passes that I am repairing the body of Emperor Loethar."

"Have you finished stitching?"

"Yes. There is little more I can do now. I've realigned the bones in that hand. They'll hurt for a while. His ribs I can do little for but he's bound. And those other wounds are now closed properly. I had to clean them though or disease would have taken him faster than you can imagine."

She nodded. "I know you had to do that. Hopefully he will forget the pain you inflicted without dulling it. I know you had the soporific in your bag."

He made a fist. "Call it a small triumph for the Valisars."

"You're a royalist?"

He shrugged. "I don't know what I am. I was incensed, though, like most Penravians, at what was done to our royals."

"I understand. But you admit life is prosperous beneath this man's rule?"

"Not for me," he said, stretching from his concentrated work.

"It wouldn't be, though, with your problem. Your fall from grace has nothing to do with Loethar."

Janus sighed. "True. I have to blame someone. Perhaps you'd let me feel—"

"And it seems you've calmed enough to be offensive again. Perhaps you should blame Lo, for cursing you with the affliction."

"Seems rather pointless."

"That's right, it is. There's nothing to be gained by shaking a fist at a god. Nothing to be gained by drinking yourself to an early death. Why not make your life count?"

"I don't know how."

She smiled. "But you just did. Not only have you helped a man in need but the man you aided is a powerful one. He will reward you for your compassion."

"I don't want his money. I want to feel the sensation of your—"

"It's as good as the next person's. And it's not money I'm talking about. Take some time to get to know Loethar and I swear, Janus, your opinion may change. Things are not always as black and white as we think."

He sat back and stared at their prone patient as Elka dribbled the dark liquid into Loethar's mouth, gently drying his lips when it was done. "You like this man," he stated.

She shook her head in slight bemusement, admiring Loethar's wiry physique. In clothes he looked surprisingly undaunting but she imagined, as she stared at him, that he was probably small and fast, probably a cunning fighter too. There was no spare flesh on his body and while it was obvious that the gauntness in his face was due to recent events, she rather liked the way his cheeks looked slightly hollow, accentuating the lines on either side of his mouth. "I do," she admitted. "There is a darkness to him but also something very pure." Janus looked surprised, and she gave an embarrassed smile. "I can't think of any other way to describe it. There is an honor to him that I like very much."

"Honor, my arse!"

She nodded despite his insult. "I don't believe Loethar lies. Maybe I'm wrong but from what I can tell he is not only a man of his word but he has no reason for guile. He is what he is, he makes no apology, he hides from no one and I regard that as a kind of purity that is attractive in a person."

Janus shook his head in confusion. "The barbarian is asleep. Move him carefully."

"You're coming too?" she asked, careful not to make him feel that he owed her anything more. "You've done what I asked of you."

"I have nothing else more interesting to do right now than hear your long tale. I'm fascinated to discover what has led up to me being here and it also gives me the ongoing titillation that I might just see your—"

She nodded her thanks and quickly said, "Follow me. And, Janus—"

"Yes?"

"If you say a word about my arse, I'll wallop you."

"Cock!"

"Pardon," she said, glaring at him as she gently lifted Loethar.

"That slips out a lot," he admitted.

She exploded into helpless laughter and as he realized the

innuendo in his words, he picked up his bag, chuckling. "I'm glad you find me amusing."

"I'm glad you've chosen to come with us."

"It's big but she does have a nice arse," Loethar murmured, drifting momentarily from his sleep before his head lolled against her breast. Elka ground her jaw.

Janus couldn't help but smile. "I'm coming along because I think he needs my assistance still," he said.

"You see, already you're under his spell," she accused.

"Rubbish! The man is a tyrant. But he is just a man and I am a doctor. My conscience won't let me leave anyone who needs my care."

"Fair enough." She nodded toward Loethar in her arms. "He can get away with it because he's drugged and isn't fully aware of what he's gabbling about, but if you mention my backside, I will hurt you."

Janus pursed his lips to make it plain to her that he would try.

Eleven

The Abbess smiled. "My, my, but I can see we have shocked you, Regor."

Corbel had stood as he'd hastily swallowed. The stew tasted sour in his mouth suddenly as he regarded the darkly attractive woman in the robes. He aged her in her fourth decade though she looked better than most women in their third. But despite her good looks there was something mean in the cut of her mouth, something cruel in the eyes that glinted defiantly. "Should I bow?" he asked, trying to buy himself some time.

"Not here," Valya replied with a lazy smile. "I am simply one of the women of the convent. As you can see," she said, pointing to the tray. "Regor," she said, tasting the name. "No relation to Regor de Vis, I hope?" she continued, raising an eyebrow.

Corbel gave a short gust of a laugh. He hoped it sounded vaguely ironic rather than angry, which is how it felt. "That's the second time the former Legate has been mentioned to me," he said, feigning bemusement. From the corner of his eye he saw Evie watching him carefully. He couldn't believe they were in the same chamber as one of the designers of the overthrow of the Valisars. Word had traveled to them through spies that Valya, princess of Cremond, was moving with the barbarian horde. It had seemed unthinkable at first but his father had then told him the story of Brennus breaking his pledge to the Cremond Crown to marry its daughter and how that had affected the young woman, broken her relationship with her parents, broken her faith. Corbel believed he could see the history of her pain reflected in the slight sneer that seemed to be her normal expression.

"He was a fine man," the Abbess commented. She smiled. "It's all right, we can speak freely before Valya; she has reason to have changed her loyalties."

Corbel was glad the Abbess had jumped to the wrong conclusion. "You knew the Legate?" he continued.

"Not personally, no. I knew of him and our convent felt the effects of his generosity and that of the Crown. Regor de Vis was a man to admire no matter what creed or race. He was one of those rare individuals who are noble in the heart, not just in name."

"Lo keep his soul," Barro said reverently.

Corbel had to bite the inside of his lip to stop any emotion showing. "I . . . er, I wish I had been named for him now. No, I'm just an ordinary Regor. Perhaps my parents were impressed by the Legate."

Valya regarded him. "You have a noble manner about you."

He made a scoffing sound that he hoped masked the choke he felt at his throat. "Noble? No, just a good family. Why are you here, if it's not a rude question?"

"I have been banished from Loethar's court," she said plainly and he noticed she didn't seem embarrassed so much as angry. "I failed him by giving him a daughter recently." She motioned toward the swelling at her belly, and Corbel realized she must have given birth recently. "She died. They say the Valisars could never hold onto a girl child but our child was not Valisar. I'm of the opinion that it's that wretched palace at Penraven. It reeks of death."

"Valya, my dear, don't get yourself upset," the Abbess soothed sounding tense. She looked at Corbel. "The empress is spending some time with us."

"Don't call me that, Mother. He doesn't view me that way any longer." Her voice sounded weary.

Corbel knew she referred to Loethar.

"And still you are the empress . . . in name, in status, and in marriage," the Abbess said in her kind tone.

Evie stood suddenly. "Are you feeling faint?"

Valya glared at her. "How would you know?"

Evie gave a crooked smile. "I'm . . . I'm a healer. Your pallor is a strong indication that you need rest."

"A healer," the Abbess remarked with wonder. "So young?"

Evie shrugged. "The empress should not be working."

Valya sneered audibly. "The people who brought me here insisted I be given work."

The Abbess nodded unhappily. "It's true. We're trying to follow orders without—"

"Low-born scum!" Valya snarled, grabbing her belly and swaying slightly.

Evie was at her side in a blink, holding her. "Please, sit," she said, indicating her chair. "Mother, regardless of what was ordered, I would hazard a guess that the empress has lost a lot of blood. She should be recuperating, not waiting on visitors."

"I couldn't agree more," the Mother said helplessly.

"Is she under guard?" Evie demanded.

"No. But we gave our word," the Abbess replied.

Evie snorted. "Well, I am giving new orders. Until Valya is fully recovered from the trials of her labor and birth, and I'm happy that her blood levels are returning to some normality, I will not permit her to be anywhere else but off her feet and resting."

Her instructions were met with silence. Corbel saw the Abbess and Valya exchange a tense, confused glance. Before they could react, Barro spoke up.

"Er, Evie is a talented healer," he explained, nodding at Corbel.

"Despite her age, she's rather senior in her sanatorium. She's used to people listening to her advice," Corbel said, apology in his tone. "Evie, you are no longer running your special healing service as you did from Galinsea."

She looked abashed. "Yes," she stammered. "Forgive me, please. I do forget myself."

"She has an almost magical talent for curing ills," Corbel explained hastily, flashing a fearful glance at Evie. "That's why I brought her with me. I'd like to set up a sanatorium," he blurted, reaching desperately for excuses.

"Lo, be praised!" the Abbess pronounced, clasping her hands. "Bless you both for such philanthropy."

Mercifully, Valya announced that she was feeling nauseous and the Abbess was diverted, springing into action and summoning help. Valya was bundled away hastily, and Corbel was relieved he didn't have to explain why Evie had left Galinsea, or was traveling with him, or even why they were in Penraven.

Once Valya was gone, the Abbess took a breath, smiled uneasily and then apologized. "I'm trapped somewhat. I gave my word to the emperor, via his emissary, that I would provide succor for Valya but that she would never leave here. It is not his intention to make her suffer physically, you see, but he is punishing her mentally I suppose. There is more to Valya's tale than she presents. She is accused of murdering the emperor's mother . . . and between us, she doesn't deny it, even though she refuses to directly answer the accusation. Frankly, I think the emperor has behaved rather decently. He could have ordered her head so easily. She is well cared for here, though she would probably argue that she is a prisoner."

Evie looked to be doing her best to understand. "But surely you can see that she is not well enough, Mother, to be doing anything."

The Abbess nodded. "I can, but you see, Evie, my child, I have no idea if the emperor or his factions have spies in here. And the emperor has decreed that Valya be useful; that she is not to be waited upon or treated with deference but that she must fit in as best she can to the life of the convent."

"I see," Corbel said, frowning.

"Why did the baby—?" Evie asked.

The Abbess held up a hand to stop Evie's question. She sighed to cover her hesitation. "Valya doesn't wish anyone to discuss it. Understandably, she is deeply upset. If she chooses to tell you more, that's her choice."

"You will have to watch her, Mother," Evie warned. She glanced at Corbel. "I may be telling you something you already know but some women can have a strange perspective on the world after having a baby. It's to do with their hor—"

She stopped herself and frowned. "Well, we're not fully sure yet," she explained and Corbel felt relief that she'd caught herself in time. "The body has its own way of tackling trauma," she continued. "Experience now tells us that some women can go mad, can certainly start acting strangely—out of character, I mean—and are capable of dangerous decisions regarding themselves."

"Waning," Mother commented, nodding.

"What?" Evie queried, looking between them.

Corbel leaped to her rescue. "They don't call it the same thing in Galinsea, Mother. Over there it's known as being depressed, as in forced down."

"Really?"

Evie nodded, looking grateful to Corbel for his help. "A depression, yes, and . . . er, well, that situation can be responsible for some unpredictable moods and actions."

"Thank you, your advice is helpful. Now, please, your food has gone cold."

"We're happy to eat it exactly as it is, Mother. Please don't worry," Corbel assured. "We are very grateful for your generosity. And speaking of your generosity, you were talking about the other Regor who was here, that he met the Qirin." She nodded. "Is it possible for us to speak with her?"

"She sees those she wishes to. I am happy to petition her on your behalf."

"Please," he said, spooning up the last mouthfuls of stew. He noted happily that Evie was also quickly swallowing down her food. They both needed full bellies and no meal should be wasted when they didn't know where the next was coming from.

She rang a bell. "Our Qirin is contrary at times but her whole reason for being is to answer the unanswerable." She looked up at another knock. "Ah, Margrey. Please take my guests to our visitor wing. See to it that they have fresh water for bathing and please launder their clothes, provide whatever they need."

Margrey nodded. "Please, follow me."

As they stood, Barro belched gently and grinned at the Abbess. "Thank you again for the meal."

She smiled at him. "I'll take that as another compliment."

Corbel bowed slightly. "Thank you, Mother."

"You're most welcome."

"If I may, I would like to leave a donation to the convent."

She smiled. "You may," she said. "Feel free to stay a day or two. I would be pleased if you would visit Valya," she said to Evie.

"I will look in on her, Mother," Evie promised.

"And I hope you will not forget us. We look forward to hearing about your progress with the sanatorium. I would recommend basing it in the north. The water is so pure here. Precisely what patients from the city require."

Corbel nodded, feeling embarrassed by his lies. "I shall do that, Mother."

"I hope the Qirin provides enlightenment."

Twelve

✦━━━━━━━━━━━━━━━━━━✦

Kirin turned to Lily. She couldn't have known. He filled his expression with forgiveness, masking, he hoped, his intense fear for her safety.

"Unless I'm mistaken," the general began, his tatua beginning to stretch with the cruel smile that was forming beneath it, "and I was only there an anni ago—there is no mill on Medhaven. Flour is brought—as are most supplies—over the small channel of water by boat from the mainland."

Kirin sighed silently as he regarded the woman he loved. His mind raced as he watched Lily hesitate before, to his enormous pride, he saw her gather herself. "Well, you're wrong, General Stracker," she defied politely. "Forgive me, but there is a small mill." She turned back to Kirin and smiled. "I'm sure you remember," she urged gently. She returned her attention to the towering general. "There has been since before I or Kirin were born. But the family didn't survive well, especially not when the miller himself died unexpectedly not long after you left," she said, glancing at him. "Link tried to keep the family business running but I'm sorry to say it perished. Of course you're right, general, that all our supplies come from across the channel into Port Killen . . . including our flour these days." She beamed him a smile. "I'm sorry that you didn't taste the Chervil Bakery bread. It was the best of the realms in its day."

Stracker's eyes narrowed as he regarded the innocent expression on Lily's face. Kirin was amazed, but covered his awe as best he could and looked straight forward. If he'd so much as caught Lily's eye he was sure he would have felt moved to applaud.

"You said this Chervil fellow *is* a miller," Stracker growled. "I might be from the Steppes, Mrs. Felt, but I understand the subtlety of the Denovian language better than you think."

Lily swallowed, smiled even brighter. "My mistake, general. A slip of the tongue. You make me feel nervous. Leak is no longer a miller, of course, but I always think of him as dusted in flour and smelling of his breads." She nodded. "Forgive me. These days I believe Leak is eking out a living as a grower. His father also owned some orchards."

Stracker's gaze slid ominously back to Kirin. "So let me get this right, Felt. You conveniently left Freath shortly before he also left the tavern to meet his fate, and you traveled to Medhaven where you coincidentally met your former sweetheart, whom you happily married."

Kirin tried Lily's tack of smiling. He hoped it had just the right amount of embarrassment in it. "General, when you put it so baldly like that it sounds far-fetched. But this is the truth. Yes, I left that evening so that I could join a merchant caravan that was leaving at nightfall. As far as I was concerned Master Freath was turning in for the evening because he had an important meeting with the mayor the next morning on behalf of Emperor Loethar. I headed south simply because I hadn't been home in such a long time. Perhaps in the back of my mind I hoped that Lily hadn't married, although I was incredibly surprised that she hadn't."

The general regarded them both with suspicion although his glance toward Lily was also lascivious. "So am I," he replied. "And you went directly south?" he added casually.

Kirin hesitated while he decided whether Stracker would know of the diversion to Woodingdene. He had to take the risk; they had to get out of this chamber. "We traveled swiftly," he said, shrugging. "I broke away from the caravan to head for Camlet." He glanced again at Lily as he crafted his lie. "I took a ferry across the river into Vorgaven and then a fast carriage south to another ferry across to Medhaven."

"You have been busy, Master Felt, over the last days. And still found time to meet, rekindle a former love and marry, no less."

Kirin smiled. "And still be back for dinner," he said, quoting an old rhyme.

Clearly the general didn't know it, for his expression clouded. Kirin didn't try explaining. He watched Stracker reach for a bell pull. They heard the bell sound distantly in the hallway outside and Kirin felt his heart skip. Perhaps they'd got through the interrogation.

"General Stracker," Lily said into what felt like an awkward pause. "I can't help but notice a wound on your forehead. Would you like me to treat that? I am a healer."

The general's tatua stretched malevolently. "What wound?"

"Er . . ." Lily glanced at Kirin, fearful. She pointed helplessly to her own head, mirroring the position of the wound. "It looks rather nasty. Perhaps a stitch or two would—"

"Mrs. Felt," Stracker cut across her words. "I am of the Steppes." He glanced disdainfully at Kirin. "We are not a soft people. If I have a wound I have not noticed it and it can wait until I can be bothered to clean up."

She nodded, embarrassed. "Of course, general. I just don't want it to get infected."

He laughed at her. "It is touching that you say that as if you really care."

Before she could respond there was a knock at the door and Kirin felt a wave of relief wash over him. Perhaps now they could escape this tense, difficult confrontation.

"Come!" Stracker bellowed, glancing at Kirin with a satisfaction that Kirin could not read. "Ah, Master Vulpan. I presume you remember Master and Mrs. Felt?"

Kirin's hopes disintegrated. The hideous blood taster nodded, self-satisfied. "Of course I do. The very handsome Vested couple I met very recently. Mrs. Felt," he said, holding up his bandaged hand. "Your magical ministrations didn't work. I'm most disappointed."

Lily looked at Kirin and he begged her through a glance to hold her nerve . . . for just a few heartbeats longer.

"You've lied to me, Felt," Stracker accused, clearly relishing the taut atmosphere and the sense of pervading fear that Kirin knew he and Lily were offering up.

He gave a tight, embarrassed smile. "Yes, I have."

"Why?"

"Frankly because I don't think you like me, General Stracker. I think you've been looking for an excuse to slit my throat for years."

Stracker laughed, loud, genuine amusement. But the mirth died in his eyes almost as quickly as it had arrived. "You're right. I don't like you, Felt."

"I don't know what I've ever done to earn your displeasure, general."

"I've always thought that you and Freath were hatching something."

"Hatching something?" Kirin repeated, as offended as he could possibly sound, despite the lump forming in his throat. "Hatching something against you?"

"Me, my brother, the empire . . ."

"No, general. You are absolutely wrong about that," Kirin said and began to feel a low protest of pain deep in his head.

At the sight of Vulpan, Lily quailed. As Kirin and the general debated a moot point that she was sure Stracker was simply amusing himself with, she watched the man of blood watching her, licking his lips in anticipation. The way his eyes moved over her she was sure that she and Kirin would not be kept together if they survived the next few moments, even though Kirin was doing his best to sound undaunted, speaking back to the general as though they were simply discussing a matter of business and not their lives.

Stracker hadn't pulled his cunning trick simply for amusement. He had wanted to trap Kirin, to give himself the formal excuse he needed to punish the Vested. Perhaps Kirin had a chance at survival if they transported him off to wherever it was the Vested were being held—somewhere in Barronel. But she? Vulpan had already accused her, in his cunning way, of cheating. Very soon they would discover that she didn't have an enchanted bone in her body. And it didn't take much imagination to visualize what fate awaited her.

"The mere fact that you have lied to me so blatantly, Master Kirin, suggests you are a man of intrigue," Stracker accused.

Kirin's shoulders slumped. "Look, general, I have no more to say on the matter. I have nothing more to hide from you. I simply didn't overcomplicate my explanation with details of meeting Master Vulpan. I'm sure he will confirm that I am Vested and that my wife and I were compliant and open with him."

"You are certainly Vested, Master Kirin," Vulpan said. "And yes, once cornered, you were compliant. But somewhere between the pair of you is a lie. I sense it . . . I tasted it in her blood. Something is not right."

Stracker's expression changed. He adopted a look of puzzlement. "Mrs. Felt, can you tell me about your brother, please?"

"My . . . my brother?" she stammered, forcing herself not to glance at Kirin. "What do you know about my brother?" she said, desperately hoping for some clues and some time to formulate a response.

"I have met him."

"I can't imagine how . . . or why?"

"Really?" Stracker asked, surprised. "He seemed very concerned for you."

She took a deep breath. "He's like that. But I haven't seen him in a while."

"How long?"

"I . . . I can't remember."

"Your mother's dead," he said, matter of factly, seeming to be enjoying himself.

Lily groped her way forward, hoping she would learn more if she offered something. Her mother had been dead for so long it was laughable. "What did my brother say? And how did you meet?"

"We met because he was trying to find you. Actually it was Vulpan he saw first."

"That's right," Vulpan said, looking smug.

Lily noticed that Kirin was very quiet. She hoped he was taking stock, listening carefully, formulating some plan for them.

"He was obviously trying to let me know about our mother, then," she risked.

They both nodded, to her relief.

"Yes, that's what he said. He had followed your trail to Woodingdene."

She stared at the general, no idea of what to say next.

"And where is Lily's brother now, general?" Kirin said.

"We'll get to that, Master Felt. I'm interested to hear from your wife about her brother."

"Why?" Lily asked. "We are not close. I have nothing to tell you about him."

"Not close?" Stracker's brow lifted. "What a pity. He seemed so concerned for you. So anxious to reach you. And here you are so uncaring of his brotherly affection?" He gave a soft tutting sound. "What does your brother do, Mrs. Felt?"

She knew she was trapped. Although the only person who would follow her was Kilt, she was sure. He would have heard by now of her questionable decision to follow Kirin Felt so closely that she had claimed to be his wife. She could imagine how he received that news—in fact she could imagine it so vividly, Lily could see the expression on his face. Gone would be the mirth that was an almost permanent quality of Kilt's sardonic expression. His face would darken, his eyelids would close slightly and his lips would thin. Again just slightly. But all of these subtle changes would occur in less than a heartbeat and everyone in his camp knew that look.

Though she hated him at times for locking her out, keeping his emotions so tightly controlled, there were other times, like now, when she loved him for risking his life so openly in order to protect her. She tried to run through in her mind all his various disguises. Which one might he have chosen to masquerade as her brother? She had no idea, but she knew that guessing wrong would be lethal.

And so she gave him only silence.

Stracker smiled and it was filled with a malevolent satisfaction.

"I'll tell you what's not right here, Vulpan. It's the fact that Mrs. Felt was being hotly pursued by a man who called himself Pastor Jeeves, who might have acted the part of a priest, but was clearly so much more by being Vested."

That shocked her. "Vested? I don't think so."

It was Vulpan's chance to turn on his oily grin. "Oh yes, indeed, Mrs. Felt. Make no mistake. The man who claimed to be your brother *is* Vested."

At first it made no sense and she began to shake her head, wanting to laugh at them for their pitiful stupidity. But then realization hit her so hard it felt like a sharp pain in her belly. Was that Kilt's secret? The possibility took her breath away. She knew her expression was sagging in its shock, that her mouth was open. Kilt . . . Vested? There had never been any sign of it. She trawled through her memories of being with him. No! He had never once used any magic.

Maybe the man pursuing her hadn't been Kilt. "Are you sure this was my brother? Was he very tall, bearded?" she said, mimicking a bushy growth. Kilt might have a number of disguises but Jewd was so distinctive that she could describe him easily. And if he had been present then she could be sure they were referring to Kilt as the pastor.

Stracker's amusement died and was replaced with a scowl. "No. That big Denovian will one day swing from a noose I'll tie myself after I've split his gut open with my blade. He helped your brother escape."

"Escape?" Lily repeated. "Was he your prisoner?"

"He *was* my prisoner."

"But why?"

"He was Vested, Mrs. Felt," Vulpan explained in his annoyingly polite way. "And he was immensely potent. He resisted blood tasting, only relented when I assured him that the Wikken Shorgan had identified him."

Immensely potent, Lily repeated in her mind. Suddenly everything she knew about Kilt seemed to disintegrate. She felt sick to the pit of her stomach. Why hadn't he shared this?

"Mrs. Felt, I think we should all stop pretending."

"Pretending?" she said, feeling annoyed at repeating so much but she was desperate for time to think this all through.

"Yes, pretending that we don't all know exactly who the man disguised as a priest happened to be. I'll stake this empire on the fact that it was not your brother."

It was Kirin who gave her courage. "You don't have an empire to stake, General Stracker," he remarked coolly.

"In my brother's absence, I am the emperor," Stracker growled. He returned his hard gaze, peering from beneath the dark green tatua, to Lily. "And I'd stake the empire again, Mrs. Felt, on a bet that Pastor Jeeves is not only no relation to you but that he is none other than the famed outlaw Kilt Faris."

Lily felt her fear so tangibly now its presence was like a person standing next to her, smiling with sinister pleasure at her spiral into terror. She reached for Kirin, grabbed his hand, and felt a spike of reassurance as he wrapped his fingers around hers.

Kirin seemed to straighten. She thought she might even have heard him sigh before he addressed their captor. "General Stracker, wherever this is leading, my wife is entirely innocent. Her brother, whom she hasn't seen for years, suddenly started looking for her to let her know her mother has died." He shrugged. "Sounds feasible to me. You say he is Vested. She tells you she didn't know this. But if she is Vested then it makes sense that he could be also. They say the power of magic can run in families. Please, General Stracker, she is a simple girl from Medhaven with no knowledge of palace life, politics or intrigues. Do you agree?"

Lily was stunned when Stracker's face clouded. He looked momentarily hesitant and then he nodded. His lips seemingly struggling to open, finally he said, "I agree."

Kirin's gaze moved to Vulpan. "You expressed some confusion, Master Vulpan, but I suspect you too can agree that Mrs. Felt has no case to answer. She should be given her freedom to leave the palace."

Vulpan's brow creased in what looked to be a momentary bewilderment. Lily's own puzzlement intensified. What was going on?

"Master Vulpan?" Kirin prompted.

"Yes, yes, I agree. So long as the general agrees."

"Thank you. General Stracker. Can we let my wife leave right now, please?"

Stracker looked fully perplexed now. He was concentrating hard but couldn't shake the mystification in his expression. "You are who I wish to talk with. I see no reason for her to remain here. She may go," he said.

Kirin turned to Lily and she saw his remaining good eye had drooped. She realized what he had done for her and felt herself crumple inside, like all the wind had been knocked out of her.

"There is no time for long goodbyes, Lily," Kirin said, forcing another of his sad smiles. "Go now." His voice was light, despite the struggle she could see he was having. "Please, Lily. General Stracker and Master Vulpan have kindly released you from here. My suggestion is that you go *home*." The emphasis he put on the word home told her that she should return to Faris, to the forests.

"Kirin, I . . ." She could hear her voice was laced with shock and regret.

"Go, my darling. I have business here to finish with General Stracker." She glanced at the two men. They looked suspended in their puzzlement. "Please hurry," Kirin urged.

She threw her arms around him, kissing his neck. "What will happen to you?" she whispered.

"Lily, just go," he begged. "It won't last. Get away as fast as you can."

She unlocked her grip from around his neck, torn. She couldn't imagine what she was leaving Kirin to face but it would be reckless for her to ignore what he was giving her—or the price he was paying to gift her freedom.

"Thank you," she said.

Gently he kissed her, their lips touching fleetingly, and

she realized with regret that she hadn't even had the opportunity to sort out her feelings for him.

"Touching," Stracker remarked. "Mrs. Felt, please return to your husband's chambers."

Kirin's look told her to disobey that command. She recalled what he'd said about the chapel and the side entrance. She had money, even her cloak was still about her shoulders. She curtseyed to both men. "Thank you, general. I'll see you later, Kirin," she said, squeezing his arm, too frightened to weep but feeling the sting of tears at her eyes. "Will we . . . ?"

He shook his head slightly, his eyelid drooping further. She had to swallow her panic and revulsion. She couldn't imagine the pain he was experiencing. "Goodbye, Lily."

She looked at Vulpan, who was still deep in puzzled concentration, and then she hurried to the door. Lily threw a final glance Kirin's way but he had already turned back to Stracker. Feeling sick to her heart, she closed the door behind her.

Leak was waiting for her. "Mrs. Felt?"

"Leak!" Stracker bellowed from inside.

"Excuse me," Leak said, his eyes widening.

"Yes, of course," Lily said, "I'll just return to our chamber." The moment the boy's back turned on her, she fled in the opposite direction.

She ran heedless of who was watching or giving her strange looks. She wouldn't waste this opportunity or the eyesight Kirin had surely just squandered on saving her life once again. Sickened and angered by their circumstances, the emotions drove her harder. Her mind in turmoil, she had to stop several people to ask the way to the chapel.

Finally, with her mind still very much with the sad yet lovely face of Kirin and his tender voice, she reached her destination. As she rounded the final corner, she collided with a priest.

"My dear, you look so worried. Are you in the right place?"

"I . . . yes, the chapel. Kirin told me to use the side gate." Then she felt alarmed. "Oh, Father, please don't tell anyone I was here."

"Lo, help me, why would I? Whatever is wrong? You mentioned Kirin. I know him well. Is he returned?"

"Yes, yes, he's back, he's in trouble. It's General Stracker . . ." And finally she began to weep.

"Let me help you. Come. You should not be seen in this state if you are trying to protect your anonymity. Here, come back here. It is safe, my dear, I promise. Please."

Meekly, all protest dissipating, Lily allowed herself to be led into a small chamber behind the chapel. She stood awkwardly in its center, regarding the priest as he closed the door behind them.

"I am Father Briar."

She nodded, gulping back her tears. "Kirin has mentioned you."

"You said he's in trouble?"

"He's with Stracker." Briar's interested expression faltered. "And that ghoul, Vulpan."

Now the priest's expression darkened. "A ghoul, indeed. I've heard of his vile practice."

"He has tasted my blood and Kirin's."

Briar's mouth twisted in revulsion. "Why is Kirin in trouble with General Stracker?"

"They think he has something to do with the death of that man called Freath." Briar looked shocked. "They are questioning him now. They . . . they let me go but only because Kirin . . ." She shook her head. "Kirin made me promise I would flee the palace. He is worried for our safety."

"As well he might be around General Stracker. The man has no conscience!" the priest spat.

She nodded. "I have to get out of here. I promised him."

"All right, I understand. I will help you as I have helped Kirin and Freath in the past."

"Are you a . . . a royalist, Father Briar?"

"I am a man of faith, that's all. I was priest to the Valisars during Brennus's reign and my loyalties are to anyone who believes in people. Stracker is not of that sort. He has a loyalty only to himself. And he hates anyone who is not Steppes-born." He gave another twist of his mouth. "He does not receive my blessing."

"How can you help me?"

"The same way I have spirited others before you from this place. I will hide you and get you out of the palace gates."

She looked at him with gratitude and disbelief. "Really? You'll get me out?"

He nodded and patted her hand kindly. "Right away. You look as though this is urgent."

"It is."

He smiled. "We're in luck, then. I have some food deliveries to make to some of the outlying villages. The palace cooks up and waste a lot of food that I can't bear to see used as currency by unscrupulous soldiers or servants. I like to load up my cart and take it out to the needy every few days if I can." He gave her a reassuring nod. "Come, we'll be on our way immediately. Er, forgive me, but I don't even know your name."

She found a grateful, fleeting smile. "I'm Lily, Father Briar. Kirin Felt's wife."

He stopped leading her and stared at her, shocked.

"I'm not sure I understand why we let the woman go, General Stracker," Vulpan whinged.

"Because I chose to," Stracker growled, although honestly he wasn't that sure either. "Why are you swaying, Felt?"

"Forgive me, general. I have not been well. In fact, I think I am going to be . . ." Kirin staggered and then collapsed, unconscious.

"Leak!" Stracker shouted. The boy took a moment or two to respond but finally ran into the chamber, his gaze drawn helplessly to the man out cold on the ground.

"Fetch the physic!" Stracker demanded.

"General, I believe Physic Chard is not in the palace at present."

"Then fetch . . . oh don't bother. I will handle it. I want this man revived immediately. I have questions for him." He shook his head, the blurriness of his confusion gradually giving way to clearer thought. "Did you see the woman?"

"Yes, general."

"Where is she?"

"Returned to Master Felt's chambers, she said."

Stracker shook his head again, clearing his throat and feeling suddenly enraged. "Aludane strike me! Put a guard on her, boy! She is not to leave the palace."

"What happened?" Vulpan asked, seemingly returning to his senses as Stracker just had.

"I let the bitch go, it seems."

"I told you not to," Vulpan snapped, forgetting himself.

Stracker lashed out, backhanding Vulpan across the cheek, then grabbing the blood-taster's injured hand and squeezing it. Vulpan looked ready to pass out from the pain.

"Vulpan, you are here at my pleasure. Your very existence is permitted only by my pleasure. Never . . . ever believe that Denovian dirt can ever speak to a Steppes-born as an equal."

"I'm sorry, general," Vulpan whimpered. But Stracker didn't want to hear it. "Leak!" he shouted. "I want you to put a permanent guard on Kirin Felt." Before the boy could answer, he strode away angrily.

Stracker was weary of being let down by others. Rather than issue any more orders he strode down to the Valisar chapel, determined to give his instructions personally. He took a wrong turn twice, on both occasions having to ask servants, terrified at coming face to face with Stracker—famed for his temper—for directions. The Valisar chapel was not a place he visited and on the rare time over the last decade that he had, he had simply followed messengers.

Finally he found himself in the familiar courtyard he had passed through on his way to view Freath's corpse. That had been a happy day, intensified by witnessing his brother experience what appeared to be a genuine sense of loss. It had amused, even pleased Stracker to see Loethar looking so suddenly bereft. It had always irked Stracker that his brother had permitted the Denovian aide into the inner sanctum of their lives. The man had already proven himself to be a traitor once and Stracker had never once trusted the opinionated, somber servant. In quiet moments he had admitted to himself that he had found Freath unnerving; the man's intelligence, his manner of speaking down to Stracker, even though the wording appeared polite, was as infuriating as his increasing closeness to Loethar. Loethar protected Freath, relied on Freath; Stracker had even caught him laughing with Freath. Loethar laughing! His brother found so little in life amusing that even the sound of his mirth was a shock.

They'd laughed as boys. They'd been real brothers then. It had never mattered to Stracker that they had different fathers. He wanted to be Loethar's best friend. In fact, although he was the eldest he had always been quietly in awe of Loethar's composure. Nothing rattled Loethar; his brother was so controlled, so clever and even though he was wiry rather than strapping, he came to be a feared warrior. Loethar had often counseled Stracker during their younger years that the only reason he won so many fights was that he used his intelligence rather than his fists.

"I beat my opponent before we strike a blow," he had told Stracker. "You have to think everything through, Stracker. That's what strategy is. Winning isn't always about leaving your rival bloodied and unconscious. Sometimes losing is winning." Stracker hadn't understood that final remark. Not until the day had come to fight for the leadership of the tribes. Then Loethar's losing streak had all made sense. The best of the tribes had gone into their fight with Loethar with a smirk, expecting to win easily.

They hadn't. Loethar had beaten all rivals for the crown of the tribes in astonishingly brutal style. He had even winked at Stracker during the combat. And then he had shocked everyone further by proclaiming that as their new ruler he was going to change their future. No longer would they be the foraging/herding tribes of the Steppes. Instead they would conquer their arrogant neighbors of the Denovian Set and enjoy the riches of the fertile soils of the west.

Stracker had to admit that his brother had kept his promise. But where had his sense of fight gone? Loethar was a king in all senses and yet he seemed satisfied, bored even, not even vaguely interested in broadening his rule or any further battles. His brother had become soft, complacent. He even seemed to like the Denovians! Stracker shook his head with disgust. He could remember a time, a decade ago, when his brother had eaten a king. Nothing had ever amused the big warrior as much as that day when Loethar had ordered King Brennus of Penraven to be roasted. Nothing ever would again.

As Stracker looked around, anticipating Father Briar to come scuttling to his aid at any moment, he realized that his and Loethar's relationship—their once fun friendship as youngsters—had been breaking down for ten anni . . . perhaps before that even.

Where was Briar, damn him to the eternal fires!

Stracker saw a lad scurrying across the courtyard. "You, boy!"

The boy hadn't even seen him, so intent was he on getting to his destination. He stopped in his tracks, a look of pure startlement on his face. "My lord, Stracker," he stammered, terrified.

"You should address me as general," Stracker remarked, enjoying watching the youngster squirm.

"I . . . I'm sorry, general."

"Where is everyone?"

"Everyone?" the boy repeated, a quizzical expression claiming him. Stracker bristled and the boy all but squeaked in terror. "Who can I fetch for you, general?"

"Where do you work?"

"In the stables, general."

"So why are you going toward the main buildings?"

"I was hoping to grab some fresh bread, general. I'm starving."

"Never could fill my own belly full enough when I was your age, boy, but I'll tell you something, it's good to be a bit hungry. It keeps you sharp, keeps you alert."

The boy nodded, still terrified. "I'll remember that, general."

"Have you seen Father Briar?"

"Yes, sir. I have. In fact, I helped to hitch his horse and cart not long ago. He was in a tearing hurry."

Stracker frowned. "Why is that?"

The boy shrugged. "I don't know, sir. He kept hurrying

me along to get the cart hitched and then he told me to leave. He . . . er . . . he was the one who suggested that the kitchens might give me some bread. I was to tell them that Father Briar sent me."

"I see. Do you know where he was headed?"

The lad shook his head. "No, sir. He normally likes to take food that the palace no longer requires out to the needy. But today is not usually the day he would do that."

"Why?"

"Today we usually check over the horses, general."

Stracker's eyes widened, and his brow lifted in mock query.

The boy hurried to explain. "I mean, we are always checking the horses, sir, but today we go over each horse very thoroughly. Father Briar knows not to request the use of an animal."

The general frowned. It irritated him hugely that Briar was not available and galled him even further that he couldn't understand what had got into his head to allow that stupid wife of Felt's to get away. They were hiding something, he had been sure. And still he'd let her go. He couldn't understand why one moment he had been feeling completely in control and the next he had been vague, making a ridiculous decision. His head still felt blurry. His mouth felt dry too.

"General?"

"What?" he bellowed, annoyed that the boy was interrupting his thoughts.

"I said the woman was in a hurry too."

"What woman?" Stracker roared, spittle flying into the boy's face.

The youngster stepped back in terror. He raised his hand to wipe his cheek but seemed to think better of it. "Er, the woman who got into the cart beside him."

"Who was she?"

The boy shook his head. "I don't know, sir. I didn't recognize her."

"Describe her!"

The boy did his best.

Stracker's gaze became distant. "Father Briar left with

this woman?" He began to feel a new sensation—a familiar one—as fury coursed through his body.

"Yes, general. It was a bit odd now I come to think of it. He dismissed me but I glanced back and saw him helping the woman into the cart. Except he was helping her into the back, not next to him. That's what struck me as odd. Perhaps she was tired and planned to lie down?"

"Or perhaps she was my prisoner making her escape with the good Father."

The boy looked shocked. His lips moved but nothing came out.

Stracker poked him in the chest. "And you helped him!"

"No, general, I . . ." The boy didn't finish because Stracker had him in by the scruff of his shirt. He whimpered as the general lifted him and then began to yell and struggle as he was raised above the huge man's head.

Stracker ignored the boy's cries. Someone had to pay for this; someone had to help quench the rage that when it came made him feel like a parched, desperate man. He grunted and threw the boy aside in disgust, feeling a mild sensation of satisfaction as he watched the stablehand's body crumple at the bottom of the wall he had been flung against.

Thirteen

Kilt and Jewd had traveled through the night, riding hard, taking spare horses and trading both pairs for a new set the following morning. Kilt refused to pause for rest or sustenance, insisting they eat and drink in the saddle. Jewd put up no resistance; in fact the big man remained mostly silent during their journey, which Kilt was grateful for. He wanted to tell Jewd—needed to tell Jewd—that he was glad they were together but right now he needed the quiet space in his mind.

They were approaching Penraven city and had slowed their horses to a trot. They needed to pass unnoticed into the general throng of dwellers. Kilt had no plan . . . not yet . . . but he had to find Lily. He had put her life into far too much danger. And she would never believe what had happened since she had left. Convincing her that Leo was now the enemy would take some doing—but that was for the future. Right now he had to find her.

As usual Jewd seemed able to read this thoughts. "Lily's not going to believe a word of what we have to tell her."

Kilt grunted.

"How much will you say?"

"Everything. She needs to know that Leo is prepared to kill me."

"Kill is probably not the right word."

"What is, Jewd? What he had in mind was nothing akin to life as we know it."

Jewd nodded, their horses moving in time with each other,

gradually slowing as the city gates drew closer. Brighthelm dominated the landscape. Kilt was overwhelmed by its size as much as its grandeur. He'd been a long time in the forest, with Francham the closest comparison he had to city life. Now he recognized it as the provincial town it was, nothing close to the noise alone of the capital. Was everyone talking at once? He could hear a drone of voices in the distance, behind the city walls, the clang of metal, the bellowing of animals. The city bell heralded midday.

They had caught up with what looked to be a merchant caravan entering the city. Jewd peeled away slightly from Kilt to flank the last cart in the caravan, as Kilt did the same on the other side. Now they just looked like they were riders in the same party. As Kilt had hoped, they were permitted to pass through without the guards so much as glancing at them. Kilt even raised a hand in thanks and realized no one was paying him any attention.

He felt the appropriate awe as his horse took him beneath the great gate, hooves echoing on the cobbles and around the stone above him. He'd seen the glorious shadow timepiece that King Cormoron had built and various royals had added to over the centuries, but it didn't fail to impress him when his gaze fell upon it again.

Kilt tensed at the thought of the Valisar royalty and without meaning to he felt his magic reaching out to test the surrounds, desperately hoping there would be no response, no alarming reaction. There wasn't, but he still couldn't shake the tension.

"Are you all right?" Jewd asked.

He nodded. "Anxious, I suppose."

The big man's expression told Kilt he understood. "We'll find her."

"Where to begin?" Kilt remarked as they slipped off their horses and began leading them through the streets.

"Stables first, a good meal and then we'll make some decisions."

It sounded like a not unreasonable plan and they found stables easily enough. Once unencumbered from the horses, Kilt's belly grumbled in anticipation of a meal. Jewd led them into an inn that Kilt paid little attention to. He even let Jewd order the food while he found a quiet corner and sipped on ale that was surprisingly strong. For some reason he'd expected beer in the city inns to be watered. He hoped Lily was still unharmed; couldn't bear to think of her trapped or frightened.

"Duck pie on the way," Jewd remarked as he joined him, sliding into the booth opposite.

"What have you discovered?" Kilt asked, knowing Jewd would have asked some leading questions of the innkeeper to get a feel for the mood of the city.

Jewd licked his lips from his first sip from his own tankard. "Well, Loethar's not here, predictably, but apparently Stracker is in the palace."

This won Kilt's attention. "He was quick to get back."

Jewd nodded. "Apparently a lot of the Greens drink here. The landlord heard just an hour ago that the general re-entered the city."

"Well, that's of little consequence to us," Kilt dismissed. "We're staying well out of his way. Anything else?"

Jewd shrugged. "There's something going on in the main square shortly. The landlord doesn't know what it is but he reckons it's connected with the palace. This place was teeming with Greens just minutes before we arrived and now look."

Kilt did. His mouth twitched. "No soldiers here that I can see."

"That's right. They've all been called."

"That doesn't concern us either."

"No, but," Jewd lifted one shoulder slightly, "you wanted to know what the landlord's saying."

Kilt nodded. "I'm sorry. I can't stop thinking about Lily. We have to presume that if she's posing as Felt's wife she's somewhere in and around his lodgings." He stroked his fake beard.

Normally Jewd would have grinned at the gesture but he remained stony-faced, barely looking up as the serving girl plonked down two steaming pies.

"Careful not to burn your lips, sir. They're just out of the oven," she warned.

"Thanks," Jewd said, distracted. Once she was out of earshot, he continued, "Well, Freath lived at the palace. And as Kirin was his close offsider I guess we have to assume that he too had rooms within Brighthelm."

Kilt blinked angrily. "I wanted to avoid the castle."

"We can. We'll pay someone to take a message."

"That's too risky."

"Not really. We'll use a child. There's always someone who knows their way around the palace who wants to earn a few extra trents."

Kilt bit into his pie, not really tasting it but knowing his body needed food. Besides, Jewd would become a flea in his ear if he didn't eat.

The innkeeper passed them and caught Jewd's eye.

"Good pie," Jewd remarked.

"My wife's. No better in the city," the man replied. "By the way, I've just heard what's going on, why the Greens left in a hurry."

"Oh?" Jewd said and Kilt noticed he deliberately sounded disinterested, more concerned with slurping up the sticky duck meat that was oozing from his pie.

"Well, word has it that there's going to be some sort of public punishment in the main square."

"Public punishment?" Kilt joined in, frowning. "Seems normal enough."

The innkeeper shrugged. "Actually, no. Emperor Loethar banned it years ago. He made an edict that anyone who is proven responsible for a crime will pay his dues behind closed doors. He didn't think families should have to publicly suffer the humiliation of their kin's deeds."

Jewd's brow knitted together. "Doesn't sound like the move of a conquering invader."

"Ah, but he's a good man is the emperor." The innkeeper put his hands up. "I know, I know. He took his crown from a sea of Denovian blood but," he gave a small shrug, "I think he rules well. We all do."

"No question of that," Jewd said, clearly choosing not to ruffle any feathers.

"General Stracker has a stomach for suffering, though,

and he's obviously decided to make a wrongdoer suffer public humiliation and pain. And with the emperor away he's in charge."

"Why do they need the Greens?" Jewd wondered aloud.

"To set it all up, keep the crowds back, I suppose," the man said.

They were interrupted by a youth. "Dad, the word on the street is that it's going to be an execution," the youngster said, eyes shining.

"Find your sisters and make sure they're indoors with their mother. They don't need to see anything like that."

"Clara would love it," his son admitted.

"Nevertheless," his father said. "Whose execution, did you hear?"

The boy shook his head. "I didn't really pay attention. A husband and wife."

"Lo, strike me!" the man replied. "It's gone to two people now." He nodded at Kilt and Jewd, and left hurriedly.

"They must be important for Stracker to be putting on such a show," Jewd remarked, tucking into his pie. "This is hitting the spot," he said through a full mouth.

Kilt had almost finished his food. "Well, I don't care about it. It just means Stracker and his Greens are looking the other way. Makes our job easier of getting word to Lily in the palace." He found a sad grin.

"I'll be finished in a blink," Jewd said, cramming what looked to Kilt to be near enough half the pie into his mouth.

"Don't rush. I always find watching you eat such absorbing entertainment."

"Go to hell," Jewd shot at him through a still crowded mouth. Then he stood. "Ready when you are." He swallowed and burped.

"You were always the uncouth one."

"I know deep down you'd rather be wearing the dress disguise than the beard, so that is probably making you cranky," Jewd replied and they both grinned, Kilt revelling in the fleeting chance to parry insults with his friend. For just a moment or two, life felt normal.

Once outside, though, that lightness evaporated and they

found themselves among a crowd of people hurrying in the same direction. Jewd pointed. "We can probably take a short-cut through there," he said, "and reach the palace without having to wade through this mob. They must all be headed to the execution."

"I feel ashamed for them," Kilt murmured. "You'd think they'd have seen enough death for a lifetime."

Jewd shrugged.

An older woman took refuge next to them. She looked thunderous. "Pah! These people. Are they really that keen to see Denovian blood spilled again?" she asked them.

"My thoughts exactly," Kilt replied.

"What do you know about the couple in question?" Jewd asked her.

"Nothing, really. I don't know her at all—to be honest I didn't even know he was married."

"But you know him, obviously," Kilt replied.

"Oh, vaguely, I suppose. I know of him, I've seen him around the city with that man, Freath. I have no idea what Master Felt has done to incur the wrath of the emperor. Maybe it has something to do with Freath's death."

"Felt?" Kilt repeated, shock traveling through him at such speed he felt his heart pounding hard in his chest. "Kirin Felt and his new wife, Lily?"

"Is that her name?" she asked distractedly, then shrugged. "I told you, I wouldn't know and I'm not interested to see anyone executed. I'm just trying to get home."

Jewd was already moving. "Excuse us, madam." He dragged Kilt through the people they'd been trying to avoid and down several small lanes. Kilt trailed behind him like a child being led.

He hauled Jewd to a stop finally. "Stracker is going to kill Lily," he said, slightly glassy-eyed. "We have to get to the square."

Kirin's mind was in chaos. He had regained consciousness on the floor of Loethar's salon only to discover that he was blind. The push of magic required to fool the rationality of two men at once had claimed a very high price. But at least

Lily had escaped Stracker's clutches. He was glad to exchange his sight for her freedom; it was a price worth paying.

He no longer cared what happened to him. Freath was dead. Clovis was dead. He was just another in the queue of loyalists who had risked their lives for the Valisars. He only hoped Lily would be able to get news of everything they'd learned to Leo.

His escort gave him a push. "What's wrong with you?"

"I'm blind," he said, stumbling again. "Where are we going?" he asked, allowing himself to be helped into a cart.

"You don't want to know."

"I see," Kirin said and then smiled grimly at the irony of his words.

He sat down tentatively and traveled in silence, amazed suddenly by how much information he was able to glean without the use of his eyes; he could work out that the afternoon was warm, that there was little or no breeze today. He knew when they were passing by the bakery, he caught a whiff on the air of the tannery to the west, and he could work out simply from the intensity of voices around him that they were approaching the central square.

Who needs sight? he thought to himself, digging deep to find his courage as the cart lurched to a halt.

"The main square?" he inquired, not anticipating an answer.

"I'm afraid so, Master Felt," his escort said.

"You sound embarrassed," Kirin replied. "Don't be. What's your name?"

"Bern."

"Well, Bern, I know you are performing your duty."

"That's generous of you, Master Felt."

"Just don't let my knees buckle. I'd rather give the impression that I was very brave at the end." He used an arch tone as though he was jesting but he was sure they both knew he was asking for help to get through whatever trial awaited.

"I won't let you fall, Master Felt," Bern assured. "Our emperor would not agree with what is happening today."

"Then you are surely not a Green."

"No. I am a proud Red. And while we accept Stracker as

our general, it is Loethar who rules us. We have not been told where he is, but you can be sure there will be a reckoning for this."

"Too late for me, though," Kirin said, angry with himself for falling straight into the very self-pity he wanted to avoid.

"Yes, for both of you, sir."

"Both?" He sensed Bern's hesitation and clutched at the man. "What do you mean, both of us?"

"Your . . . your wife as well, Master Felt."

Kirin felt the bile rise to his throat. "Lily?" he choked out.

"Is that her name? She is a very pretty woman, Master Felt. I am very sorry for both of you. Here she is. Aludane save me, there looks to be a third prisoner too."

But Kirin couldn't care less about another prisoner. He strained to see her even though he knew he couldn't. "Lily! Lily!" he cried.

And the one voice he adored with all his heart but hoped he would never hear again cut through the rabble of excited voices. "Kirin!" he heard her answer in an anxious shriek.

"Please, Bern, please, let me speak with her."

"Master Felt, I—"

"I beg you! One favor for a condemned man."

Once again he heard his companion hesitate and then he heard Bern speaking in the guttural tribal language. Moments later he felt Lily's familiar hand grasping his.

"Lily!"

"I'm so sorry," she choked out, her voice trembling. "They hunted us down."

Another voice broke in. "Kirin, forgive me."

"Father Briar?" He frowned, turned to the voice, his staring eyes seeing nothing.

"What's happened to you?" It was Lily again. "Your eyes, Kirin. Can you not see?" She sounded even more anguished.

"It's not important. My eyes are nothing. I would give my life for you, Lily."

"Oh, Kirin." She broke down.

He couldn't bear to hear her weeping and hugged her closer, despite the trauma, helplessly glad of one last chance to hold her tight. "I'm so sorry I brought this upon you." He kissed her head. "I love you, Lily. And I will love you through eternity. I will bargain for your life."

"Too late, Master Felt," said a chillingly familiar voice. Stracker laughed. "This is a very touching scene, I must say. And Father Briar. I've long wanted to see you pay your dues."

"Dues?" Briar said, his tone querulous.

"I've never trusted you, priest. You and Freath . . . and Felt . . . conniving, I thought."

"May Lo forgive you," Briar said firmly. Kirin silently applauded his friend's courage.

"I don't need his or any other gods' forgiveness, priest."

"Perhaps you'll need your half-brother's, though, Stracker," Kirin joined in, enjoying the sound of defiance in his voice.

"Too bad for you Loethar's not here now," Stracker cackled. "Let's begin . . . perhaps Mrs. Felt first?"

"Be done, general," Lily railed at him, clearly finding her own well of courage. "You and your kind sicken me. It was merely a charade that you primitive people could live within a civilized structure."

Kirin heard her cry out. She had been struck. The crowd began to protest.

"Yes, we'll do the slut first, shall we? Obviously your dark magic takes its price. Pity you can't watch, Master Felt, but I can assure you you'll fully experience all that Mrs. Felt does very soon." Stracker laughed close to Kirin's face.

"I enjoyed tampering with your mind," Kirin said, shocking himself by admitting the level of magic he had guarded so rigorously for so long. There was a telling pause from Stracker and Kirin pressed on. "Yes, general, I manipulated you and the disgusting creature known as Vulpan. And we nearly got away with it. Perhaps you should have slaughtered me along with all the innocents ten anni ago."

"I've changed my mind. We will execute Kirin Felt first. His wife can go next."

"For what crime, general?" Kirin challenged as loudly as he could make his voice carry.

"Treason!" the general roared.

"Can I not defend myself?" Kirin demanded.

"You are guilty!" roared Stracker.

"We cannot call ourselves a just society unless we allow the people to hear all sides of any argument." Kirin turned his blind eyes to where he knew the crowd stood and used all his strength to challenge Stracker's charges. He could feel the discontent rippling through the audience. "Emperor Loethar would permit me to answer all accusations levelled at me. His general does not. All of you bear witness to this charade. This is simply an excuse for the general to get rid of anyone who challenges him as he makes his attempt to usurp the throne from his—" Kirin felt the side of his head explode in sharp pain and he fell to his knees, feeling dizzy.

"You brute!" he heard Lily hurl at the general.

"Get him in position," Stracker ordered. "I'll do him myself."

Kirin was hauled to his feet and dragged forward. He realized death was hurtling toward him.

"Spare my wife, General Stracker, and I will admit to any accusation you care to level at me."

"Too late, Felt. She defied me."

"But that's her only crime. Do you hear that, Denovians? General Stracker is executing Lily Felt simply for being my wife and trying to escape an unfair death."

The crowd roared its disapproval. Kirin felt a small stab of satisfaction. As hollow as it was, it was a tiny triumph to hear them turning against the ruling authority.

"Kirin Felt has been proven guilty of treason. You should all be howling for his head."

"What did he do?" someone yelled.

Stracker shouldn't have fallen for the baiting, but he did. "The man was plotting to kill the emperor," he yelled.

"Where's the proof?" shouted another voice from the same region, Kirin thought.

"Let them go! Let them go!" the first man chanted.

The second man joined in the demand and within a few heartbeats the crowd around them had picked up the mantra and was yelling it back.

Kirin felt the sound like a wave of noise that almost made him sway it was so loud, so intense. He began to grin.

The chant had picked up momentum and it was now sounding angry. The crowd was raising its collective fist, many individuals punching the air. Lily was sorry Kirin could see none of it. She wasn't sure if the tears she wept were for his courage and the sorrow of his new affliction, or for the recognition of two voices that she loved in the crowd.

Kilt was here. And so was Jewd. She would know their voices anywhere. She could pick out Kilt now with his ridiculous dark beard and thatch of dark hair. Not far away stood huge Jewd. He couldn't hide his size but he was in full disguise with his own long, dark wig of dun brown hair and robes that suggested he belonged to the church—not a priest but . . . She mentally shook her head. What did it matter! They were here. And, bless them, they were urging the crowd to revolt.

Stracker looked like a man possessed by a devil. The tatua of his face was contorted as his mouth pulled back in an angry snarl. He was barking orders in the tribal language of the Steppes that only his soldiers understood.

And now Lily felt her panic take flight because darling Kirin was being pushed to his knees. She watched, petrified, her screams dying in her throat as General Stracker drew his huge, ghastly sword. She'd heard the rumor that he sharpened it but never washed it and, true enough, there were spatters of dark, dried blood at the top of the sword and over its hilt. Its edge looked keen, though, as though sharpening it kept it clean of all guilt from its battles.

Do something! her desperate glance at Kilt begged, but he too looked shocked, either mesmerized by the chanting of the crowd or unaccepting that death was really coming. She looked at Kirin and was glad he appeared lost within himself and his prayers.

There was nothing anyone could do. She knew that now. Kirin was about to lose his head and she was next. Father Briar had his eyes closed and was murmuring in prayer for all of them.

She wanted to close her eyes too. She couldn't bear to watch Kirin die but she needed to bear witness. She was his wife. *Until death part us*—wasn't that part of her vow?

"Lily," he called in her direction, just for her hearing, and her heart broke. "I love you."

Her tears flowed freely now for him and she shocked herself by responding so affirmatively. "I love you too, Kirin."

And Stracker's gleeful blade swept down.

Even more lost than he had felt when his aegis magic had responded to Loethar's Valisar magic, Kilt watched with a sense of guilt as Kirin Felt paid the ultimate price for his loyalty to the grand royal dynasty that most people had already set aside. He gave the signal to Jewd.

The idea to use a catapult was about as desperate as they had ever stooped. It would bring a pile of soldiers crashing into the crowd seeking out the attacker and they had to at least injure Stracker enough to stall proceedings. But Kilt wouldn't see Lily fall to this bastard's blade, not for any reason.

He heard Kirin yell his love for her and Kilt's gut twisted when he heard her anguished response.

The crowd too had fallen silent as in a single vicious blow General Stracker cleaved through Kirin Felt's neck. Kilt looked down at the moment of execution. He didn't want to see the man's head spin from his shoulders. But he knew it had occurred when the people who had gathered gave a collective groan. Swallowing, he raised his gaze to see Stracker holding up Felt's severed head.

"This is what we do to people who commit treason against our emperor. We did him the honor of executing him in the Denovian way. He would have suffered far more if we'd punished him in the manner of the Steppes."

"Thank you for your leniency, general," someone yelled out, sarcasm cutting through the hush.

Kilt didn't have to look around, as those in front were, to know it was Jewd. He also knew Jewd would have rapidly changed position, melting back into another area of the crowd so that locating him would be difficult.

Stracker kicked Kirin's fallen body out of his way and flung the head into a waiting basket as he turned now to Lily. She looked pale and suddenly paralyzed; her mouth was forming words but no sound issued as far as Kilt could tell.

"Bring her over here," Stracker commanded, "I've got a taste for it now."

Kilt felt the panic rise. For what felt like the first time in his life he had no cunning plan, not even the seed of an idea. The catapult was useless in this crowd. His attempt to use the mob's opinion as a tide of conscience, a way to make Stracker reconsider had resulted in only stalling proceedings.

He watched, stunned into inaction, as Lily was dragged to the front of the small landing where Stracker was having his fun. She'd roused herself from whatever stupor she'd been plunged into at Kirin's death and seemed to be finding a depth of courage he could only marvel at, shoving away the hands of her minders, lifting her chin in clear defiance of the bullies around her. And then she shifted her gaze and looked directly at him. He was devastated to see forgiveness in that look, as though she did not blame him for how events had turned out.

In the forest Kilt's outlaw gang used a silent sign language. He and Jewd had developed it in their youth and they'd taught it to those they trusted. Lily had been a fast learner. Kilt's heart felt as though it was being torn to shreds as she looked away from him, so as not to incriminate him, and signed into the air.

This is not your fault. Do not do anything that puts either of you in jeopardy.

"What's that she's doing?" Stracker bellowed. "Stop her!"

Lily burned an angry stare at the general. "I am permitted to say my final words. I choose to say them silently."

The crowd's murmurings swelled in approval. Stracker gave a wave of dismissal. "Get on with it, Mrs. Felt. My sword, sticky with your husband's blood, looks forward to being stained with yours."

"How romantic," she threw at him with such damning disdain that many in the audience laughed.

Stracker snarled at her. "Be quick. My sword is thirsty."

Lily yelled loudly at him. "Loethar is the head of this empire but you are its arse."

Delighted laughter erupted across the crowd but she paid the price of a belt around her ear for her daring. From her knees, Lily stole a surreptitious glance at Kilt as she signed. *Make our deaths count and put a Valisar on this throne. I have loved you both.*

She looked at Stracker. "Do what you want," she said as carelessly as she could. She hauled herself back to her feet. "But I will not kneel for you, Stracker. You will have to cut me down as I stand and look at you."

Kilt couldn't fathom where this bravery was coming from but it inspired him. He covertly signed to Jewd.

Ready?

The big man nodded above the heads of others.

Kill that bastard.

You grab Lily.

Kilt nodded.

Then I might take some others down too.

Kilt signed rapidly. *Split up.* Kilt began moving forward but just as he was easing his way closer to the stage, a familiar sensation doubled him over. He took a couple of deep breaths and straightened but he was dizzy. It couldn't be. His eyes roamed the square as he swayed like a drunk, trying to regain control. People began to push him. He stumbled and fell; crawling through the legs of the crowd he realized too late that he was moving back the way he came. And in fact the crowd, irritated by his behavior, had managed to shove him so far to the side that he had no time now.

He tried to find Lily but his gaze was locked onto Jewd's face, which was frowning at him. Kilt took deep breaths and was back in control, but already it was too late.

Jewd glanced her way and saw that Lily was staring with revulsion at the general.

"You'd have made a good Steppes execution with your defiance," he laughed. "Go ahead, let me be the last person your eyes see as you die."

Lily turned away, searching the crowd. Jewd was torn.

Was he still supposed to take out Stracker or would it be better to go to Kilt's aid? His friend seemed to be in trouble . . . but Lily. Lily needed him! In his hesitation he lost his clear line of sight and attack; it was too late for him to take aim and fire at the general with the pebbles he always kept handy in a pocket.

In fact, the general was already taking aim at Lily's neck. Lily had closed her eyes. Jewd held his breath, transfixed with horror.

The sword cleaved through the air with horrible certainty. And stopped.

Everyone gasped.

Stracker regarded his sword in comic confusion. It looked like a piece of tomfoolery, as though he was going to suddenly mug at the crowd and grin, winning huge applause for the jest.

It was so silent in the main square that Jewd could hear his own ragged breathing.

Stracker looked again at his blade, at his men, at Lily Felt's exposed neck and back to his sword. He blinked angrily as a soft murmur erupted through the crowd, then roared his perplexion and took another swipe. Again the sword stopped just a hair's breath from Lily's unharmed neck.

"Is this a jest?" Lily begged into the silence. Her voice was shaking and it was obvious that so were her knees.

Kilt knew this feeling. But it was impossible! He heard Lily ask the question but then he began to chuckle darkly, helplessly, as someone at the back to one side of the square began to clap.

Heads turned, searching for who was applauding in such ironic fashion.

"Ho, General Stracker! Or should I say General Dungheap?"

Kilt thought he recognized the voice. A fresh gasp erupted, as well as a few outbursts of laughter.

Jewd was suddenly at his side. "What the hell is it? What's happening to you?"

"Not it," Kilt groaned. "Who?"

Jewd looked puzzled.

"It's one of the Valisars. The world is crawling with them, it seems," he choked out. "It's not too bad. I can control it. Lily?"

Jewd's brow furrowed. "Her head's still on her neck. She's fainted and safe for now. What do you mean, Valisar? Loethar or Leo?"

"I have no idea. You have to get me away from here fast. I . . . I have to think."

Jewd wasted no time. He picked up Kilt as though he was a bundle of rags and ran him away, down backstreets, into the safety of anonymity.

Fourteen

➤➤————————————————————————◄◄

Lily had swooned into the large puddle of Kirin's bright red blood but Stracker barely noticed her. Heads were turning to the sound of the man clapping in a jeering fashion, daring to make fun of him.

In fact, Stracker noticed, there were two people approaching. He was so confused, though, that he couldn't even respond to his men, who were looking to him for instructions. He was even ignoring the man poking fun at him. All he could do was stare at his sword, bamboozled.

The strangers walked right up to the podium. People parted for them, falling away to ease their path up onto the structure.

"General Stracker?" the man said.

It was only then that Stracker came out of his stupor, and stared at the young man who stood before him.

"Perhaps you remember me?"

"Impress me!" the general spat.

"I'm Piven. And this," he said, gesturing at the man beside him, "is Greven."

"And what in Aludane's Fires are you doing here interrupting me?"

Stracker's voice sounded as though he was in control but inside he was filled with turmoil. Piven? The halfwit! It couldn't be and yet there was no mistaking the familiar face, still such a youth; just a few straggly hairs around his jaw but otherwise still that baby-faced boy. But that was where similarities ended; he was tall now and looked strong—his body had filled out in a way that Stracker recognized could only be achieved from manual work. Stracker blinked. It didn't make sense. Piven was not Valisar. He realized he was staring blankly but he promised himself he would not cower to the youth, no matter what dark magic was at work here.

Piven made a tutting sound. "Come now, general, that's not a very warm welcome back for me, is it? I've been missing for a decade. Aren't you even vaguely intrigued?"

"You might have intrigued my brother—"

"Half-brother," Piven corrected.

Stracker snarled. "But you hold no interest for me. Throw him in the dungeon until I'm ready to deal with him."

Soldiers immediately moved at Stracker's command, but he was surprised to see Piven benignly smiling.

"Kill them, Greven. But, Greven . . . save Stracker for me."

And at this new order, Greven—an old man as far as Stracker could tell—began to fight. He fought ruthlessly and with no expression on his face. He made no sound other than the odd grunt. His strength was remarkable. He didn't need a weapon; his fist was a killing device, breaking bones, crushing limbs, snapping necks.

The most alarming fact was that no matter how many men rushed at him with their weapons, their swords could never touch him—or Piven—and their arrows appeared to bounce harmlessly away once they arrived within a hair's breadth of their target.

"What is this?" Stracker cried above the sound of the slaughter and the crowd's yells of fear as it dispersed, mothers grabbing children and running for what they thought was their lives; men pushing back, ringing the square now with a collective look of dread on their faces. The square, though not empty, was suddenly cleared of the press of people.

"This, General Stracker," Piven said with a mirthful expression, "is the Valisar magic working."

"Valisar?"

Piven nodded. "Greven is an aegis," he said calmly while men died around him. Then he smiled and there was ferocity in it. "Now keep up, general. I know you don't have the capacity of your brother's cleverness but you must at least try and pay attention because I won't be explaining this again. An aegis is the ultimate champion, available only to a Valisar." He paused a moment. "Ah, excellent, I see the obvious is registering with you. Yes, indeed, shock upon shocks, I am a Valisar." He tapped his nose. "Or I wouldn't have the benefits of an aegis at my disposal. Oops, that's at least a dozen of your warriors, general. Would you like me to stop him? The best way is for you to call your soldiers off."

Piven paused again.

Stracker's mouth moved but he couldn't think of what to say.

Piven began to chuckle. "You know, general, another dozen could die while you make up your mind. I suggest you give the command. There's no point in losing many more lives this day."

Stracker found his voice finally. "Step back!" he shouted to his men.

"Well done. You see, Stracker, you should have remained as your half-brother's second. These delusions of leadership you have are ill-advised; you're at your best when you are taking orders from a higher source." He smiled again. "A higher source such as I," he finished. "Greven, leave us but keep me shielded."

The older man removed himself to the shadows of the arches at the very back of the main square. Piven sighed pleasurably and surveyed the scene.

Lily Felt chose that moment to moan as she came back into consciousness.

"Would someone please pick up the fallen Mrs. Felt," Piven commanded. "There will be no execution for her today—or indeed any day, general. From what I gathered watching your theatrics unfold, and how your audience was reacting, she is innocent . . . or at least, unworthy of execution. And she's far too pretty to be killed off for no good reason. Now her husband I liked. Kirin Felt never did me a wrong. To be candid with you, general, I'm a little angry that you executed him. The least you could have done was offer him a trial."

"Who are you?" Lily Felt was sitting up, her obvious confusion reflecting Stracker's.

"Your savior it seems, Mrs. Felt. I am Piven, one of the Valisar princes."

Her eyes widened. "Piv—" She stopped herself.

But his eyes narrowed. "You sound like you know me, Mrs. Felt, and yet I am sure I have never seen you until this day."

"I . . . I know *of* you, of course. But no, we have never met, highness."

Piven spun around on his heel like a child, laughing. "Highness?" he repeated and then he ran up onto the scaffolding and helped Lily to her feet. Without turning he addressed Stracker. "Don't try anything, general. I should warn you that I cannot be killed. And for each attempt from now on I will have ten of your Greens slaughtered before you. Are we understood?"

Stracker paused. He was so angry he could feel himself shaking. But Piven didn't notice, wouldn't even look at him. He was staring at Lily.

"Do you understand, Stracker?" he repeated.

"Yes!" the general roared.

Piven ignored him, kissed Lily's hand and stared into her eyes. "Thank you for paying me the courtesy of my true title. You are the first to utter it."

The woman found a tentative smile and despite the streaks of dirt on her face and the blood over her clothes, she inclined her head politely. "Thank you for saving my life."

Piven grinned, his face young and full of mischief. "It was nothing," he said, waving away the thanks. "Forgive me for not acting sooner. Your husband was killed as we arrived into the square—shame on them for making you kneel for his death—but I could hear all the shouting as we were approaching. Just a few minutes earlier and . . ."

"Please, your highness, don't say it." She looked down at her blood-drenched clothing and gagged. "He didn't deserve to die."

"No," Piven replied gently. "I knew him in childhood and he was a decent man. But he is dead, Mrs. Felt, and there is nothing to be gained from dwelling on it. Come, let us get you out of those clothes, bathed, rested. We shall talk shortly." He looked around. "You, Father Briar."

"Is it really you?" the man stammered.

"No one else," Piven replied. "Now, take Mrs. Felt and see to it that she has all that she needs."

Briar nodded dumbly, seemingly awestruck by Piven.

As Father Briar and Lily helped each other away, Stracker rounded on Piven. "He was helping her to escape in the first place!"

Piven regarded Stracker. "So what?"

"They are traitors to the emperor."

Piven cocked his head to one side. "And you're not?"

Stracker remained silent.

"Keep doing as I bid, general, and perhaps we can work together. You have to stop occupying your very small reasoning capacity, Stracker, with people who don't matter. I can tell that Mr. and Mrs. Felt have offended you on some level but they are merely pawns." He took a step forward and Stracker actually flinched. "They are unimportant people often sacrificed by the more important players in the deadly game of power, but whose deaths are meaningless in the greater plan."

"What is the greater plan?"

"Ahh, now we come to it, general. Why, to rule." Stracker felt shock run through him like ice water. Piven chuckled and continued, "But people like Father Briar, Kirin Felt, his wife, are unimportant."

"Who is important, then?"

Piven smiled wolfishly. "Clear the square, order your men away and get this scaffolding dismantled. There will be no more executions for the time being."

Stracker regarded the young man for a long time. Piven didn't so much as blink beneath the scrutiny, patiently waiting until Stracker made his decision. At last, Stracker barked orders in Steppes language and soldiers leaped to his command, immediately dragging away Kirin's corpse, herding onlookers away and summoning carpenters to take down the makeshift stage.

"Good," Piven said, "that was your first wise move. Walk with me. I will answer your questions."

Stracker fell in alongside him like an obedient dog. The aegis, Greven, followed at a short distance behind.

"Tell me about him," Stracker said, thumbing over his shoulder.

"He's not much fun, as you can tell. But he's the father who took me on when you and your half-brother decided to kill mine."

"But you're adopted," Stracker said.

Piven sighed, loudly theatric. "That was the ruse, General Stracker. I am Valisar."

"Valisar?" Stracker queried, totally lost. Then he gathered his thoughts, punching the air with a finger. "I may not have the cleverness of my brother but you were a halfwit last time I saw you."

"Yes, now that probably is the best secret of all. Not only was lucidity hidden from my family but it was hidden from me for many years. Unhappily for you, Stracker, I am far from the smiling monkey boy I think I once overheard you refer to me as. It seems I am Vested and Valisar. Hmmm, that is a potent mix."

"And him?"

"As I explained, he is an aegis. He can singlehandedly fight his way through your army if he so wishes and he won't so much as break a sweat. And, I might add, will not sustain even a scratch. And because I have trammeled him I am invincible as well. You cannot touch me."

"What do you want?"

"To rule. I'm vastly better equipped than you. And with Greven, I am now stronger than your brother and his entire army."

"Then why haven't you killed me?" Stracker demanded.

"Because, although I don't think you're capable of ruling with any effect, I do like your anger. And if it's channeled properly, you are useful."

Stracker broke the first hint of a smile. "It's my brother you're after," he stated, feeling smug.

Piven tutted. "He hates being called your brother. Your half-brother is definitely one of three people I intend dealing with and you seem rather pleased about that."

"I am."

"Then you shall have the pleasure of killing him." Stracker grinned. "But only if you are prepared to take instructions from me and follow them without question," he added. "Think about it."

"No need." He shrugged. "When Loethar is dead I will return to the Steppes with those among our kind who also wish to go back to their home. You can have all this," he said, waving an arm through mid-air. "But I will want terms."

"Terms," Piven repeated, as though testing the word. "Are you in a position to demand them, I wonder." They had entered the palace and Stracker noticed Piven looking around, his expression distracted as though remembering earlier days here. Suddenly he swallowed and turned back to Stracker.

"Tell me your terms, general."

"Free trade."

"Granted."

"My people have rights into and out of the empire but are not ruled by you."

"Granted, but they abide by the rules of my empire when they enter it."

"Agreed," Stracker replied. "One tenth of all yearly palace income is to be paid to the Steppes people annually."

Piven smiled. "Audacious, but I'll grant it."

"And you will marry a daughter of the Steppes."

"Marriage?" After a moment's thought, Piven waved a hand. "Fine," he said, sounding disinterested. "She must be at most my own age, not older. She will not bear the tatua. And, general, she must be dark and pretty, like Mrs. Felt, with small breasts and clear skin—as opposed to someone who could be a daughter of yours . . . if you understand me right. Take heed or I will send her straight back in pieces!"

Stracker actually laughed. Then he nodded. "As you wish, highness."

"You see, Stracker, so much can be solved without having to resort to bloodshed. Who knows what simple promise you could have made and then kept Kirin Felt as one of your own, working for you. So much more powerful to have a fox in dog's clothing, don't you think?"

"How old are you?" Stracker demanded.

Piven laughed. "Use your fingers and toes, general, and I'm sure you can work out how many anni I am."

Stracker shook his head. "I like you and I'll be your general. Just give me my . . ." He thought about his next words. "My half-brother to kill."

"There you go, general. You got it right at last. Well, I'll make you this promise. Loethar is all yours, but my full brother, Leo, is all mine . . . as is my sister."

Later, bathed and in fresh clothes, all her tears for Kirin done, with no more strength to weep and her sorrows firmly and determinedly buried for now, Lily presented herself before Piven. He was such a surprise—seemingly a man trapped in a youth's body, and yet while he spoke in such a mature way, some of his mannerisms were still juvenile. She noticed he fidgeted like a typical youth; she remembered how he'd spun around with pleasure at her using his title, his clapping, the childish joy in his eyes to best Stracker. And unlike any man she had known, he appeared entirely unaffected by the earlier bloodshed.

"Your hair is still damp," he noted, gesturing toward a seat.

Lily touched her hair self-consciously. "Thank you, your highness. I feel much better for the bath." Kirin had warned her about Piven and his suppositions, which had seemed so wild, had been borne out. He was all Valisar—but he was also clearly in league with Stracker now, which told her plenty about where Piven's loyalties lay. No doubt a deal had been struck.

She wished Piven weren't so attentive. It was hard enough trying to keep the shock and confusion of losing Kirin under control. Her final words to him spoke of love; he had died believing that she loved him as much as he had loved her. And she had to admit Kirin had got under her skin with his vulnerability and courage, his constant sacrifice for her and his obvious love. She had felt love in that moment of unashamed terror. Later, sitting in the tub of warm water, alone and watching specks of his blood float off her skin, she realized that Kilt would have heard their exchange. Was it possible to love two men with the same intensity and yet very differently and for different reasons?

Lily realized she'd not been paying attention, had been staring absently out of the windows of the beautiful room.

"I'm sorry, I know we're all being rather hard-hearted about the fact that you've lost a husband, Mrs. Felt," Piven said, "but I cannot return him to you. I can only offer to do my utmost to make this difficult time as easy as I can. What can I do for you?"

"Do?" she repeated. Lily frowned. "Why, nothing. I want nothing from you. *You* did not kill my husband, your highness, and you saved my life. I owe you a debt of thanks."

He regarded her soberly. "Do you like this room?"

She blinked, unsure of the sudden change in topic. "Yes . . . yes, I do. It is very beautiful. It makes me feel . . ." She didn't finish but shrugged instead.

"Go on, please. How does it make you feel?"

Lily frowned as she thought. "Well, highness, I was going to say that it makes me feel as though this room belongs to a woman. But I do not wish to insult you."

Piven smiled. "This room is—was—my mother's suite. I spent a lot of time in this room with her. The witch Valya took it over for a while but I'll soon have all remnants of her gone." He closed his eyes and inhaled. "I can almost still smell my mother's perfume."

Lily wasn't sure what to say. If Kirin was right, this boy standing before her, looking forlorn and wistful, was the enemy. She fell back onto her manners. "I'm sorry for you."

"Don't be," he said matter of factly. "Are your parents alive?"

She sighed. "My mother died when I was newborn. My

father?" Lily looked down. "I'm sorry to say that I don't know how he is or even where he is. We have lost contact. But he and I were very close."

"How did you lose contact?"

Before Lily could contrive a lie the door that led into one of the sundry rooms opened and to her disbelief her father walked in. Seeing Lily, he nearly dropped the tray of food he was carrying.

"Ah, Greven," Piven welcomed. "Thank you. Just put it there, I'm ravenous."

Lily's shock numbed her so rapidly even her lips wouldn't work. She stared at her father, who stared back, looking terrified. He regained his wits first and shook his head at her once. She knew that look and obeyed it even though it took all her will to close her mouth and bite back the torrent that was desperate to explode.

"Greven, this is Mrs. Felt. We saved her life. I don't think you saw her properly when we arrived." He looked at Lily. "Whatever is wrong, Mrs. Felt?"

Lily gulped. Her treacherous eyes were watering. "Er, forgive me. I know this sounds far-fetched, your highness, but your servant, Greven, just fleetingly reminded me of my father. Perhaps it's because we were talking about him."

"Really? Greven here is my adopted father, actually, not my servant."

"I *am* your servant," Greven said pointedly, scowling. "Let's not pretend otherwise."

Piven gave Lily a look of soft exasperation. "Greven raised me." He smiled. "He has been a father to me and I love him but Greven struggles with the new me—the one that talks and thinks intelligently, the one that turned into a real Valisar."

She stole a glance at her father. He wore a grimace but again in his eyes was only warning. Though his leprosy was gone the decade seemed to have turned him haggard and he was shockingly missing a hand. She realized she was holding her breath, feeling herself on shakiest of grounds.

"My father was a bit younger, now that I look at you, sir, and he was . . ." She hesitated.

"Whole?" Greven asked.

Piven tutted. "Let's not go into that now, Greven, shall we?"

"Why not? Are you concerned by what people might think?"

"You know I'm not, old man!" Piven snapped, then took a breath and composed himself. "Forgive us, Mrs. Felt. I'm sure you didn't fail to notice the carnage in the square."

It wasn't a question but she shook her head silently anyway, trying not to look at her father.

Piven continued. "It's a long story that I won't bore you with but it is connected with the Valisar legacy of aegis magic. Greven is an aegis and he is bonded to me."

Lily swallowed. "Through magic?"

Piven nodded. "Indeed. A very powerful one. And Greven doesn't care for these new circumstances. But he will get used to them over time. We are going to be together for a long time."

"That means you are Vested, sir?" she asked Greven.

She watched her father's face soften. "Yes," he admitted. "But I hid it well."

She nodded and quickly wiped away the tears that she couldn't keep from falling. "Forgive me, highness. Now I feel sad for Greven, sad for myself, sad for my husband. I'm quite a mess really. I will take my leave with your kind permission." She stood.

Piven did also. "Are you sure I can't offer you anything—refreshment, accommodation, money . . . a position?" He shrugged, and Lily realized Piven seemed desperate for friendship. Why in Lo's name had he chosen her?

She gave a humorless smile. "No, highness, but thank you. I wish to return to the north, if I may. I have good friends there and they will help me to start again."

"Then travel safely, Mrs. Felt." He cocked his head to one side. "May I know your first name? You seem far too young to be a widow and I do hope our paths cross again. I will look you up when I'm in the north."

Lily panicked but hoped it didn't show on her expression. "Of course," she replied. "I am Maera." She squirmed inwardly. Why the name of Kilt's favorite whore from the Velvet Curtain in Francham would spring to mind at this juncture was anyone's guess. Of all the names she could have chosen!

"Maera." Piven gave her a curious look.

"Is something wrong, highness?"

"Not at all. I . . . I'm not sure that name suits your beauty."

She blushed. Surely this youth was not flirting with her? "I promise when I meet my father again I'll ask him about it. Thank you, your highness. You've been very generous to me." She hoped he couldn't sense her urgency to be gone from here.

"Do you know your way out of the palace?" He took her hand and kissed it lightly, courteously.

"I'll find my way easily enough, I'm sure."

"Greven, please escort Mrs. Felt to the stable and ensure that she is given one of the palace horses. Maera, I only ask that you tell people I am the new ruler of the Set as you head north." He sighed. "We might as well spread the word."

"Good luck then, your *majesty*," Lily replied.

Piven's face lit with amusement. "You are the first to use that title."

"This way, Mrs. Felt," Greven muttered, pushing past them.

Piven gave her a final look, begging tolerance. "Please excuse Greven. His way is very gruff. I can only control him to a point," he said.

She waved the apology away, desperate to be gone, thrilled and yet daunted by the opportunity to speak with her father alone.

"Don't be too long, Greven. You know I don't like you to be far. Just go to the stables, no further."

"You forget, your majesty," Greven replied acidly, "the magic does not permit me separation from you for very long."

Piven ignored him, already turning his charm to Lily. "Farewell, Mrs. Felt," Piven said and Lily took her leave, hurrying away, trying not to make it obvious.

Once out of sight, Greven dragged Lily into a small vacant chamber. They hugged and Lily wept silently.

"Your hand?" she said, after they'd finally let go of each other. She was exhausted from tears.

"It's called trammeling. That how he has bonded me. He ate part of me." Even as he said it, Greven's face convulsed and he appeared to gag.

Lily felt momentarily dizzied from shock. "Ate you?" she murmured, wondering if she'd heard right.

He nodded, stifled a sob. "I am his to command, Lily. He must never know who you are, or he will use you against me. Forgive me."

"So you're Vested," she repeated, resigned.

"And so much more, I'm afraid. I knew it; I just never acknowledged it to you, or your mother. I thought if I could just keep myself to myself, live a simple life, stay well away from the palace and never cross the path of a Valisar I could live our lives in peace."

"And then Leo came along," she said.

He nodded. "That was hard for me."

"What do you mean?" she asked, frowning.

"My magic responds to the Valisars. Fortunately Leo has no power at all, not a skerrick of magic in him other than the dormant Valisar Legacy. That was lucky. I realized immediately that he wasn't sensing me but I was very glad that he spent the night in the crawlspace."

"Why didn't you tell me?" she groaned, twisting around and holding her head. "We could have—"

"Done nothing," he interrupted. "We had to help those boys. I hated being an aegis but I was a loyalist."

"What happened to you? You know I tried to reach you time and again."

He nodded sadly. "I knew you would. But I held to the notion that you were safe with those outlaws. I never wanted such a solitary life for you. I wanted you to find a good man, enjoy family life." He looked down.

"So you left our hut?"

"Yes." He tried to cover his emotion with a soft cough. "I walked for days and days, feeling drawn toward Brighthelm even though all my life I had avoided it. And then I came to the edge of the woodland that surrounds the palace and I saw him."

"The prince."

He nodded, tears welling again. "He was pitiful, Lily. Abandoned, dirty, hungry, his face filled with joy, his tiny hand in mine. He was drawn toward me too. Even though he couldn't speak, he filled my heart with pleasure. I knew I had to look after him, get him away from that terrible place."

"But didn't his magic—"

"Not initially. He was an invalid. The shortcomings that kept him safe also kept his magic masked. My magic didn't react to him in the dramatic way it should have. Instead it happened gradually, over the years." He shook his head. "I think without really being aware of it I was throwing up stronger and stronger shields as he emerged gradually out of the prison of his illness. I suppose I taught myself how to be around him. But tell me about you. You found your way to Kilt Faris, obviously?"

Lily quickly told him a drastically shortened version of her life over the last decade, ending with her convenient marriage to Kirin Felt.

"What an amazing tale. And there's me claiming what a royalist I am when you've spent these past ten anni plotting against the empire," he said, envy in his voice. Then he actually smiled. "I wish we could have more time for me to tell you how beautiful you've become but, Lily, you must leave now. Flee. You've escaped him once. Get as far away from Piven as you can."

"But you—"

"There is nothing you can do for me. It's magical, Lily. I belong to him now."

"Dad—"

"No, listen to me. I have to finish this. I'm no longer frightened. Seeing you has stiffened my resolve to find a solution to Piven. I . . ." He shook his head. "I feel responsible. But you now have an important role."

"Me?"

He nodded. "Pay attention, Lily. This all rests on you now.

You have to find his sister." He held up a hand. "Come, I'll explain as we walk. No, my dearest one," he said, kissing her head. "No more tears. We leave now. You must get away and you must listen to what I have to tell you."

Piven was listening to Stracker. Though the big man was doing his best to rein in his anger and appear reasonable, it was clearly a struggle. The conversation had become tedious long ago and Piven's mind had strayed quickly. He couldn't place why but he felt vaguely preoccupied with the woman, Maera. She was lovely and far too old for him but it wasn't her beauty that was gnawing at him. It was something else; he had been teasing at it for most of Stracker's discussion but it was not yielding to him.

He sighed. "All right, general, then why don't you go out and slaughter the same number of Denovians to match the loss of Greens?"

Stracker looked back at him, dumbfounded. "Do you jest?"

"Do I look like I'm amusing myself?" Piven asked.

Stracker shook his head. "How do I choose who dies?"

"I don't know, general, and frankly I don't care. This is your burning need. Go out, kill and make merry. I have other pressing things on my mind."

"But if we kill without reason the people won't trust us, won't recognize us as the authority."

Piven smiled at him. "Ah, that is a dilemma for you, Stracker. Suddenly you're racked with a sense of rightness. Loethar would be proud of you. I'm surprised. I had you down as someone without conscience." He laughed at the general. "You don't have to kill anyone, of course. But I'm giving you permission to do so—so that you'll stop your irritating bleat."

Stracker looked confused. Piven sighed, tired of the big warrior already.

"Look, Stracker, there will be plenty of blood to stain your sword soon. You've told me Loethar escaped you— where would he head, do you think?"

Stracker shook his head. "I don't know. I told you he was taken by a huge woman and a Denovian man."

"Huge woman. You mean fat?"

"No. She was as tall as I am, as broad and lean. She was strong, used a catapult like a warrior."

Piven thought about this. "Sounds like a Davarigon. My father took us north one year when I was very young, maybe three anni. He met with a group of Davarigons at the base of the mountains." He frowned. "Is there a monastery at the entrance to the Teeth?"

Stracker nodded slowly. "A convent. It's where, I believe, Loethar's wife, Valya, has been banished to."

Piven's face lit. "Excellent. Now there's someone I'm looking forward to executing."

"She lost Loethar's child."

"Good. I hope she's suffering."

"He let her off easy. She poisoned our mother."

"Good," Piven said savagely. "Now, general, remember what I told you. Every attempt on my life is worth ten of your Greens."

Stracker made an animal sound, close to a growl. "Maybe I will kill some Denovians. I'll make sure it's done in your name."

Piven shrugged. "Tell them what you like. I am all they have now. I am emperor."

"It's going to be entertaining watching you tell that to my Loethar." Stracker smirked.

"Then let's go find him, shall we?"

"You think he's in the mountains where the Davarigons live?"

"It's a place to start. And while we're up there, general, we will also be hunting my brother."

"Yours?"

"Leo is alive. He has been harbored by Kilt Faris and his outlaw gang."

Stracker's mouth had fallen open. "You have confirmation of this?"

"I have no reason to lie to you, Stracker."

"But how do you know that?"

Piven shrugged. "My companion, Greven, harbored my brother when Leo first escaped your clutch. He was instrumental in getting Leo to safety."

Stracker gave a low snarl of disgust. "How does your companion know Kilt Faris?"

"He doesn't."

"Then how did the Valisar scum meet up with Faris?"

"Greven's daughter. She . . ." Piven never finished. The pieces of the puzzle he had been absently pondering seemed to suddenly fit into perfect place. "Lily took him," he said, as if in a trance, no longer looking at Stracker but searching his mind for further clues.

"Er, what do you—?"

"General Stracker," Piven suddenly interrupted. "What was the name of the woman who married Kirin Felt?"

Stracker frowned, thought about it for a short pause. "Lily."

"Lily! Are you absolutely certain of this?"

Now Stracker looked puzzled. "Yes, why?"

Piven's expression had turned dark. "Crafty old Greven. He thinks he can thwart me but he has played into my hands more than he might imagine." He sat forward. "Pay attention, general, this is what I want you to do . . ."

Fifteen

Gavriel had sufficient money on him to buy a horse but he'd opted against going back into Francham. His mood was pensive, his thoughts so fractured that he'd found it easier to keep to the comfort of the forest. Without any real direction in mind he'd instinctively headed north, toward the Dragonsback Mountains.

His time with the Davarigons had taught him all that he needed to know about surviving in the mountains. He knew food, water and even cover for the the night was accessible to anyone who had the knowledge of what to look for and where. He was moving quickly, unencumbered by anything but his sword and his heavy heart.

He missed Elka desperately and he hated what had occurred between himself and the king. But the more he thought about Leo's intentions for the young lad, the more Gavriel quailed at the notion that he had almost been party to something so savage.

It began to make sense now, all these years later, why Loethar had committed the truly barbaric act of consuming some of King Brennus. Gavriel could now understand how the man had been driven to such lengths after years of such enmity. He was the true king—and Brennus had probably known of his elder half-brother's existence.

Gavriel found himself torn. Just a day ago he'd had no doubt in his mind about his loyalty and then within hours it had been turned upside down. Suddenly Leo seemed to be acting like a villain—grasping for rulership, prepared to take any route to kingship he could, even if it meant the most ignoble of behavior.

Gavriel spat on the rock he was clambering up. Regor de Vis would surely squirm to know that either of his sons had any part in this, Gavriel thought, and was reassured by his decision to let the young lad Roddy go. But then the nagging notion occurred to him that his father had obviously urged Corbel to follow Brennus's order to kill a child and get the princess to safety.

Gavriel was suffused with anger and confusion. Nothing was as it seemed. He couldn't shake the deeply personal revulsion that his family had been forced into such dishonorable behavior. No matter what his circumstances Gavriel didn't believe he would ever deliberately attack a child, especially one who was defenseless and blameless of any guilt. And as much as he found Kilt Faris an arrogant sod, he wouldn't be party to maiming the outlaw either, on the presumption that it might transfer some legendary magic.

But this stance now left him not only without a single companion but, more disturbing, without any reason not to just disappear into one of the compasses with a fake name. It was tempting. He could vanish, live a quiet existence under whomever ended up ruling or he could board a ship and sail away from his homeland. That option hurt, though. He'd never see Corbel again if he fled.

Besides, Elka also loomed large in his mind. She was now on the run with the Emperor, his former enemy. The worst aspect of this whole mess with Leo was that Elka no longer trusted him; she was now as much on the run from Gavriel as she was from Leo.

Where would she be? Loethar was injured. Knowing Elka, she would head for the mountains. That's where she felt safest. But she may have needed supplies; she may even have sought help. Francham was the closest town big enough that she could achieve some anonymity—although Elka was hardly easy to forget. If she had gone into Francham then he suspected she would likely retrace the steps they'd made just days ago, back toward the convent and into the foothills of the Davarigons. She wouldn't have access to horses unless she stole them so he guessed she would be moving relatively slowly and that gave him an advantage to catch up with them.

Feeling calmed that he'd made a decision, Gavriel found new vigor in his stride. He sped up his pace to a trot and turned east, determined now to hunt them down.

Leo stewed. He'd forced himself to sit and calm the anger that had enveloped him at Gavriel's betrayal. This was war! Why couldn't Gavriel see that a Valisar must do whatever was required to preserve the family name? His father had drummed into him that the king was expected to be resourceful, courageous . . . ruthless.

Leo shook his head at Gavriel's lack of spine. He himself had no trouble accepting that war had its casualties. And he wasn't even asking either Roddy or Kilt to die—why couldn't everyone accept this? He felt his fury rise again and quickly put Roddy out of his mind so that he could find calm to think. He needed a clear head to plot his next move.

It was the first time in his life, he realized, that he had been alone. It was odd. It was certainly lonely. He missed Jewd and Kilt even though he knew they were lost to him, were now his enemy. And Gavriel had proved himself a traitor as well. What would Lily make of all this? He could imagine her repugnance at how everyone had turned on him.

He was the true king. They owed him fealty, irrespective of his hard approach. He shook his head with disgust for the umpteenth time and closed his eyes to find his sense of calm again.

He needed an aegis. That was of the highest importance. If Loethar trammeled Faris, Leo knew he could wave farewell to any chance he had of actually sitting on the throne that he rightfully owned. But where did one begin to look for someone who refused to declare himself? Faris, after all, had lived alongside him for ten anni without revealing even a sign of his hidden life.

Leo pondered as he chewed on some stale bread and his

favorite fally paste that Lily made up in jars for him. He was on his last jar. And the fally didn't grow again until next leaf-fall.

Where would I hide if I was an aegis?

He kept returning to this question. Initially Leo was convinced that the best place to hide was out in the open. If you lived among others in a busy town, you could virtually disappear. If, like Kilt, you were strong enough that you never used your powers, no one would suspect anything; you'd just be the local miller with a family, or the blacksmith who drank hard at the inn. He frowned. Should he start looking in Francham? Perhaps an aegis had passed him in the street on the occasions he'd been allowed into the lively town.

Leo tried to recall if he remembered anyone shying away from him or whether anyone found it difficult to be in his presence. But he came up blank.

He sighed, tossed aside the knuckle of bread and stood. He needed to make a firm decision about where to go. He couldn't remain here in hiding, waiting for someone to come and make an attempt on his life. He had to at least go out and try and find an aegis. No one knew what he looked like. He didn't even need a disguise.

He gathered up a few belongings into a sack and then looked around at his home of ten anni. There was little to show that he'd ever been here. But although it was no palace, it had been a good home to him. He was sorry that he was leaving under these circumstances, all but hated by everyone. He didn't deserve that. But kings couldn't trouble themselves with whether they were liked or not.

He reached for Faeroe, feeling the familiar thrill of pleasure whenever he wore his family's sword. As he buckled up the belt, a fresh thought breezed through his mind as though his inner voice had found inspiration.

If I were an aegis I'd hide among the Vested and appear to have only the most simple of powers.

Leo straightened and blinked.

Among the Vested!

Hadn't Tern said that when Lily had followed Felt they were interrupted by two wagonloads of Vested being transported from Brighthelm and the south? He searched his memory. Where had Tern said he'd overheard they were headed? His fingers drummed against his lips as he searched back over old conversations, certain it would come to him if he nagged at it long enough. Barronel, that was it.

The more he rolled this notion of heading to Barronel around in his mind the more right it began to feel. At least it was somewhere to start.

With one final sentimental glance back at the camp, Leo was gone. He headed north. Once he was out of the forest he would begin to track west into Barronel. He needed protection and he prayed that Lo would have an aegis waiting for him soon.

Loethar had begun to feel the positive effect of Janus's ministrations. He liked the doctor and inwardly considered himself very fortunate to have these two companions. Elka's strength, physically and mentally, was a gift from the heavens. And she was beautiful—inside and out. Even through his pain he had developed an enormous admiration for the Davarigon woman.

When her laugh came it was hearty and infectious. It made him feel warm for the first time in so many years that he only now realized how unhappy he had been, even before war was declared on Denova. He trusted Elka, he realized. And he had never placed full trust in anyone before, so this was an unnerving new experience for him. But she had proven herself to be someone who valued her own integrity and he respected her for her capacity to make her own decisions. It was obvious that she and de Vis were very close; he didn't believe they were lovers but there was something wistful and sad about Elka whenever she spoke of him. Perhaps she loved him and it was unrequited? Nevertheless, she had chosen Loethar over de Vis, a decision that, he suspected, cost her dearly in her heart. But he sensed she walked with a clear conscience, and he respected that.

Elka could make the hardest of decisions when she felt she was right and she made them using only her head, not her heart. She was calm and always composed—he liked that aspect about her perhaps more than any other. When he thought of Valya's temper, wreaked on the most pitiful of people—like a messenger boy, or a maid—it made him feel almost jealous of de Vis having the attention and loyalty of someone as special as Elka. She certainly deserved better than she was getting from him.

She was tracking back toward him. He'd insisted on walking on his own and while it was hardly comfortable he refused to be carried any longer. Janus remained ahead, and although the doctor was grumbling loudly Loethar suspected he hadn't had so much fun in ages. And his hands were steady for probably the first time in an anni.

"All right?" Elka asked as she drew back alongside him.

"Just rosy," he replied, using an old Denovian phrase that made her smile. "So where are we now?"

"Well, much against my wishes we are now fringing the Dragonsback Mountains. Hell's Gate is just ahead but we're approaching from the west—and few do—so that's why it's deserted." She looked up. "By midday we'll be seeing a lot more people."

"Coming into Francham?" he inquired.

"Both ways. In this milder weather the traffic into and out of the mountains triples, quadruples even. Bigger caravans, more people on horseback traveling alone or in wagons."

"And how will we go—" He stopped and straightened, concentrating.

"I hear it, too," she acknowledged. She frowned and listened. "Two voices, I think," she said, concentrating again.

Loethar felt vaguely blurry. He blinked a few times, wondering if the seeds Janus had given him to suck or the bitter plant concoction he'd had him drink might be taking a late effect on him.

He shook his head. "Forgive me."

"What is it?"

"I'm not sure. I feel . . . dizzy."

"Sit down." He obeyed without protestation. "Any better?"

"Not really." Loethar felt his bile rise and suddenly he knew what this was. "Elka, go and stop Janus. I don't think he's realized we've stopped."

"I'll call—"

"No, don't. Just in case. Go and get him. I'll wait here."

She frowned as she regarded him. "You're worrying me."

"I'll be fine. I'll just sit here and let this pass."

Elka nodded and began trotting up the incline toward Janus, who had disappeared over a ridge. Loethar didn't pause. He withdrew the dagger that Elka had entrusted him with and, ignoring the nausea, and the increasing sense of distraction, he hurried, as best he could, straight toward the source. If Kilt Faris could withstand it—and not show it—so could he.

Their voices were loud enough now that he could hear individual words. They were close; a man and a child. Which one was it? He crested the rise and then he saw them. Something about the man resonated deep inside but it was the child on whom his eyes helplessly locked.

Heedless to his injuries and engorged by the desire he had recently become familiar with, he began to run, lopsided and aching, ignoring the pain. They were strolling, the boy eating as they walked. Neither carried any belongings. The man, dressed in black with a long stride and powerful build, looked like someone who was used to fighting, which made it seem all the more odd that he carried no visible weapon.

Neither saw him rushing from the side and neither heard him; a well-trained warrior of the Steppes could move soundlessly.

With a snarl of triumph as much as despair at his nausea, Loethar snatched the boy, dragging him away as though he were a predator bringing down a helpless calf. The boy screamed and his companion stood suddenly still, looking confused more than shocked.

"Stop struggling!" Loethar roared at the child squirming in his clutch. At his commanding tone the boy instantly fell still. Loethar watched the man warily as every fiber of his body responded to the child. It was like a drug. No, it was worse than that. It was desire, passion, lust, rage . . . it was compulsion!

"Loethar?" the man murmured. He sounded calm but he threw worried glances at the child. "Please do not hurt him, your majesty."

Loethar's shock at being recognized and addressed so politely nearly undid him. He almost let the boy slip from his arms but the wave after wave of sickness crashing against him reminded him of the prize he held. This was an aegis in his clutches.

The boy had stopped screaming but was now retching and moaning.

"Please set Roddy down," the man pleaded.

"Roddy?" Loethar repeated.

"Yes," the boy choked out. He was dry retching now. "I know who you are. Please, please don't hurt me."

"Who is your companion?" Loethar demanded, unsure now of himself, of his intention, of everything.

"He is my friend, Ravan." He was surprised the boy could still speak; he could feel him trembling in his arms.

"And I am *your* friend too, your majesty," the man added.

Loethar frowned. "Stop speaking to me as though you know me. I don't know you."

"You do," the man called Ravan said. "I know you better than anyone else."

He didn't have time for this. The sickness was claiming him. How had Faris withstood this for so long? Perhaps he was weaker than the outlaw. "Who are you?" Loethar demanded.

But before the man could answer Loethar heard Elka.

"What are you doing?" she yelled, running down the incline, Janus following suit far more clumsily. Even in this tense moment he couldn't help but notice—and admire—that Elka was every bit as noiseless as he was. She too was a good hunter, a fearless warrior and right now a very angry-looking giantess.

"Elka, stay back," he warned.

"What's happening here?"

"Help!" Roddy cried, his arms outstretched to Elka.

Clever boy, Loethar thought, reaching out to Elka's maternal instincts. Right enough, Elka's eyes narrowed. He knew that look. She could probably snap his bones with all that strength she possessed.

"Put the child down," she said quietly.

All he could do was shake his head.

"What has got into you?"

"He's an aegis," Loethar said bluntly. He watched her balk at the mention of the word.

She watched him carefully, her face serious. Janus muttered something to her that Loethar couldn't hear. She shook her head.

Her gaze bore into him, her eyes dark and angry and filled with loathing. "Loethar, he is a child. You are better than this."

He licked his lips, hating himself for what must appear a sign of weakness. "Everyone wants to kill me, Elka. I need protection. The child gives it to me."

"I'm promised to someone else," Roddy cried, squirming uselessly.

"Leo?"

"Not Leo," Ravan answered for his friend. "And not you, either."

Loethar knew his grip slackened momentarily. There were no others. What was the man talking about? Roddy had gone limp in his grip. He looked pale.

"Loethar, may we please be seated and talk?" Ravan asked, his tone reasonable and polite though his worried glances at his friend suggested he felt otherwise.

Loethar began to shake his head but his nausea had intensified again. He didn't know how long he could hold it off. "The boy stays with me," he said, more to gather time for himself. He backed away. Roddy rallied and began to struggle again. "If you don't stop squirming, I will kill your friend," he murmured to Roddy, and the boy fell instantly still. Loethar continued to back away as Elka and Janus joined the man.

"Sit!" he commanded. They did so. "You too," he instructed Roddy but didn't let go of his thin arm. "Remember my warning."

Everyone warily regarded the other.

"Let's start with you," Loethar said, pointing at Ravan. He was struggling to master the dizziness and nausea but was proud of himself for doing this well. "How do you know me?"

"And you know me, your majesty. I am Vyk."

"Vyk?" Loethar laughed. "I haven't seen Vyk in a while but my last recollection is that he was a bird, not a man."

"Your majesty, I am Vyk. My real name is Ravan. The story of my change is long, if you would hear it."

Loethar stared at him. The man must be mad.

Roddy coughed weakly, wiped his mouth with his sleeve. "It is true," he croaked. "I was there. I watched him change from a raven to a man. Are you really the emperor?"

"What?" Loethar said, turning, confused, to Roddy. "Yes, I am the emperor. So watch yourself."

Roddy's eyes lit. "You're scary, but not as scary as I thought. You're not even as big as Ravan." He frowned. "You look alike but he looks more like a king, doesn't he?"

Loethar nodded, despite the confusion. He kept staring at Ravan. "We do," he replied, baffled by how right Roddy was. "And yes, I'm disappointed to say that he does look more kingly. How do I trust that you are Vyk?"

"Because you trust no one but me. You whispered that often enough during our life together. You named me for your child-hood friend, the one Stracker accidentally shot dead with an arrow. You told me Stracker wept over it but you never believed it to be an accident. You thought it was jealousy."

Loethar gave a low growl of frustration. No one but Vyk could know this. "How did this magic come about?"

"It is a very long story, your majesty," Ravan replied. "But I will gladly tell it to you. You do trust me, don't you, high-ness?"

Loethar hesitated. "Can you understand why I need your friend?"

The man nodded. "Leo wanted him too. Gavriel de Vis let us go."

"Gavriel," Elka whispered. "Why?"

Ravan shook his head. "Because he recalls his noble roots. He retains his honor and felt what the young king planned to do contravened that honor."

Elka nodded unhappily. "Which is more than I can say for some," she said sharply, her glance toward Loethar so cutting he could swear he would bleed from it.

"Roddy, you said you were promised to another. Who are you promised to?" Loethar demanded.

Roddy didn't answer.

Loethar turned to Ravan, and the two men stared at each other for what felt like a long and uncomfortable time. Loethar ignored everything but Ravan, the shock of him sitting here as a man, derived from a bird, very unnerving and yet somehow it all seemed curiously plausible. Vyk had always been unusual to the point that Loethar had thought of him in terms of another person, who could hear him, understand him, even if he couldn't respond in similar fashion. "Whose magic turned you into a man?" he finally asked.

"The magic of Sergius. The same person who has sent us on our new journey. Before you ask, Sergius is dead, killed by your enemy."

"Leonel?" Loethar sneered. "Leonel is—"

"Not Leo, your majesty," Ravan interrupted. "Your real enemy. Piven."

Loethar felt like he'd been punched in the belly. *Piven?* Piven was surely dead. "Piven, if he still lives, is an incapacitated youth. You believe he could be my enemy?"

Ravan nodded. "He is. He plans to kill you."

"And Leo," Roddy added, panting as though exhausted or dying, Loethar couldn't tell which.

He ignored Roddy for now and instead quickly explained for Elka and Janus's benefit all that he knew about Piven. They asked no questions but he could see Elka was turning over the new information in her mind. She looked at Ravan.

"Are you Loethar's enemy in any shape or form?"

"I am only his friend," Ravan said. "I always have been."

"Where were you were headed?"

"Into Lo's Teeth."

"Why?"

"Don't tell him!" Roddy exclaimed, rousing from his stupor, eyes wide with panic.

Vyk levelled his gaze at Roddy and there was tenderness and love in it. "Roddy, I will always tell the truth. I have no reason to lie to Loethar."

"He is our enemy, surely?"

Ravan shook his head. "Not ours. Yours, perhaps."

Loethar felt guilt fluttering on the edges of his mind. He looked at Elka, whose gaze was riveted on him. Her expression was hard, not angry; if anything she looked disappointed. For a reason he couldn't explain to himself at that moment, her sorrow hurt more than any of his injuries. Shocking himself and all around him, he let go of Roddy.

The boy rubbed his wrist, unsure.

"I'm sorry," Loethar said. He had not said those words many times in his life; in fact he couldn't remember the last time he'd said them with such sincerity. He looked at Roddy fully now. "Forgive me, Roddy."

The boy gagged again but he had nothing left in his belly. He looked back, confused but also teary. "Am I free?"

Loethar nodded. "Go to Ravan. Being this close to you is too hard." He stood and walked away, this time so that he too could retch. How had Faris been able to resist Leo? It had to be that Leo had so little magic to respond to.

He was relieved when they left him alone, especially Elka. He began walking. He didn't know where to. Suddenly survival didn't seem so important. Let Leonel trammel Faris. And then let both his half-brothers fight it out. He suddenly no longer cared.

Sixteen

❖━━━━━━━━━━━━━━━━━━━❖

Loethar had staggered well away from his companions and no longer had his bearings. That didn't matter. At least the nausea was passing, although he would be lying if he didn't admit he could still sense Roddy's nearness, like a seductive lover beckoning to him.

He would resist. He smiled inwardly. The barbarian tyrant—the monster—had surely surprised them all.

Loethar started when he felt a hand on his shoulder. Elka had stolen up on him so silently it was frightening.

"What can I do for you?" she said softly.

He shook his head, annoyed that she could move so much faster than him but pleased he could say farewell. "You've done more than enough." He paused. "And so have I. I've had ten good anni as emperor and I can genuinely take comfort that I have done as good a job—if not better—than Brennus in unifying the lands of the Set. Perhaps it's time to let someone else take over." He stepped onto an old tree stump, leaned on a branch and stared into the distance.

"Am I hearing right?"

He sighed with a small smile. "I know, sounds odd even to my ears but, Elka, I'm tired. And I think I've finally reached a level of disgust with myself that even I can no longer live with. I've spent those ten anni with a woman I loathed, a half-brother I had no respect or love for, a mother I was fond of but who constantly manipulated me and people who were, at best, confused by me. I was a Steppes warrior and yet

I wasn't. I'm weary of it all. To think I was about to sentence a child to the life of a living corpse . . . that would have truly been my worst act."

"Really?" she said, her tone sharp but not cutting.

It won the desired effect. Loethar laughed sadly. "I've got a lot of 'worst acts' to answer for, I know."

"Not the least of which was the slaughter of Regor de Vis."

The shame pinched at his cheeks. "Yes, that was perhaps my darkest hour. I want to say I was a different man then but that wouldn't be the truth. I was a younger man, perhaps too motivated by the smell of blood in my nostrils and the wrong people around me but I made my own decisions. I regret it and have done since the moment I swung the blade."

"You should share your regret with de Vis's son."

He turned. "Will it make a difference?"

She eyed him with a hard stare. "Do you want his forgiveness?"

He shook his head. "No. Nor do I deserve it."

"So you give up?"

He shrugged. "Elka, I'm your enemy, remember? You're not meant to be acting as my conscience."

"And still I do." She gave a soft sound of scorn. "What is it about you that makes me *want* so much more from you?"

He raised an eyebrow. "What's that supposed to mean?"

"You're such a mystery. I want to hate you and yet I find myself leaving Gavriel for you. You're supposedly my enemy and yet I want to heal you. You kill hundreds of people, you slaughter kings, you have so much blood on your hands and then moments ago, when I can believe I am watching you at the height of your cruelty, you surprise me with tenderness and brilliance." She gave a huffing sound filled with despair.

He gave Elka a searching look, his mind rattled. The woman standing before him made him feel special in a way he had never felt before. Why did compassion or understanding mean so much more coming from her . . . and why did impressing her feel so rewarding? Without warning, without giving himself even a moment to weigh his action and judge potential repercussions, Loethar leaned forward and kissed Elka.

It was a soft kiss, not exactly hesitant but certainly not swaggering. The sensation was entirely different to how it had felt when he kissed Valya—which had been rare. Bedding Valya was raw lust. There was never any feeling above the need to sate himself; kissing her was always a chore. But it felt unique to kiss Elka—he felt tenderness and affection and desire rather than a rutting lust. He wanted her forgiveness, her smile, her understanding.

She didn't pull away, which was encouraging. He risked deepening the kiss but only permitted himself the pleasure momentarily before he pulled away, anticipating a slap or a rebuke.

Her expression was unfathomable. He waited for her to speak.

"I guess that tree stump was handily positioned," she remarked.

Loethar looked down, then back up to her face and exploded into delighted laughter. "I never was the tallest among men but how embarrassing . . . but then I guess you must be used to towering above your men?"

She was grinning at him. Her smile faltered. "Not with Gavriel." He waited, wondering if he'd just made a huge blunder. "We are not lovers, Loethar."

He said nothing immediately, then cleared his throat. "I think I should apologize for taking advantage of you."

"No," she rushed to say. "Not at all." Elka looked uncharacteristically flustered. "I . . . I'm just a bit surprised."

"That I found such a novel way to reach your lips, you mean?"

She chuckled with delight. "That you wanted to reach my lips at all."

He grew serious. "Until that moment I wasn't sure."

"So why did you?"

"A moment of insanity."

"Ah," she replied, turning away, but he caught the hurt in her eyes.

"Elka, wait," he said, reaching for her. "It *was* a moment

of insanity. I know how you feel about de Vis and I took advantage of your compassion for me. But it felt like I was in the grip of a momentary madness. I had to kiss you or risk never knowing."

Her face softened. "Never knowing what?"

"Whether you'd welcome it."

She touched his face. "I'm confused but I'd be lying if I said I wasn't glad you risked it. Thank you for freeing the boy."

He sighed. "I must leave."

"To where?"

"I'm not sure. Perhaps in disguise I can make it to a port and then board a ship for somewhere far from here."

She looked suddenly anxious. "Don't go."

"I can't stay."

"So the whole idea of empire is suddenly cast aside?"

He looked at her, aghast. "Forgive my surprise but weren't you part of the conspiracy to overthrow my rule? Isn't this what you want?"

"I was part of nothing, other than helping Gavriel de Vis find his past. I didn't really care who ruled Penraven or the new empire. It has little impact on my life in the mountains. I was dragged into this struggle but I'd be lying if I didn't admit that I was on Gavriel's side."

"And now?"

He watched her chest rise and fall as she appeared to grapple with an internal battle of conscience. She shook her head. "Now I'm quietly confused. Your ability to rule is not in question here. The truth is you have done a lot for the former realms. The unification into empire, while brutal, has also given all the people of those lands a brighter future."

He sighed, noticing that she had sidestepped his question. "Let my family fight over the scraps. I am done."

She took him by his shoulders and he winced. "That's a strong grip you have there, Elka." She laughed and he was sorely tempted to kiss her again but the moment passed and she began talking again, desperate it seemed to push sense into him.

"Now listen to me, Loethar, when I took you away it was for a raft of different reasons. These last days I've begun to see a whole new side to you. The very fact that you are Valisar convinces me that you have every right to fight for rulership—and perhaps, I've begun to accept, you are the rightful heir."

The rightful heir. "You stagger me."

"Listen, I've spent ten anni getting to know and love a man called Regor. Everything changed—he changed—when he discovered his past and that gave me pause. In defying him I have discovered that you are not the monster you are painted and although you have done things that chill me to the marrow of my bones, I can begin to see why you've been driven to such lengths."

"You want me to fight for the crown."

Elka looked up to the sky. When she returned her gaze to him it was unwavering. "Slinking away to ultimately vanish is not the answer. You have a duty to your people—all your people—to protect them from whatever is coming. If Leo and his brother are going to slug it out for sovereign right, you should do all in your power to keep everyone—Steppes or Denovian—safe from the wrath of kings."

"The wrath of kings," he repeated quietly. Then he sighed.

"Do you really no longer want to rule?" she asked pointedly.

"Elka, I had everything as emperor, or at least I thought I did. The truth is I had an empty existence. People were scared of me and I was surrounded by either sycophants or traitors. Love has never been in my life. I can count my friends on two fingers, and of those the one I genuinely admired was working behind my back to bring me down; the other, it now turns out, was a magical bird. The only person I can count on is you . . . and I'm your prisoner, not a friend, and we barely know each other." She raised an eyebrow but he didn't pause. "So, no, ruling hasn't satisfied me. I am more bored, more at odds with myself than ever. I thought killing Brennus and humbling the Set would reward my years of isolation and despair but it has made me feel more empty than I thought possible."

"So disappearing is the answer?"

"Only if I want to live. Leonel can—"

"Leo has no vision, Loethar, and you know it. He is a boy and his motivation is based on pure hate and revenge."

"So was mine."

"No. If I understand you correctly, your motivation was your right to rule. You *are* the true heir; you always were. Neither Leo nor Piven is fit to rule. You are! And Stracker needs to be stopped. You can stop him."

He stared at her with a searing gaze. "You want me to take responsibility for all the claimants, is that what you're saying?"

"Yes, that's precisely what I would want from you. You set this chain of events in motion. You made war on Denova. And you've unleashed Piven in his madness and Leo on a narrow-minded trail of revenge and Stracker's sudden elevation from tattooed brute to a pretender for emperor. This is your mess, Loethar."

"But you have taken away my own means to clean it up."

Her eyes narrowed. "You would use a child?"

"I didn't—but it would be for the greater good, Elka." He ran his bandaged hand through his hair. "What do you want from me?"

"This is not even my war, not my land but I'm now helplessly involved against my better judgment and—"

"Involved? Why? Because I kissed you?"

Her expression turned wintry. "You flatter yourself."

And now he did kiss her again. This time he meant it. There was nothing exploratory or tentative about his ardour; his embrace was tight and demanding. And Elka responded. She moved beneath his mouth, closing her eyes and melting around him. He felt as though he was losing himself and for the first time he wanted to.

He pulled away savagely, before it went too far. He glared at her. "Gavriel de Vis is a fool!" he growled and walked away, using the time to calm his mind.

Eventually he made his way back to where he was surprised to still find Ravan patiently waiting. Roddy sat encircled by

Ravan's long arms, rocking back and forth. As Loethar approached he stood, alarmed.

Janus was dozing, eyes closed and snoring lightly as if entirely bored by all the drama surrounding him.

"Why are you still here?" Loethar demanded, the seductive call of magic as repulsive as it was compulsive. He was using all of his inner strength to resist Roddy now and was deeply disappointed that the pair of them had not taken their chance at escape.

Loethar noted how Roddy looked toward his friend nervously. He watched Ravan gracefully unfold his long limbs to stand.

"I wouldn't desert you, Loethar," Ravan replied.

The words were so kind that they tore at Loethar's heartstrings. No one but Vyk had ever stuck by him. And here was his bird—in a new form—still holding to their friendship even though Loethar had threatened his well-being.

"You should have escaped when you could."

Ravan shook his head. "I knew you wouldn't do it."

"I would have!" Loethar insisted, angry that everyone was making presumptions about him.

Ravan's expression didn't shift. "Then why is Roddy standing here whole?"

There was no snappy, neat answer for that. How did he begin to explain that a giantess from the mountains had got beneath his skin and was now affecting his conscience, his way of thinking? Damn Elka and her high principles!

"Just go," he said, waving his hand. "Roddy makes me feel sick and I know I do the same to him."

Elka reappeared, throwing a soft, somewhat sheepish glance his way. He wasn't sure what her look meant. He had no doubt that her emotions were as mixed and confused as his were. He watched her nudge Janus, who snorted awake.

"Ah, forgive me," the doctor said. Then his eyes widened. "From this angle, Elka, your—"

"Janus!" she snapped and he flinched. "Get a hold of yourself. There's a boy here."

Janus looked mortified. "Forgive me," he said, struggling

to get to his feet, prompting Elka to sigh and help him. She hauled him upright.

"Just try thinking first."

"I do," he mewled. "It doesn't help. I just catch sight of your big, perfectly sculpted br—" Her scowl stopped him but Loethar was sympathetic; Elka had a similar effect on him.

She turned, having regained control of her calm countenance, and looked to Roddy. "You are free to go. The Emperor will not claim you."

Something bit at Loethar's mind as she said this. "Wait!" Everyone turned nervously toward him. "You said you were promised to someone. There are only three Valisars that I'm aware of, which includes myself. But you denied you were meant for Leo or myself and it is obvious that Piven has no need for you."

Roddy's eyes lit up. But he glanced at Ravan first as though seeking permission. Loethar noticed the man give the boy a small nod.

"I am promised to the princess."

"Princess?" Loethar murmured, his throat tightening.

"You explain, Ravan," Roddy said. "I feel too dizzy and sick to talk anyway."

Ravan obliged. "Your majesty, the daughter of Brennus and Iselda survived."

Loethar looked at his old friend unblinking. He ran the words again through his mind and still they made no sense.

"Loethar?" Elka asked.

"That can't be right. I saw the dead newborn. I watched the tiny girl cremated. I witnessed Iselda casting her daughter's ashes to the four winds from the palace battlements."

"I was there too, majesty. Except that was not the royal child. It was a newborn girl, yes, but not the daughter of the Valisars. The princess was secreted away to safety on the night of her birth, before you'd even reached the gates of Brighthelm."

Loethar gave a groan. He walked away a few paces, then he spun around again, pointing.

"Tell me everything!"

Ravan nodded. "I will tell you what I know. Corbel de Vis was charged with the task of getting the princess away to safety. I have no idea where she was taken. King Brennus made the arrangements."

Loethar's gaze narrowed. "No woman could feign the heartbreak I watched Iselda go through. I saw her change from a strong, courageous queen into a shell of a woman."

"The queen's grief was likely real, your majesty. She believed that the child she cremated was her daughter. I think it was the losses of both the princess and her precious Leo that gave her the excuse to die."

Loethar looked at Ravan, aghast, as he let the concept settle into his mind. Then he turned to Elka. "And you think I'm cruel. I can't hold a candle to my half-brother Brennus," he snarled. "Did he kill a child for the ruse?"

Ravan nodded. "I believe he did, though he did not dirty his own hands with the deed."

"No, of course he wouldn't." Once again he turned to Elka. "This is the king you all admired. The king the whole Set looked up to and took its lead from. The king everyone mourned. He is as guilty as killing innocents as I am. But at least I did it honestly. Everyone saw my bloodied blade. I was at war. Brennus was simply a murderer!"

Elka swallowed and took a few steps toward him, laying a hand on his arm. "It's why you must not walk away from this. No one knows the truth. The real story is only now emerging. Your agile mind is every bit as clever and cunning as Brennus's. People should know that you are Valisar and that you are the rightful heir to the throne, that Brennus effectively stole it from you."

Loethar blinked. The notion wasn't new but when it was put to him as Elka had just outlined, he could suddenly believe that Brennus was the villain of the tale, not him.

She hadn't finished. "We've now got four people on the loose who all think they have a right to rule. But only one of them has proven he can, has absolute right on his side, and frankly is the best Valisar to sit that throne."

"The princess didn't choose to oppose you," Ravan counseled.

"That's right," Roddy said. "She can only be ten anni. She probably doesn't understand any of this."

"I'm not levelling any blame at the child. She was another of Brennus's pawns. Even Leonel is a pawn. He didn't choose this path—his father pushed him onto it. Piven . . ." He shook his head. "Piven I don't understand. I had a bond with that boy. I couldn't bring myself to kill him even though I knew I should."

"So you humiliated him," Ravan remarked, no accusation in it but also no tenderness.

"That was the excuse I used. Valya, Stracker, even my mother would have happily had him smothered, not because he was an invalid but because he was linked to the Valisars. But I couldn't hurt that child. There was something so intriguing and charming about him. I grieved at his loss."

Ravan shrugged. "Well, now he's your enemy, Loethar. Don't be fooled. Piven is not the sweet smiling innocent you remember. He walks in the body of a youth but he has the mind of a wily old man."

"And now he has his aegis," Loethar murmured. "Be on your way, Roddy. Go find your princess and give her your magical protection if you still wish to. In all of this mess, she is truly the innocent."

Roddy stared at him. "Although you make me feel so sick you really aren't nearly as frightening as I thought."

"It must be my handsome looks," Loethar said and caught Elka's smirk. Even Ravan chuckled silently.

"No, that's not it," Roddy continued, sounding serious. "I just don't think you were ever as bad as you were said to be. You did a very good job of making everyone fear you."

Loethar gave a lopsided smirk. "I did, didn't I?"

"Er, well, you killed several thousand people," Elka reminded.

"Stracker did most of the killing," Loethar said absently. "But yes, I am responsible for it. I planned it. I sanctioned it."

"The thing I'm trying to say," Roddy said, looking exasperated, "is that I don't think the Princess needs protection as much as you do."

Loethar's gaze flicked back to the boy. "What are you saying?"

"You are not a bad man. Not as bad as I have always thought, anyway. You let me go. What would you do right now, if you could do anything?"

Loethar frowned. "I would leave this empire to Leonel and Piven to fight it out. I would find the princess and take her to safety; she is the only kin I have who might give me a chance at being part of a family. And I would disappear." He saw Elka's chest swelling; she was preparing to launch a fresh tirade. He wanted to smile because Janus saw it too and his eyes were nearly out on stalks. "But," he said, holding a hand in the air to her, "Elka will not permit that. So, taking her wishes into account, I would still protect the princess. But I would also likely find myself doing battle with my two nephews because I don't think either of them is a suitable ruler. And . . . I would kill my half-brother, Stracker. His death has long beckoned and I am the right person to deliver it."

He threw his hands up in the air, wincing at the pain in his shoulder. "But this discussion is of no consequence. Go, you two. Find your princess and run away with her. Keep her safe while her two brothers fight it out using their famed Valisar magic. Janus, thank you. Elka . . ." He hesitated. "I hope our paths cross again." It sounded pathetic even to his ears but he really didn't know what to say to her. "I hope you can find de Vis again. Tell him I'm impressed he let Ravan and Roddy go."

"Tell him yourself!" she snapped. "You are not just walking away from this."

"I don't know what you expect of me, Elka. I am not in a position to do—"

"With me as your aegis, you will be," Roddy said, cutting across Loethar's words.

The boy's words silenced everyone.

Finally, Ravan spoke up. "Did I mention that Roddy is a very brave soul?" he asked conversationally.

"I absolutely will not agree to this." Elka's words cut off Loethar's reply.

"Giant! This is not your decision!" Roddy hurled at her. "Ravan and I have discussed it. We want to do this." He pointed at Loethar. "I want your word that you will help the princess."

Loethar's eyes squinted as he focused only on Roddy.

"I will give myself to you if you share the same cause as us," the boy said. Glancing at Ravan, he continued. "I won't be giving up my life, just my freedom. And freedom is a sacrifice I'm prepared to make for the princess, for Cyrena, for Sergius who died so terribly, for the man called Clovis." He pointed at Loethar. "He can make everyone feel safe because he wants the barbarians and Denovians to live as one. It's his half-brother who wants them still at war. And Leo would want the same. Piven . . . I don't know what Piven wants."

Ravan joined in. "Piven wants chaos, I think. He has no conscience."

Elka turned to face Loethar. "Not this way. Please, Loethar . . . he's just eleven anni."

Loethar felt trapped by their individual demands. It was Janus who broke the standoff.

"Elka, I've been thinking, while I would gladly chew your toenails—"

"Not now, Janus," she hissed at him, looking fraught. "Can't you just for once measure your words?"

He blinked, stung by her waspish attack. "But, Elka, it's a good idea," he stammered. Then he straightened. "I may have a disease but that doesn't mean I can't offer up useful—"

"Be quiet, Janus. My patience with your lewd comments is sorely tested," she warned.

He wasn't to be deterred, though. "Go ahead, then, maim the boy—but don't ask me to clean up the mess," he said, waving his hands as though tired of all of them. "It was good feeling needed but as usual my ailment has trespassed. Farewell, all. I shall try not to miss your breasts, Elka. By the way, that last comment wasn't my illness talking!" He made another dismissive gesture and began walking away.

"Wait, Janus!" Loethar called. "Lo strike me! Why didn't I think of such a simple solution?"

"What are you talking about?" Elka said, looking between them.

"I understand," Ravan said, nodding to himself. "Why shouldn't it work?"

"What?" Elka demanded.

Loethar moved to her and calmed her rising fury with a hand on her arm. "I consume something non-fleshy from Roddy's body."

Dawning spread across her face. "Like a toenail," she finished, sounding embarrassed.

"If Janus is right then there is no need to hurt Roddy."

"But he still loses his freedom," she persisted in a much smaller voice now.

"That is true. It's up to Roddy now."

Roddy shrugged. "I had no other plans," he admitted, prompting Loethar and Ravan to share a sad smile. "At least this way my life becomes exciting, even important. I'll make my mother very proud. Protector of the emperor!" he said, triumphantly jabbing a small fist in the air.

"Oh, Roddy," Elka said, and Loethar noticed her eyes were misty.

"I won't hurt him, I promise you, Elka," Loethar said. "And I'll abide by your wishes," he added before nodding at Roddy, "and his rules."

He gave her an encouraging small smile as he squeezed her arm and then walked over to Roddy, amazed by the powerful surge of desire and nausea. He crouched on his haunches before the child.

"I know this is as hard on your health as it is mine, Roddy, so let's do this quickly before we both start rushing for the bushes again. Are we in agreement?"

Very solemnly and clearly fighting his own revulsion, Roddy nodded. "We are."

Loethar held out a hand and Roddy placed his small one in it. Surprising himself as much as everyone around him, Loethar changed position so he was kneeling before Roddy and then pulled the boy to him and hugged him. "I kneel humbly before the bravest person I have ever met. We will do only good things with our magic, I promise."

Roddy hugged him hard back and Loethar felt choked by the affection and the youngster's trust.

"We'd better hurry," he said. "I think I'm going to vomit!"

Seventeen

They'd remained in disguise and booked themselves into a room at an inn that was so far on the outskirts of Penraven's main streets that in Kilt's opinion it shouldn't rightly call itself the city's "Northern Gate Inn." It would take a guest the better part of a bell to walk to the northern gate proper, which meant the inn was closer to Gormand's border than to Brighthelm.

"Why here?" Kilt asked, somewhat ungratefully.

"Here is as good as any," the big man answered, handing him a mug. "Keep drinking. The nausea passed last time because we kept you topped up with lots of water."

"There is no nausea. I told you, I just felt dizzy momentarily in the presence of the magic. But it passed very swiftly. I think it was shock that undid me."

"Nevertheless," Jewd persisted. "Lily always says that water is the best tonic."

"I can't imagine what is happening to her."

"Then don't try. Whoever that was interrupted for a reason; for now I think we can count on her being alive."

Kilt looked back at him in disbelief. "Why? How can you make such a dangerously sweeping presumption?"

Jewd sat down opposite Kilt on the other small cot. "Because the timing was too critical for whoever that was to not intentionally be saving her life."

Kilt grunted his acceptance of Jewd's logic. "It was a Valisar, I tell you."

"Then it has to be Leo. It couldn't have been Loethar—he's badly injured and the people and Stracker would have recognized him. And you'd be writhing in a gutter."

"Unless he's got access to magic. I'm pretty sure I read something at the Academy that said once bonded the Valisar magic doesn't search out any other aegis. I think that's right." He shrugged. "The sickness didn't linger, Jewd. I recognized it and I think I panicked."

"Not like you to panic," Jewd replied.

"I've never been under threat of being eaten before."

"It was a younger voice, Kilt. Loethar speaks softly, his voice low and mellow. This had the pitch of a much younger person, even a squeak in it as though the voice was newly broken. Come on, think clearly now."

Kilt nodded. "But Leo's voice is fully broken."

"Agreed," Jewd said. "But it sounded more like Leo than Loethar, right? And he knows and cares for Lily, which might explain why she was saved. So she's safe for now and more to the point, so are you."

"Still, you didn't have to insist on us coming this far away," Kilt said, looking unappreciatively around the room.

"You weren't making any decisions."

"I was confused."

"Same thing! Totally unhelpful, so stop complaining. In any event, we are not going back into the city. Someone may be there who could butcher you and commit you to a living death. I don't care if it didn't feel threatening."

"It didn't. It actually—"

Jewd ignored the protest. "We *don't* risk it. Are we agreed on this?"

Kilt nodded.

"All right, so that leaves us with the choice of heading west, or sitting around in disguise and hoping we can spot Lily heading back."

"Pathetic options and you know it."

Jewd ignored him but Kilt noticed the flicker of triumph in his eyes. "Or," he said, sticking up a second finger, "we can try and learn some more about your situation. We've said for a long time that we should take a break and journey to the convent in the foothills of Lo's Teeth."

"Well," Kilt began, exasperated. "I'm really glad you're in the mood for visiting our old friends the nuns. That's definitely my favorite heroic alternative, really action-packed."

Jewd stood and flicked Kilt's ear in the way they'd admonished each other since childhood.

"Ow! You sod!" Kilt said, rubbing at the side of his head.

"Now you're just being thick," Jewd said contemptuously. "And you keep telling me how smart you are. We go to the convent and pay the Qirin a visit."

"I've told you before—"

"Yes you have. But now that won't wash. We need information, Kilt. We need to know what we're up against here and whether she has some insight into how we can protect you."

Kilt scowled. "For protection I've got big-fisted you, haven't I?"

"Me and my fists aren't enough when we're up against magic. There are Valisars out there who are hunting you down while we sit here. They want to eat you, Kilt! We can be very sure that Leo will not sit back and lick his wounds now that you got away. And Loethar has nothing to lose by coming after you. We need magical advice on how to outwit those who want your magic."

Kilt nodded, realizing that Jewd was thinking very clearly. "All right. In the absence of a better idea, let's go visit the Mother and her girls."

Jewd's relief was written all over his face. "Good. I've already organized horses. We can leave immediately."

"I hate it when you assume you know how I'm going to react."

"Kilt, we're like an old married couple. We've been together for far too long to pretend that we don't know what the other is thinking."

"For appearances you could just pretend."

"Well, now you're just acting pouty. Do you need me to

find you a skirt?" Kilt glared at him in reply. "Come on. We can ride hard and be across Gormand through the night. If we change horses and keep going we can be in the foothills by tomorrow evening."

Eighteen

Elka couldn't help the smirk.

"I suppose it is amusing," Loethar said dryly.

Now she laughed as she stirred the contents in the small flat cooking pot. "They are some of the strangest ingredients I've ever used in a meal."

Ravan twitched his nose. "Makes me glad I don't feel hunger," he offered.

Loethar threw him a look of scorn. "So . . . magic means you don't consume carrion any longer, digging about in the entrails of some long dead vole?"

His old friend didn't react other than to smile softly. "Nothing you say is going to make it easier to eat toenails, fingernails and hair . . . even insulting me."

They glanced over at Roddy, who sat far enough away from Loethar that both could control their nausea.

"I'm glad he and Janus are getting on so well," Elka mentioned.

Ravan nodded. "I suppose Roddy has found a kindred soul in Janus. The doctor must understand what it is for Roddy to live with his palsy, how he's tried to hide it, why he's such a loner."

"Did you notice the relish Janus took collecting Roddy's toenails and throwing them into this brew?" Loethar demanded.

Both Elka and Ravan laughed aloud now.

"Luckily you weren't awake when he was sewing you up

and fixing your other injuries," Elka warned. "He really enjoyed hurting you."

"Hmmm," Loether pondered. "And still I like him."

Elka nodded. "He is a good man. Well, I'm sorry to tell you that we're nearly ready here, Loethar. Are you?"

He looked into the pot and felt his stomach turn. "You can't pretend to me that you can cook toenails or hair," he grumbled. "I'm going to know they're there."

"I'm not trying to pretend anything. I'm simply disguising them in a savory porridge. All you have to do is hold your nose and swallow the brew."

"Don't think, just swallow," Ravan echoed. "And, Loethar?" Loethar looked up at the man who was once his bird and held his gaze. "Don't set aside what Roddy is gifting you. To give up one's freedom willingly is extraordinary. This is the least you can agree to."

"I know," Loethar said, feeling suddenly embarrassed. "He shames me by his courage."

"Which is why humbly eating his toenails should be easy for you," Elka said with a wicked glint in her eyes. "I can't say I'm not going to enjoy watching this."

Loethar grimaced again. "Does anyone know what's supposed to actually happen when this works?"

"We don't even know if it will," Ravan cautioned. "And Roddy's the only one among us who seems to instinctively know the process."

"Well, we're ready here," Elka said, tipping the gruel into the only bowl they had, the same one that Janus used for his work. "Let it cool slightly and then just tip it down your throat as quickly as you can," she repeated. She set the bowl down in front of him and then, without being able to disguise any of the humor she had clearly hoped she could, she added, "Just don't chew on anything in there." She walked away chuckling.

"When I'm filled with my magic I shall turn you into a donkey and make you carry me up a mountain," he threatened.

"So what's new?" she threw back at him over one shoulder.

He growled before looking at Ravan, who regarded him with the same blank expression he'd possessed as a bird.

"She's good for you, you know."

Loethar rocked back on his heels. "Whatever made you say that?"

Ravan shrugged and it struck Loethar that his old friend had very quickly picked up the habits of men. "Not all that much has changed for you. All the people you despise still despise you. You remain the loneliest man who walks the land. You are still the most feared, the most single-minded, the unhappiest man. You forget I've not only known you for most of your life but you have confided in me. You have never loved anyone. But now I watch you with Elka and you are different with her."

"In what way?" Loethar asked, stirring the gruel, not wanting to meet Ravan's searching look.

"In so many ways. You listen to her, you set store by her remarks and advice, you seem to care about what she thinks and how she reacts, you even banter with her— unheard of in my time with you. I don't believe any woman has ever even vaguely amused you, or aroused your interest beyond the carnal. I've only been in her presence for the briefest of times and yet your gaze follows her helplessly, your whole body responds to her in subtle ways you likely don't even realize. But I do. I know you, Loethar. And I know this woman," he said, glancing over at where Elka sat flanking Roddy with Janus, "has a genuine effect on you." He paused and sighed. "It is a profoundly positive effect too."

Loethar's eyes flashed up. "You approve?"

Ravan gave a soft laugh for their hearing only. "It is not for me to approve or disapprove. And since when was my opinion that important?"

"Since you turned into a man! Whose form do you take anyway?"

"I am told it is of Cormoron, First of the Valisars."

"Truly?"

Ravan nodded. "I have seen my image in a mirror and I can see elements of it strongly reflected back in you. You must not doubt your claim to the throne of Penraven, to the empire you have built."

Loethar swallowed. "And that is why your opinion is important. Because you walk in the body of my great-great-great-great-great-great . . ." he looked up to the sky, his eyes squinting as he calculated, "grandfather! And you speak in what is presumably his voice and you've most importantly shared my life for years."

"In that case I should tell you I approve of Elka wholeheartedly. Most of the women in your life have been purely for sexual release—even Valya, though she was given the prize of being your wife. And as much as she worshipped you, you reviled her in equal measure. It was sad really."

"Sad?"

"Well, I despised Valya too but there's no denying her intelligence, cunning, beauty and suitability as a mate for you."

"She left me cold."

"I know. But around Elka you are full of warmth—a quality I doubt many believe you possess. I've known Elka for barely a day and yet she impresses me more than any other woman I've observed and probably for all the reasons you cleave to her. So yes, if it's important to you to know this, then I approve. She's very tall but perhaps it's time you looked up to a woman."

Loethar chuckled. "I think I love her and that's such a difficult concept to wrap my mind around. But she belongs to someone else."

"And that stops you?"

"It's Gavriel de Vis. He and I are not friends but I have come to respect him."

Ravan gave him a sympathetic glance. "I see. If not for him Roddy would be bonded to Leo." He nodded toward the bowl. "It's cool enough," he said and grinned.

Loethar grunted unhappily.

"If it's any consolation, Loethar—and I've studied people and their habits—I don't think you have to worry about where Elka's feelings lie. She might once have believed herself in love with de Vis but all of my instincts tell me her affections are for you. She tries to hide it but she can't hide it from a practiced observer such as I. Now eat your porridge and good luck." He stood and went to join Roddy's group.

Loethar stared at the bowl, tried not to think about what it contained or whether this was a good idea. He looked at Roddy, so small and puny, the tremor in his hand so noticeable now that the boy no longer tried to hide it.

How was this child to fight off those who would kill him without thinking?

With magic, a voice inside encouraged.

Loethar ground his jaw, angry with himself for the lack of courage. "Ready?"

"Ready," they all answered with a collective gleam of humor.

He picked up the bowl. "Roddy? Are you sure?"

"Do it, your majesty," the boy urged. "Be done with this."

Loethar took a deep breath, tipped the bowl, closed his eyes and began to swallow. He momentarily felt the need to gag at the thought of toenails and hair but then words began to enter his thoughts. Words he didn't know he knew, words of binding. He began to say them silently while he swallowed repeatedly until the bowl was empty of the small helping of porridge.

He threw it aside with a groan of disgust. "It is done." And as he said the words he heard Roddy cry out as if in agony and then within himself he felt as though an opening was being rent. He didn't think he made a sound, but his audience reacted anxiously and then a new sensation hit him; that someone else was beside him . . . no, inside him. He could hear nothing of the outside world but in the world of his body he could now hear two heartbeats, could feel them match each other's rhythm, could feel the rush of blood around two bodies. There was darkness for a few frantic moments of confusion and then he heard Roddy speak to him in his mind.

"We are one, your majesty. It didn't hurt so much because I wanted it to happen . . . so I didn't fight you." Loethar's eyes flashed open and he saw the row of faces before him, all fearful except Roddy's, which wore a smile of pure sunshine. "Your aegis awaits your command."

And Loethar didn't know whether to laugh with glee or weep with disgust.

Greven stared into the blackness of night to where stars winked and whispered of worlds beyond his own, and he prayed for his daughter. For at least the hundredth time he replayed the events of the day in his mind. After tearfully hugging Lily farewell he had returned to the chamber where Piven and his hateful new partner-in-rule awaited.

"You've been gone a while, Greven," Piven remarked.

"You asked me to see Mrs. Felt safely away."

"That I did. And she's on her way?"

"Yes."

"Did she say where she was going?"

His heart skipped a beat but his words did not. "She was headed south as I understand it, back to Medhaven. Not much for her anywhere else now that her husband is dead . . . murdered." He watched the general's tatua twitch as his mouth moved into its comfortable snarl. "Her family is the best place for her."

Piven grinned malevolently. "Oh I couldn't agree more," he said expansively. "Which is why she should be right here with us . . . with you in fact."

Greven felt his throat close. "Me?"

"You are her father after all." Piven took a step forward. "Well, aren't you? Dare you deny it? No. I can see the fear on your face. I can feel your loathing, Greven. You almost did it, you know; you almost pulled off a very clever ploy. But I am much smarter than you can imagine. We'll give Lily some time, shall we? That way her pulse can calm, her breathing become deeper, her sense of security feel real."

"I should kill you now," Stracker hurled.

Greven gave a low growl of protest, laced with anger. "I'd love you to try, you tattooed lout."

Stracker lurched forward.

"Stracker!" Piven snapped, as though calling back a dog. The general halted. "Clearly this needs to be explained all over again. You cannot hurt Greven. Not because I don't give my permission—which I don't—but because you are unable to wield any injury against him. For the last time, Stracker, this is magic you are up against, not flesh and blood. Is that clear?"

Stracker nodded, silent.

"Then don't let's have these scenes again. Greven is untouchable and it's because of his magic that I am too. Behind me, following my commands, is where you need to be. Don't think, general, just do. And as long as you do as I say, you will get everything you want, including Lily Felt's body to play with if that's what takes your fancy."

Stracker laughed at the look as Greven blanched, unable to hide his fear.

"She'll head north, general. It is tempting to imagine she'll rush to somewhere like Francham, where she could lose herself and where I gather the town would protect her secret, but somehow I suspect she'll be fleeing to that convent where they take in strays and women in trouble. She wouldn't think it's a place we might think of to search but I know how Greven thinks. Do you remember, Greven? You mentioned several times as I grew up that you hoped your daughter had gone to the convent, that it was a place you would encourage her to flee to if trouble found her. Oh dear, I see you'd forgotten that. We've shared so much, you and I. Isn't the convent where that witch Valya is?" he added, turning to the general.

"Yes," Stracker nodded.

"Well, you have my permission to retrieve both women. As long as they are in one piece for presentation to me, with all their faculties intact, what you do with them afterward is your business."

A smile stretched across Stracker's face, the tatua changing shape and mocking Greven.

He looked away. "One day I will take my revenge upon you," Greven said, turning to Piven.

"I know, I know," Piven said, sounding weary of the repetitious threat.

* * *

Lily had wasted no time paying for a ride in a carriage headed east but she had taken the precaution first to visit a place whose services were only used by men.

Although she didn't know it, The Honeypot was arguably Penraven's most famous brothel; it was certainly its wealthiest, catering to a more affluent clientele. She approached it from the rear of the property, where she expected to find and did find women of various ages washing clothes, dusting linen, peeling vegetables and generally going about their daily chores. She smiled tentatively at the striking red-head who approached.

"What's the cat dragged in here, then? What's your name?"

"Lily Felt. I was hoping—"

"Yes, darling, we know what you were hoping but we have more than enough of what you're offering. Besides, I don't need your sort of competition."

The other women laughed. It was a compliment of sorts but somehow the rejection knocked the wind out of her, and suddenly, with disgust, she realized she was crying.

"Lo, strike me, look what you've done to her now, Julee," someone said. "She's just like any of us—you were her once." A woman pushed past the speechless Julee and put her arm around Lily. "Come on, lovely, let's get something stiff into you." She winked at the girls, who laughed at the old joke that they'd probably heard a hundred times. "I mean a drink, darling," she whispered. "A little tot of green reffer and you'll be able to face the world a little easier, I promise."

Lily allowed herself to be led into the laundry area and to be sat down. "Wait here, love," her new friend suggested. "Master and Mistress Glendon aren't generous to strays unless there's money to be made from them. And somehow I don't think you came here to offer yourself as a new worker, right?"

Lily sniffed and shook her head.

"I'll be back. I'm Lizbeth . . . Biddy is what I'm called, though."

She returned soon enough with a small glass of the green reffer that Lily had never sampled but knew would taste strongly of eucalypt. "Get that down you. No sipping, just knock it back."

Lily did as she was told and in a moment the liquid, deliberately kept cool in water, turned into a fiery channel opening up her throat, clearing her nose, blowing out the cobwebs of her mind. She gave a groan.

"That's good. You feel alive now, don't you?" Biddy asked.

Lily coughed. "Perhaps I don't want to be."

"Oh come on now. Nothing's that bad. Why did you come here?"

"I need to change my appearance."

"Lo's balls! That's the last request I would have expected to hear. Are you sure? I mean looking how you do . . ."

"Can you help?"

"How much of a change? Just clothes?"

"Clothes, hair if we can, anything you can suggest."

Biddy frowned in consternation. "Well, the clothes are easy. Anything else will cost money and—"

"I can pay," Lily hurried to reassure, reaching for one of the small pouches of coin. She jangled it. "I can pay well for your help and the brothel's secrecy."

"Secrecy? You'd better tell me what I'm getting into here. Start by telling me who you are."

Lily told her companion everything she thought she could without compromising anyone else. When she was done, Biddy sat back on the floor looking astonished. "I knew Kirin Felt, though not very well. I don't think I . . ." She faltered, looking embarrassed. "Well, you know. I think he favored one of the other girls. But he was a gentleman, a good man."

"He was," Lily said, trying to tamp down an unfair flare of jealousy. "Will you help me escape the palace's clutches?"

Biddy looked immediately fearful. "The palace," she breathed. "That awful Stracker."

"He doesn't need to know anything about me being here. Just help me and I'll be gone quickly . . . in moments if I must."

"All right, all right. But we need someone else's aid."

"No one else!" Lily begged. "The fewer people who know, the better."

"All the girls saw you arrive. Let's talk to Julee. She can probably give you one of her wigs, which is quicker than us dyeing your hair."

"Call her, then. Please hurry."

Less than two bells later and distinctly lighter of purse, a flaxen-haired woman dressed in a dark blue traveling skirt and a black jacket with a bonnet was seen demurely emerging from an alleyway that was nowhere near The Honeypot. She looked behind her once and waved before hurrying to the pick-up point where travelers boarded the carriages that would transport them out of the city and beyond the borders of the compass of Penraven.

Nineteen

➤➤————————————◄◄

It was Janus who broke the lengthening silence. "Are either of you unwell?"

Loethar shook his head and, next to him, Roddy did the same.

"Good, then I'm not required."

"How are you feeling?" Elka asked.

"I rather like to feel your breasts," Janus replied.

"Not you. I'm talking to Loethar."

Loethar felt vaguely perplexed. "I'm spectacularly aware of Roddy but other than that, there's not really much difference."

"Shall we put your bond to the test?" Ravan queried.

Elka frowned. "What do you mean?"

"Let's try and hurt Loethar."

Her expression turned to offense. "You'll do no such thing! We're only just getting him back to strength, he's got weeks of healing to—"

"Elka," Loethar cut in softly. "Elka," he repeated, winning her attention. "I'm healed."

"Healed? What's that supposed to mean?"

"The magic . . . the trammeling. In the exchange I have been made whole again. I can't feel a single hurt anywhere."

"Well, that's impressive," Elka admitted, regarding them both with a mixture of suspicion and awe.

"So Ravan's right," Loethar continued. "Let's test it."

"How?"

"Loose one of your arrows at Loethar," Ravan suggested.

She looked appalled. "So it's not just Janus, but everyone's afflicted with a form of madness now, is that it?" Janus gave her a glance of injury and she returned it with a glare of exasperation. "Oh, I'll make it up to you, I'll let you watch me bathe or something." She stared at Ravan, then Loethar and Roddy. "I am not going to fire an arrow at you," she said, returning a hard gaze to Loethar.

"I will," Ravan said.

She stepped away. "Not with my bow or my arrows," she warned and no one was going to argue with the look she was now giving off.

"All right, a stoning it has to be," Ravan suggested without any hint of recrimination in his voice. He moved to select an appropriate weapon.

"Is this a joke?"

"Elka, relax," Loethar calmed. "Just watch. We have to be sure."

"And what if this doesn't work?"

"Janus can earn his keep and fix me up again," he replied, winking.

"No. I'll forbid him to so much as lay a finger on you. Do you hear me, Janus?"

The doctor smiled. "I dare not ignore you, Elka."

"And don't say you know where you'd like to lay a finger on me either."

"I wasn't going to," he said, looking around them all as if wrongly accused.

"Sorry," she said, suddenly embarrassed. "It just sounded like a perfect opening for you. Oh, Lo, please don't jump onto that either."

Loethar began to laugh. Janus waved Elka away. "Do you really trust this magic?" he asked Loethar. "Because it's a lot of mess coming up for me if it doesn't work."

"Watch," Loethar said and startled everyone by leaping around in a mad dance. "Could I have done that earlier?"

No one answered.

Finally Ravan said in a dry tone, "Well, that was something to store away. It was definitely worth witnessing."

Ravan's understated manner clearly amused Elka, as did his sarcasm. Her laugh gurgled through her worry and she pointed at Loethar. "That looked ridiculous. What was it? Some sort of barbarian war jig?"

Now Loethar felt offended. "I was simply demonstrating that all my limbs are working perfectly, in harmony and without any pain. Let me assure you, I'm perfectly capable of graciously twirling around a ballroom if called upon. Ask Ravan. As Vyk he watched me dance."

"Loethar is suggesting he danced regularly," Ravan assured the audience. "That's not true. Yes, he can dance, rather elegantly in fact in the Denovian style—I've seen him practice alone. But the truth is he refused to dance at any of the formal gatherings at Brighthelm. I think the only time I've ever seen Loethar move to music with a woman in his arms was on his wedding day. And that seemed purely dutiful rather than enjoyable."

At the mention of his wife Loethar felt the good spirits between himself and Elka plummet. Disappointment knifed through him as he watched her drop her gaze and the amusement flee from her expression. "Your wife? I hadn't . . ." Why hadn't he told her about Valya? He should have, especially as she'd been so honest about de Vis. He tried to catch her eye to apologize silently but she refused him eye contact. "Well, you're right, Ravan, we'd better test this magic," she said matter-of-factly.

Ravan weighted a large stone he'd been holding in his hand. "This should do," he said, innocent of his part in tearing a rip in the special bond that Loethar and Elka shared.

"No need for that," Elka replied. "I think you were right: the arrow is a better idea. A much cleaner wound," she emphasized. "Besides, I haven't had much target practice in a while." She threw an angry glance toward Loethar, who sighed. "Shall I aim for your heart?" she asked, her sugary voice defying her expression.

Roddy, who had been silent, flinched. "Best not, Elka. I would feel responsible if the magic failed and you killed our emperor."

"Don't worry, Roddy, I don't think our emperor has a heart to hit."

Loethar gave her a pained look but she still refused to meet his gaze and busied herself selecting an arrow and flexing the string of her bow for its tautness. He didn't think anyone else noticed what had occurred but he'd forgotten how connected Roddy was to him now.

"Don't worry, your majesty, Elka can't hide how fond she is of you."

He gave his champion a sad grin. "But does she know how fond I am of her?" he whispered only for Roddy's hearing. "How do you feel about what we're about to do?"

"It makes sense to see if the magic has worked. Although I can feel you without touching you, so I think it has."

Loethar nodded his agreement. "Do you know how to protect me, though?"

Roddy grinned nervously. "No idea. I'm scared that you'll be hurt and it will be my fault."

Loethar felt deeply touched. "Roddy, if this is going to work, our magic will know what to do."

"What if she kills you, majesty?"

"She won't."

"She looks frightening."

"Elka *is* frightening. She always looks like that," he murmured. He winked at the youngster and they both grinned. "It's going to work, Roddy. Your instincts will know what to do. I trust you completely."

Roddy's eyes clouded with anxiety but he nodded gravely. "I won't let that arrow harm you, your majesty."

"Are you both ready?" Ravan called from where he stood next to Elka, who was already taking aim.

"Ready," they called in unison and Loethar felt his heart give a little to realize that Roddy had taken his hand and was squeezing it. He looked around and realized for the first time in his life he had real friends and people he genuinely cared about.

"Wait!" he commanded. Elka lowered her bow and their gazes finally met. "Whatever happens, happens because I've permitted it. No one here is to blame for anything that goes wrong. Does everyone understand?" He looked at each of them and they nodded gravely. "Good. Aim for my heart, Elka. I promise you it's there and Roddy will keep it safe. Trust him. I do."

"I hate you for this," she said.

"No you don't," he said softly back at her.

They all watched her take close aim. Loethar held his breath and as he did so he felt a change come over him, a gentle warmth. Elka loosed her arrow and it felt to him as though it took an age to fly through the air. He could take in its detail, acknowledge that it was on the mark, that her aim was true. He watched it arrive a few hairs' breadth from his chest and he saw it bounce uselessly away.

For a few heartbeats there was a stunned silence and then Roddy started whooping and jumping up and down in celebration. Ravan was laughing, Janus looked too shocked to comment and Elka remained still, staring at Loethar. He couldn't read what her look meant but her eyes looked misty and then she turned away. Ravan had lifted Roddy into the air and they were both grinning like loons.

Loethar couldn't help but join the elation; Roddy deserved that much.

"We did it, your majesty!" Roddy yelled.

Loethar nodded, grinning helplessly. "Thank you, Roddy. Thank you, Ravan." He moved toward where Elka stood near Janus and without any warning he hugged them. "Thank you."

Janus looked awkward but he seemed to enjoy the moment nonetheless. Elka remained silent.

"I know that was hard for you," Loethar said.

Elka bit her lip, suddenly pensive, but nodded. "In more ways than you can imagine."

"I'm sorry."

"We had to test—"

"I mean I'm sorry about Valya. I want you to know something important. She—"

"Loethar!" called an angry voice. Loethar swung around, startled to see its owner brandishing a sword and advancing on him purposefully.

* * *

Barro was singing in a tub of water as Corbel finished up shaving. The convent had provided surprisingly decent garments that fitted even his tall frame reasonably well. It felt deeply comforting to be back in the genuine clothes of his homeland and he smiled as he fingered the toggles that served as buttons and the handsewn, roughish fabric of his shirt. He would need to buy new boots; the ones given were tight. But all in all he looked like he belonged again.

It was as though Barro could hear his thoughts. "Now you look like you come from these parts," he said, interrupting the lusty ballad he'd been performing before picking up its threads again and singing even louder.

Corbel recognized the song and had to admit that he not only found his new companion amusing but he had a manner about him that was hard to dislike. Plus it was useful to have him as an ally—yet another protective ring he could throw around Evie.

As he tossed the linen that he'd been using to dry his now shaven face into the nearby basket, he turned back to Barro.

"I'll see you soon."

"Where—?" Barro stopped short.

Corbel looked at him quizzically. When Barro didn't respond he shrugged in question.

"Uncanny," Barro breathed.

"What?"

"It is like Regor de Vis stands before me."

Corbel made a scoffing sound but then his gaze narrowed. "Really?" he asked, turning back to the small looking glass he'd balanced on the windowsill.

"Can't you see it?"

He shook his head sadly. "I've forgotten so much detail about his face, his voice. It's the same with my brother. I can't bring his face fully to my mind. But I carry them both in my heart."

"We'll find your brother, I promise you. But we need to be watchful. You might startle the wrong people looking as you do. You have grown into your father's image."

"I'm done hiding my face," Corbel replied. "There is someone here I must speak with. I shall not be long."

"Are you taking my lady with you?"

"You have to call her Evie."

"I'll try harder."

"Yes, I'll have her with me, so take your time . . . and, Barro?"

"Mmm?"

"Do not even entertain the notion of what you had in mind for Valya," Corbel warned.

Barro spat into the water. "Her throat should be slit."

"She is nothing but another pawn and I will not have our position compromised because of your feelings."

"That woman is one of the reasons the Denova Set no longer exists."

"That woman is an outcast from her family in Droste and an outcast from the barbarian she aligned with. She has no power any longer. Leave her alone. We have much bigger fish to fry."

Barro nodded. "I see you haven't forgotten how we speak here."

"It's coming back to me," Corbel said dryly. "Heed my warning."

"As you wish."

Corbel left Barro singing at the top of his voice and heedless of the spy who had been eavesdropping his conversation, went in search of Evie. He found her already waiting for him in the main courtyard. She was sitting alongside the cloisters, admiring the well-tended gardens. Her head was bent, looking at what he suspected was a frond of herb, because she kept smelling it, presumably trying to recognize its fragrance. He smiled, taking in all the details of the woman he loved. Her hair was damp and tied loosely back and while she was never one for makeup, he loved that her complexion was clear of even a hint of lip color. She was now very appropriately dressed in a plain-ish dress which despite its best efforts couldn't hide what she worked so hard to do—her high, full breasts and her neat but curvy figure.

"Hello, Evie," he said softly, forcing his gaze away from her chest.

"Ah, Corbel, I—" She stopped and blinked.

"What's wrong?" he asked, instantly worried.

"Nothing," she stammered. She looked more carefully. "Is that really you?"

He gave a small laugh. "Yes, last time I checked it was."

"But . . . but look at you."

"I suppose it is a bit of a shock," he said, feeling suddenly self-conscious.

"A bit of a shock? You're joking, right? You're . . . well, you're er . . . almost handsome," and she now sounded self-conscious. "I won't say altogether handsome because it will go to your head."

"Never did before."

"When all the girls at the palace used to swoon over you, you mean?" she said tartly.

He grinned. "Gavriel and I were in great demand, I'll have you know."

She threw the herb frond at him in reply.

"That's called feremore. It's used to help cry-babies."

"Cry-babies?"

"Infants who can't settle, feed badly, cry a lot. Your mother used it a great deal for Leo, I seem to recall. Although I was very young, I could be making this up."

"Oh, what we'd call colic, I suppose."

"You know, you need to forget about who 'we' are," he cautioned.

"Yes, sorry. I really will be more careful." She smelled her fingers. "It has a lovely fragrance, part citrus, but a soft note of aniseed there. Is it used for anything else?"

"I've only ever known it to be used for squally newborns, crushed into a drop of honey to sweeten."

She shrugged. "There's only one small plant of it. I guess they don't have much call for a cure for infant colic in a convent. Anyway, you look much younger, much happier."

"Barro thinks I'm the image of my father," he murmured.

Her gaze softened. "Well, that must feel good to know, right? You really are very handsome." Her tone was bright but Corbel could tell she was trying to cover her embarrassment.

He nodded. "It means a lot to know," he said and hoped she didn't realize he wasn't answering her question but responding to her comment.

"Hopefully someone might recognize you, lead you to Gavriel."

"I'm not sure that's such a good thing right now. If I'm recognized it could signal all sorts of problems. Loethar, for starters, would want me dead."

Her eyes widened. "You say that so calmly."

"It's a fact. Anyone as close as we brothers were to the Valisars is probably long dead. I'm just hoping with all of my heart that the man who was here not so long ago might just have been Gavriel . . . and that he survived."

"Master Regor? Miss Evie?" a newcomer inquired.

"Yes, that's us," Corbel said, swinging around to see a young nun.

"I've been asked to take you to meet the Qirin. Please follow me."

They made small talk as they fell in step alongside her, she inquiring that their bathing facilities were comfortable and them asking her about life in the convent.

"This is it," she finally said, gesturing at a door. "Ah, here is the Mother."

"Well, well," the Mother Abbess said, regarding Corbel with deep interest. "And how are you both feeling? Much refreshed, I hope?"

"Thank you, Mother," Evie said. "I will never again take a bath for granted."

This made the older woman laugh. "I'm glad that you will take away a lesson from here, my child." She looked again at Corbel and again he felt the scrutiny of her gaze.

He spoke to prevent her from mentioning how he looked; it was obvious she wanted to. "Thank you for your generosity. And my apologies that our companion, Barro, is making so much noise."

"We have asked him to calm his volume," she admitted and smiled kindly. "And you, Regor? Feeling like yourself again?"

It was a pointed question and even though it was cunningly buried beneath innocence, he could not avoid answering. "Very much so, Mother," he said and held her gaze firmly.

The Abbess stared at him a moment longer and then nodded. "I'm pleased to hear it. Perhaps now you're back in the region, you'll hunt down all the people you used to know."

"I plan to."

"Do make sure you have an audience with the emperor. He is very supportive of anyone who wishes to improve services to the needy. Anything to escalate care, education, health, he is a strong advocate for. It is a surprise, I know, given that he was considered a barbarian warlord; I must admit, though, that the emperor is full of surprises, particularly his generosity to his people—all people, not just those from the Steppes."

"He wasn't so magnanimous to the Valisars, Mother."

"No," she admitted. "He was ruthless where they and indeed all the royals of the Set were concerned. But that is past history," she said, eyeing Corbel hard. "It does no good to dredge up what I'm relieved to know is well behind us." It was a veiled message.

"Not everyone can leave the past behind."

She nodded. "Those with hatred in their hearts will never go forward. Loethar is a good ruler. It always startles me to hear myself say that but I stand for the truth. He has achieved some amazing advances for the union and people are generally happy with the way of things."

He knew he couldn't win this discussion, certainly not with the way Evie and the young nun were staring at them looking baffled. "I will consider your good advice and no doubt the Qirin will open my eyes too."

She inclined her head gently in a bow of acknowledgment. "I hope she answers all of your questions, Regor. And you too, my dear. I feel sure this new land you've chosen to leave Galinsea for will be good to you."

Evie smiled. "Do we go in alone?" she asked, frowning.

"One at a time is how the Qirin prefers. Regor, why don't you go first? Perhaps while you do, Evie could quickly check on Valya?"

"Er, I'd rather she wait here—"

"I'll be glad to," Evie said before he could finish. "Regor, I'm in a *convent*," she reminded. "Nothing will happen to me."

"You are not to fret, Regor," the Mother assured. "Your beautiful young physic is very safe with us."

He hesitated but felt trapped by the Mother's ever so slightly condescending tone. Plus he was outnumbered; three pairs of female eyes regarded him with a definite "hurry along" expression.

"See you soon, then," he said and knocked at the door.

"Just go in, my son," the Abbess said. "She will already know it's you."

He nodded and opened the door. The darkness inside was complete and swallowed him up.

Evie smiled expectantly at the Abbess, not really sure of the protocol now that her guide was gone.

"Amely, will you take Evie to see Valya, please. Not too long, mind. I don't want to keep the Qirin waiting as she tires easily during tellings."

"Of course," Amely replied and nodded her head. "Come with me, Evie. It's not far away."

They passed the ablutions block before approaching a series of small, joined, hut-like buildings. "These are some of the elders' accommodations," Amely explained. "Valya lives here. Can you just wait a few moments? I'll just check she's ready to see you."

"Happy to," Evie said, inhaling the sweet smell of the nearby climbing jasmine. At least she recognized this plant and its perfume. The jasmine's familiarity was comforting especially as she remembered the day Reg had given her a small pot of the climbing plant. "It will remind you of me," he had tried to pass off casually but his grave face defied the intended quip. Reg . . . no, Corbel! was such an enigma. The unruly beard, the shapeless clothes, that shambling walk, even the stoop—it had all been an act. How had he maintained it for all that time? He was still quiet but now he walked tall and strong with confident strides. She thought about the curious

conversation between the Abbess and Corbel, deciding that
the old girl had not been fooled. If he looked as much like his
father as Barro seemed to think, it might have been better if
he'd remained hidden beneath his beard.

Evie had always wondered what he might look like beneath
his trademark scruffy appearance but she hadn't expected
him to look nearly as young or handsome. He wasn't twenty-
eight for sure, which was the age he claimed he should be, but
he didn't look as though he was closing on fifty as she'd originally aged him. He could easily pass now for a youthful,
good-looking man in his late thirties. And he was tall and so
broad. He'd managed to hide his body convincingly for all of
those years that they'd been friends—she realized she had
never once seen him without his greatcoat, even in the heat of
the summer.

The violence that had found him, and the relish with which
he had faced it, frightened her. And while she was making a
concerted effort to leave that episode behind, she remained
unnerved by his vigorous new way of giving orders and expecting to be obeyed. A sort of arrogance had closed itself
around him.

Another thought struck her. If she was to go along with
this bizarre new life—not that she had much choice just
now—then Corbel believed he'd been away for a decade of
his land's time he had aged two decades. She caught her
breath. That meant anyone in this world would, if they didn't
believe her dead, expect her to be ten going on eleven, not
nearly twenty-one. She sighed with the confusion of it all
and pinched herself to just be sure she was here. Yes, she
could feel that, and it all felt horribly real.

She frowned and turned. Amely was taking much longer
than she had expected. She wondered if something was
wrong. Just as she took a step forward and was reaching for
the handle of the door, it opened.

"Oh!" she said. "I wasn't sure if something had happened."

Amely regarded her with a curious look but then smiled
kindly. "I'm sorry we kept you." She hesitated. "Valya was
changing," she said, unconvincingly.

"Shall I come in?" Evie asked.

"Please do. She's waiting for you."

Evie allowed herself to be ushered in. Valya was standing to greet her in the middle of the austere room.

"How are you feeling?" Evie immediately asked.

"Fine. There was no need for anyone to worry. Dozens of women all over the land must give birth each day. I shouldn't be considered different."

"No, of course," Evie soothed. "But some women birth with ease and others have varying degrees of complications. Yours . . . well your experience, aside from the physical toll, is emotionally very complex. To lose a child is—"

"You sound very knowledgeable," Valya commented.

Evie was startled by the woman's hard attitude but then again she had learned that people cope with their grief in myriad ways. Some found it easier to simply pretend it hadn't happened, to distance themselves from their loss.

"I'm not a midwife," she admitted. "But I have enough knowledge to be helpful on the subject. Would you like me to examine you? It's important we make sure that your—"

"Not just yet."

Evie was astonished this time at the way the woman coldly cut her off. She took a silent deep breath.

"May I ask you something?" Valya said.

"Of course," Evie replied. She glanced behind and noticed that Amely was near the door. She frowned. Something was not right.

"Thank you," Valya replied. "Oh, how ungracious of me. I should have offered. Can we get you anything?"

Evie shook her head. "Forgive me, Valya, but I promised the Mother I wouldn't be long. This is not a social call." She bit the inside of her lip. That sounded officious and typical of the way doctors were encouraged to speak in order to distance themselves from emotional involvement with patients. Softening her tone, she explained, "Sorry, what I mean is, the Qirin is waiting. My companion has gone in to speak with her first and I was asked to be quick. I can come back later if you wish?"

"No, that won't be necessary. I imagine you have much to talk with the Qirin about."

Evie shrugged. She really didn't know what the Qirin was supposed to achieve. "I'm not sure, to be honest," she said.

"And I imagine your friend has plenty to ask her about."

Evie started to feel a whisper of uncertainty. "I honestly wouldn't know."

"Really? I would have thought his first question might be where his twin brother Gavriel de Vis might be found?"

Evie felt herself blanch and then her face grew warm with embarrassment. "I . . . I don't know what you're talking about."

"Oh come, come. Evie or whatever your name is, or whoever you are, you are under the spell of Corbel de Vis, who has miraculously returned from his long-believed death."

"I think it's time I left," Evie said. But Amely was on her in a flash and had pushed her to the ground.

"Wait! What are you—?"

"Quick!" Valya urged. "Make her drink it."

Evie was so shocked she could barely struggle. Before she knew it a vile dark liquid was being forced through a tube down her throat by the no longer soft and smiling Amely.

"Henbane, mulberry, hemlock, mandragora, ivy and poppy," Valya recited. "All in?"

Amely nodded.

"Excellent. Just enough time to tell her."

Evie was coughing, desperately trying to vomit, but it was too late; she'd swallowed plenty in her struggles. She knew the drug was already moving grimly into her system, recognized enough of the herbs to know that together they would knock her out.

"Why?" she spluttered angrily.

"I have no certain idea of who you are but if what Amely tells me is true then," Valya laughed with wonder, "incredibly you are the Valisar daughter who supposedly died and was cremated, her ashes blown to the winds from the top of Brighthelm."

Evie began to feel light-headed. "I have no idea what you're talking about."

"Well, you wouldn't if you were secreted away at birth. Could he have done that?" She gurgled with delighted laughter. "Brennus, you old fox, you might just have pulled off the second greatest ruse in the history of the cunning Valisars."

"Please," Evie began.

"No! Don't beg me, Valisar slut! No one listened to me when I begged. I am the empress! I was meant to be a queen of Penraven but your father fell for that Galinsean whore and I was cast aside. So I have double the reason to hate any Valisar but especially anyone who wants to lay a claim to my rightful throne. Stay awake and listen, you wretch! You are my bargaining stick, Evie. Is that even your real name? Not likely. Not Valisar enough," she spat. "You're coming with me. I can't imagine what he'll offer when I tell him of the prize I have for him."

"Who?" Evie whispered groggily.

"Emperor Loethar. My husband is going to crawl back and beg to be in my favor. And isn't he going to relish knowing that Corbel de Vis has re-emerged as well. He will finally see the importance of me as his wife . . . by his side."

"You're mad," Evie croaked. Her head was spinning now. She could see Valya spitting saliva as she spoke but it sounded like a senseless babble now, and unless she was dreaming it, she thought she could hear a baby crying. *Colicky cry,* she thought to herself as the drug claimed her. "Stew some feremore," she mumbled as she lost consciousness.

Twenty

Barro had finished bathing and, after witnessing de Vis's transformation, had decided he too must make today the first day of a new life. That began with a trim to his beard and mustache that had long ago stopped being lustrous and had simply become unruly.

He realized now, staring into the looking glass, that his fall from grace had been virtually complete. His terrible choice of loutish companions aside, he really had looked a state. But now after a long soak, with clean hair neatly tied back and his beard trimmed, he felt like a new man. He went to put his old clothes back on with a trace of sadness but smiled when he noticed that the nuns had delivered a fresh shirt for him to use. It was well worn, darned many times by the looks of it but it was soft on his skin because of its age and if there was one thing Barro of Vorgaven couldn't bear, it was an itchy shirt. He preened, admiring his fresh image in the looking glass.

"Not bad at all," he muttered to himself and would have lingered longer if his attention hadn't been caught by the sight of Genevieve, the Valisar princess, walking alongside one of the nuns. He could see her reflected in the looking glass, talking amiably with the young woman. Barro swung around and paused. The princess was meant to be with Corbel, surely? He watched them disappear from sight through the window and looked down to his old scuffed and terribly worn boots as he considered the somber words of Corbel de Vis.

At no time—no time, Corbel had impressed—*is she to be unescorted by one of us. Evie is arguably the single most important person in the entire empire right now. She can bring down the barbarian horde single-handedly.* Barro remembered how he had scoffed at the last sentence and how his amusement had died as he was regarded by the somber face of de Vis.

You have no idea of her power; none of us do. But I am telling you that she has the potential to wield a magic like this world has never seen.

They were chilling words and there was no doubting that Corbel de Vis deeply believed in what he was saying. There was also no reason to doubt him, especially as Barro had been on the receiving end of some of that power. He fully believed the woman he was traveling with possessed magic; she had brought him back from the dead, after all. And for that reason alone he believed and he trusted . . . and he obeyed. If this girl was Valisar, then he owed her his fealty as well.

He blinked. She hadn't looked uncomfortable or scared. De Vis had gone to meet her so presumably he had sanctioned their splitting up. Barro bit his lip as he wavered. Finally the soldier in him won through. Orders were orders. Whatever she was up to with the pretty nun, he was obliged to follow, even if he remained hidden.

His sword had been removed and handed over at the gate. The Abbess would not brook any weapons walking beyond the entry compound and de Vis had nodded that this was agreeable. He had duly given over his weapon but the nuns were perhaps a little naïve and hadn't insisted on a thorough search. No soldier worth his salt didn't conceal a weapon and Barro checked his dagger now, glad that he had always kept the blade keen.

He slipped out of the ablutions block and followed the women, careful to remain hidden. The nun knocked on the end door of what appeared to be a compact row of accommodations but he was surprised when she left Evie alone while she went inside. He frowned as he waited and watched, torn as to what to do. Just when he felt he should make himself seen and have a word with the princess, the door opened again and the pretty nun appeared, smiling broadly and clearly apologizing for keeping her waiting.

It all looked innocent enough. So why did he feel something was wrong? Regor de Vis had always impressed upon his men to trust their instincts first before their eyes. And now his gut was giving him an entirely different message to what he was seeing.

Barro tiptoed up to the door and listened. He could hear two women talking but he couldn't hear what they were saying. The window was not open so he couldn't eavesdrop. He crawled beneath it, hoping that no one spotted him creeping around a nun's room—how bad would that look, he groaned inwardly—and silently crept around to the rear of the building. As he'd anticipated, this end chamber had a back door. He was surprised to find an old nag tethered to a cart waiting patiently just outside. Carefully and out of sight of the women inside, Barro prised open the back window.

What he heard made his belly do a flip. He no longer cared if he was seen as he leaped up to look squarely through the window. The young nun was on the ground, shoving something into the princess's mouth while the bitch-empress stood above and hissed threats.

Without a further thought, Barro heaved his shoulder against the door and arrived theatrically into the chamber with a thunderous crash as the door not only gave way but flew off its hinges. Barro had hit the ground rolling but was back on his feet in a blink, dagger in his hand. Two women were screaming at him and above was a high keening sound that he fought the temptation to turn toward.

In a blink his training allowed him to rapidly assess that the young nun, who looked terrified, was no threat. The bitch-empress was already in a high dudgeon and his arrival had fueled her mad state.

Everything then happened so quickly he reacted purely on instinct. The front door of the accommodations opened and what looked to be a herd of nuns rushed in. At the same time Valya ran at him, screaming obscenities. He had just a heart-beat to see her bared teeth, hands turned to clawlike weapons.

He didn't move; he didn't have to. Valya flung herself blindly toward him, not noticing the blade in his fist.

She gasped at its impact. Barro looked down at the same time as she, and almost comically they both looked back up at each other, as though surprised to find themselves separated by the hilt of a dagger. He caught her as she fell and although he knew he shouldn't remove the blade, he did. Nothing in his life had given him greater satisfaction than to stab the high-born woman who had betrayed the Set and revelled in the downfall of his beloved Penraven. It flashed through his mind as women clustered around him, shrieking, one battering at his shoulders, that the princess could likely save Valya if she laid her hands on the empress. He would not give the princess that opportunity.

Lo, forgive me, he asked his god, as he withdrew the dagger and Valya's lifeblood began pumping out over his hands, soaking his new shirt and leaking her life into the rushes on the floor.

And above it all, he realized a baby was wailing.

Corbel found himself absorbed into a womb of darkness.

Aha, I wondered when you'd turn up, said a voice into his mind.

He paused, startled, a pit opening in his stomach as the magic surrounded him.

And I was under the impression you de Vis boys feared nothing, the voice teased.

Qirin? he asked into the void, tentatively reaching out to touch that magic.

Who else did you expect? Aludane?

He laughed nervously, then caught himself. *I . . . I didn't really know what to expect.*

And now you sound like your brother. Easy to tell you're twins, you even tiptoe in here alike. However, he thought I could hear. At least you shifted easily to mindspeak. I'm impressed.

The hairs on the back of his neck rose at the mention of his brother. *You have seen Gavriel?* he asked anxiously, the mere mention of his own family like a touchstone to his heart.

I spoke too soon about you. You are tarred with the same brush. Of course I haven't seen him. I'm blind!

He stammered his apology. *I meant—*

I know what you meant. But I enjoy making people squirm, especially young men. What other sport is there for a decrepit, blind old woman?

He held his breath, unsure of how to answer.

And now you've lost your tongue. Not used to being spoken to so rudely eh?

May I start again, Qirin?

She chuckled in his mind. *Well, if you're his twin then you're as handsome as Gavriel de Vis. And I don't get enough men here to flirt with.*

He tried a different approach. *Would you like me to tell you that you are beautiful?*

Now she laughed. *Yes, I would, though I suspect you lie, especially as you cannot see in this gloomy world I live in.*

Corbel knew he surprised her when he used his senses to guide himself to where she sat. He reached for her, careful to find her hand, and he took it. *I meant that you are beautiful inside. I do not know you, Qirin, but I'm sure you were very kind to my brother. Won't you tell me about him? Like you I have been deafened and blinded to the world I love for years. To know my brother is alive would be a great comfort.*

What do I get in return?

Name your price.

He felt her amusement touch his mind.

Let me touch you. She felt for his face. *Ah, yes, newly shaven. And your hair is damp, so newly bathed too. Thank you. I appreciate a clean man.*

He laughed. *Were you always locked away in your mind?*

Not always, she whispered and she sounded momentarily forlorn. *And I have known the love of a man. It is enough.*

He didn't pry. *How can I pay you, Qirin?*

You are a good man with a good heart and a ferocious loyalty. I like this about you. I liked it in your brother too. I will tell you about him.

And then she started to speak.

Corbel held his breath throughout the telling. Only when

she had finished did he let it out; it came as a sigh. He was thrilled that Gavriel had mentioned to the Qirin that Leo had survived the barbarian invasion but he was distressed to hear of his brother's loss of memory—ten anni of not knowing who he was.

You are sad, she said.

He was here so recently. It has been . . . He couldn't finish.

Too long, she said gently into his mind. *Where you have been time passes quickly, Corbel de Vis. You have the lines on your face of a man older than his twin.*

He nodded. *I know.*

How can you if you have not seen your brother?

He trusted you to tell you about the young prince. I know I am older than I should be because I was charged to take care of the prince's baby sister. She was born twelve years after her brother but while she should be just ten, she is now twenty anni.

She said nothing for a long time. He waited out her silence.

You sons of Regor de Vis have had weighty burdens placed on your young shoulders. Your own lives have been been forfeit while you have carried out your roles.

They are our duty to our king.

Who is long dead.

To the new sovereign, King Leonel, he corrected.

Who does not sit the throne.

We will put him there, he countered.

He felt her hesitate in his mind, as though changing her own. *You came here to ask me questions. What do you wish answered?*

You have told me my brother is alive. Do you know where he is?

He is not far away. Now that I have touched Gavriel's mind, I can reach out and feel his presence.

Where is he, Qirin? Corbel squeezed her gnarled hands in a mix of anxiety and excitement.

Once again she paused. He felt the ripple of magic in his mind but could neither touch it nor understand it. Then she chuckled again.

What is amusing?

I'm not sure you will want to hear what I have to tell you.

Tell me, please. Is Gavriel injured or—

He is physically sound but he is troubled. She sighed. *But then you brothers have been troubled for many anni. You are used to it.*

What of him, then? Where is he?

He is with another whose mind I have touched.

The girl, Elka?

No. Curiously I have never met her even though she has been here several times.

Who then? Who is Gavriel with?

He is with Emperor Loethar.

Corbel felt as though all the wind had been punched from him. He heard himself gasp with the shock of her words. Gavriel and Loethar? Impossible.

Before he could press her for more information there was an urgent banging on the door.

That sounds like trouble, the Qirin prodded. *No one bangs like that for me. It must be for you.*

His eyes had become more accustomed to the dark by now and Corbel realized a small opening cut into the stone at the top of her dwelling not only acted as an air vent but permitted a tiny amount of daylight to seep into the chamber. Though it hardly counted as light it nevertheless helped him find his way to the door without groping. He opened it roughly, desperate to return to the mindlink with the Qirin. "Yes?"

A young nun stood before him. "The Mother has sent me, sir. Forgive the interruption but your companion Evie is—"

He pulled the door wider. "What? Where is she?" he demanded, looking around, noticing that she wasn't there and suddenly feeling fearful. He just stopped short of shaking the stammering nun.

"She is drugged and the empress is dead, killed by your male companion."

"What?" he whispered.

If only drugged then I'm sure the princess will survive, Corbel. Fret not. But you'd better go to her now. I know you had more questions and I suspect they are concerned with that aching heart of yours. The answer to your second question is yes, with all of her heart but not in the way you hope. She is destined for another.

With a pain like a knife in his chest, Corbel ran out of the door, away from the Qirin's tellings, away from the reality of something he had known for much too long already.

Twenty-One

Elka knew that lovely voice. "Gavriel!" she exclaimed as she swung around, instinctively stepping in front of Loethar to protect him.

"Step away from him, Elka," Gavriel warned.

She felt Loethar's hands on each of her arms. "Yes, my love, step away from me," he said gently, pushing her aside. Elka hardly heard his words, so angered was she by Gavriel's violent stance and order.

"Get your filthy barbarian hands off her," Gavriel warned.

"Or what, de Vis?" Loethar baited.

"Or I'll kill you where you stand."

"Gavriel," Elka began but his sharp, angry words cut her.

"You be quiet. You betrayed me."

Before she could respond, Loethar replied, "In more ways than you can imagine." Elka glared at him but his attention was focused on Gavriel. "Well, what's stopping you? Strike me down. I'm unarmed and you're much bigger, stronger than me. It's what you've wanted for years, surely. Here's your best excuse, de Vis . . . my permission."

"I don't need it."

"Stop this!" Elka said, stepping between them. "I did not betray you when I left, Gavriel. What you and Leo were about to do was unforgivable. But that aside, this man was our prisoner. He deserved fair treatment and he certainly wasn't going to get it from your exiled, out-of-control king."

"Really? Fair treatment? Like he treated my father, or King Brennus, or the queen, or all the royals of the Set? Ask him about the children he murdered in cold blood, killing boys of Leo's age in order to hunt him down one by one. Ask him—"

"You know something, de Vis? I'm getting very tired of that repetitive accusation. I was responsible for all of those deaths, yes. It was war and if you had worn my boots you might know what it was like to walk in them, be a Valisar, be treated like scum by the great Brennus you admire so much but who plays as dark and far dirtier than I ever would, perhaps ever could. I might not have behaved fairly in your estimation, de Vis, but you're choosing to ignore that I live by the same code of honor that you do. I'll say it again: I regret the death of your father deeply. He was an honorable man. Brennus cared not so much for his family as his family name. He would kill just as easily as I, except the man I killed would know who wielded the sword and why I sought his death . . . and I would face him, meet his eyes. That same man would not even see Brennus coming. Your king would lurk in the shadows and use someone else's hand to wield the killing blow . . ."

Elka watched Gavriel blink angrily. Something Loethar had said had resonated but she couldn't be sure which part.

"Do you think that speech excuses you?"

"Not at all. Killing your father in the manner I did was honest but it was shameful. I live unhappily with that shame. And for that alone you have a right to try and exact my life. But you've had chances before and not taken them, and I suspect you won't take the chance now either. So stop bleating."

"How do you know what I will do?" Gavriel demanded.

"Then surprise me, de Vis, and make good on your threat," Loethar said, sounding weary of him.

"Listen to me," Elka urged. "I had to leave with him to prevent you making a mistake, clouded by your devotion to Leo. And I was right to get Loethar away because I knew you would follow the Valisar before you followed good sense."

Gavriel turned a look of pure scorn at her. "As you did!"

It broke her heart to see him this distraught. He looked exhausted. He must have run across country for miles, for hours without sleep or sustenance. "So you came all this way to cut Loethar down?"

"I came for you, Elka," he said and it sounded like an accusation. "I thought he might have taken advantage of you."

Elka's cheeks burned with the memory of Loethar's kiss and how she had wanted it, welcomed it, not wanted it to stop. After believing herself in love with Gavriel for so many anni, how had she swapped her allegiance in a heartbeat for Gavriel's sworn enemy? How could she look at Loethar and feel so protective, so committed to him? Now that she was faced with Gavriel she did feel like a traitor and her heart hurt for him.

"I did what was right," she tried. "And he has stuck to my rules. Did you trammel Faris?"

He shook his head. "He escaped."

"But you would have," she persisted.

The fight seemed to desert him. "At that moment, yes, I would have."

She frowned. "But not now?"

"Now I'm just confused, Elka. The king I have devoted my life to protecting has told me he will kill me the next time he lays eyes on me. The man I swore I would kill next time I lay eyes on him is not only urging me to do just that but damn it, Elka you're on his side!"

She took a step forward. Yes, she definitely knew him too well. He was holding something back, not yet ready to share. "No one's taking sides, Gavriel. I know you put your lot in with Leo but you've also searched your conscience and come up wanting. Leo isn't the man you hoped he'd be. He doesn't hold to the same sense of duty as you. For Leo, it's rule at any cost. For you, it's about honor. I know you better than anyone."

"Then why I am here?" he asked, suddenly aware of the others. "Ravan . . . Roddy, you're here too?" he said, his voice small and shocked.

"Er, I'm Physic Janus, if you're interested." Elka held her

breath; knew the poor man would fight his affliction as best he could. "And I'd like to . . ."

"Janus is a friend and has helped us," Elka cut in. Janus gave her a look of gratitude and she smiled back sadly at the damaged man.

Gavriel nodded at Janus before returning his injured expression to her, awaiting his answer.

Elka took a deep breath. "You are here because you know I did the right thing. You have discovered perhaps that the Valisars—including Loethar until recently— all suffer the same delusion: that the crown belongs to them . . . that they have a right to simply take it. They are happy to allow the rest of us to be pawns in their squabbles. You have to decide, as I have, as all of us have, which is best suited to rule, most deserving of your support."

"Loethar has earned that right in your estimation?"

She shrugged. "Loethar doesn't even want the crown any more."

Gavriel shot him an angry glance. "What?"

Loethar nodded. "It's true. But I don't need Elka to speak for me. Sit with me, de Vis. Let's talk."

"Talk?" Gavriel repeated as though Loethar was mad. "You want me to parley with you, as you parleyed with my father? Perhaps you'll split me in two just for some entertainment for your followers."

Everyone sighed, including Roddy.

"Here we go again, de Vis. Your father is dead, man! Dead. He understood war. He took his chances with Brennus and he paid the price for being your cunning king's stooge. Sooner or—"

Loethar didn't get any further. Gavriel was upon him at such speed that Loethar, mid-sentence and glancing toward Elka, barely had time to blink.

"Roddy!" she screamed.

In spite of his limp, shockingly fleet for his height, Gavriel demonstrated why he had been the most celebrated of King Brennus's up and coming brood of young warriors. And as sharp and agile as Loethar was, he was older and could never be as fast as the young, strong de Vis who was upon him, his primeval roar of rage driving the force of his sword's killing blow, both feet off the ground as he swept the long blade in a mighty horizontal arc.

Its aim was true. It should have hacked Loethar's head from his shoulders and sent it flying into the undergrowth. He should have watched the arrogant Valisar bastard's body crumple to its knees before the headless corpse accepted defeat and slumped at his boots.

All of that should have happened.

Instead he stared at his sword as it stopped a finger-width from Loethar's neck. It struck what felt like a cushion of air and then slid gently away. He couldn't believe it. Again and again Gavriel raised the sword, hacking uselessly at Loethar, never getting closer than the elusive finger-width.

He refused to accept what was happening, never actually allowed the notion that magic was at work; he just kept striking pointlessly until he found himself spent and on his knees, a deep sob escaping him. He was the one staring at boots. He was the one whose body was accepting defeat.

Into the tight silence he let out an animal-like howl of despair, and it was Loethar—of all people—the man he hated most in the world, who bent down and offered comfort.

"I'm sorry, de Vis," was all he said but it was said so tenderly and he heard such deep sincerity in the man's softly spoken words that he didn't need any more words to be spoken. He understood that Loethar's apology referred not just to the death of his father but to the loss of a brother, the loss of his memory, the disillusionment of his newly found king and the humiliation here today before Elka, now weeping herself.

He angrily hauled himself to his feet, pushed away the helping hands—especially Elka's—and stepped back. He sniffed, wiped his face with his sleeve and refused to shed another tear. He swallowed hard and took a moment in the horribly awkward quiet to gather up his bared emotions and put them away.

With his jaw grinding he looked at the thin, elfin form of Roddy.

"So you lied. You are an aegis? I defied my friend—my king—and earned his wrath and enmity to win your freedom from this imprisonment."

Roddy looked deeply guilty. "Ravan trusts him," he said softly, glancing toward Loethar.

Gavriel's gaze did not waver from the boy. "Ravan was his pet bird. Ravan doesn't exist other than through magic! He's not real."

Roddy reached for Ravan's hand. "He feels real enough to me and that's all that matters. Ravan doesn't scare me like everyone else does because Ravan isn't doing anything for himself. He is fair to everyone. I trust him and he trusts Loethar."

"But why, Roddy? Why do any of you trust Loethar?"

The lad sighed. "He doesn't want the crown but he doesn't think Leo or Piven should take it either."

"Neither are fit to rule," Elka said quietly.

"What would a Davarigon know?" Gavriel hurled at her. "Especially one who aligns herself with a tribal barbarian with a bastard claim to the throne."

Elka flinched as though struck.

Ravan took a step forward, his expression dark and foreboding. "I'm afraid you are wrong there," he said and in that moment, as he stood alongside and much taller than Loethar, Gavriel was aware of how similar in features the pair looked. "I can assure you that the unethical claim always belonged to Brennus."

Gavriel stared at the man made of magic, uncomprehending.

Ravan continued. "And you are confused in believing that Leo has any right to claim over Loethar, for Loethar's claim to the throne precedes Leo's by a generation." He paused. "I can see you don't follow. Let me be clear. Brennus knowingly usurped the Valisar throne." As Gavriel's mouth opened in surprise, Ravan held a hand up. "Brennus was Valisar through and through; that is not in contention. But so is Loethar Valisar through and through. He is also the son of Darros the Eighth, older than Brennus by several moons. I might add, the identity of the women who gave birth to either heir has no bearing on the weight of the child's claim. According to Valisar law there is no such child as a bastard heir. If your father is Valisar you are Valisar and heir to the throne of Penraven."

"If you feel this way why did you try to help Leo all those years ago?" Gavriel demanded.

"I don't feel any particular way," Ravan replied evenly. "On the Steppes my role was to watch over Loethar. When I came to the palace instinct prompted me to watch over all the Valisars. I helped each as best I could. That Piven has come into his powers so strongly and with such a savage view of life is not my doing or my concern. That Leonel has disappointed you with his one-eyed approach to taking back the crown at all costs is of no consequence to me personally. But the fact that Loethar is hailed as a usurper I do find inaccurate and I must uphold his claim. As to the princess, she—"

"Princess? Well, you didn't waste any time," Gavriel sneered, casting a sarcastic look toward Ravan and Roddy. "Happy to share your secrets with Loethar but not Leo."

"It seems the Valisar princess did not die," Loethar said in his quiet way, seemingly unoffended by Gavriel's recent attempt to hack him to pieces.

"So I gather. But do we know that for sure?" Gavriel said, his breath sounding suddenly shallow. He began shaking his head, his loyalties feeling as though they were swinging like a pendulum: one minute keeping information from Leo, the next feeling offended when others did. He didn't want to be discussing this matter of Leo's sister in this company and yet he couldn't help himself. He was involved in that episode, his brother, his father too. "I was there," he growled. "I stood next to my father when King Brennus told us that his daughter had to die. He looked at Corbel as he said it. We were shocked. I mean, I knew my duty was to protect Leo at all costs but Corbel's role—to protect the princess by killing her . . ." It sickened him to even recount the words. Had Corbel known it was a ruse? He couldn't have, not when he threw that last disquieting look at Gavriel.

"And what happened then?" Loethar asked, clearly unable to disguise his own intrigue in the tale.

"Er." Gavriel swept a shaky hand through his hair. "Dragging my mind back . . ." He shook his head, trawling through memories. "After the king told us the terrible plan, Corbel and my father were excused."

"Why?"

"King Brennus wanted to speak to me privately."

"So you never actually discussed the death of the baby with your brother?" Loethar prompted.

"I never saw my brother again." He shook his head and his voice shook with it. "It was a terrible thing to ask of Corbel. He was quiet, prone to a darker temperament than I was, but that didn't make him capable of killing a child in cold blood. I hated the king in that moment."

"Then hate him more," Ravan replied. "Because in holding you back on the pretext of needing to speak with you in private, he was actually preventing you from learning the truth of what your brother was genuinely charged to do."

"To save her," Gavriel said in a dead tone.

"No, it was worse. Brennus did ask your brother to murder a child. A baby girl was killed by his hand; I remember a terrible ruckus on the night of Loethar's attack, a woman screaming that her newborn daughter had gone missing. But her wails were lost in a much larger tragedy for the walls were breached shortly thereafter. Your brother was charged by your father to kill the peasant child purely for appearances."

"Appearances?" Gavriel murmured, his heart pounding.

"Queen Iselda, even Leo," Loethar began, then shook his head. "Actually everyone, including myself, believed the baby dead. She was cremated and I stood and watched her ashes cast to the wind. I know the queen believed that was her child; her trauma was not feigned and therein was Brennus's masterstroke. Even his family believed. No one could give away the secret that the child was alive and being hurried away."

"By my brother," Gavriel finished. "Why couldn't they tell me?"

Loethar shrugged softly. "I suppose for the same reason they couldn't tell the queen. The grief had to be genuine. If you knew you might try and comfort her or get word to her; and you would surely have told Leo. You might have tried to speak with your brother, be overheard, risk the plan being discovered. Brennus was heartless, de Vis. He didn't care about how any of you suffered. He didn't care that he imposed a weighty burden on a young man, asking him to murder a newborn baby stolen from her crib. All that mattered was his crown."

"So what of the princess? You are all sure she has emerged?"

"Apparently," Loethar replied.

"She has," Roddy confirmed. "I know she has."

"Then you can be sure that whoever is behind her claim is chasing personal glory," Gavriel warned.

"Were you chasing that same personal glory when you gave up everything to protect and aid Leonel's claim?" As Gavriel de Vis ground his jaw in barely restrained contempt, Ravan continued. "I say that only because it is your twin brother who is—"

"You've seen him?" Gavriel demanded.

"No. I promise I have not."

"But he's alive, he's—?"

"I cannot say. But Roddy and I both experienced a disturbance—a powerful magic. It is our belief the Valisar princess has re-emerged. As she was taken somewhere safe and secret by Corbel de Vis, he is the only person who could have brought her back."

"How do you know all of this?" Loethar and Gavriel asked together. Gavriel didn't miss that Loethar threw a wry glance his way.

Ravan shrugged again. "We know things. As we travel I will tell you about a man by the name of Sergius. He is the reason I am of this plane and how I now walk in the guise of a man; how I am drawing upon his knowledge. Sergius is the reason Corbel and the princess are safe and why they were called to return."

Loethar was frowning. "Where is this Sergius?"

"He's dead," Roddy answered. "Murdered by Greven."

"Greven?" Gavriel said, leaping onto the name. "Greven

is the man who helped Leo and myself when we were first escaping your clutch," he said to Loethar. "It was his daughter who introduced us to Kilt Faris. It seems Greven then met with Piven, although I can't give you any detail."

Ravan continued. "Sergius died at the hands of Greven but not by his will. Greven has been trammeled by Piven and is now entirely under his command."

"And he's going to kill his brother and sister," Roddy said.

"And his uncle," Ravan added tonelessly.

Roddy sighed. "Which is why I had to give myself to Loethar. It's the only way we're going to save Leo and the princess."

"Save . . . ?" He turned first to Loethar, then glanced at Elka.

"No more killing," she said.

Gavriel finally looked Loethar directly in the eye. "And you are in agreement with this? Or are you pulling one of your cunning tricks over unsuspecting people who really do care about others?"

"There's not much for me to live for, de Vis," Loethar said. "In fact, I've tried meeting death head on—Stracker tried and you stopped that; Leonel tried and Elka prevented a sure death; you've had your opportunities . . ." He paused, for once looking unsure of what to say. "Stracker has to be stopped. So does Piven by the sounds of things and he's got his aegis and is presumably already at Brighthelm. It's anyone's guess what havoc he is wreaking."

"And you will not harm Leo?"

"I will not," Loethar promised. "I always keep my word."

Gavriel stared at him, taking a measure of that promise. "I'll hold you to that."

Elka let out a breath. "So?" She looked unsure. "Are we all agreed? We work together, I'm taking us to Lo's Teeth?"

Everyone nodded except Gavriel. He turned to Ravan. "Is my brother in the mountains?"

"That's where we believe the princess is, and while I cannot promise, I have to presume he will be too."

"Then yes, I will come with you."

"De Vis, that does not answer Elka's question. She asked

if we're working together. We are committed to the Valisar princess. Have you agreed to join us in that goal?" Loethar demanded.

"If you swear before the people here that you have no intention to take the crown, then I will work with you. Leo might want me dead but I don't want to see his blood shed. And I certainly don't want to allow my brother's suffering to be in vain. I will do anything I can do to aid his duty."

Loethar shocked them all by kneeling, looking at Roddy as he did so. "I swear to everyone here, and in the presence of my aegis, that his magic will be used only in the protection of the Valisar heirs and not to claim the throne."

Janus began clapping. Elka looked stunned.

"And now you, de Vis," Loethar encouraged. "What is your pledge to our witnesses?"

Gavriel gave a tight smile of scorn. "If you're asking me if I'll attack you again, the answer is no. Everyone here seems to trust you so I'll let someone else, in due course, deal you your just deserts."

Twenty-Two

—»»—————————————————————————————«‹—

Corbel burst into the chamber like a man possessed. "Where is she?" he yelled.

"Calm yourself, Regor," the Abbess warned over the others' heads.

Most of the nuns who had crowded anxiously into the chamber were being banished, herded out by one of the Mother's senior aides. Corbel could move more easily into the chamber where Evie was laid out on a cot.

"She has been sedated heavily, but she is physically unharmed," the Abbess said before he could speak again.

His fears abated as fast as they'd risen and now he was able to coldly take in the rest of the terrible scene. The Abbess was crouched next to Valya, who was prone on the floor, a pillow beneath her head. Corbel didn't need anyone to tell him that she was moments from death, if not already gone. He swung around and only now noticed Barro, sitting in the corner, his head in his hands. He looked shaken.

"Barro?" he murmured.

The older man looked up. "I followed orders," he murmured.

Corbel was by his side in a heartbeat. "Tell me."

"She threatened my lady. I had to stop her but all I did was enter the room and challenge her. She attacked me, she hurled herself at me. I was holding the knife and she threw herself on it. I certainly had no intention of killing her."

"She's not dead yet," the Abbess murmured. "Hold this,

Agetha," she said to her aide. "Keep the pressure on that wound."

"What are you going to do?" Corbel asked as he saw her stand. Her old knees popped with the effort and she sighed as she turned an accusing glare on Barro.

She shifted her gaze to Corbel. "I'm going to our apothecary to find someone who knows anything about this drug," she said, pointing to the glass tube that still had remnants of dark liquid splattered on it. "If we can revive her," she said, pointing to Evie, "she might be able to help Valya. She's a chirurgeon you said, didn't you?"

Corbel nodded. He glanced at Barro and was impressed by how they seemed to instantly and instinctively understand each other. Neither of them cared a whit for Valya; neither would lose sleep if she took her final breath right now. Her history of cruelty and violence and her total lack of compassion had earned her the title of being the most hated woman in all of the empire. "It looks far too late for that now, Mother."

"We have to try," the Abbess urged. "This is the empress, after all. But I don't know where our apothecrist even is. Do you know, Agetha?" she asked her companion, her voice filled with anxiety.

"She's most likely to be with her herbs but you know Herry. She likes to roam the foothills looking for her tiny petals and special leaves."

"You both go. I'll keep up the pressure and do my utmost to keep her alive," he lied. In fact, as soon as the women turned their backs he planned to smother the empress and make sure she didn't live to spill their secret or have any further opportunity to hurt Evie.

"You don't go near her," the Abbess warned, pointing at Barro.

But as Agetha was about to let Corbel take over the pressure a moan from behind told him that Evie was stirring.

"She's waking!" Agetha said excitedly, no longer relinquishing her post, and the Abbess swung around.

Corbel's heart sank and he stole an anguished glance at Barro, who looked equally disappointed. The Abbess was already splashing Evie with cool water and gently slapping her cheeks to bring her back to full consciousness.

"She couldn't have swallowed enough," she remarked. "Quickly, help me, Regor, call to her. She might recognize your voice more readily than mine."

Reluctantly he gave his aid, furious that the Mother would expect Evie to help someone who just moments ago had wished her genuine harm.

"I'm surprised you haven't asked Master Barro more about what happened, Regor. Surely it's not normal for an empress to attack a stranger in this way." She looked at him with an arched eyebrow.

He reached for an excuse. "Perhaps I'm too shocked. My mind is reeling from what I learned from the Qirin and now this attempt on Evie . . . It's too much to take in. I'm sure Master Barro has already explained to you what happened. Soon enough he'll tell me."

"Yes, but I wonder if the stories will match?" she queried. "Come on, Evie, wake up now. Try again, please," she urged him.

Evie moaned groggily.

"Evie, it's Reg," he said, falling back on his old nickname.

"What? Reg . . ." she called out, her voice croaky. "The drug."

"You're safe now," he murmured and wrapped his arms around her. "No harm, I promise you," he soothed.

Her eyes flashed open, frightened, and she began to cough and speak at the same time. "They forced drugs down my throat . . . Valya and her—"

"I know, my dear," the Abbess reassured her. "Amely is being held in a locked chamber, although I rather think her terror of Master Barro will keep her confined better than any key or bars." She smiled kindly as Evie's terror began to subside.

"You're safe," Corbel repeated, more for his own comfort than Evie's. "How are you feeling?"

"Drowsy. Let me sit up." They helped her to do so. It was obvious she wasn't fully awake. "I think . . ." She stopped, a look of pure horror coming over her face. "Valya!"

"She's not dead," Corbel said, hoping his disappointment wasn't evident in his tone.

"But very nearly," the Abbess hurried to add. "We need your help, Evie. Please. I know you should not feel obliged but . . ."

"What happened?" she asked, shaking her head, trying to wake herself up.

Barro explained. "She ran at me screaming, clawing. She didn't see the dagger in my hand. I was only holding it to scare her."

Evie looked at the dying woman with contempt. "She deserves to die," she began and Corbel felt his spirits lift, "but I am obliged to save her life."

"Evie," he began, a warning note in his voice.

"If I can," she added as qualification. Corbel closed his eyes in dismay.

"I just need you to look at the wound and tell me if . . ." The Abbess shrugged helplessly. "If there's anything you can do."

"Help me down," Evie said. "I have no real feeling in my legs."

Corbel half-heartedly offered a supporting arm and Evie near enough collapsed next to Valya.

"Do you want to see the wound?" the Abbess offered, nodding at Agetha.

"No," Evie replied. "That won't be necessary. I know what a stab wound looks like and I can see a lot of blood has been lost."

"So you can't help her?"

"Clear the room, please," Evie said. Corbel looked at her in surprise and knew that everyone else's expressions mirrored his own. "Quickly!"

"Evie," Corbel tried again.

"You too," she said to him. "Barro, you can stay. If she tries anything, you can have another go at killing her."

Barro smiled grimly and stood.

"Everyone out," Evie repeated. "We have only moments if I am to save her." Corbel could tell she was already losing herself in the medicine. "We are losing her."

"But what—?" the Abbess began.

"Go!" Evie hurled at all of them. Agetha fled as Evie took over staunching the hole in Valya's belly, followed by the Abbess, confused and startled. Corbel, furious, trailed after the Abbess, but at the door he stopped and turned back to Evie.

"If you do this, you will start a tidal wave of danger for us."

She nodded. "I have to," she replied and he could tell there would be no further argument. He threw a look of disgust that was shared by Barro and then he stomped out behind the Mother.

"What is she going to do?" she said, turning, perplexed and staring at him.

"She's going to do what you asked her to. Save the life of the empress," Corbel snapped, and then he loped away, angry and filled with a fresh dread.

Leo had traveled constantly. Without companionship or belongings other than Faeroe to slow him down, he moved at a steady speed, his long legs moving easily over terrain he had become so accustomed to he hardly noticed the steep climbs and unsteady footholds. His time with Kilt and his men had also taught him precious survival skills; he knew how to forage for food and to keep his small water skin topped up at every opportunity.

He had learned long ago that in lean times a certain type of oily nuts would fool his belly into thinking a rich meal had been consumed, while berries and fruits laden with sweetness restored energy. A single rabbit, skinned and cooked, kept him in a frugal supply of meat that he chewed on as he walked.

While he stopped to rest only during the darkest, coolest part of the night, he did pause once as he took advantage of a tiny village to take some fresh milk. There he met a man who was also inquiring after some fresh milk from the farmer who had clearly been quenching his own thirst from a pitcher.

"Not unless you've got coin," the farmer was saying as Leo strolled up.

"I don't," the man replied evenly. "But I will do a reading for you in exchange for a small cup."

The farmer had gruffly waved the man away and turned his attention to Leo. "And what are you after, traveler?"

"The same, I think. A cup of milk, perhaps some cheese if you have it."

"Aye, I have plenty."

Leo frowned, recalling how even during lean moons Kilt would drop coins into the outstretched palms of stranded travelers or those who had fallen on hard times. He had never asked about their lives, simply given generously even if it meant Kilt's men had to go without some staple such as flour for another moon. He couldn't help himself. "Then spare a little for my fellow traveler. Lo will reward you for the gesture."

"Ho! Who are you to lecture me? I have a farm to run and six children to feed and a permanently angry wife who is still waiting for the new silk hanky I promised two namedays ago. No, traveler. You spare some of yours. Let Lo smile upon you."

Leo had cursed the farmer silently for his selfishness, particularly as he looked well fed and the sons he assumed who worked in the field beyond looked strong and healthy. "Two cups of milk and a block of cheese," he said, not showing any of his disgust.

"I'll see your money first, stranger," the farmer said.

Leo palmed two coins from a pocket. "What is your name, farmer?"

"Sawberry, though why that's important I can't imagine," he growled, pouring the milk into a cup. "Here," he said, taking the money before he handed it over.

Leo wiped the rim of the cup and handed it to his nameless companion. "After you."

The man nodded, a look of soft surprise creasing his eyes before it turned into a smile. "Thank you, young man."

Leo turned back to the farmer. "Why? Because I want to remember you."

The farmer laughed. "Here's your cheese," he said, having hacked off a piece from the block he had laid out on a nearby stump. "My sons won't be happy to go without their midday food."

"I'm sure they'll manage," Leo said, turning to take the cup that his companion had drained.

"Thank you," the man said.

"Refill it," Leo ordered and this time the farmer said nothing. "Here, have the cheese. You look like you need it more than I do."

"I couldn't," the man replied.

Leo took the refilled cup and drained it easily in three gulps. He gave the farmer a scathing look. "A pox on you, Sawberry."

Sawberry laughed again, turned away and pocketed the money.

"I meant it, you have it," Leo said, beginning to walk away.

"There must be a fair exchange," the man said. "Let me do a reading."

"A reading. You're a seer?"

"Of sorts."

Leo shrugged. "All right. While the milk settles, I'll let you earn the cheese."

They settled themselves on the rim of a copse, having walked away from Sawberry's farm and although Leo was not in the slightest bit interested in the reading, he took advantage of the rest.

"My name is Darry," the man said, making himself comfortable on a tree stump. "I'm from—"

Leo held up a hand. "It's all right, Darry, I don't need to know anything about you. Our paths will not cross again. I am doing this simply to make you feel easier. Shall we get on with it?"

"As you wish. Would you like to give me your name?"

Leo shook his head. "Let's see how good at reading you are, shall we?"

The man nodded, seemingly unoffended. "May I?" he said, his palm hovering over Leo's hand.

Leo shrugged and Darry placed his on top and his eyes grew distant. Then they seemed to flash with a recognition before the man looked down and cleared his throat. "What would you like to know?"

"What am I?" Leo said baldly.

"That's an odd question."

"Ignoring the obvious. Tell me what I am—what dark secret do you see within?" he replied cryptically, knowing the man had seen or felt something.

"You are of blue blood."

Leo's eyes glittered now. "Tell me what that makes me."

"The family's chalice," the man said uncomfortably. "But don't ask me what it means. The word has sprung into my head, won't leave, but won't reveal itself either."

"The chalice," Leo repeated. "Anything else?"

The soothsayer shook his head and while Leo suspected there was more, he didn't care. He was on his path now. "Just tell me if I'm heading in the right direction for what I seek."

Darry bit his lip. "I don't know what it is you seek but there are plenty of people who wish to avoid you."

Leo smiled without humor. "Is one of them in Barronel?"

"Possibly. I have no clear reading on it."

Leo stood. "Then you have earned your milk and cheese, Darry. I will ask you not to speak of this to anyone or I will hunt you down and kill you."

"I believe you. I have no reason to share this knowledge."

Leo nodded at him, turned and strode away without so much as a glance behind him. *The chalice*, he muttered, not understanding it at all but his spirits leaped that the soothsayer had seen something of what sounded to be a magical quality in him. Perhaps he wasn't entirely without powers after all. Time alone would tell.

His sense of direction was reliable and he'd skirted the Dragonsback Mountains with ease and found himself in Barronel within a day of leaving the camp. His shortcut route over higher country had cut days from the traditional traveler's route of passing first through Francham and Hell's Teeth before veering west into the mountain pass.

The time alone had given him space that he'd never known previously to lose himself in thought. Life with the outlaw gang had its freedoms but he'd never had a moment alone and he'd got used to growing up under a constantly watchful eye.

It niggled at him that he had not been able to sense Kilt's magic. And the more he thought about it, the more furious he was that though he was the rightful heir he also seemed to be the least magically talented Valisar. Piven had somehow emerged from his madness and had already secured himself an aegis; Loethar the bastard claimant would likely find a way to hunt down Kilt. And he was left searching for a glass bead in the rain. That's how it felt. Impossible!

At least he had a place to start looking. And there was the marking, wasn't there? Some sort of giveaway signal that you did possess the aegis magic. What was Kilt's sign? He had never noticed anything untoward or odd.

His reflective mood dragged his thoughts forward, daydreaming of wresting back the crown. He felt no pain at the loss of Gavriel, he realized; as far as he was concerned, his former friend was a traitor to the Valisars. He had given his loyalty to the Davarigon slut.

Women!

Leo was glad he'd not yet fallen under the spell of a woman. When he thought about those terrible days stuck in the ingress, how he and Gav had to trust one another only, it beggared belief that Gavriel would choose a woman over him.

Leo shook his head in disgust for the umpteenth time over this topic. But it had prompted his memories of the ingress that he hadn't thought about in so many years now it had almost taken on an unreal quality—as though he had imagined those frightening days; the stuff of nightmare.

With all those people, and even that damn magical Vyk, it galled him to think that he'd never felt his own magic respond to anything. It actually turned his stomach with rage that Piven had so much power to draw upon—if what Roddy and that strange Ravan fellow had said was true—and yet he, the whole and very dutiful Valisar son had never felt even the pinprick of a . . .

Leo stopped still, his arm poised to reach for a branch, but he never actually touched it. Instead his hand slipped down the bark until it lay flat against the trunk, his expression faraway and distracted.

A recollection had come back to him; hit him like a punch in the belly. There had been something once though. He'd felt it, but paid scant attention because the rest of his life had been balanced on such a knife's edge, fraught with tension and anxiety. The pull at his magic—and he did remember now what it felt like and how he'd registered it, but instantly dislodged it from his mind. He concentrated hard. He'd been alone. Gavriel was on one of his "ranges" as he called them. He'd been left alone too long and become bored. The tedium of the darkness, the cramped space and the lack of activity, not to mention the constant hunger that every boy suffered, had contrived to make him break the rules.

He never did tell Gavriel that he had gone on a small exploratory tour of his own. With a tiny nub of candle and a small flame lighting his way he'd followed one of the chalked maps. It had taken him to a dead end so he hadn't felt quite so guilty by then and he knew it was of no help to their cause so there was no reason to visit it again or even mention it to Gavriel. But he had felt the smallest hint of a breeze on his exposed leg where he'd torn his trousers. Examining closer he'd found a spy hole that required him to lay flat on the ingress floor to peer through it. He understood now its curious positioning, for from this angle he could just see a tiny picture of the entrance of the bailey, just beneath the famous timepiece that decorated the grand arch into Brighthelm.

The frame was minuscule but he was still amazed that a perfect little glimpse of who was coming and going through this entrance could be gauged. In truth all one could see were the heads and shoulders but it was enough to thrill Leo to see people on the outside.

It was not a happy time for any Denovian. The bailey was overrun with the tattoed barbarians but even seeing prisoners led through the gates helped to shore up his spirits because it fueled his determination to escape and one day return to humble the Steppes tyrant.

Yes, it came back to him now, as he stood by the roadside entering Barronel more than a decade on, how one group of what was presumably prisoners were led through. He blinked as he replayed it all in his mind, realizing he had forgotten none of the detail. That group had contained Kirin Felt, one of the people he thought was another grasping traitor who had joined forces with Freath. He knew differently now and perhaps Felt had been a royalist and someone working behind the scenes in his favor and keeping the faith that the Valisar throne would be returned to the rightful heir.

But that wasn't what he'd been searching in his thoughts for. It was the girl.

A young woman, who as she'd been led into the bailey, along with the other Vested, had for some curious reason sharply looked up. He remembered now his shock. It was as though she'd sensed him there and she had looked directly at him! She couldn't see him, of course, but still he'd rocked back, his heart pounding. And there was something else. Think, Leo, think! Yes, there was something else all right. Inside he'd felt as though his mind had been charged with a blinding light and he felt a strong wave of nausea pass through him. It had lasted for less than a blink, had happened so fast it was logical to believe it was connected with the shock of her looking up and feeling as though his hiding place had been discovered. That or his intense hunger!

But now he knew different. Since then he'd witnessed what had happened to Loethar and Kilt Faris when they'd met; and he stupidly hadn't fully recognized the feeling of being drawn to Roddy. It wasn't strong and he could be reaching but now that he really thought about it the feeling the girl prompted in him that day had felt similar to what Roddy prompted except supremely more intense. In that blink of an eye, that single brief glance she threw his way shocked him but at the same time seemed to enter him, know him! And then it had passed as she looked down, walked hurriedly on and then he'd been distracted by hearing Gavriel calling out in the dark and he'd rushed away, forgetting about her and his exploratory trip almost immediately because Gavriel had returned with food.

He hadn't known anything then. He had no idea of what had just occurred or what had reached out to him because his own magics were so weak, even his instincts weren't relaying the important prompts to him. But he was older now, less frightened now, more experienced with the touch of magic.

Well, he had to hunt down the one person whose destiny was to help him take back the crown. His aegis had to exist for him and now he had to find him or her. His Valisar blood would seek the aegis out more surely than his eyes could.

"If you're in Barronel, I'll find you," he murmured.

Valya sucked in her breath and her eyes flew open. They registered Evie's presence and she gasped. "I thought I was dead."

"I certainly wish you were," Barro remarked over Evie's shoulder. Valya made a move as if to rise but he put a grubby boot against her shoulder.

"Oh no, empress, you can stay right there." Without warning he moved Evie aside and flipped Valya onto her belly.

"What are you doing?" she screeched.

"Just making sure you don't try anything stupid again," he said, locking metal cuffs around her wrists. "I carry these with me. Heavy but very handy," he remarked and dragged her back around to face Evie.

"There, your majesty," he said to Evie. "Now talk to the bitch."

"Your majesty? You mean *her*?" Valya repeated, enraged. "I am the empress."

"A dead one again if you're not careful," Barro warned.

Evie grimaced. "Is the binding of wrists really necessary?"

"Entirely," he assured. "And I've got the key. They don't come off without my say so and I have no intention of releasing her."

"I'll see you gutted," Valya snarled at Evie, "but he'll be first and I'll dream up something tailored to make your final seconds as painful and repulsive as possible," she hurled at Barro.

He simply laughed at her. "Oh, I don't doubt you would. Pity you'll never get the chance."

"What did you hope to gain by drugging me?" Evie asked, as Barro hauled the now hale and uninjured Valya to her feet.

"I thought it was obvious."

"Whatever makes you think the man who threw you in here in the first place would take you back simply because you give him me?"

"Oh, my dear, you have so much to learn about Loethar. I think he'd sell his soul to the devil to destroy a Valisar. And you got away from beneath his very nose." She leaned closer to Evie. "Don't think flashing those big eyes at him would appeal to the softer side. There is no softer side to my husband."

"Valya, isn't dying fun?" Barro baited.

Evie looked at him with consternation. He winked back.

"You see, you're not dealing with any pretty girl. You're up against a very powerful magic. Ah, I see in your eyes that you are not a disbeliever. That's good. Evie here used the most powerful magic of all to heal you, so I'd back down if I were you. She might have given you back your life, but I'll happily take it again."

Valya blinked. It seemed only now she looked down at where her wound should have been. Her white robes were garishly soaked with blood and her own sticky blood was pasted in rivulets to the earthern floor. She looked back up at Barro, her face pale, confusion creasing it now as realization hit. "I don't understand."

"Didn't think so," Barro said, obviously enjoying himself.

"I ran at you," she whispered, and then as if remembering the shock of the blade penetrating her flesh, she gave a tight gasp. "You stabbed me."

"No. You impaled yourself. Same outcome but a very different intention."

She shook her head. "I felt life leaving me." Then, shocking them both, she began to weep. "My daughter . . ."

"Daughter?" they murmured together.

"I heard a baby crying," Evie suddenly recalled.

Barro nodded. "Come to think of it . . ."

"Where is she? She was . . ." Valya spun around and Evie followed her gaze to the door of the chamber, which was off its hinges and resting at a strange angle. Valya's hands flew to cover her mouth and she groaned. "Here," she said, finishing her sentence, tears streaming down her face. "Her crib . . ." she stammered. "It's beneath there," she pointed.

"Barro!" Evie said. She didn't have to say anything more. He crossed the room swiftly and pulled the door up, peering in.

"No baby here."

"They've taken her," Valya said, fright overpowering her.

There was a knock at the door. "Valya?" the Abbess's voice called.

Evie nodded at Barro and he moved to open the door.

"What's happening?" the Mother asked, entering the chamber hesitantly. Corbel followed. It was the Mother's turn to gasp at the sight of Valya alive, standing near Evie. "How can this be?" she uttered. She shook her head as if seeing a vision. "You were so close to death, Valya, I . . . I . . ."

"I am whole, Mother," Valya assured. She threw a cruel sideways glance at Evie. "She uses magic."

The Abbess's eyes widened in shock. "What?"

"Abbess, if you'll let me ex—" Corbel tried but Valya cut him off.

"There's no stab wound," she hissed.

Barro took a step forward. "Well, let's just rectify that, shall we?"

"It's her filthy magic, I tell you," Valya added.

Corbel looked down, so distressed he couldn't meet Evie's gaze. This was exactly what he had feared.

"Stop this!" the Mother commanded. She turned a horrified stare on Evie. "You are Vested?"

"I don't know what that means. Do I use strange powers to heal? I suppose so. I don't imagine it's everywhere someone who was stabbed and lost so much blood that her heart was about to stop can look as healthy as Valya does right now."

Evie had her cool surgeon's air pulled around her now. Corbel could tell she was unhappy at being challenged like this.

He didn't like the sound of where this was headed. "You demanded her help."

"But . . ."

Valya gave a sly smirk toward Corbel. "What she's struggling to tell you—although I'm surprised you don't know this—is that the Mother is now obliged to report you to General Strack—"

"General Stracker can kiss my arse if you think we're going to let you turn my lady over to him," Barro interrupted.

His vulgarity prompted a brief, somewhat shocked pause, before Evie helplessly smiled.

"Let me get this right," she said, holding up a hand to prevent anyone interrupting or speaking for her. "You feel obliged to turn me in to the authorities—that is, Emperor Loethar—for using 'magic,'" and she loaded the word as she said it. "And in return I should feel equally obliged to inform the same authority that his daughter, believed dead, is alive and well and secreted away in the convent where he imprisoned his grieving wife, bereft of her child and husband. That's about the sum of it, am I right, Mother?" Her words were said so dryly that Corbel, despite being shocked at learning of the daughter's survival, broke out in a wide smile. This was Evie at her best, her mind as sharp as the scalpel she wielded with equal dexterity.

"No!" Valya yelled.

The Abbess looked horrified. "You told them about Ciara?" she asked, aghast.

"We guessed," Evie said. "I heard the baby crying, so did Barro."

Corbel couldn't believe what he was hearing. "Loethar thinks his daughter is dead but you are keeping the truth from him? Why?"

"He might have named her but he didn't even want to see her," Valya snarled. "He was happy for her to die; he never gave her a chance and if you want the truth, everyone gave up on her—even the midwives, the physic. I suckled her and kept her going, only me. Where is she?" she demanded.

"She is safe, Valya," the Mother promised. "I've sent her with the woman you trust—Dilys—to the scriptorium."

"Oh not to that girl!"

"She has a rare ability to calm Ciara. And the little mite needed calming. We couldn't think straight for her crying, poor little thing."

"She needs to be fed, comforted."

"The wet nurse went with Dilys. If feeding is all that's required, that's good. She was terrified by the noise and disturbance."

Corbel had tolerated enough discussion about wet nurses and calming scriptorium workers. "Abbess," he said, "we need to talk."

He noticed Valya blanch. "Lo save us! Mother, this is the son of Regor de Vis. Look at him!"

Corbel flinched.

"And this," she said, struggling with her bonds, jutting her chin toward Evie, "is the Valisar daughter everyone believed dead."

Corbel closed his eyes. He hated Valya. Why couldn't she have been generous and just died!

Silence descended on the room and lengthened uncomfortably as the Abbess considered what she'd just heard.

"Is it true?" she finally asked Evie.

Evie shrugged. "Forgive me, Mother, for sounding repetitive but I have no idea." She theatrically pinched herself. "Apparently I'm here. But you know as much as I do."

The Abbess turned to Corbel.

"You *are* one of the de Vis sons, aren't you?"

There was no point in denying it any longer. Corbel nodded. "I am Corbel de Vis."

The older woman sucked in air and shook her head. He thought he saw tears.

"Why did you lie?"

"I have been lying since my youth, Mother," he admitted sadly. "All for the Valisar cause."

"And the man who was here recently, also called Regor?"

"My twin brother, Gavriel, according to the Qirin."

Valya made a hissing sound.

"So what is going on?" the Mother asked. "Is something afoot?"

"Can't you tell, Mother? They plan to steal my child's throne and put this girl on it!"

Corbel flung up his hands. "Forgive me but this woman is beneath my contempt. She may call herself empress and may have once been a Drostean princess but now she is nothing more than a barbarian's whore. I refuse to discuss anything more with her spewing her poison around me. She is a prisoner of her own empire and now she's a criminal and should be treated as such."

"How dare you—" Valya raged.

"He's right that I gave my word to the emperor to contain you, Valya, and it seemed to me that you were prepared to throw all our generosity to the wind in order make some sort of escape with your child and Evie here," the Abbess cautioned. "I would suggest you go to the misericord and say some prayers, consider your situation, have some quiet time."

"Mother, I—"

"Take Valya away, please." She motioned to two of her helpers. "Master Barro, as I'm sure Master de Vis will insist, you may keep guard of the empress but this is to be a silent guard and an invisible one. You are not to look her in the eye to taunt her, neither are you to so much as utter a sound to her to bait her. Is that clear?"

"It is."

"Then please help escort Valya to the chapel and take those cuffs off her."

"Mother, I must insist—" Valya began.

"On nothing, my dear. You have no rights, other than what I grant you and until I hear all that my guests have to say, you are granted none . . . other than your infant, who will be brought to you soon enough. Now go."

When everyone had trooped away, leaving only the three of them, the Abbess regarded Corbel and Evie sternly. "You have a lot to explain. We shall walk the cloisters together and I will expect to hear your story—your whole story—before I make a decision."

"On what?" Corbel asked.

"On what to say in my message to the palace."

Corbel shook his head. "With all due respect, Mother—"

"I know. You could simply walk out of here. That's quite true but you won't, not immediately. You will do the right thing and do me the courtesy of an explanation. Your name is de Vis and we both know what that stands for."

Corbel acquiesced. He nodded at Evie and they both fell in step behind the convent's mother like scolded children.

Twenty-Three

The soldiers picked him up not long after he'd walked into the main street of Barronel's Royal Straight. He'd only been to this realm once as a young child and remembered very little although the tall trees lining the impressive and elegant long street did prompt a memory of riding on a shiny black stallion between his parents. They had been here to meet with the royal family of Barronel.

Now it looked very different. The Straight was still an elegant concourse but now it seemed to be a region inhabited by barbarian soldiers, mainly Reds it seemed. The truth was the once grand capital now felt like a ghost city. The soldiers he did see were few and far between.

Two soldiers emerged from an alley and approached him. "Ho there, traveler," said an older Red in heavily accented Denovian, stopping him in his tracks.

Leo had to look up at him, atop his fine horse. He was glad he'd taken the precaution to hide Faeroe for fear it would be confiscated.

"Yes?" he said, trying his best to sound deferential.

"No civilians here," the man said. He had clearly not made the transition easily to the Denovian language.

"Oh?"

"Are you Vested?"

Leo considered this. It was really his only way into the camp. "I am. I was told to come here."

The Red and his companion laughed.

"What's amusing?" he asked.

"None comes willingly."

"Is that so?"

"But now you're here," the other soldier said, his tongue handling the colloquial Denovian much more easily, "we'd like to extend an invite for you to join your fellow Vested."

Leo nodded. "Fine. I have no family, no friends, no work, no income. I might as well be looked after by the state."

The two men smiled. "You're a strange one," the youngest said.

"So I'm told," Leo admitted.

"I'll take him," the companion said to the old Red. "You go on. Take my horse." He hopped down from the animal, retrieving his sword. "Hope I won't be needing this," he said to Leo, glancing at the blade.

"You won't. I haven't come here to make trouble," he lied.

The Red nodded and took his arm. "Come with me," he said.

Leo hated even being touched by one of the barbarian invaders. He shook the man off. "That won't be necessary. I have willingly offered myself."

"Orders," the man warned.

"I will walk into the camp without any trouble but don't push me, pull me; in fact, don't manhandle me at all."

"Or what?"

"Or perhaps I'll turn you into a rock; I told you I was Vested."

The man sneered.

"Or I know, I'll turn your tatua permanently green. How would you like that?"

This won the soldier's attention. "Do not *touch* the tatau!"

"Then do not touch me," Leo warned.

The man nodded, taking him a lot more seriously now. Leo was impressed that just the mention of magic seemed to have these simpletons believing him. If he could find his aegis, he would kill this man first as an example of his power. "What's your name?"

"Welf," the man replied.

"I won't forget it."

They walked in silence, veering off the seemingly haunted Royal Straight toward open fields.

"Where are all the people?" Leo asked.

"Which people?"

"The Barronese," he said, surprised.

The man gave a careless shrug with one shoulder. "No one lives here. They left a long time ago. Our emperor made this a compass where we brought, how should I say? . . . *your* people. As they grow in numbers, their families expand, we can accommodate them."

"Keep an eye on them, you mean."

The man shrugged again. "Either way, now that you're here you won't be leaving. Let's get you registered."

"What does that mean?"

"We check that you are genuinely Vested and then you are given a number, assigned accommodations. We find you work that suits your talents if you'd like, or more usually you are left alone to live as you choose."

Leo felt the first hole in his plan erupt. "How do you check my magic?"

"Through your blood," the man said, as though Leo was dim. "We have a blood taster. His name is Vulpan. He will know that you have magic."

Leo recalled Freath's warning with a stab of guilt that he quickly banished. "To what end?"

The soldier looked at him, baffled.

"I'm not complaining—after all, I came here—but I've never quite understood the concentration of Vested. Why bother gathering up these people? What's the end result?"

"I'm a soldier. I don't ask questions, I follow orders. But I suppose one reason is that should the empire ever be attacked, then we have, I suppose, an army of sorcerers."

"Army?" Leo echoed incredulously. "How many Vested are there?"

"Here, gathered and registered, it's getting close to three stacks."

Leo understood the slip into Steppes. He'd heard the term before. *Three hundred Vested were here and tested for having magic.* "That's impressive," he replied.

The man laughed. "You're strange," he accused. "Come on, it's just in here," he said, pointing.

They'd left the city center behind and the landscape had changed.

Leo noticed that they were approaching a barricaded area.

"This is your new home," the soldier said.

Behind the barricade it was like a beehive. Everyone was going about their own tasks; shops were open, the smell of fresh bread overlay the smell of human crowding. In the distance Leo could hear the clang of the blacksmith's and the bray from stables. Children and dogs played harmlessly.

But while everything looked normal, there was an unnatural quiet to what to all intents was a thriving community. The air should have been filled with voices and the sounds of their endeavors, but the atmosphere was leaden with what could only be described as a unified sorrow. Even the children at play appeared curiously quiet. Each Vested was dressed in identical robes, some shabbier than others—perhaps attesting to how long they'd been held here—but with no clarification in styling between men or women.

The single most distinctive sight, however, was the mark that everyone inside seemed to bear.

"That symbol," Leo murmured.

"It's how we would know should anyone from here escape." Leo stared, disturbed, as the man continued. "All children of Vested are regularly tested and given tatua if they show powers." He shrugged. "But the Vested have their own color—yellow—so they are not forced to belong to one of our tribes."

Leo stared, shocked.

"Still glad you came?" the soldier said, in a slightly mocking tone.

"Of course," Leo replied without hesitation, resolute that his crown depended on getting inside what he now realized was a guarded compound, nothing at all like the place of endeavor the rumor mill had led most in the empire to believe.

"A new one," Welf called out to the guard on duty.

"Name?" the fellow asked, entirely disinterested.

"Cadryn," Leo replied easily. *Battle king*, he translated from Ancient Set silently.

"From where?" the bored man inquired.

"Medhaven."

"You'll find plenty of company from there," he said, sighing and gesturing Leo through the gate. "You can take him through," he said to Welf. "Put him in the admissions building for full registration."

Welf nodded and with soft pressure on his arm, Leo was ushered into a whole new world of imprisonment.

In a quiet dwelling on the very rim of the Vested compound a young woman worked her plot. She had a way with vegetables that was nothing to do with her being Vested; she simply had an affinity for growing food. She also liked the peace of the plot; no one troubled her here and her small powers of forecasting were accepted and considered, for the most part, useless to the empire.

If she could just *see* the future that would be helpful, the revolting man called Vulpan had told her when he'd finished licking his lips clean of the blood he'd sucked from the webbing between her thumb and forefinger. The action of his putting her fingers on both his cheeks so he could get at this tender spot with his tongue and lips had been clearly carnal, and the sensation of his mouth on her had repulsed her. It was true that she had never been intimate with a man through choice, but even so, this oily creature feigning tenderness and polite manners hid what she could tell was a grasping nature. And what he most tried to hide—his underlying pleasure of his own evil intention—sickened her. Thankfully he could only linger with her for so long before he put a mark by her name to say she had been "tasted." She had read the runes to demonstrate her skill, and had predicted that Master Vulpan would suffer a toothache in the coming moon, which he had, much to her intense pleasure. Then a new mark had gone next to her name, confirming that she was indeed proven Vested, and with that came a third and final mark—this one on her forehead.

Being pricked and pierced by the sharp needles, the

wounds then being doused with colored ink, was the greatest injury of all. She could cope—even quietly accept—the loss of her freedom but the marking of her skin was something else. She wept most nights quietly into her pillow over this degradation in her always tense but very sheltered life.

Her garden plot was her escape and she was humming quietly to herself, not exactly happy but definitely not especially sad today, as she tended to some of the more aggressive weeds choking her new plantings. Nearly six anni she'd been here, picked up in a sleepy hamlet in Vorgaven where she'd fled to after the invasion. She'd managed to avoid attention for more than four years, working quietly in a distillery helping an old herbalist extract the liquor from various plants for his unguents and treatments. He was a popular man in Vorgaven, his preparations well known all over the former Set, even the Empress Valya swearing by his treatments for warts, apparently, although that was a closely guarded secret. She had felt safe with him, and he had treated her with just the right amount of distance combined with genuine regard for her well-being, which she was grateful for.

He had two apprentices and while they were both male and shared accommodation, as a woman she had a private room next door to where they stayed. It was an idyllic time. The herbalist was a quiet man and noticed her propensity for silence from the outset; it encouraged him to give her more and more tasks that brought her into closer contact with the more fascinating aspects of his work.

Now and then he would consult her about a plant and seemed impressed with her knowledge. His wife had died early and childless in their marriage and he showed no inclination to marry again, and certainly no interest in her, so this only added to the attraction of her situation.

Once only—and it was her downfall—did she quietly admit one day to the two apprentices that she could read the runes. They begged her to do a reading. She refused but they had persisted, badgering her daily until they wore her down. She gave them none of the dark news that she saw on the horizon; one would die in his thirty-seventh anni through accident, the other, seduced by liquor and womanizing, would never actually reach his full potential. That was another reason she hated performing readings; seeing the bad events was not reward enough for giving people positive news. But as she told her two companions the good things she saw for their lives she also foresaw her own demise. One of the apprentices she knew was intensely jealous of her relationship with the herbalist. It had not occurred to her that he would tell the authorities about their harmless fun.

With a heavy heart she packed up her few belongings, knowing it was time to move on. But she hadn't foreseen or counted on just how quickly the apprentice would act. Soldiers were at the doors of the distillery within hours and before she could even find tears, she was in a cart alongside men wearing tatua, being borne away from the place she had called home. She would never forget the herbalist's distress and how he'd raged at the soldiers who took her away.

Perhaps there was some affection after all; she'd often wondered about it. They could have been happy together with their strange relationship of respect and fondness, without the need to be intimate. And from the moment she'd waved her last goodbye, she realized she had loved him in her own curious way, never quite sure if it was for the father she'd never known or the potential husband she'd never thought to want.

Since then she'd kept her head down and lived an even quieter life, hardly communicating with anyone other than the woman called Reuth, who had been brought to the encampment only a couple of years ago with her children. Though she had hardly recognized the older woman, Reuth had recognized her immediately; after much prodding and prompting they had put together that they had been initially incarcerated together at Brighthelm. If not for the man called Freath and the help of Father Briar, they would likely not be alive today.

Freath had given her four years of freedom and a happy life and she had often wondered what became of him, living his dangerous double life. She couldn't imagine he had survived but the empire had flourished and life for most people—unless you were Vested—was unchanged if not much better for the arrival of the man who had once been hailed a tyrant.

It was Reuth who interrupted her quiet musings now.

"Are you there?"

"Out here," she called and as she stood to wipe her hands on her apron, a hint of a sensation she had only felt once before passed through her like a ghost. She trembled.

"Hello!" Reuth said, breezing down the garden. "How are the runner beans getting along?"

"Oh, it will be the usual fine crop," she stammered.

"What's wrong? You look unwell."

"It's nothing. Just a slight dizzy spell. I think I stood up too fast," she said and indeed the sensation passed so quickly, she could believe she had imagined it.

"At my age that's the norm even just getting up from my chair," her visitor said brightly.

"Children working?"

"Yes."

"Has it got worse for Ory?"

Reuth nodded, her chin trembling slightly. "Oh, look at me getting upset. I shouldn't be surprised with both Clovis and I being Vested."

She nodded. "But Lars has shown no sign."

"Not yet," Reuth said. "Won't you—"

"No, Reuth, I've told you before. What will be, will be. If you can't see it with your skills then my runes will tell us little."

"I'm sure you play down your skills, my girl."

"Think what you will. I grow better runner beans than I tell people's future, believe me."

Reuth admired the trellis and the plants growing strongly up them. "Well, you do have the best in the whole region," she admitted.

"Time for dinch?"

"Always." She followed her friend back into the hut. "I've got some new gossip too."

"Oh, good."

"A new and very eligible Vested bachelor has arrived,"

Reuth said triumphantly. Perl gave her a pained look and Reuth sighed. "Oh, come on, Perl."

"Reuth, stop. I've told you how I feel."

"No, you've fobbed me off with excuses." Reuth began to mimic her. "I don't like anyone here, there's too few men my own age, I still have feelings for my herbalist, I don't like being touched."

"It's true."

"Fair enough, but that shouldn't stop you enjoying marriage and children . . . and—"

"Both of those things involve touching."

Reuth grinned sadly. "Yes, they do. But you don't mind when I hug you."

"That's different."

"Oh," Reuth groaned. "He's very handsome and right about your age, I'd say."

"And what's more," Perl said, as though Reuth hadn't spoken, "look at me. Which husband wants his wife to wear a scarf permanently? Men like women's hair, Reuth."

Reuth sighed audibly.

Perl sighed privately. Her baldness alone would be hard enough for any man to look past but the strange birthmark was something else entirely. Her herbalist had tried several remedies to ease its intensity, with no results. If he had been shocked when she finally and very reluctantly permitted him to see her complaint, then he didn't show it. And she had loved him for that.

"I am not lonely, Reuth, and I don't live here wistfully hoping for my prince to come along," she said. "Life is just fine—well, I could make it better leaving here—but it's hardly unbearable. I have you, and Ory and Lars . . . you are my family."

"That's sweet," Reuth said and squeezed her hand. "Anyway, can you believe he just arrived moments ago, brazenly walking in and presenting himself to the gate?"

"He came willingly?"

Reuth nodded. "Handsome but stupid, obviously. What possessed him?"

"What's his name?"

"Cadryn, I think. They've taken him to the newcomers' section."

"And his meeting with Vulpan, Lo rot his soul!"

"Vulpan's not here, so he'll have to wait."

"Do you know everything that goes on here, Reuth?"

"I do my best. You never know when we can take advantage of information."

Perl poured the dinch, throwing a dry glance Reuth's way. "You continue to hope you can bring the empire down, don't you?"

Reuth sighed. "I've never given up hope. I'd love to hound every last one of the barbarians out of the Set."

Perl smiled indulgently. "I wish I had your vigor, sometimes." Reuth looked at her, perplexed. "You know, your energy and your anger is like sustenance to you. I'm sure it's what wakes you up each day and keeps you going."

Reuth nodded. "I have to look at life that way, Perl. Very soon now my beautiful child is going to have a tatua marked permanently on her forehead to brand her Vested. I live with the dream that one day we can return our land to a free one, a democratic one where everyone has the right to speak for themselves, lead their lives as they choose, use their magic if they possess it." She shrugged. "Surely you can't want anything different."

"I don't. I just don't have your strength or belief."

"That's because you allow yourself to be a victim. Sometimes you have to stand up to the bullies. I will keep searching for a weakness and I will exploit it fully. Anything that keeps the tatua from Ory's forehead is worth fighting for."

"How long do you think you have?" She pushed the mug forward to her friend.

Reuth blew on the hot dinch and sipped, the steam making her blink. "If she gets through this anni without being marked, I'll consider us lucky. They want to re-test her in the Freeze. I will keep hoping."

"I envy you your resolve and your optimism."

"Good, then you'll agree to meeting the newcomer, perhaps invite him over for some dinch," Reuth laughed.

Perl laughed too, but the nausea she had felt earlier nagged at her mind. The last time that had happened, she had been in the process of being escorted into the once proud Valisar stronghold of Brighthelm. And anything connected with the Valisars frightened her.

The Abbess sat and stared at both of them, dumbfounded.

"This is the truth, Mother," Corbel assured.

"But even she doesn't believe you," the older woman said, noting Evie's skeptical look.

"She's struggling to, that's true, but so far everything that has happened should be telling her that I am not lying. Her magic alone should inform her."

"This magic troubles me."

"Because of your faith. And that's understandable but, Mother, you have seen Valya returned to full health. You have to trust Evie's magic is real."

She nodded.

"That I can't dispute," Evie admitted. "Valya was seconds from taking her final breath."

"You cannot tell anyone about us," Corbel pressed.

The Abbess pondered. "Understand my position here, the . . . Oh what now? Yes, Marybel?"

"Visitors, Mother."

"More? What's got into everyone? It's like a continuous stream of callers. Does it need me? Can't you just give them alms?"

"Charity is not their reason for calling, Mother. And they've specifically asked for you."

"Oh very well, then, who are they?" She gave Corbel and Evie a look of apology.

"Two men, Mother. One very big."

She smiled. "Ah, I think I know who this is. It's been a long time." She turned back to her guests. "If you'd both wait I'd be grateful." She gave them a kind look and said gently, "It would be in your interest not to steal away."

"We understand," Corbel said, his hopes dashed.

"Come, Marybel, if I'm not mistaken these are good friends of ours."

Jewd grinned when the gate of the convent swung back to reveal the Mother.

"Ah, Heremon and Beven, I knew it would be you! Welcome, welcome. It's been too long."

"We're sorry about that, Mother," Kilt said, giving her a big kiss.

She giggled like a young girl. Jewd gave her a brief hug.

"I'd forgotten how tall you are, Beven."

"Or are you shrinking, Mother?" he replied and winked.

"Oh, go on with you. Which wind blows you both our way?"

"A very blustery one," Kilt admitted. Suddenly, with a shocked glance toward Jewd, he swayed and then staggered. Jewd caught him just before he fell.

"Lo, save us, what's happened, Beven?" the Mother asked. "Quick, Maribel, water please! And you'd better fetch Evie."

"I don't know," Jewd stammered, frowning. "Heremon!" He shook him. But worry overtook him as Kilt began to spasm in his arms. "Kilt . . . Kilt! Damn you. What's happening?"

"V . . . ar?" Kilt mumbled.

"What? Kilt, say it!" Jewd cried, anguished.

"Valisar!" Kilt choked out, convulsing. His body seemed to lose all control; he doubled over, retching and gagging.

Jewd swung around to the shocked and terrified gaze of the Abbess. "Is there a Valisar here?"

"What?"

"Valisar . . . one of the royals? A . . . child?"

"We have a baby here but it's not Valisar," she stammered out.

Jewd's lips pursed. "Actually, a young girl. Perhaps ten anni?"

"No, no one at all like that."

"Jewd," Kilt croaked, grappling at his friend's arm. "It's Valisar, it's getting worse."

"Jewd, Kilt, what are these names?" the Abbess murmured. "Ah, wait, wait, here comes Evie. She's . . . well, I'll let her tend to Heremon. If anyone can help, she can."

Kilt began to writhe as the woman called Evie approached. "Jewd!" he all but shrieked.

Without waiting another moment, confused and frightened for his friend, Jewd once again picked up Kilt, settled him in his arms and prepared to run from the convent.

"Wait!" the young woman yelled. "Don't move him, he could be injured."

"He's not injured. He's, he's . . ." He looked down. Kilt was slack in his arms. "Kilt!"

"Please, let me examine him," the dark-haired beauty asked. "My name is Evie and I'm . . . er . . . well, I'm a physic."

A tall man loped up behind her. There was something familiar about him but Jewd couldn't place it, couldn't even think. He really didn't know what to do. He looked back at the woman.

"Please put him down on the ground. He's not dead," she assured. "Look, even you can see his chest moving. But he's breathing in such a shallow way that it's not a good sign. Let me see to him," she urged again and Jewd was at last persuaded to place Kilt back down.

"Has he eaten anything suspect?"

Jewd laughed. "That's an odd question."

"Bad food," she snapped, "toxic in any way?"

Jewd looked around at his audience. "Who is this?"

"Just answer!" the man suggested. "Evie, a lot of the food in the inns and . . ." He shrugged.

"Has he been sick?" she persisted.

"He was trying to vomit," the Abbess offered.

Evie lifted up Kilt's shirt and placed her hand on his belly. Instantly, she pulled her hand back with a gasp as though she had been burned as Kilt came back to consciousness, screaming so violently that everyone leaped back. Both he and Evie began to heave helplessly.

In the cacophony of panic and voices calling to the two who were sickening, Jewd made the connection.

"You!" he said, pointing at Evie.

The woman looked around, trying to dry her mouth on the back of her sleeve. Her face was suddenly pale and she looked weak. "What's happening?" she murmured, struggling to get the words out.

But Jewd had Kilt by his ankle and without any further care began to run, dragging his helpless friend back deeper into the convent and away from the danger.

In the carriage following in Lily's wake, Piven gave Greven a look of sympathy. "I know you want to strike back at me but you have to accept it's not possible."

"If I could take my own life I would."

"I believe you."

"Why is he with us?"

Piven looked across at Vulpan. "I find his magic incredibly intriguing. What a find by Loethar. And I know he has no problem with switching allegiance, do you, Vulpan?"

"Not at all, your majesty. I always found Emperor Loethar to be rather . . . um, distant, for want of a better word."

"You see, already I am his sovereign in his heart. It's so much easier, isn't it, Vulpan, to offer obeisance to a Valisar than a barbarian?"

"Oh too true, majesty. I was always a loyalist," the man said, clearly not noticing the wry glance Piven threw at Greven. "But I was found and ordered to perform these services for the empire, like so many others. None of us had a choice but to dig in and get on with living beneath Loethar's rule."

"It doesn't seem to have done you any harm," Greven scorned.

"My skills are useful to the empire. I tell you I had no choice. It was provide them or die."

"I would choose death."

"Yes, this is now old ground, Greven. Don't be boring when we're cooped up in a small space," Piven admonished. "Let's talk instead about what we'll do when we catch up to Lily at the convent."

Greven eyed him. "She could be going anywhere."

"Yes, she could. But Stracker has already sent horsemen ahead to follow at a much closer distance. We know which carriage she was on, despite her silly wig, and if she alights before its final destination the soldiers will report back."

"Where's your dog?"

Piven laughed. "That's a very good description of him. He's riding with the horsemen tailing Lily. But I keep my dog on a very short leash. Stracker's not allowed to lay a finger on her. Our sweet and desperate Lily will lead us directly to the heart of the action—where the other Valisars lurk."

"Piven, you are delusional and your bedfellow is unhinged. I don't know how you reckon Lily knows anything about the Valisars. She spent most of her life in the forest."

"Well, you are connected to the Valisars, and you're her father."

"She didn't even know I was Vested! That's how much she knew."

"Ignorant, living in the forest and still she claims to be married to Kirin Felt within hours it seems of meeting him. It doesn't add up, Greven. Why would she put herself through all the trauma she did for a relative stranger? I think Lily was a puppet and someone else was pulling her strings. We now know Freath was taken by someone. If that party was cunning enough to whisk him away under the very noses of his own escort, then that same party would have been more than capable of keeping a close eye on Felt, Freath's partner. When Felt parted company with Freath I suspect whoever was watching them had him followed . . . and who better to follow—and get information from—an unattached man than a very attractive single young woman?"

"You're incredible!"

"I know."

"No, I mean, you're mad!"

"I was once. But not now, Greven. Now I'm seeing things clearly. Lily was someone's spy. I don't fully understand how or why Felt went along with her story but at some point he fell for her. And who could blame him? But my point is that whoever Lily was working for obviously had something to do with why Freath and Felt were in the north in the first place. And I suspect that person was aligned with the Valisars, because I know that's where Freath's loyalty lay."

"That's where we found the trail of the infamous outlaw Kilt Faris, your majesty." Vulpan spoke up. "I tasted blood he left behind during a skirmish in the woodland outside of Francham."

Piven turned with a look of intrigue. "The plot thickens, Greven. Perhaps our puppeteer was Kilt Faris."

"Why would Faris involve himself with royal squabbles?"

"I can't answer that," Piven admitted. "Not yet, anyway."

"Is that why we have the Green army trailing us?"

Piven shook his head. "That's all Stracker's doing. He's got a hunch that his half-brother is in the north, too, and he wants his Greens nearby so that when Loethar is humbled, they'll be there to witness his downfall."

"I don't know who I want to fall more, you or Loethar," Greven grumbled.

Piven stared out the window at the passing countryside as they began to bear west toward Lo's Teeth. "I was born near the mountains, you know. Well, the foothills anyway, north of Velis in Gormand. My mother came and got me after leaving me with a wet nurse for nearly a whole anni. I recall feeling confused and frightened to leave that woman but I was locked in my mind then and couldn't express myself. I have never been back." He sighed.

Greven ignored him.

"Do you know what I think?" Piven said after a long pause. He didn't wait for Greven to reply. "I think whoever the puppeteer is, he has been protecting my brother all of this time. And if that puppeteer is the wily Faris my father spoke of often, how fascinating is the proposition that Kilt Faris might have been harboring an heir to the throne of Valisar for all of the time that you harbored one too?"

Greven felt a yawning pit open in his stomach. He was in awe of the clever connections Piven could make but he feared it too. "You're just reaching now," he said, trying to sound disinterested.

"Am I? The more I think about it, the more I think Freath contrived to go north to meet with Leo. How or why he met his death really does baffle me, as does Felt's part in all of this but this, dear Greven, is why I am taking us north, following in Lily's footsteps."

"Because you think she'll lead you to Leo?" Greven asked, using a tone of disdain to cover his dread. What if Piven was right again?

"That's precisely what I'm hoping. And then it will be one claimant dead, one more to go."

"You're forgetting your sister," Greven said acidly.

"She's a child of ten at most. She's the least of my problems. Shall we sing, Greven? Remember how we used to sing when we walked through the woods collecting mushrooms? You said it made the journey shorter."

Greven looked at the youth and wondered how he could ever have loved him the way he had. If he could kill him, he would do it this second with his bare hands.

"Leave me alone," Greven said. Piven laughed and began the first strains of a repetitive tune Greven had taught him as a child. It disgusted Greven even more that Vulpan was smiling indulgently, moving his hands as though conducting Piven, encouraging him all the more.

Twenty-Four

―→―― ―←―

Evie had recovered to some degree but she was still looking very ashen. Corbel sat in the dust with her and the two nuns, all of them staring in shock at the cloisters the pair of new-comers had used as their escape.

"What just happened?" Corbel wondered aloud.

"That man," Evie said shakily. "Who was he?"

The Abbess shook her head, her hand covering her heart. "I don't think I can take much more of these events. Those were two men I've known for a number of years. I've only ever known them as Heremon and Beven, wealthy men who donate to the convent frequently. They have called upon us now and then when passing through the northeast. But today they were using different names."

"What happened to you, Evie?" Corbel asked.

"I . . . I can't really say. I was examining him. I lifted his shirt," she said, frowning as she recalled the events. "I wanted to check for swelling in his ab—" She glanced at the Abbess. "In his belly. As I touched him this immense sensation overwhelmed me." She stood. "I have to see him again."

"What? No!" Corbel said, holding her back.

She shook him free. "Let me go. You don't understand. I need him. I have to see him. I have to talk to him. I have to . . . have to . . ." Her face creased in frantic confusion. "He is mine to bond with," she said, her expression telling Corbel that she hardly understood what she was saying.

He reached for her but she was gone, lifting her skirt and running after them.

"Corbel, what is happening here?" the Abbess demanded.

"I don't have even the slightest clue," he said, and then he took off too, his long strides easily hunting down Evie, disappearing into the dark of the cloisters.

Kilt had regained his wits but still felt very weak and ill.

"Who was it?" he struggled, his breath coming in shallow gasps. "Which Valisar?"

"A young woman," Jewd replied. "How is that possible? You're sure this is the Valisar magic?"

"Have you ever seen me behave like this other than in front of Loethar?"

Jewd dragged him into what looked to be a small storeroom. "She and that man are hardly going to leave us alone, then. Think, Kilt, you're our hatcher of plans. You're going to need a good one to get us out of this situation."

Kilt looked around. He was slumped on the floor of a room containing fruit—mainly apples—that the convent obviously stored through the Freeze. Stocks were low by this time of the year and the apples looked very old and brownish.

"Smells nice," he remarked.

"Don't you dare start to joke around now. This is serious, Kilt. If that's who we think it is, then she—just like Loethar or Leo—has the ability to trammel you."

"I know, I know, it's just that the smell has made me want a cider. I'm parched."

"Stay parched. Think, damn you!"

"Bad news, Jewd."

"What now?"

"The sickness is returning. She must be coming close again. Tell her to stay back or I'll kill myself," he said, dragging a dagger from a strap around his thigh. "She'll believe it. Because if I'm feeling this, so is she. Go, tell her. I need distance to think. Get her away so I—" He couldn't finish; overcome by the presence of the Valisar royal approaching, he began to retch.

Jewd stepped out of the storeroom.

*. * *

Corbel had caught up with her. "Evie."

"I can't stop, I'm sorry. I don't—"

The big man, Jewd, stepped out of the shadows. He had an arrow levelled at Evie, his bow pulled taut. "Stop!" he said in the most reasonable of voices.

Corbel grabbed Evie. "Wait!" he yelled, trying to keep Evie still as she pushed against him.

"Get her away."

"All right, all right. Please. Do not loose your arrow."

"Then start moving."

Corbel wearied of Evie's struggles and picked her up in a bear-hug. It was easy enough. None of her protests were effective, simply irritating.

"Keep going," Jewd warned.

"We need to talk," Corbel said.

"There's nothing to discuss. We're not sticking around for a chat. I'll fight our way out if I have to," Jewd threatened.

"My sword's ready any time you want to take it on," Corbel said. He shook Evie. "Be still now!"

He'd never spoken to her like that ever and she instantly obeyed, looking almost perplexed as she regarded him.

"You reckon you're better than me and my arrows?"

"I'll take my chances."

"You're very cocky," Jewd snarled.

"You have a Penraven accent. Are you from there?"

"Why? Do you think you know my aunty?"

Corbel smiled without humor. "Does the name de Vis mean anything to you?"

Jewd lowered the bow slightly. He looked suddenly unsure.

"I am Regor de Vis's son, Corbel. I thought it worth mentioning only so you know my fighting pedigree."

The bow lowered even more. "You are lying."

"It's an outrageous lie if I am. Why would I lie about that? Why would I gamble on anything but the truth?"

"Because, *Corbel*, I happen to know your brother."

"Gavriel? Where is he?"

"Congratulations on knowing his name. Now I'm really

convinced. Hey, Kilt. Everything's fine," he yelled theatrically. "Apparently Gavriel's brother Corbel is out here and we're all going to be friends."

Evie began to struggle again. "I must see that man, I need to—"

Corbel scowled. "Give me a moment, will you?" he said to Jewd, and turned to Evie. "Your majesty, I'm going to ask for your most sincere forgiveness."

"Why?" she said angrily, trying to twist away from his grip.

Corbel pulled her close and, reaching nimble fingers around her neck, he muttered, "For doing this."

Evie collapsed and he caught her, laying her gently at his feet. He looked up. "We don't have long." Before Jewd could speak, he undid his sword belt, removed all his weapons and threw them to one side. "I'm unarmed. I need to talk to you."

Jewd looked surprised.

"I don't understand what's happening but it seems to me that you do. Now I've told you the truth about who I am. Do you really know my brother?"

"Yes. I saw him only days ago, in fact."

Corbel gave a nervous sigh that came out almost as a bleat.

"But you must be lying. Gavriel is not yet thirty anni. You look well past that."

Corbel nodded sadly. "It's a long story and it involves the Valisars, as I suspect you have guessed."

"What makes you say that?"

"If you know my brother you know of our connection to the former royals."

"And current ones."

Corbel frowned but before he could reply Evie began to stir.

"Tell me that isn't the Valisar princess," Jewd said.

Corbel hesitated. If Jewd and his friend were already aware of Evie's presence perhaps they were not enemies. And if they were, there was no point in keeping up the pretense. He sighed. "I would have to lie to you, then," he replied.

Jewd rolled his eyes and dropped all tension on the bow's string. "Lo damn you!" he cursed.

Corbel wasn't ready for this. "I don't understand."

"You have to get her away from Kilt."

"What do you mean? And be quick—you have to explain to me what's going on before she wakes up or we're going to be right back where we started."

"In a nutshell, then." Jewd pointed at Evie. "That's the Valisar princess, hungry for her aegis. In there," he pointed, "is my closest friend for the past thirty-six anni. He is an aegis. But she's having him for dinner only over my dead body. Do we understand one another?"

Corbel frowned. "No."

Jewd took a step toward him.

"Wait, I don't know what you're talking about. Why would she want to eat him? Who is he to her? I didn't even understand the word you used. Ayjess? What's that?"

"Do you jest?"

Corbel shook his head. "Can we just sit down and—"

"No more talking, de Vis. Your brother's thrown his lot in with Leo and is hunting my friend. Loethar wants him too and now she does also. You can all go and—" He stopped. "What's so funny?"

"Behind you."

Jewd never had the opportunity to discover what Corbel meant. Barro hit him so hard with a club of timber that the big man fell like a stone.

"That was fun," Barro admitted.

"I thought you'd never come."

"The Abbess found me and pointed me in the right direction. Though I'll admit I didn't understand most of what she was muttering."

Evie was coming to fully. Corbel knew he had to move fast. "Barro, I need you to do something for me. It means defying the princess and whatever orders she gives you."

"Why?"

"I'll explain everything later. But right now we need lots of rope."

* * *

Later, with Jewd tied up but his head being seen to by the nuns of the apothecary, and Evie equally restrained and behind a locked door, Corbel finally entered the storeroom to confront Kilt Faris. The outlaw was sitting up, and though he looked dazed he certainly had his wits about him.

"Corbel de Vis, I presume?"

"Correct."

"Even if I hadn't heard who you were, just looking at you tells me who your father is. And there's no doubting who your reckless brother is either."

"I'm the handsome one," Corbel said dryly.

Kilt gave a tired chuckle. "So I'm now your prisoner?"

He shook his head. "I don't need encumbrances."

"Then you plan to give me to her?"

"Her name is Genevieve. Before I do anything I want you to explain everything to me."

"Where is she?"

"Well away from you."

"It can never be far enough. I can feel her presence. Her magic reaches through stone for me."

"Then you need to be quick. I need to understand what we're up against here."

Kilt shook his head. "Where have you been?"

Corbel slid down the wall to sit opposite him. "A long way away for a long time."

"Then I have a long story for you."

"Lo, I'm parched. Is it me or does this make you want to swallow a cider?"

Kilt laughed. "I'll tell you everything I know."

All of Leo's nerves were on edge. He was desperate to feel even the slight giveaway tingle that might suggest he was in the presence of the Valisar magic. So far he'd been asked a series of questions by an older man who looked more like a civil servant than one of the barbarians. He'd explained that he was one of the former realm's nobles. When his lands and assets had been seized by Loethar's people he was given the choice of dying for his Crown or living for the new regime.

"I'd had a lot of disagreements with our sovereign anyway, and I wasn't going to lose my family over what I had begun to believe actually had nothing to do with Barronel." The man looked embarrassed as he said this, not meeting Leo's eyes. "We were the innocents, caught up in the emperor's bid to demonstrate to Penraven that he could crush and overrun any realm he chose. We were an example, you could say, that he set for Brennus's interest."

"How did you know?" Leo asked.

"There were a lot of rumors coming out of the Steppes that the young hot-headed new chieftain had some sort of personal vendetta with Brennus. But our king ignored the information and trusted Penraven because he was very thick with Brennus—trusted him implicitly—and it's true the Valisar king had never even set foot on the plains."

"But you believed it all the same."

He shrugged and nodded. "One of the merchants who brought the information of the east was a man I knew and liked. He had no reason to lie. But mine was one small voice among too few, and because my disagreement with our own king was widely known about everyone thought I was being affected by that."

"But you fought," Leo insisted, quite convinced he would kill the man with his stylus if he said he'd given up on that as well.

"Of course I fought!" he said indignantly. "I was loyal to the Crown, even though our General Marth believed we were getting involved in a hopeless war, one that Barronel could not win. In the end our king surrendered, which was the right thing to do, given the circumstances. Our soldiers had been massacred. I lost all my sons. My wife was never the same. I think she eventually died of heartbreak rather than a sick heart as the physic declared."

"Well, I suppose you're happy that Ormond lost his life."

"No! Not at all and certainly not in the way his body was defiled. Ormond wasn't a bad man; he was even a good and beloved king. His ties to Brennus were perfectly natural and I'd be lying if I didn't say our realm benefited hugely from their friendship. But he was blind to the truth and made errors in judgment. His best decision was to surrender." He sighed. "Such old history. Forgive an older man his indulgence."

"Not at all, sir. We are all in much the same boat."

"Alas, you don't have your freedom, young man. I hear you offered yourself up. What's in your head?"

"It was getting tedious staying on the run and living wild." He shrugged. "At least now someone will feed, clothe and keep me warm. It's no longer my problem."

The man gave a nod of surprised agreement. "I suppose that is a way of regarding your situation."

"What happened to General Marth?"

"He was murdered by Stracker's mob, despite the surrender. It was a terrible time. All of Ormond's family was slaughtered."

"But here you are working for the barbarians," Leo remarked.

"I often daydream of breaking free of their shackles. The problem is the empire is prospering and people seem content with Loethar's rule."

"Except here," Leo said.

"Yes, except here. Though most of the Vested are quite helpless there are also a few who think themselves militant."

"Really?"

The man nodded. "There's a woman called Reuth who never lets the rest of the Vested forget what has happened to them. Both her husbands have been killed—the first in the initial wave of interest in the Vested, and then her second not so long ago actually. Her losses keep the fire in her belly well stoked, as I'm sure you can imagine. Actually Reuth's a good person for newcomers like yourself to talk to—she's full of help. Look out for her."

"I will," Leo said. "Are we almost finished here?"

"Just about. We have all the details you've given us and at some stage we do look into them but your next stage is to be tasted by Master Vulpan. It's revolting but it seems to work and it's all over quickly so don't be too unnerved by it."

"Vested turned viper. His name suits him."

"Indeed, but don't say that too loud. I've just got one last question to ask you. What magic do you claim to possess?"

"Well, it's a strange one, I'll grant you—and not that much use in an everyday way—but I suspect the authorities will be intrigued. I'm connected in a curious magical way to royalty and those who rule."

The man's head flew up, his expression shocked. "What?"

"Yes, I feared that reaction."

"Explain yourself."

Leo feigned embarrassment. "Look, it's hard to explain but they say the heir to the throne—Leonel, is that his name?"

The man nodded dumbly.

"They say he disappeared ten anni ago."

"All believe him dead."

"Quite. Well, I know he's not. He's alive and has been hiding out in Penraven for all of the time. I don't really know where but I see him in my dreams all the time. The forest I think is where I saw him last."

"You see him?"

Leo nodded, helplessly enjoying the man's look of bafflement. "I hear him talk too. He talks about killing the emperor."

"Lo, strike me!"

"And I think there was another member of the family that was an invalid."

The man nodded. "The youngest son. He was adopted. Not really Valisar but," he shrugged, "he was very popular I gather. A charming sort of child from what I heard. A sort of smiling idiot you could say, but a very sweet boy."

"And everyone believes he too disappeared."

"Perished is probably more to the point. He was just a little boy of around five anni when he disappeared, wandered off into the woodland near the palace. I mean, his parents were dead, brother gone; no one was really looking after him I suppose and I doubt very much whether anyone cared anyway."

"I shall shock you again, sir. He is alive. And far from an invalid."

The man stared at him with a narrowed gaze, an angry set to his mouth. "Oh, this is preposterous."

Leo shrugged. "He was taken south. He's now very able and also very keen on the throne."

"Is this some kind of a joke? Because if so Vulpan will soon see through—"

"No joke at all, sir. I'm deadly serious. The emperor should be made aware of it."

"Oh I doubt very much whether the emperor would be at all frightened by this . . . this frankly unbelievable news of yours. And in any case he is very well protected. He has an army behind him. Look around you, Cadryn. These are all loyal soldiers. No one can touch him."

"Is that so? Then I'm not sure how you explain that the emperor has gone missing, captured in the forest."

"Young man, you are—"

"I'm telling you only what I see. You asked me my magic. This is it. I see the Valisars and those closely connected to them. Check the facts if you don't believe me, sir. I think if you ask in the right circles you may find some embarrassed answers from the emperor's men. I'll bet no one knows where exactly he is right now and that will be because I know he has been captured by a Davarigon."

"You've seen this?"

Leo nodded. "As clear as I see you sitting before me, sir. He is her prisoner."

"Hers!"

"Yes, sir, a woman."

"Wait! You said you dreamed about Valisars. Why do you dream about Loethar?"

"Because he rules," he said evasively. "And by the way, if anyone is looking for Gavriel de Vis—that is, the son of Regor de Vis, deceased Legate to our former king—they'll find him probably traveling in cohorts with the Davarigon."

"Right," the man said, standing abruptly. "You are coming with me. As much as I want to, I can't ignore this news."

"Well, actually you can, sir."

The man paused, suspicious. "And what's that supposed to mean?"

"You can write down anything you like as regards my magic. Is your blood taster here?"

The man shook his head. "He's in Penraven."

"Then we're in no immediate hurry. I have time."

"Time to what?"

"General Marth, do you really think you could keep up this disguise?"

The man sat down again, looking around fearfully. "Keep your voice down. What did you just say?"

"You heard me. I must admit I never for a moment thought I'd have a stroke of luck like this."

"Young man, I think you've made a mistake."

"No, sir, I have not. I have a perfect memory for faces and you are General Marth of Barronel. How you have kept this a secret from the invaders must make a good story."

"I don't recognize you at all. Should I?"

"You should, yes, but I doubt you could. I was perhaps ten when I was presented to you."

"Presented?"

"Yes, general, at Brighthelm, during one of the gatherings of the Set. All the royals brought their closest aides, their families. If Loethar had done his homework properly, he would have known far less blood needed to be shed if he'd simply struck one of these lavish occasions. He could have killed all the royals of all the realms in one fell swoop."

"And what were you in the palace? A page, a messenger, a stablehand, what?"

Leo laughed. "No, sir. I was attached to the royal retinue."

"One of that man Freath's team, eh?"

"He was one of mine, more like."

The general blinked.

"I shall put you out of your misery because time is against us. I am Leonel, true Valisar King of Penraven."

The man stared at him, dumbfounded.

"Close your mouth, sir. We don't want to attract attention, now do we? I can prove it; ask me anything about the Valisar household. I was privy to a lot of my father's private information, the sort he would have shared with King Ormond."

The general couldn't help himself. "There was a pact—a plan that went to hell it seems once the barbarian horde struck. It was between Ormond and Brennus. What was it called?"

Leo nodded. "Their code for it was Biramay—after the sweet dessert liquor they were both partial to but one needed an acquired taste for. I myself loathe it."

The general's eyebrow arched. "What was the name of the horse Brennus gifted to Ormond at the birth of his third child?"

Leo frowned. "Frolic . . . er no, forgive me, that was for his second. It was Nightmoon. I chose the name," he said, shrugging.

Marth sat back and regarded Leo somberly. "Something happened in their childhood—as princes—that made Ormond and Brennus special friends. Very few people know."

"I do, sir. There was a picnic in Barronel. The royal children were playing on the lake near the palace. They were forbidden to take out a boat but they defied their minders. There were three of them. Your king, my father and another high ranking noble's child—a daughter I seem to recall. The boat capsized. Ormond was a good swimmer and saved my father's life but they never spoke of it outside the immediate families because he chose to save my father over the child of Barronel, who drowned."

The general nodded, looking stunned. "This is just not possible."

"I think I've just proven it is."

"But why have you decided to declare yourself now?"

"That really is a tall tale, sir. But in short, when Leothar conquered the Set I was child. I had to wait to grow up before I could make a real challenge. And now everything I've told you about Loethar is true. He has been taken. The empire is now being run by Stracker, except no one probably realizes this yet, and I don't think even Loethar would stomach that."

"Absolutely not. I don't think any of us would."

"Us, sir?"

"Those of us who have learned to accept Loethar's rule. The people."

Leo smiled. "Well, why don't you do some digging around

to see that the new information I've given you is true. In the meantime can you make it possible for me to roam the compound?"

Marth looked back at him quizzically.

"You know: meeting the others here, getting to know all the different areas. I'm actually looking for people I might have known once. I'm sure the person you mention—Reuth—could help."

The former general looked relieved, Leo knew, because his request sounded innocent enough. "Yes, of course. And I will see what I can discover. You are still an inmate of the compound er . . . Cadryn."

"Of course. Calling me your majesty is probably a fraction presumptuous yet."

Marth blinked uncertainly.

"General Marth," and Leo paused as the man looked around, worried, "I won't call you that again, I promise. I do understand that I am not your sovereign. But you need to keep in mind that you have no sovereign any longer. If all of Ormond's immediate kin was slaughtered then a royal family exists no more. You might as well throw your support behind Barronel's closest ally."

"Who should have come to our aid when we cried out for it!" the older man growled.

"I understand why you might think that. But you must remember that it was war. I cannot know all that was going on in my father's mind, but neither do I think I should be held responsible for his decisions. And I can assure you that our only chance to depose Loethar is through our union. If I can win back my throne, who is to say Barronel's Crown cannot be reinstated through a distant family line, or Vorgaven's, or Cremond's?"

His companion snarled. "Cowards that they were!"

"Dregon, Gormand, then? Each realm has its own sorrows. We have to start somewhere. And right now you have a king sitting before you, not an heir. On my father's death I assumed his crown. I watched him die, Marth. I knew from that moment I had become king and my right to rule has burned with a passion the same way that you describe Reuth's belly still burning from the loss of her husbands. You've lost sons and a wife. It is surely worth their memory to at least undermine Loethar. Do you want to be remembered only as the man who surrendered to a barbarian?"

He watched the old soldier fight the emotion wrestling inside; his lips moved with his internal battle.

"Marth, my family sword has been buried for safekeeping not far outside the city's entrance. Will that help convince you? That and the confirmation that Loethar is not available for any meetings, any orders, any form of communication?"

"You are not Vested, are you?" Marth asked with a heavy voice.

Leo smiled evasively. "I could be."

It was clear Marth didn't believe him but regardless he nodded as though resigned. "Tell me where to find the sword."

"Give me that stylus. I will draw a map of where to find Faeroe. The rest is up to you."

"All right, Cadryn, I will give you access to the whole compound. I'll take your map. I'll look into your claims. And I will find you. If any of this is a lie, you will disappear from this camp and it won't be because you were allowed to walk out of it. You will be buried somewhere in an unmarked grave."

Leo nodded. "So be it. But for now find me Reuth."

Kilt looked back at Corbel gravely. "That's the most outlandish tale I've ever heard. It would make an excellent bedtime story for childen."

"Making fun is not—"

"I'm not making fun. I'm simply astonished at the breadth of Brennus's vision and his cunning . . . but mostly his ruthlessness. I should no longer be surprised by the emerging Leo. Blood will out."

"What's that supposed to mean?"

"Simply that his desire to wear the former crown of Penraven outweighs all empathy. He is his father's son."

Corbel nodded. "I do not know Leo any more. I knew only the lad. But given what Brennus demanded of me I think we can safely say that the king was able to sacrifice empathy for what he believed was his duty as a Valisar. And still he was a good sovereign to his people."

"I hate to say it but Loethar is better."

Corbel's head snapped up.

Kilt shrugged. "It's true. If you had the time I'd make you canvass as many ordinary people as you cared to in any part of the old realms. I'd stake my life that almost all of them—peasant to merchant to noble—will say that life under Loethar's rule has been good . . . better even than under Brennus."

"How can you say that when he's a barbarian? An impostor, a tyrant—"

Kilt held up a hand to stem the barrage, his tone patient. "Corbel, if you think your story had the capacity to shock, what I shall now reveal will stun you. It did me and I am not easily stunned."

"Go on."

"Loethar is no impostor. He is the first son of Darros and as much a Valisar as Brennus with, I might add, a far stronger claim on the throne than Brennus or Leo."

Corbel stared at him, his face a mask. The silence lengthened.

"I am not lying to you," Kilt continued. "I have no reason to."

"How can you prove that?"

"You accept the Valisar magic? You've witnessed what happens to Genevieve . . . to me? I've explained to you all about my difficult relationship with Leo and I've given you as much as we know about the aegis magic."

Corbel's expression turned pensive, his voice sounding perplexed. "I'm coming to terms with it," he said slowly. "There is no explanation for Evie's behavior; she looked to be in some sort of pain and yet she couldn't keep away from you."

Kilt had regained enough of his composure to wink. "I'd like to claim it's my irresistible charm or my dashing looks. Alas, though I do have both of those, it is the call of the magic that draws Genevieve to me. I can explain it only one way—it feels like a tortured rapture. It hurts more than I describe but you want more and more. If Jewd hadn't dragged me away I would have just given myself to her."

"Meaning?"

"She could have done whatever she wanted with me."

"And it will always be like this between you?"

He nodded. "And any other untrammeled aegis, I suspect. I could resist Leo. His magic is all but not there; he never once suspected who I was although it still hurt me to be around him. But I quickly learned to cope and taught myself how to resist the magic's pull. The princess is brimming with a magical force I have never encountered previously. I have no chance against her. I would simply drown in her magic."

"You would let her maim you?"

"Not happily but willingly, if she is near enough."

"But you and she were next to one another. How come she didn't react? It was only when she touched you that her response began."

Kilt frowned. "I can only put that down to her being taken away from this plane before her magic woke fully. Touching an aegis awakened it, I'd guess, like suddenly igniting a flame in a barn of straw."

Corbel blew out his cheeks with a big sigh. "And so now you're going to tell me that you have reacted the same way to Loethar."

"I hate to be predictable but yes. My reaction to him was less hysterical, I suppose, than to the princess but it was the strongest I've ever felt. Even Brennus, all those years—his magic was very weak, like Leo. Anyway, that's why I'm here and on the run. Loethar nearly had me in his clutch and Leo saw that and got the same idea."

"And Gav's with Leo," Corbel said, thinking aloud.

"The last I saw."

"We were called back through magic. Do you know what is expected of us?"

"I suppose only that fellow Sergius you've told me about can explain that. I can't guess, other than for Genevieve to attempt a coup."

"Putting Evie on the throne by force?"

Kilt shrugged. "I can't imagine her father went to all the effort of hiding her simply because he was so in love with his hours-old daughter. He was very calculating, both as a man and as a ruler. So," he sighed, "I suspect she was sent away to be kept safe, so that she could rule if her brother couldn't. As a contingency."

"She will not want the throne."

"But you knew that before you returned. So I presume you don't care what she wants. If you're anything like your brother you're all about duty."

Corbel scowled at him. "That's not how it is."

"It is, de Vis," Kilt said wearily. "You surely didn't think being brought back meant there would be a parade and people flinging flowers for Genevieve to tread on all the way to her coronation, did you? Genevieve smiling indulgently as she is crowned beloved new queen?" He kept his tone kind although the words were sarcastic. "At the back of your mind you had to believe there was a fight waiting."

Corbel gave an angry groan. "I don't want her life threatened."

Kilt made a soft scoffing sound. "And now you're just deluding yourself. You knew from the moment she was given to you as a newborn that her life was threatened. But you weren't emotionally attached to her then. Now you clearly are," he said lightly. "It's harder to risk someone you . . . care about." He smiled. "And yet risk her you have because it is your sworn duty."

"We were not living a real life. When I recognized the magic reach out and call to me I had to answer it. I didn't have a choice."

"Didn't you?" Kilt broke the awkward pause that followed by hauling himself to his feet. "Lo, but I'm getting very weary of how this Valisar magic leaves me so helpless. I think I would happily kill all the Valisars myself if it meant ridding myself of this weakness . . . not that I can get within howling distance of them with a weapon." He winked at Corbel. "Come on, de Vis. It's no good moping. Something very strange was happening at Brighthelm a day or so ago and it involved the throne. We have to make some decisions. I think another Valisar has crept out of the woodwork."

Corbel looked at him from where he still sat. "There isn't one."

"Well, I'm afraid that doesn't wash at all. We didn't know Loethar was Valisar, did we? And yet Valisar he is. No one knew that the princess was alive and well and capable of claiming the throne, and yet here she is. Leo has always spoken fondly of Piven and we don't—"

"Piven?" Corbel shook his head and stood easily. "Piven was lost in his mind. He was a complete invalid. If it wasn't for his mother he would have been kept on a leash or caged. It beggars belief that he didn't kill him."

"Indeed. But now we could hazard that he perhaps felt a vague family connection, especially as Leo tells us that Piven was so affectionate to Loethar. The boy was no threat, after all, clearly a helpless innocent." Kilt flashed a wry glance at Corbel and his mouth twisted into a brief crooked grin. "Or was he? Has he got everyone fooled?"

"Impossible!" Corbel snapped.

"I'm telling you, de Vis. I have no control over how I respond to Valisar magic. And there *was* a Valisar in the square yesterday; it was a male and he wasn't scared of anyone. He sounded like Leo, but younger. I can assure you it wasn't Loethar."

"It wasn't Piven," Corbel growled, but he no longer looked as sure.

Kilt gave a small shake of his head. "Fair enough, but if you follow that theory, you now have a fifth Valisar running around—a dangerous one, by the sounds of things. And he's in the capital and he's got an aegis already trammeled, from the little I could tell. That spells real trouble for everyone."

"What do we do?"

Kilt had been thinking of nothing else since he regained his wits. "I need some time to think. Will you give me that?"

Corbel nodded, his expression somber.

"I'm going for a walk. I will not disappear, I give you my word," he said, holding out a hand. Corbel took it. "Tell my large companion Jewd—who will likely be foaming at the mouth with rage—that I'm sorry and I'll be back shortly."

He left Corbel in the storeroom looking confused and staring at its contents.

Twenty-Five

Leo walked with Reuth through a small orchard. They were alone; Marth had seen to it. "Be warned," he'd cautioned Leo.

Reuth, looking surprised to even be introduced to the newcomer so soon, had turned to Leo. "What was that about?"

"You'll understand after we've spoken," he had said cryptically and then proceeded to ask her a number of questions about her life, her loyalties, and most importantly, her despairs and dreams. Satisfied that Marth had been correct to mention her as a potential ally, he had told her his story.

As it had unfolded and mid-morning had passed through midday well into the afternoon, Reuth had become pale. Even the few questions she'd asked began to give way to a stunned silence as the gravity of what she was learning began to sink in.

After Leo had finished with his reason for being in Barronel, he'd given her time to digest everything.

He felt the silence between them become pensive.

"How can I trust this?" she whispered.

"Why else would I give myself up to the authorities?"

"I don't know—I certainly can't understand willing incarceration!" she snapped.

"I'm offering you a chance to fight back, Reuth."

"I don't see how one man—exiled king or not—can make a difference." She turned away. "We are not soldiers or fighters; we have no weapons—"

"You have magic," he insisted.

Reuth swung back. "Yes . . . some people can actually make the plants grow faster, others can predict the rain, or talk backward, or have an impossibly amazing memory that cannot be tripped up. I know someone here who can make a ladle stir a pot without having to lift a finger—although she has to then recover for more than a day from the headache it provokes. I can see just how jolly useful stirring pots and making plants grow can be when it comes to overthrowing a tyrant with a powerful army and the majority of support from the very people he has cowed!"

Leo stared at her. The deep breaths she was taking revealed just how helpless she felt, nor could her stinging words disguise the passion she tried so hard to cover. Oh yes, Reuth wanted revenge all right . . . and he had the means to give her that revenge.

He smiled. "It would take only one of you . . . if I can find the right person."

She looked at him as though he had lost his mind. "What are you talking about? One of us?"

Leo nodded. "A very particular person. Vested, secretive, probably unassuming; in fact the least obvious person you could imagine may well be the most powerfully endowed person in this camp."

"I don't understand," she whispered, but Leo could see her desperation to believe in him, to nibble from the carrot he seemed to be enjoying dangling before her.

Before anything more could be said, Marth found them again.

"Well?" Leo said.

"It is all as you promised."

"Do you believe me?"

"Have I a choice?"

Leo impaled the man with a steely glare. "Do you think I'm lying about anything I've told you?"

Marth shook his head without hesitation. "I am with you."

Leo nodded once. "Thank you." He turned back to Reuth. "Now," he began more gently. "I know you don't understand because I haven't explained it fully. Have you heard of the aegis magic, Reuth?"

Her frown deepened. "No."

"Then let me explain."

Later, when Leo finally paused, Reuth looked even more dumbfounded than she had earlier.

"How do you know it works?"

"I've watched its effect on an aegis and a Valisar."

"Which Valisar? There aren't any alive except you or your adopted brother."

Leo hesitated, covering his error with a blink. "I meant me." He cleared his throat and moved quickly on. "I had an aegis within my grasp just a day or so ago. I—"

"Then why didn't you—what was the word?"

"Trammel?" he offered patiently.

"Yes. Why didn't you trammel that Vested, seeing as you are old enough, look strong enough, felt secure enough and clearly don't lack for arrogance."

"Careful, Reuth," Marth counseled. "You're talking to the Valisar king."

Reuth laughed. "And look how scared I am! Besides, he is not a king, he is a man who believes he has the right to claim kingship. The last I took notice we were living under an emperor." She turned to Leo. "I didn't even have the chance to hug my husband farewell. While you were safely hidden he was dragged from my side and unceremoniously slaughtered in some dingy outhouse of your palace by Stracker and his thugs. Don't talk to me about respect for the Valisar throne. You Valisars did *nothing*; nothing to save the other realms and nothing to save your own! Your father let all of us take the consequences of his inaction."

She poked Leo in the chest, unafraid. "In the early days I cared about the Valisar name. Really I did. But since I've lost my second husband, since my children and I were transferred here, treated as prisoners, I've come to believe that it doesn't matter who is ruling when no one is looking out for the helpless. And I am helpless, as are most of us Vested. My ability to predict the weather accurately has been enough to have me incarcerated and tattoed, my children growing up as prisoners in a downtrodden camp of people who have no use until an upstart comes through with a claim on the throne and a grand idea to use one of us to further his own importance." She spat on the ground and then impaled him with a glare. "Why didn't you grab hold of your own sorcerer the other day?"

Leo felt as though he'd just been chastised like a child getting his letters or numbers wrong. This older woman wasn't at all impressed or in awe of him or his title or his pedigree. He felt his cheeks burn with humiliation as he realized that no one would take him seriously until he stopped believing that everyone owed him their fealty.

Freath had tried to explain it, Kilt had angrily told him much the same and then Gavriel—his most loyal friend, someone who considered Leo's safety more important than his own—had conveyed the identical message. It was time now for honesty with himself, he realized; time for him to really behave as a king should. He knew his mother would want him to lead by example and his father would expect him to brutally take control and prove his leadership skills, not simply expect people to follow because of his name, or his bloodline. But Brennus would tell Leo that he must be cunning. And so Leo told himself that so long as he convinced people of his sincerity, he was giving them what they wanted while at the same time achieving what needed to be done . . . for the good of the Valisar throne.

He looked down, striking a humble tone. "I wasn't quick enough, Reuth. I have been outwitted at every turn. An aegis is constantly hiding his or her magic; they've spent a lifetime concealing the truth. I don't know what I'm doing; I don't recall my father ever seeking his aegis and so I have no experience with this whole notion of magic. I don't even know if this trammeling can work but I'll be damned if I'll just grow old in the forest, hiding from the soldiers, forgiving myself my fear of declaring myself. Better to die on the end of the blade fighting for my birthright than to fade away an old man who spent his life wondering."

Marth shifted uncomfortably where he stood; Leo sensed

he had the general on his side. But it seemed Reuth wasn't ready to give up fighting back yet.

"Why haven't you tried any earlier?" she demanded. "You speak as though you have wanted revenge against Loethar since the day of his arrival into Penraven."

"I have," Leo said quietly, recalling how Loethar used a soft voice to intimidate. It worked; she bit back on whatever retort sprang to her mind. "But I was a child for the first five anni and the last five have been spent maturing, finding the right moment to strike." He was pleased with that; it sounded not only reasonable but almost like an admonishment.

"And this is it?" she asked and he saw a glitter in her eye that told him Reuth simply needed a worthy, reliable excuse to help attempt a coup.

He nodded. "This is it," he answered gravely. "I happen to know that Loethar is under siege." He held up a hand to stop more questions. "Forgive me, I have no time to explain everything, Reuth. In this you must trust me. I know that Loethar is on the run."

"Stracker," she breathed. It was not a question but Leo answered as though it was.

"Yes, his half-brother has taken over the rule of the empire. No one has realized it yet but by the time they do it could be too late. Now, during these days of confusion, while Stracker is keen to keep the compasses peaceful while he shores up his allies, it is the perfect time for any loyalist of the Valisar throne to strike. He will not expect it."

"But what makes you think we have the solution . . . here, in sleepy Barronel?"

"I can't be sure you do but I had to start somewhere. If Loethar has spent the last decade rounding up everyone Vested, there's a good chance that I'll find an aegis here."

Reuth looked between the two men, astonished. "And now I see you trust him," she said, cocking her head toward Marth.

"I do," Marth replied. "Are you going to help, Reuth? No one here knows the Vested better than you. You've made it your business to know everyone, be trusted by everyone . . ."

"Even you," she said harshly.

He nodded. "And I have never treated you badly."

She looked back at Leo. "What am I looking for?"

He gave a mirthless smile. "Therein lies the key. I don't know because an aegis, whomever he or she is, will cover his or her tracks so well as to be almost invisible. But if I were an aegis I would probably live alone, certainly quietly. I would prevent people from getting to know me terribly well." He shrugged. "That way I wouldn't let anything slip about the very topic that I'm working so hard to keep secret. Remember, the aegis spends his or her life protecting this secret, always on guard. So perhaps someone who is hard to penetrate or read, someone who shrugs off his or her magical talent, playing it down as not being magical, simply a learned skill."

He paused. Reuth was nodding. "Unfriendly, withdrawn, quiet," she recited. "Most likely a man?"

He shook his head. "No. Neither man nor woman is more likely. It could be you, Reuth, or it could be that young lad over there stealing pears from the orchard."

"How many of these people are there?" Marth asked.

Leo shrugged. "Perhaps three," he said carefully, avoiding the truth.

"One for you," Reuth counted. She looked at him, baffled, clearly unable to go on.

"Another for my father," he continued without hesitation. "My father didn't trammel an aegis so his, whoever it is, lives on quietly. And the same goes for my sister."

"The princess who died . . . of course," she replied sadly. "So an aegis was born for her too."

"Yes." Leo was glad he didn't have to mention about Loethar or Piven.

Reuth seemed lost in her thoughts. "I was taken into Brighthelm the day your sister was cremated. It was the same day my husband was murdered."

Leo's breath caught in his throat. "The day my sister was cremated was the very day I first felt the presence of an aegis. I didn't know it at the time and I was young, frightened, but I've felt the sensation again since, but not nearly as strong as on that occasion."

Reuth looked at him quizzically. "And you'd not felt it previously around the palace?"

"Never."

"Well, to my knowledge there was only one largish group of Vested who were brought into Brighthelm that day."

His hopes flared. "What can you tell me?" he urged.

"That plenty more than half disappeared almost immediately. And who knows how many of that big group were slaughtered within moments of their arrival." He watched her purse her lips as she reined in her emotion.

"I am sorry about your husband, Reuth . . . about both of them."

She moved on. "The rest of us were taken to a holding room in the palace proper and that's where we met Freath. When he chose Kirin and Clovis as his helpers, we all thought we were going to be killed. Freath was so sinister. But as it turned out I judged him badly. The rest of us were to be killed but he found a way to save us . . . all eight remaining." She sighed. "Clovis is now dead, of course."

"As are Freath and Kirin Felt, I'm sorry to tell you."

She didn't look surprised. "They were living in the eye of the storm. I'm surprised they lasted as long as they did; Freath in particular, working as he did daily under the eye of the dragon who created the storm. He was an amazing man, Freath was; such courage, such tenacity. I owe my life to him and he gave Clovis and myself a chance to find happiness again."

Leo swallowed. He begged inwardly that she would not ask how Freath had perished. He would have to skirt the truth if she did. "Of the eight, are any of them here?" he asked, hoping to draw her attention away from Freath.

She nodded. "Yes. Three, in fact. Tolt, Perl and Hedray. All have valid but fairly curious skills. Hedray can communicate with the animals, Perl reads the runes—very rarely now though—and Tolt can dream future events although less as he's aged. Hedray does not fit your criteria. She is friendly and very much part of the fabric of the Vested community. She married another Vested but he died last year. They have several children. I know her too well, know her background, have seen no sign of the caution you suggest she might show."

He shrugged. "That gregariousness could be her disguise, of course," he warned. "My criteria was based on guesswork but there's no telling how someone would choose to hide; sometimes out in the open is the most effective. What of Tolt and Perl?"

"Perl is twenty and five summers. She's quiet and yes, I would agree withdrawn but then so are many other Vested I could name. With me she is more than friendly enough and we are close. I like her very much but, as I say, others find her awkward."

Leo didn't think anything Reuth had said about the woman was particularly inspiring although Perl intrigued him. "She reads the runes, you say?"

Reuth shrugged. "So accurately it's chilling. She has no reason to do so here . . . and in fact now refuses unless a soldier will pay her to. She donates the money to the good of the Vested. That is her saving grace, and why people haven't entirely cut her off."

"All right. Tell me about Tolt."

Reuth took another big breath. "Tolt is a year or so younger than she is. How old are you?"

"Twenty and three anni," he replied.

"Then you and he are the same age."

Leo leaned forward, intent on her words; this was sounding more promising. "Go on."

"His visions come through dreams; nightmares, to tell the truth, for they are never happy. He has accurately foretold a pestilence that took a flock of sheep, one of our Vested dying from a seemingly harmless fall, that sort of thing. The older he has become, the more withdrawn he is and the fewer visions he has. In fact, I don't remember when I last heard Tolt's voice, and he used to be such a sunny youngster. Now he nods or shakes his head. He lives alone very much on the rim of the camp. He has no friends to speak of. I make sure he eats properly and I generally keep an eye on him but otherwise he wants nothing to do with any of us. He tolerates my intrusions, but no more."

Marth nodded. "I know which lad you mean. Tall, scrawny fellow who scowls a lot."

"Mmm, yes, that sounds like Tolt," she admitted.

"And he certainly fits," Leo said, determined not to rule anyone out. "Can I meet him?"

"Why not?" she replied. "I suppose you'll know soon enough if he is whom you seek."

Leo fought to control his eager expression. "Reuth, it's highly unlikely but if he *is* an aegis, you did understand what I told you earlier today about the bonding process, didn't you?"

She looked down. "Let's worry about that, your highness, when you know for sure that Tolt is who you seek. Until then, this is all just idle conversation between two prisoners and their keeper."

He gave her a reassuring nod, thrilled by the breakthrough with her. She had accepted him; he could see it in the set of her mouth and the glimmer in her eyes. She wanted the aegis almost as much as he did. Reuth Barrow had revenge in her heart and she was going to use a Valisar king to achieve it.

Kilt had strolled the surrounding fields deep in thought; he'd sat for what felt an age in a small gully, watching water from the mountains make its way down. He'd lain in the grass and leaned against a tree. All the while he'd turned the same question over repeatedly in his mind. He didn't think he had a choice but he was desperate to find an excuse, a way beyond what appeared to be the obvious. If anyone could find it, he could.

He'd come north to the convent hoping to find an escape from the Valisar magic but all he'd found was entrapment. And he'd lost Lily; he knew that now.

What he'd seen in the blind eyes of Kirin Felt had looked like love and what he'd heard in that poor fellow's voice had sounded like love. He didn't think he'd ever looked at Lily or spoken to her in that way. Or any woman, for that matter. He had known many women, slept with many women, been affectionate to perhaps far too many, and flirted shamelessly with all women, but the truth he realized was that he had loved none.

Love was a luxury he had never believed he could afford— not with the dark secret he carried in his life. The closest he had come was surely with Lily but he knew she had never felt loved and that was guilt he deserved. Perhaps the love he would only ever know was the love of his mother and that of a friend. Jewd loved him, that he knew.

Just as he was thinking how good it was to feel well again he felt his bile rise and his heart began to pound. His head snapped up as he instinctively searched for her. There she was, sitting down on the other side of the brook, far enough away that he could barely make out her features.

"Please . . ." he called out, his hands out as if to shield himself. Even he could hear a plea in his voice he had never heard before.

"No further," she said. "I promise. I just want to talk, that's all. How are you feeling?"

A Valisar who cared. He gave a lopsided grin. "I've had much better days," he admitted.

He watched her smile gently. "I'm really sorry about coming here. It was not my idea. Corbel said I should talk with you. He said he thinks you need to know me." She shrugged, looked embarrassed. "I'm not sure what it can achieve."

She had a nice voice. She was still young, perhaps just into her third decade but nevertheless far older than she should be. In his estimation Leo's sister should be ten anni. He regarded her and she didn't seem to mind the silence; she was not tall from what he could tell and she was slim. Her hair was tied back but he'd wager if it were loose it would be that slippery shiny hair he adored in a woman. And it was dark, almost black like her father's. Instantly he felt a stab of guilt on behalf of Lily, who had thick, coarser hair that turned wavy the longer it was allowed to grow.

"If I told you about myself you might understand that I am feeling as frightened and as confused as perhaps you do," she offered.

He nodded. "Tell me about your life," he said, liking that

despite her claim to fearfulness she was direct, her voice clear and calm.

"All right." She looked down, seemed to gather her thoughts. "I grew up feeling lonely . . ." she began.

And as she continued Kilt was soothed by her even tone, impressed by her candor. Her sorrows and sense of dislocation resonated strongly with his own.

"The hospital became my haven and the quiet man I knew as Reg," she gave a soft shrug, "Corbel de Vis, I mean, became my anchor. He made me feel steady and safe. The hospital and my one friend—they were my life."

He didn't interrupt as he listened, falling deeper and deeper under her spell. As her story continued he realized that Princess Genevieve was every bit a victim of the Valisar curse as he was.

Tolt refused to come to him but Leo only had to clap eyes on the young man, working quietly at his labors, to know that this fellow had no connection to the Valisars. He looked at Reuth and gave a soft shake of his head. While her expression didn't change, the set of her shoulders drooped, telling him she was every bit as disappointed as he must appear.

She muttered something to Marth, who in turn urged forward the two men they had decided to bring in on the plot. Leo had been firmly against expanding his secret's reach but Reuth and Marth had held firm to the belief that should one of these Vested prove to be the one he sought then they would surely need restraining beyond what the three of them could provide. And Leo had to agree. Going by Kilt's reaction alone, there was a good chance his aegis would make a dash for freedom or fight them to the end.

It seemed Marth and Reuth were taking his idea seriously; his arrival and his challenge had obviously spoken loudly to their deep-seated hatred of the barbarians and their long disguised passion to strike back. He, on the other hand, held out little hope now that he would find his aegis here and he moved with a slightly heavier heart, following Reuth to where she said they would find the young recluse called Perl.

"She's on the other side of the encampment," Reuth warned. "It's a bit of a hike."

Leo shrugged and turned to Marth. As he was about to speak, a sensation he had not felt since he was a twelve-anni-old youth reached its tendrils around his gut and squeezed.

He stopped dead; took a steadying breath. This felt utterly unlike what he'd felt with Kilt, Greven and Roddy. In truth his response to being in their midst had been virtually silent, certainly invisible; he'd had no physical reaction to them at all even though Kilt had admitted he had always felt repulsed in his company.

But this! It was euphoric. And very powerful.

"What's wrong?" It was Reuth and he realized she'd been shaking his arm.

Leo began to retreat.

"Where are you going?" Marth asked, expressing a look and tone of concern to match Reuth's.

Four steps back and the feeling of euphoria subsided. Leo let out his breath, his face breaking into a hard, tight smile. "I've found my aegis," he uttered.

Questions fell from his companions but he ignored them, asking his own. "It's her. It's the woman Perl. How far are we from where she lives?"

Reuth stopped her gabbling. "We're now about four perhaps five hundred steps from her tiny half cottage."

He nodded. "Then she already knows. She might be already preparing to flee. You had better get over there," he said to Reuth and Marth, whose faces were identical studies of confusion. "Reuth, you go in alone. She trusts you. Calm her. You must stall her while I think this through. Hurry ahead."

"But how do you know it's her?" Reuth persisted.

"You are going to have to trust me and the Valisar magic. You have nothing to lose and everything to gain by doing so. But you're also going to have to convince her to make the sacrifice. I'm sure you can be very persuasive, given that this is your dream coming true. I promise you, Reuth, Marth, with Perl's help, you will be able to take your revenge. Now go. Do not let her escape."

And Reuth was running, Marth following at a safe distance with his minders in tow. Leo did not hurry. He needed to stay back, well out of the magic's sensitive reach, until he knew Perl was fully captive.

They had been sitting for so long he was sure her backside was as numb as his but neither moved. Her voice was beginning to lose its smoothness, was sounding vaguely gritty from her long period of storytelling, but still he was anchored to it.

"In pain, aren't you?" she said. "And that troubles me. I'm a doctor, after all." She stopped, looked up from where she had been fiddling with the grass between her boots.

It was the pause he heard before the question filtered through the layers of thought, mesmiration, lull of false security, and joy and fear of her presence. "Pardon?"

She shrugged. "I'm a healer of pain, not a bringer of it."

"If it's any consolation, it is a rapturous pain."

Evie grinned. "Like an orgasm," she said, sounding embarrassed.

"What's that?"

"Well," she started slowly, reassuming her physician's countenance, "during sex, either or both partners may experience a euphoric rush of sensation that—"

He began to laugh. "I know what it is, your majesty, I just wanted to know if you did."

She gasped and gave him a look of pure murder rimmed with embarrassed amusement too, standing and surging forward as she did so. "You sod!" she said, uselessly flinging the grass in her hand at him.

He too stood, laughing, but then doubled over. "Oh, no closer, highness. That magical orgasmic feeling isn't nearly as much fun as the physical."

She stuffed her hands into her skirt pockets and stepped back a few yards. "I wouldn't know."

He blinked. "But from what I can see you are beautiful. What do you mean, you wouldn't know?"

"Kilt—may I call you that?"

"You may."

"Well, Kilt, where I come from we aren't all married off or pregnant or indeed even eligible for either by the time womanhood first shows its signs of emerging. Women choose when they will lose their virginity. Some of us wait."

"For what?"

"To find the right person who is worth giving it up to."

Kilt hesitated. "Are you talking about falling in love?"

She shrugged. "Yes. Although, not necessarily with the person you might want to spend the rest of your life with but most women want to feel very fond, even be in love, for their first time."

"That's quaint."

"Are you making fun of me again?"

"I'm not sure. You seem so awkward and embarrassed about something so natural. Men and women fu—"

She cleared her throat, interrupting him. "That's such a typical man's response. It's the perfect excuse."

"Really?"

She shook her head. "Oh, I don't know. My whole world is upside down, Kilt. I don't know what I'm doing here or why you have to feel pain when you're near me, or why I am so strongly attracted to you."

"Attracted to me. That's such a gracious way to say it. It's more like compulsion. But that's the magic at work."

"Is it?"

He stared at her. "I . . ." He hesitated, his gaze narrowing. "I'm not sure what you mean, majesty."

She sighed. "Oh, I don't know," she said, looking around. "There is no getting away from the fact that I am drawn helplessly to you and you to me. I am resisting the urge to leap over this waterway and . . ."

"And what? Eat me?"

She made a groaning sound. "No! Maybe. Corbel told me some ridiculous—no, outrageous—and hideous tale about how I must bond you."

"He is right. Every fiber of your body must want me."

She laughed. "Now where I come from that sort of line would get your face slapped."

He grinned. "I mean—"

"I know what you mean. It's true, but I have a much higher threshold of resistance than people arc giving me credit for. I will not be ruled by a magic. I refuse to capitulate to it. I will show it that I am in charge of it and not the other way around."

"Do you feel sick?"

She shook her head. "No, it's more of a hunger . . . a pang. If you got up now and walked away I would feel an intense desire to hunt you."

He nodded. "That is its way; how I've always imagined it must feel to be Valisar. For me it is similar and yet somehow opposite. I am drawn to you but the feeling, though one of rapture, is mixed with fear and loathing. And the pain is intense and yet I can't help myself. We are far enough away . . . just . . . that I have a smidge of resistance. I have exercised control over your brother and your uncle but they are merely men," he said with feigned condescension. "They can't hold a candle to your power."

"Why is that? Chance?"

"Not chance," he said, smiling crookedly. "Fate perhaps. Obviously no one has explained much about your magic to you."

She shook her head sadly. "I've lived oblivious for nearly twenty-one years . . . er, anni, I gather I'm supposed to say."

"Then let me educate you swiftly and concisely."

She smiled and although he couldn't see her eyes, he felt the radiance and kindness in her gaze.

"So," he began, "let us sit down again on our respective banks." He did so and watched as she followed suit. "I shall tell you everything I know about you Valisars—and especially the female power—and as much as I can about myself."

She lay back, gazed up at the sky and listened as Kilt began a story he admitted he had never told anyone in its entirety before.

Perl had been shelling peas when she sensed it. She cried out and doubled over as what felt to be her very spirit surged out, seeking, questing . . . and finding. She felt pulled in different directions—an overwhelming desire to race toward the source of that joy and the compulsion to run as fast as she could away from it, away from the feelings of dizziness and nausea that had since followed.

When she straightened, breathing heavily, everything was normal and that previous stark sensation had dissipated; she waited, not sure of what she was waiting for. There was no sound but her breathing and the birds squabbling outside. She had begun to doubt that the sensation occurred at all when she heard Reuth calling from the front door.

"Perl? Are you home?" came the familiar voice.

"Where else?" she replied, relieved that she was not alone any longer.

"Ah, there you are. Goodness me, you look like you've seen a ghost. Everything all right?"

Did she detect a false note in Reuth's voice?

"Yes, yes, I'm fine."

Reuth took her hand. That was unusual.

"Are you sure?" the older woman continued. "Because you look a bit peaky to me."

"I . . . I did feel a bit faint a moment ago but I always forget to eat when I'm busy . . ." She looked down. Reuth's knuckles were white against her hand.

"You're hurting me," she said, confusion claiming her. "What are you doing?"

"I'm sorry, Perl. I'm so sorry," Reuth said and then she looked toward the front door. "In here!" she called. "I've got her."

Perl reacted like a burned cat, clawing and shrieking, but suddenly men were upon her, holding her down. Then the vile sensation claimed her again and she knew why they were here.

"Where?" she groaned.

"He's coming, my girl. I'm so sorry," Reuth said.

"Who is it?" she cried.

Marth growled. "Hush now, keep your voice down, lass, or you'll have us all killed for our trouble."

Reuth stroked her face, begged her to be still. It was hope-

less anyway, she knew it. She'd avoided this all of her life.
Maybe it was easiest to just give up and give in.

"That's it, that's it, Perl. You be calm now, my girl," Reuth
said, tears streaking her cheeks. "It's Leonel. He's young
and he's handsome . . . and he's—"

"Valisar!" Perl groaned. "Please, I beg you, don't do this
to me. You're my friend." She began to tremble, choking on
the words as the pain intensified.

"You're already dead in your heart, Perl. Already a prisoner. What difference does it make?" Reuth pleaded.

She was pinned down on her cot, her head flung back,
and the men did not let up on their grip even though she had
stopped struggling. The tears dripped from either side of
her eyes into the scarf that covered her head. "But not in my
mind, Reuth . . ." she cried. "I'm free in my mind."

And she began to retch helplessly as a shadow fell across
her doorway.

Twenty-Six

Lily was tired. It had been a long and dusty journey. In an attempt not to draw undue attention to herself she had engaged in conversation with an older couple going north to take a dip in the mountain springs famed for their therapeutic effects. Though Lily was sure she could achieve similar, if not better, results with one of her unguents, she didn't mention it. All she wanted to do was talk pleasantly but not too animatedly or expansively so that no one became too intrigued by the quiet woman, traveling alone in the corner of the carriage.

"Not long now," the old man said genially.

"I imagine you'd know the journey well," Lily replied, having learned that this was their sixth pilgrimage.

"Oh yes," his wife confirmed, "although each anni we see some change in the landscape." She pointed out of the window. "Those little dwellings weren't there last anni and you know the town of Lower Flitchington that we passed through?" Lily nodded. "Well, that was little more than a dusty two-horse village when we first began coming through these parts."

"And now look at it," Lily finished for her and the woman smiled triumphantly.

"Exactly. Next time I might suggest to Burnard that we overnight there in one of its inns and not make this such a dash to the north."

Lily smiled. "That would be nice," she said, trying to keep up her polite interest.

The fear and shock of Stracker, of Piven, of her father, not to mention the stress and adrenaline of outwitting her captors, was giving way to despair at Kirin's brutal death. The more she thought about him the more convinced she was that somewhere in the traumatic but brief time they had been together she had fallen in love with his unassuming quiet strength and his tender, affectionate way. She'd always thought she loved Kilt but she now understood that what she had with Kilt was a great friendship. They had trusted each other, found each other amusing, and they were safe together. He had been good to her and while his remoteness had infuriated her, it was perhaps, she now realized, the aspect that she found most intriguing about him. She liked his mystery and his dangerous lifestyle, his recklessness and his sense of fun. She had confused excitement and his entertaining manner for love. But he had never loved her, she knew now. Love was what she had for Kirin and he'd had for her; Kirin had died because of her, selflessly protecting her.

She felt a sob rushing to her throat and caught it just in time.

"There's the marker," the man said, pointing with enthusiasm to the stone boulder. "You'll be at the convent before you know it."

Lily was grateful for his intrusion, swallowed her sob and took a deep breath to steady herself. Kirin was gone. She hoped Kilt and Jewd had stayed safe in the crowd and that one day soon their paths would cross. But now all she wanted was to take some time at the convent if they would permit her to stay for a while. She needed a quiet, uneventful stay.

Leo looked upon the woman writhing before him. He could see the revulsion and fear in her eyes but he felt only an immense feeling of pleasure. All nausea had fled, replaced with a rapture. This woman was his aegis; not just any aegis but the aegis born for him.

He had owned her from his birth. He could hear Reuth's voice murmuring and cajoling; he could hear Marth giving orders to the other Vested and to Perl. He could hear Perl begging for pity that no one would extend. But he knew these things only through their tones, not their words; his hammering heart and his rushing blood were muting the sounds of the words. He could not focus on anything but his desire to trammel Perl.

"I must consume her," he said. The words sounded as though he was talking in a tunnel or beneath water.

He watched Reuth whisper to Perl, saw Perl open her mouth to scream. Surprisingly it was he who reacted the fastest, covering her mouth quickly so no sound came out. He saw everything in intense detail—her nostrils flaring with her labored breathing, her chest rising and falling so fast she looked like a panicked bird, her eyes widening in horror as Marth lifted a small pair of shears from his back pocket.

"Just a sting, Perl, I promise," Leo lied. He nodded to Marth. "Do it!" he commanded and once again pressed his hand hard over her mouth.

Without any ceremony or hesitation Marth reached for Perl's ear and in a trice, despite her hysterical squirming and the silent shrieks behind Leo's palm, snipped off an earlobe.

Blood gushed, Perl retched and the bloodied piece of flesh fell into Leo's free hand. Leo wasted no time. He threw the earlobe into his mouth and closed his eyes as he swallowed without chewing.

As he felt the small piece of flesh slip down his gullet, feeling neither remorse nor repulsion, he heard the words of binding arrive in his mind in an old language he knew he shouldn't know. And yet, without conscious effort he began to murmur them. Perl instantly began to arch her back despite her captors' efforts, the whites of her eyes showing from her agony. Leo let out a silent cry of his own, feeling only the ecstasy of the magical Valisar bond as his aegis became truly his.

Kilt had finished talking long ago but they'd both kept a comfortable silence since, reflecting on all he'd said.

Evie raised herself to sit with her arms pulling her knees tight to her chest. "Can you imagine how this all sounds to me?"

He shook his head. "Highly improbable, I should imagine."

"So ridiculous in fact that I feel I have no choice but to believe in it. I'm here; this isn't the dream or the nightmare I hoped I'd wake from. You're here and I am so aware of you on every level that it's making my hair stand on end." He gave a sad smile and nodded silently. "And so let's say I now accept my bloodline, let's say I even accept that I am the only daughter of the Valisars to survive and that I am the wielder of this profound magic that no one seems to understand . . . what am I supposed to do with it?"

"I don't know, Genevieve."

"You're the first person to ever call me that. I thought my name was Evie."

"Genevieve is a beautiful name. I like saying it." He looked up and straight at her. "You wear that beautiful name very well." He knew she blushed by the way she suddenly looked away from him. "As to what you should do with your magic—I suspect your father always imagined that if his son were unable to do so, you would use it to seize back the crown."

"But you're telling me that Leo is more than capable."

"Yes, he is."

"Then let him have it. I don't want it. If my father wanted his son to rule, shouldn't we all just help Leo achieve that?"

"That's exactly what I was doing until a few days ago. But I have seen elements in Leo that I don't like. There's a real sense of duty that walks hand in hand with a devastating lack of empathy for others."

"He's selfish," she said simply.

"No, it's more than that. I now believe that Leo is capable of tremendous cruelty—violence, even—if he feels the ends justify the means. Now maybe that's what ruling actually boils down to."

"The bigger picture."

He frowned. "Yes, that's a very good way of describing it. Perhaps that's exactly what is needed, but it's not the king I had hoped he would grow into. Leo would, I think, sacrifice his soul for the crown. He is so suffused with the notion of power that he's not going to let anyone stand in his way."

"And?"

"You are standing in his way, Genevieve. You are now his greatest threat."

"Me? I don't even want the wretched throne. I don't even want to be here."

"Well, that may be but you are. If Leo finds himself an aegis, then there's every likelihood—if Loethar hasn't found one of his own, that is—that your brother will simply take the throne. He will be unstoppable. And he will set about destroying all the other contenders simply as good housekeeping."

"Even if I assured him I had no desire to play royal?"

"He is Valisar, and he shows his father's traits. He will leave no stone unturned in cleaning up his new empire and that will include you, your uncle and potentially his adopted brother. Beyond that I suspect there will be plenty of blood-shed as he wreaks his new-found power against the barbarians."

"You said they were well integrated though."

"Most are and the fact is most people of the empire are very content with the ruling power. Loethar is, dare I say, a damn good emperor and more than worthy of his bloodline. I admire what he's achieved since he took over."

Evie sighed and shook her head. "So it sounds like I must go on the run. Corbel and I can—"

"De Vis has a sword. That will be worthless against this level of sorcery."

"So I'm hunted and already murdered in your scheme of things whatever I do?" she said. It sounded like an accusation.

Kilt stood and stretched to buy himself a few more moments. "No, your majesty, it is not your only option. Why don't you join me on this side of the rivulet?"

"But you can't—"

"Well, I've been practicing for all this time. And yes, I'll probably suffer but I think we should formally meet."

"I would like that." She stood. "Is there anything I can do to make it any easier on you?"

He gave a lopsided grin. "Oh well, you could say you find

me irresistible for my handsome physique, my dashing charm and unequaled looks. We don't have to discuss the dirty words of Valisar magic."

She was moving toward him and he had to lean against a tree to steady himself.

"Keep coming, Genevieve," he urged, his voice tight.

She lifted her skirt and easily skipped over the narrow gully. Kilt doubled up.

"I must say, this is all very complimentary," Evie quipped. "Next you'll vomit."

"Well, the nausea's arrived," he admitted. "Don't feel sorry, just walk straight at me. I'm doing better than previously."

She was close now. "Kilt," she stammered. "I have to admit that it's getting hard for me to retain control."

"All right, stop," he said, putting a hand up, breathing with difficulty. "Let me look at you, the first Valisar princess to ever survive." He straightened with difficulty. "Lo, please don't strike me blind!" he begged, his discomfort forgotten for a brief heartbeat. "You are beautiful."

She blushed furiously. "Shall I go back?" she asked. "Let me, Kilt. I hate doing this to you." Her voice was trembling.

"No, no. The pain is exquisite but looking at you makes it a tad more bearable."

"Stop it, this is insufferable! I refuse to be a part of this. If I can't get back and I can't go on the run, why don't I just make it easy for everyone and kill myself?"

"Genevieve, wait!" he begged, breathless. "There is a way for you to be safe, for me to be well."

Her gaze narrowed as she paused in thought. Then her dark eyes widened. "No! Absolutely not!"

"It is the only way," he said, slipping down the tree trunk in weakness until he was on one knee.

"Eat you?" she asked, her voice brimming with disgust. "Hurt you? I took an oath, Kilt. I don't expect you to understand but what you're suggesting goes against everything I stand for, everything I am."

He laughed mirthlessly. "I was born an aegis. Consuming me is your birthright."

"Not this princess," she hissed, pointing a finger in warning to him. "I want to be your ally, not your jailer. We've both shared secrets and fears, parts of our lives with each other that we both admit we haven't shared with anyone else." He nodded, incapable of speaking. "I want to be your friend, Kilt. I cannot be convinced to hurt you, not even if my pathetic and intensely protected life depends upon it."

"Bravely said, your majesty."

"Don't call me that. I like to hear you call me by my name." There was something in her voice that stirred deep within him, calmed his pain slightly and gave him the strength to straighten and look at her. "I too have been practicing while we spoke," she said. "And while you trained yourself to show some resistance, I've been training myself to withdraw my magic. Did you feel anything different then?"

He nodded. "I did. The pain has subsided slightly."

She took a deep breath. "How about this?" She frowned, waiting.

Kilt paused, even managed a smile. "Better, much better."

"Right, one last mighty effort then. This is all I have, Kilt," and he could feel her pull the grasping magic back into herself.

It didn't leave entirely, the nausea didn't disappear, but she now felt like Leo had to him—bearable.

He tested it, realized he was wearied but back in control. "How . . . ?"

She gave a wince of regret. "I'm sorry I didn't think of it sooner."

"Think of what? How have you done this?"

"I'm a doctor . . . healing is what I do for a profession. And it seems healing is also the magic I possess."

"And?" He still didn't understand.

"And . . . I'm counteracting your sickness with my healing power."

He stared at her, dumbstruck. Finally, he managed, "I'm just in awe of you."

"Awe of me?" she queried, looking confused.

"Yes. Your intelligence, your generosity . . . your strength."

"Oh . . ." She looked away.

"I'm making you blush."

"Yes . . . yes, you are. So you're feeling all right?"

He did a small jig and then mugged for applause. "How's this?"

"Now that's embarrassing," she admitted, giggling.

"This is truly amazing. You are amazing!"

"Stop now, please," she said, holding up a hand of protest.

"But how long can you do this for?"

She shrugged. "I don't know. It feels . . . um, comfortable for now. The main thing is, you can get away. You and your friend, run for your lives and disappear. I'll never know where you are and I give you my word I won't look for you." She smiled. "And that's the word of Valisar royalty," she added with a dry edge to her voice." She looked down. "Go, Kilt. Go right now."

He took a breath to speak and then closed his mouth. Instead he took a step forward and took her hand, bent over it and kissed it gently, lingering his lips on her soft skin. He straightened, still holding her hand, and stared into her soft brown eyes. "You would do this for me?"

She nodded. "It means I beat the magic. I win."

"Is that all it means?"

She shook her head and her breathing changed. "No. It's very important to me—as a doctor—that I find solutions for people's ails."

His stare intensified. "That's it?" For what felt like the first time in his life Kilt acted impulsively. He lifted her hand to his lips again and softly but sensually let them mold gently around her small, neat row of knuckles. Then he placed her hand against his stubbled cheek, sighing. He let her hand go. "Forgive me, your highness. I . . . er, I'm not sure what came over me then. Relief, no doubt."

She blinked, looking unsure of herself, of him. "You should go. Run, Kilt. Please, run from me."

He smiled sadly. "I should but I don't want to."

She shook her head slowly. "Please, it's your chance."

Still surprising himself, still unsure of what he was doing or why, but feeling a fresh intoxication—nothing to do with his magic—he drew her back beneath the cover of the small orchard that the nuns tended.

"Genevieve," he murmured, "I . . ."

"Just kiss me," she said and then added, "Please," as though her urgency matched his.

He paused for a heartbeat as his eyes drank in the sight of her own closed eyes, long dark lashes resting against the creamy complexion, her cheeks infused with a blush of desire. Their lips met, soft and hesitant. And then Kilt had no further rational thought; instinct took over. Suddenly all those emotional responses he had never paid attention to welled up in him and spilled over; yearning, passion and a longing for love overwhelmed his control. He kissed the Valisar princess more tenderly and yet more deeply than he had ever permitted himself to kiss a woman previously.

He felt naked. It was as though Genevieve had stripped back all the disguises, all the barriers he had spent a lifetime guarding. She had found him. He was hers. He couldn't run from her even if he'd wanted to.

Kilt didn't know how long they kissed but their ardour had intensified. There was nothing hesitant about their longing any more. And it took his entire reserve of will to pull his head back from hers, sighing as he did so with deep regret as he felt the loss.

"Don't say anything," she whispered. Her face was cupped in his hands, her eyes were misted with emotion. "Do you believe in love at first sight?"

His mouth feeling deliciously swollen from their kissing, he twitched a grin. "I didn't."

"I always have. I've always wanted my Prince Charming to come along, sweep me off my feet."

He looked back at her, frowning quizzically. "Who is Prince Charming?"

She chuckled. "No one real. Someone many women dream of." She shrugged. "We like to believe there is someone perfectly matched to our needs, our wants and desires . . . to who we are. Someone who will protect us and always love us, want us, never tire of being with us . . . even when we're old and fat."

"I could never tire of you. If you're not making me feel nauseous, you make me feel drunk. Either way, I'm dizzy and light-headed around you. And no woman has ever done that for me."

She gave a soft smirk. "I'm not sure I can believe that."

Kilt clasped her hands, searching her face. "You can. I have pushed away every woman I've known . . . walked away from more than you could count."

"Then you would walk away from me."

"No," he insisted. "I don't think I can. You own me now and in more ways than are obvious. I have never looked for love. I didn't think it existed. I was prepared to settle for affectionate companionship."

She shrank. "There's a woman in your life? How silly of me. Look at you. Of course there would be." She tried to pull away but Kilt held her hands too firmly, pulled her back.

"She loves another. She married him, even. I have been coming to terms with losing her but, Genevieve, the truth is, I was never good enough for her because I only pretended to love her."

Evie's eyes narrowed as she considered this, her gaze never leaving his.

"But . . . but this bond, this amazing feeling I have with you has shocked me," Kilt finished.

"It's the magic, it's—"

"It's not the Valisar magic. It's not my magic or your magic. It's our magic, the magic two people feel when they find the person they want to share everything with. I've never had that with anyone until now."

Her eyes flashed with a fiery spark. "The moment I was close enough to see you clearly I felt a catch in my throat. Once I'd touched you, I was struggling to be matter of fact about it, but magic aside, I loved you on sight."

"I can't be without you," Kilt admitted.

"Do you really mean that?"

He nodded. "I'm helpless." He shrugged. "You might as well hack off a piece of me now and cook it."

"Don't ever speak to me of that again."

He pulled her close and wrapped his arms around her, kissing the top of her soft shiny hair. "I will not leave you.

I cannot. I . . ." It felt so strange and clumsy to try and attempt to say it. "Genevieve, I . . ."

She pulled back. "What?" she said, searching his eyes.

"I want to be with you. I believe myself hopelessly in love with you."

"You don't even know me."

"I know everything about you that's important. You've told me all the elements that make you who you are. The rest, if you belch like a man or pick your nose while I'm eating . . ." She began to laugh. "Well, let's just say I'll discover that as we grow old together."

"Grow old together." She gave a start.

"What's wrong?"

"Corbel. He'll be worried. I made him promise to leave me alone with you. How long have we been alone?"

"Long enough that a man in love would be anxious."

"A man in love? What do you mean?"

"For an intelligent woman, you surprise me. Isn't it obvious to you that Corbel de Vis worships you?"

"No, no," she said, smiling, embarrassed. "Corbel's looked out for me for so long it probably looks that way but we're just close friends. He—"

"Genevieve . . . the man is deeply in love with you. Either you're highly insensitive to the relationship you have with him or he works very diligently to hide his true feelings."

She stared at Kilt with a look akin to sorrow. "Has he told you that?"

"He didn't have to. You can hear it in his voice, see it in his eyes—just as I told you about Kirin and how he felt about Lily."

"Lily's the woman you mentioned?"

He nodded. Then gave a small, mirthless gust of a laugh. "Gavriel de Vis fell for her when we were briefly together but she chose me. Now I'm stealing Corbel de Vis's girl too."

"Are you?"

He stared deep into her eyes. "If she'll agree to being stolen."

"I love Corbel but not in the way you think he may love me." She shook her head. "I love him as a brother."

Kilt smirked, but not unkindly. "Please don't ever say that to him. Those are words that chill a man who loves a woman."

"I'll trust you on that," she said, her voice full of sorrow. "Why didn't he ever say anything?"

"You know him much better than I but from the little time I've spent with him I know he's a very private, very reserved person. Very different from his brother."

"Gavriel? That's a nice name."

"And like his twin he's a good, loyal person. But you know what Gavriel is thinking because he tells you. Corbel might be saying one thing but thinking another." He held up a hand. "I'm not calling him a liar. What I mean is, he doesn't allow anyone to see the real him. I know the feeling and I think it's why I find him easy to like."

"Back . . ." she sighed. "Where we've been living he had no friend but myself. I mean no one. He was a loner."

Kilt nodded. "Try and put yourself into his position. Imagine what he has had to do for his sovereign, the price he's paid and continues to pay for his loyalty. He's given up his life, his family, his world."

She looked suddenly guilty and turned away. "I haven't really paused to consider any of this from his perspective."

"Well, the Valisars are known to have a selfish streak," he replied, his tone dry.

Evie turned and punched him lightly. "I am not one of them."

"Oh, my sweet girl, I'm afraid you are. But, to the business at hand. Thank you for releasing me from your spell but I cannot accept the gift."

"Kilt," she began, shaking her head, a look of plea in her eyes.

"Listen to me," he said. "My feelings, de Vis's feelings, your feelings aside, we must return to the original problem—that you are in mortal danger. Whether or not you care about your crown is not the issue. You could be killed for simply being a Valisar heir." He inhaled and made a tutting sound as she began to protest. "Wait, let me finish. What has happened between us changes everything. I want to be bonded to you. Trammel me now or break my heart forever."

She swallowed. "I refuse."

"You can't. You cannot ignore my feelings for you. I will wear down your healing resistance. And even if I can't, even if you can keep channeling that healing magic, it can't stop my loving you. Either way, magic or through love, I am yours."

"I should heal you of your love, then!"

"Is that what you want?"

"I don't want to trammel you."

"I don't want you to die. And die you will when Leo or Loethar catches up with you. But if you have an aegis, no one can touch you. You don't have to do anything with that aegis magic except use it to defend your life and those of the others you care about—Corbel de Vis for instance, or me. If you care a whit about me, trammel me. I never thought I'd hear myself beg for such a thing but, your highness, I'm urging you to use the magic bond for good, to save lives."

She bit her lip. "I won't eat your flesh."

"You have to!"

"Wait. Listen to me now. I've been thinking. This great aegis magic you tell me was conceived hundreds of years ago."

"Correct," he said.

"And so presumably you would consider the era that you live in far more advanced and civilized than then, right?"

"Right. That was the time of Cormoron, First of the Valisars. My reading of history tells me he was something of a barbarian himself in the way he invaded and cowed the tribes of the region that he ultimately called Penraven."

"Good, so try and follow my line of thought here. I am imagining that this whole idea of the aegis was written down somewhere. And wherever it was first put down, it was recorded in a more ancient language. What if that language needs to be interpreted?" He frowned at her. "Hear me out," she continued. "From what you've explained the key word regarding the aegis magic is that the Valisar must *consume* his or her aegis."

"Or any aegis," Kilt corrected.

"But they must be consumed. Am I right, that's the term?"

"Yes," he said, looking bewildered.

She smiled ferociously. "Kilt, the word consume doesn't just mean to eat. It can mean destroy, as a fire might consume all in its path. And it can mean to spend . . . as, as . . ." She searched for the right comparison. "As in consuming all one's money in worthless goods."

He blinked.

"And it can mean to devour . . . as in to eat or drink—but it could also mean to be engrossed," she said, almost lecturing him. "As in you and I are so consumed by each other that we forgot the time. To consume can mean all of those things but it can also mean to absorb," she said, slowly, clearly, as though holding his hand and leading him down a path. "Will you accept that?"

He considered her premise. "To absorb?" She nodded and he echoed her gesture. "Yes, absolutely it could mean that, but I don't see how this relates to—"

"Hell, men are dunderheads sometimes. Think, Kilt. How else can I consume you if I don't eat or destroy or devour you?"

He shook his head, lost.

She gave a groan. "All right, make me say it, then!" She turned away and leaned against the nearby tree. "If you made love to me, I would not only take your living flesh inside me but if we do it right," she said, turning back, cheeks flushed with embarrassment, "then you would leave behind a part of yourself that I would absorb . . . that I would consume into my body."

"My seed," he said, enlightenment dawning.

She smiled. "Yes."

His gaze snapped back to hers and he kissed her hard. "Amazing, just amazing! You are easily the cleverest and most cunning of all the Valisars. I think you've just found the secret to outwitting their own clever magic!"

She shrugged. "It's just a theory."

"It has to work. It has to. There is nothing in anything I've read about my aegis magic that specifies I have to be eaten. The word is consumed and you're so right, it's open to interpretation. Perhaps the devouring of an aegis by gorging on it was always a poor interpretation. Genevieve, you're incredible."

She grinned and there was a wicked sparkle in her eyes now. "I just didn't think it was worth wasting that," she said, looking down and pointing.

His laughter echoed around the orchard.

Twenty-Seven

Perl slumped in a corner, motionless. She hadn't spoken since the trammeling and everyone had wisely left her alone, even as they had tested the magic.

"Protect me, Perl!" Leo had commanded. She made no sound, didn't even glance his way, but he nodded and beckoned to Reuth. "Now, Reuth. Come."

Tentatively, then with more and more force, Reuth tried to stab the king. Leo had laughed the loudest of all when the blade slid away, time after time.

"Now do you see, Marth?" he raged, pacing the small hut, puffed like a mating raker bird, swelled with his importance and invincibility. "Now we have our king, we have our weapon, we have our means to simply break free of the shackles of the barbarians."

"Perl," Reuth tried. "You did it. And now we can be free."

"You maybe, Reuth, but not I. I am more of a prisoner than I have ever been previously," she said, her formerly distant gaze suddenly viciously focused.

Leo threw her an offhand look of disdain. "Stop bleating, Perl. This is war. And I need you."

"So much for the famed Valisar magic," she sneered.

Reuth looked at her, aghast. "He's the king, Perl. Show some care."

"Why? What do you think he's going to do to me? Hurt me? Kill me perhaps? Make my life miserable? He's already done the worst he can and now I have to protect him anyway.

So no, I don't believe I have to show care at all toward our merciful Valisar king!" She spat on the ground. "You have no magic to speak of of your own and if I wasn't your true aegis, I could have evaded you entirely but not the others."

Reuth, still looking shocked, blinked. "Others?"

"Loethar and the halfwit child," Perl said matter-of-factly.

"Be quiet!" Leo warned, taking more notice of Perl now.

But Reuth couldn't let it go now. "Loethar isn't Valisar."

"Isn't he?" Perl asked, looking around at everyone. "Why do you think he's trying to shut me up?" she said, nodding at Leo with her own measure of disdain. "Loethar *is* Valisar, you poor fools. Look at him, look how angry I've made him." She laughed, genuine delight creasing her face. Reuth had never seen her so animated.

It was Marth who was most intrigued, though. His face had grown heavy with concern. "How do you know this, Perl? Er, no," he said at Leo's attempt to interrupt. "I need to hear this. I told you, while you may be Penraven's heir, you are not my king. My king is dead. And while I am loyal to the Set and thus the Valisars, I will still satisfy myself."

Leo's scowl intensified. "So what if he's Valisar. He's not the rightful crown bearer. I am!"

Reuth gasped, genuinely shocked.

"You knew?" Marth asked, sounding angry and confused.

"He's a bastard son. Darros must have idly cast his wild seed on the plains and promptly forgot about the bitch he lay with."

"The bitch being Dara Negev, presumably?"

Leo shrugged. "She deserves no title but to be remembered as the old whore who treated my mother—your queen, Reuth," he said, pointing an accusing finger at her, "like scum. My mother didn't have to steal a throne, she didn't even need a Valisar marriage; she was a royal in her own right!" His voice broke with the emotion fueling his rage.

Reuth nodded. "We all understand how you feel, majesty. But you are relying on us to win you the throne. The least you can do for us is honesty. You should have told us the truth about Loethar."

Marth still looked dumbfounded. "He's Valisar. How can we be sure?"

"The magic doesn't lie," Perl snarled. "I know, I live with it. When I was taken to the palace, we were led to some rooms in a far wing and we saw the man that I later learned was the self-proclaimed emperor cross one of the courtyards. My reaction was instant."

"You swooned, that's right," Reuth said, wonder in her voice as she recalled the memory of many anni previous. "Hedray and I helped you."

Perl nodded. "If it was just one of them I might have caught my reaction in time but not two of them." She smiled maliciously at Leo. "Truth time, your majesty," she said, pronouncing his title in a tone loaded with derision.

Leo regarded the stares of inquiry and shrugged. "Then she knew long before I ever did."

"What?" Marth demanded. "What is Perl alluding to?"

"She's enjoying her knowledge that my brother, Piven, who we all believed was adopted, is in fact a blood brother."

"Clovis was right," Reuth said, bewildered. "I never believed him but Clovis was right. He knew that lad from the south was the prince."

"Well, Reuth, I was going to spare you this but since we're on this pathway of honesty now you might as well hear it all. It was Piven, my true Valisar brother, who slaughtered your husband, Clovis."

The blood drained from Reuth's face. "What?" she whispered.

"Clovis was unarmed, Reuth. He simply wanted to talk to Piven. And here's another truth for you all: Piven is no longer the halfwit everyone believes him to be. He is now whole and what's more he's on a killing spree. He has his aegis and he is crazed with his new-found power, hellbent on revenge."

"Revenge?" Marth asked, his face a story of his own series of shocks.

"Yes, revenge on Loethar, revenge on me, revenge on anyone who stands between him and the throne of Penraven. He has simply replaced one form of madness with another. And now he has the capacity to kill at will whomever he chooses."

"So do you," Perl snarled.

"I am rational, Perl. I am returning order to Penraven and ultimately the Set. General Marth here will be able to reinstate the royal bloodline of Barronel—I will help him to do just that. My intention as king is to return all the realms to their rightful royals. I do not want to rule an empire."

Marth sighed. "Well said, majesty. Despite the shock, I think we know we're doing the right thing. Perl, it is done now. I am sorry for your suffering but it was for the greater good, not just for the Vested or the royals but for all the people of the Set."

"And with Marth and Reuth as my witness," Leo said, "I give you my word that I will do everything I can to make your life pleasant. You may live as far away from me as you can stand; you will have all the comforts and wealth that you desire, or don't . . . as you wish. You will lead your own life, Perl, as much as the magic will permit. I will make no further demands upon you once we have won back the throne. Do you all hear me?"

Reuth nodded, and saw that Marth did too. "We hear you," they repeated.

Reuth touched Perl, looking amazed by her clean scalp; the birthmark that anointed her as an aegis had disappeared with the trammeling. "He's being fair. Can't you move past your despair and be optimistic; help us to help yourself?"

Perl had been jingling her runestones in her pocket and now she cast them on the table nearby. "I will consult the stones."

Reuth sighed and looked up at the others, shaking her head. "So what now? We know you are invincible, Leo, but how do we now take on the barbarian army? Perl can presumably protect some of us but what can a few of us achieve? We are still vulnerable to their arrows, their swords, their numbers."

"How many people are in the camp here?" Leo asked.

Marth shrugged. "Around four hundred Vested, including children and infirm."

"So perhaps two hundred and fifty useful bodies?"

"I'd say that, yes," Marth agreed.

"None of them fighters," Reuth qualified, glaring at Marth.

"Farmers, bootmakers, tanners, bakers . . . They can't wield swords and wouldn't anyway."

"Think about the magic that is here, though," Leo tried. "Think hard. Does anyone have a magic that we can use against the barbarians?"

Reuth shook her head. "Unless it hasn't been declared or discovered, the most intriguing is someone like Tolt who can correctly predict events. The rest is all practical but harmless magic like weather reading, water divination."

Perl smirked. "I can assure you that half of the people here probably possess more interesting powers but won't admit it. I have seen it in the stones."

"Why haven't you ever said anything?" Reuth asked.

Perl touched her damaged ear. "Because people are not good to one another if they know too much." She stared at one of the stones she'd picked up, blood from her fingers wetting it, and suddenly laughed mirthlessly. "The solution is staring at us."

"What did you just see?" Reuth said, grabbing the pebble from her friend's hand. "Tell us."

Perl was still smiling. She shook her head. "Why should I?"

"What do you want?" Leo asked, his voice betraying his frustration with her.

She shrugged. "What every girl wants I suppose."

Everyone looked at her slightly befuddled. And then Reuth scoffed. "Perl, you've never shown any interest at *all*," she claimed, staring around at the men.

Perl's expression became uncharacteristically petulant. "Well, maybe now I do. Why shouldn't I ask for this? I'm giving my life for it anyway. Who deserves it more?"

"What in Lo's name does she want?" Leo asked. "If you have a solution for how to make us all safe, Perl, please share it with us. I will grant you now whatever you want, if it's within my power."

She laughed and clapped her hands. "Oh, it's within your power, your majesty," she said, again adding a snide tone to the royal title. "Where is Father Cloony?"

"Father Cloony?" Marth repeated.

Leo looked between them in consternation. "Why do we need a priest?"

"So we can be married immediately, majesty. I'm going to be Queen Perl as of today," she declared. "And then you will be as trapped as I am," she snarled.

Evie sucked in a helplessly deep breath and then even though she didn't mean it to happen, a small ecstatic shriek escaped her. Kilt Faris clung to her, rigid. She felt the pulse within her and forcing her eyes open she saw her lover grit his teeth as he began to groan. It was partly the pleasure of his release, she knew, but mostly terror of the final imprisonment as she sensed a pain rip through him and the bonding process begin.

"It's happening," Kilt murmured, still in the midst of his ecstasy but plummeting fast into the trammeling.

And then she too was lost. She could feel her heart pound and was sure she could feel his heart hammering above her chest. They clung to each other as Evie heard strange words enter her mind and without any control she began to recite them in a language she didn't recognize. Meanwhile, Kilt, his mouth pulled open now in a silent scream that looked nothing akin to pleasure, held her tight, and then tighter still until she was sure she could no longer tell their bodies apart; they felt as one.

And as one they became, their ardour spent as their connection to one another was no longer physical but mental and indeed spiritual.

"That's like no other finish with a woman I've ever experienced," his voice murmured, muffled, near her neck. "Was it good for you too?"

She laughed helplessly despite the gravity of their situation. She knew also that even though she was now magically shackled to Faris, he would be very hard not to love. His charm, his manner, his ability to amuse her even in dire circumstances only made her feel even more drawn to him.

"Genevieve, I know you're new to this but you're not meant to laugh," he groaned, reluctantly withdrawing from her. "You're meant to now be telling me that I am the best lover you know."

Her amusement increased. "You're the only lover I know."

"We shall be keeping it that way," he said. Then he lowered his head to kiss her tenderly again. "I am entirely yours now . . . body, mind, soul," he added, his arch tone gone.

"Kilt, I can hear your heartbeat," she whispered, wondering if his pain was over.

"And I can feel you, without having to touch you, although touching you is a very special bonus to this whole aegis arrangement."

She grinned again, feeling like a loon. "I'm not using any healing power. Has the pain stopped?"

He nodded. "Gone."

Evie hugged him. "Suddenly coming here doesn't feel so bad."

"I hate to spoil our tender moment," he said reluctantly. "We should be languishing in a tangle of naked limbs instead of partly dressed and in quite such a hurry, but I think we do need to get back."

"Yes, yes, of course," she replied, hurrying to straighten her clothes. "All these fasteners," she complained and then looked at him, imagining how to explain buttons, let alone zips. And then she let it go; easily, let everything about her former life go. Suddenly all that mattered was Kilt; she didn't care at all about being Valisar or claiming thrones or righting the way this world should be. She was in love, she realized, and she felt deep within herself a private glow at finally giving up something she had always thought precious and had begun to wonder whether she would ever relinquish.

"I should tell you I think we were seen," Kilt admitted sheepishly.

"Who?" she said, spinning around. "Corbel?"

"No, another fellow. He doesn't realize I glimpsed him." He shrugged. "Habit," he admitted, "ever cautious. Anyway, it wasn't de Vis but neither was it my friend, Jewd."

"Barro probably," she said. "He's traveling with us. How much did he see?"

"Only us disappearing into the orchard."

"Then he can't tell Corbel anything."

"But we must," he warned. "He deserves that much."

"I plan to, but, Kilt, after what you've said about Corbel, can you let me tell him, please?"

He nodded. "It's not something I relish telling any man, so go ahead. But it has to be done immediately."

She nodded. "How do you feel?" she asked, unable to help the doctor in her.

"I don't think any aegis could ever feel as fortunate as I do."

She nodded gravely. "Me too; I feel very lucky. I'm so glad Loethar didn't get you."

"Indeed. He doesn't have such great tits!"

Princess Genevieve's delighted laughter filled the orchard.

Twenty-Eight

——➤➤——————————◀◀——

They arrived back into the convent, holding hands, to find everyone waiting for them. The atmosphere felt tense.

Corbel had been sitting with Jewd, away from the other pair of Barro and the Mother, who were talking quietly. Corbel and Jewd appeared silent, deep in their respective thoughts.

She sighed as they approached. "Corbel must know."

"If Barro's any sort of friend he would have told him some of it."

"And your companion looks rather grave too."

"Mmm yes, don't be fooled. I'm in as much trouble as you."

They shared a sympathetic smile. "Marry me, Genevieve," he said on impulse. He gave a soft shrug. "We might as well make it official and really get their tempers warmed."

She nodded. "All right. I've never done anything spontaneous and certainly nothing reckless. I've also never felt like this before . . . so aware of my own life's fragility. So yes, why not marriage to a man I met hours ago? I'm up for it."

As a group, the others noticed them. Everyone shifted but it was Jewd who was upon them first, Corbel hanging back.

"Kilt, what the f—"

"Jewd, I'd like you to meet Princess Genevieve. I doubt you were properly introduced."

Jewd caught himself, but with a scowl dark enough to sour milk aimed at Kilt, he bowed. "Princess," he said.

"Hello, Jewd. You don't look very happy to meet me."

Kilt made a tutting sound. "Don't be fooled. This is Jewd's normal look of rapture, isn't it?" he said, scowling straight back. "Manners, old friend."

"What the hell's been going on?"

"Well, the princess and I have been getting more closely acquainted." He threw her a look but while she refused to look at Kilt, she blinked, embarrassed, at Jewd.

Jewd ignored her and stared at Kilt as though his friend had turned loopy. "You had me bound and tied to a wall!"

"Yes." He nodded seriously. "Yes, I did. And I'm sorry about it and we will discuss it and I will make amends but for now you should perhaps be happy to see that the princess is not trying to gnaw my leg off and that I am not writhing on the ground or screaming to get away from her."

Jewd seemed to realize this fact only now. His mouth opened in shock. "You let her do it to you?"

Kilt nodded. "I did. I let her do it to me twice in fact," he said, feeling like a naughty youth, and felt his new love pinch him surreptitiously but hard.

Jewd scanned him briefly, not understanding. "Where is the wound?"

The others had drawn closer but Corbel still hung back and Kilt decided it was time to be less flippant.

He made his voice serious. "Listen . . . all of you. Genevieve and I talked for a very long time, as you probably know because you've all been waiting for us to reach some sort of resolution . . . and we did. As you've witnessed, I'm helpless in her presence and the fact is she is helpless without mine." He looked around and Barro and the Mother nodded; Jewd just stared at him in a mix of disbelief and anger, while Corbel seemed to seethe in the background. He took a breath; it was more difficult than he'd thought it would be. "I am prepared to throw my lot in with hers." He looked at Jewd as he said this. "We had to support one of them, Jewd. And it could no longer be Leo."

"Why any of them?" the big man demanded.

."You know why and I know you haven't changed your loyalties to Penraven or the greater Set. Besides, she's blameless, she's innocent, and she's helpless."

"So you trammeled him," Jewd accused her, "just like that?"

"Not without his permission I didn't," Evie qualified, an edge to her tone.

"Jewd. It was my decision. Genevieve did not ask me for it. In fact—and I don't care if you don't believe this—she made it possible for me to escape."

Corbel looked up sharply, as if stung. "What do you mean?"

Kilt shrugged. "Your Evie is too clever by half, de Vis. She used her healing magic to give me enough relief to recover, more than sufficient for me to make a run for it. I should add that she also gave her word that she would not look for me."

"Then why—?" Corbel began.

"Because as you are, de Vis, I too am loyal to Valisar and it was the cowardly way out."

"It had nothing to do with the fact that you both seem so easy with each other then?" Barro said.

Kilt's gaze slid to the other big man. "Oh, she is very easy on the eye."

"You bastard!" Corbel said, advancing.

"No!" Evie said, putting a hand up to stop him.

"Not in this place, you won't, Corbel de Vis," the Mother said. "There has been enough blood spilled today."

Kilt watched the man's face cloud, his jaw working overtime to keep his anger in check.

"I think you need to speak with the princess alone, de Vis. And by the way, noble or not, if you ever raise your hand against me again, it will be the last time you raise it against anyone."

"Don't threaten me, Kilt Faris. You're a lowlife outlaw."

"This is true. Strange though that the lowlife outlaw is the one the Valisar king ran to when he needed to protect his crown prince. And here is that same lowlife outlaw now giving his life to protect that same king's rather amazing daughter."

He sighed. "Now, de Vis, hear out your princess. Jewd and I need to talk. Mother, please forgive us all this trespass on your convent, your time, and your patience. All will be explained."

"I can't wait," she said dryly.

Corbel found it hard to even look at her. He sat on a wide windowsill, his arms crossed, a sense of dread in his heart.

"Won't you even look at me?" she tried, and he could hear the hesitation in her voice.

Angry and unsure of what had occurred between her and Faris, he reluctantly raised his gaze to meet hers.

"Thank you," she said. "What's happened between us, Reg?"

"I do prefer Corbel."

"And I preferred my Reg."

"Your Reg? Really? More like your Kilt."

She blinked with irritation. "You know, for someone who has put me into this situation—bullied me into it—you're playing the victim rather well."

He ignored her barb. "I want to know how it comes about that not only can he now stand to be next to you, but two perfect strangers have become such close allies."

She nodded. "You certainly deserve an explanation. You've heard most of it from Kilt. I used my new-found healing powers to rid him of his weakness and pain long enough for him to get away. He stupidly refused to take the option, based on some misplaced sense of loyalty to King Brennus or the Valisars . . . or perhaps it's just that he's loyal to his land. Whatever it is, he wouldn't go. But he did suggest a way that I could consume him without a need for maiming, or even any sort of injury or agony."

Corbel sighed. "You're hedging, Evie. You're usually far more direct than this."

"Well I always thought you were too."

"What's that supposed to mean?"

She advanced on him, pointing a finger. "We were the closest of friends, you and I. I've shared everything with you. But you were full of dark corners, shadows and shades of gray. How dare you accuse me of hedging!"

"Aren't you?"

She pursed her lips and then pushed him, both hands flat against his chest. "Ooh, Reg, you're such a—"

He grabbed her hands but there was only tenderness in the way he held them there against his body. She looked up at him, clearly stunned, swallowing hard. Looking deep into her eyes, he lifted her hands and kissed them gently before he placed them either side of his face with a sigh. "I so prefer it if you'd think of me as Corbel."

"Corbel . . ." He saw tears well, almost spilling over down her cheeks.

"Is it such a surprise, Evie?"

She searched his face. A heavy tear slipped off a lash, down her cheek as she nodded. "You are my best friend, my conscience, and my rock. I'm sorry that I never guessed."

He felt sorrow strike him deep in his heart. "I was in love with you when you were a newborn and it just got worse, changing from adoration as a guardian to the adoration of a lover as you grew and turned into a woman. I hated not being able to tell you the truth of our shared background but truly, Evie, there was no point; I couldn't be sure we'd ever return and frankly after twenty years could you blame me?"

"No," she said, her lips trembling as she cried.

"And how do I tell the young medical student I've watched grow from a distance, whom I've had to contrive to meet and befriend very carefully, very slowly over years . . . how do I tell her that I'm really Corbel de Vis and that I love her with all of my heart—that I always have, that I always will? Tell me how you would have reacted."

"Oh, Corbel," she said and broke down, hugging him close and allowing him to hold her. "I'm so sorry."

He kissed the top of her head, loving the feel of her close against his body even has he was convinced that he could hear the sound of his heart breaking. She would never be his . . . not in the way he'd always dreamed. The Qirin's words echoed in his mind.

"So am I," he said softly.

She hugged him closer still, her weeping deepening and as he wrapped his arms fully around her small frame and laid his head against hers, he realized how his Evie had trammeled Kilt Faris without bloodshed. Barro had said they'd disappeared into the orchard, she following willingly, but he hadn't connected everything in his mind until this moment.

"You slept with him?" he murmured, astonished, agony ripping through him.

She nodded against his chest, hiccupping through her tears. "It was the only way I'd agree to bond him to me."

"This was your idea?"

"No, his," she mumbled, sniffing and getting control of her emotions. She sniffed again. "He wanted to be trammeled."

"I'll bet he did," Corbel said angrily, a vision of Kilt Faris rolling in the grass with Evie claiming his mind's eye.

"No, wait, Corbel. You're missing something," she said, sniffing hard and sighing. "I have to explain this properly."

"What's to explain? This is rape! I'll kill him!"

She shook her head wearily. "This was . . . well, it's hard for me to say this to you now."

He returned her gaze with confusion. "Say what?"

She appeared to find the courage after an awkward pause. "That I love him. That I wanted to be with him in this way."

Corbel repeated the words silently, testing *that I love him* on his tongue as though the phrase made no sense.

His voice was tight and strained when he finally was able to speak. "You don't know the first thing about him! You've just met him."

"That's the whole thing, though. I know everything about him. I can feel him right now, Corbel; I can feel his heartbeat. I can feel his presence as though he's standing right next to me, in me."

"In you . . ." he repeated in an angry whisper.

"We talked first. He told me so much about himself that he had revealed to no one before. And I did much the same for him."

"I've obviously flattered myself that I was that person with whom you shared your deepest thoughts."

She nodded. "It's true, there is nothing I told him that you don't already know, other than perhaps how much I love you." He had been looking out of the window but now his gaze snapped back to hers. "As a brother, though," she added.

Corbel felt his insides do a flip and thought he might be sick. He pushed her away.

"Please, Corbel."

"No, don't say any more. You've been clear and I will say in your defense that I have been far from clear in my affections for you. You are a young woman with all the yearnings of youth. Lo knows I've suffered them long enough in my loneliness."

"Corbel." She reached for him but he stepped aside.

"It's only natural that you would respond to the advances of an older, more worldly man who—"

"Don't," she warned.

He stared at her, his breathing feeling labored but mercifully silent.

"Don't presume to know how I should feel. I'm so sorry that I can't return your love in the manner you wish but please don't denigrate what's happened between Kilt and myself as something petty or as a girlish nonsense. I need to be very honest with you now." She took a deep breath as though steeling herself. "And you need to know this, no matter how much it hurts. I fell in love with Kilt on sight when he was in agony on the ground. And when I rolled up his shirt and touched him I couldn't breathe for how I felt about him." She stepped back. "And it was nothing to do with the Valisar magic!" Evie's ire was up; her eyes were stormy and he spotted familiar high spots of color at her cheeks. He loved her all the more when she was this passionate but he hated that it was anger, and directed at him for the first time in their history. "It had nothing to do with my healing, or his Vested powers or whatever you call it over here. It was plain and simple chemistry, Corbel de Vis, something I understood from my world. My body, my whole being reacted to him in the most primeval, instinctive way. Take away the magic, take away the bonds and the need to be protected. Strip it all away and I would still feel the same way about him."

"Evie—"

"I love him, Corbel. I cannot help it and while I *know* it sounds ridiculous and childish and probably pathetic given the time frame, I do truly believe in love at first sight. I always have. And I always hoped it would happen this way for me. This is the first time in my life I have felt love of a romantic kind for anyone. I'm sorry—a thousand times over I'm sorry—that it's not you, but I love Kilt Faris and yes, we made love in an orchard and we are now bonded as much as by this wretched magic as by our beautiful affection."

Corbel ground his teeth. The old saying of pouring vinegar on a wound had never felt more real, and Evie was emptying the vinegar jar into the gaping wound that his heart had become. "And he feels the same way, I presume."

"He wants to marry me."

He nodded as he let the reality sink in. "Then you have no need for me any longer, your majesty. I will take my leave," he said and bowed, not giving her a chance to say anything further.

His heart was already hardened when he heard her choked sob and he refused to turn.

Loethar stood on the rise, looking down toward the convent. It was not the familiar, welcoming sight of the series of buildings that had his attention but the chilling vision of his own army advancing on Lo's Teeth.

He felt Gavriel's body stiffen alongside him. They'd achieved an awkward but nonetheless easy sort of truce since de Vis's confrontation. Leo appeared to have reconciled himself to walking alone. Loethar couldn't help but feel private sympathy for both; Leo was, after all, doing what any royal in exile should . . . work toward securing the crown at all costs. Loethar had once pursued the same.

What Loethar had discovered, though, and Leo didn't yet know, was that the price of the throne—the cost to one's soul—was too high. Loethar pitied him even as he understood what drove him. Leo had nowhere to go, no reason to live except for finally grasping that crown, making his struggle of the past ten anni count for something. Loethar could forgive Leo his hate.

The truth was, he couldn't help but like de Vis now too. But the former noble of Penraven had a new reason to detest him. He might have turned down Elka's love—that much was obvious—but that didn't mean he approved of whose arms she had since turned to. Nothing had been made obvious; Loethar and Elka had barely stood next to one another during the journey here, but their bond was obvious. De Vis did not have to be too attuned to sense their emotional connection.

And so now Loethar presumed that de Vis would stare down at the advancing imperial army and assume the worst. He was right.

"You've led us into a trap," Gavriel said, sounding resigned, as though it had been inevitable.

Elka swung back to stare open-mouthed at Loethar.

"If you believe that, Elka, you're a fool," he said softly.

"Why am I staring at your men in such large numbers?" she asked.

"It seems they are no longer my men."

"But why would they blindly march when presumably there is no war?"

"No, it's not that. They think they are following your orders, Loether," Gavriel said, and both men shared a glance of understanding.

Elka looked between them.

Gavriel gave a barely discernible shrug and Loethar took over. "Stracker must not have mentioned my disappearance to anyone. The men would believe their emperor has commanded them. They trust Stracker; they always have, just not before me. So Stracker has cunningly just kept the chain of command as though he has been instructed by me. The men have no reason to query it. And unless my eyes are playing tricks, those are all Greens I see . . . Stracker's most loyal."

Gavriel squinted into the distance and nodded. "All Greens."

"All right," Elka said, sounding relieved. "That makes sense." She threw Loethar a look of apology and he returned it with a brief smile that came helplessly to him. *What is happening to the renowned icy heart of mine*, he wondered dryly.

"But that doesn't explain why they're here," Gavriel reminded.

"Indeed." Loethar considered. "Stracker has absolutely no reason to come here . . . unless," he paused, his mind searching.

"Unless what?" Elka prompted.

"Unless he intends to kill Valya. I told him she was incarcerated here."

"Why would he kill your wife?" Gavriel asked, and it was not lost on Loethar how he subtly emphasized the final two words. He glanced at Elka and noticed the barb was not lost on her either.

"Because she murdered our mother. And whatever Stracker is, he loved his mother," Loethar said, giving Gavriel an icy stare.

"What about you—didn't you love your mother?" Gavriel continued.

"I did, but I wouldn't need anything more than a small blade—my bare fists even—to deal with her murderer."

"Stracker would not be here to kill her with an army behind him," Elka said.

"No, he would not. He is not scared of Valya."

"So someone else has put him up to this," Gavriel said slowly.

"It's Piven," Roddy suddenly piped up from the background.

They swung around. "What?" Loethar queried. "You're sure?"

"I feel him too," Ravan admitted. "He and I have somehow been connected since I shared the trammeling of Greven."

Roddy stepped forward. "I no longer feel him as a threat because I am now bonded but I recognize his . . . his magical 'scent,'" he explained.

"Piven?" Loethar murmured, amazed. "I can't sense that. But then my magic is nonexistent, it seems. So we have to presume that he knows I'm here?"

"He couldn't," Ravan admitted. "He can only know that I'm here and with me likely will be Roddy. Though he won't know Roddy's scent because Roddy was not trammeled when he met him."

"So, again, why is he here?" Gavriel demanded. "He's hardly tracking you and Roddy. We know he wants Loethar and Leo dead but Leo is certainly not here, not yet. Or we would know it."

Loethar's gaze narrowed as he shifted it back to the convent. "Then something he wants is in there," he said. "Come on, it's going to take him a little while yet to reach the convent. I want to find out first what he's after."

"Wait, Loethar, surely this will trap us?" Gavriel said.

Loethar turned. "Then stay here with the others out of sight. Keep them safe until Roddy and I return."

"No, I refuse to cower in the bushes," Gavriel challenged. "Anything could happen and we won't know what's going on," he added.

Loethar nodded. "Then follow us, but be quick, everyone. Elka, you're going to have to pick up Janus." She nodded. "Ravan, grab Roddy. De Vis, you're known and mustn't be spotted."

"I'm known?" Gavriel all but spluttered. "Don't be heroic, Loethar. Elka, grab him, will you, and run. He's the one who will be recognized in a blink. If we're seen now, we're doomed. Come here, Roddy," he said, and swept the youngster onto his back. "Ravan, you're the strongest of all of us, I'm sure. Grab Janus, he's not going to be quick enough. This is not about protection—it's about speed and not being seen by that army."

"Lo's Balls and Gar blind the lot of you!" Janus yelled as he was suddenly effortlessly picked up. "What is going on?"

"Hush now, doctor." Gavriel nodded at Loethar and Elka. "Go! Run for your life. Elka, you know your way in. Jump the wall if you have to and open that damn gate yourself. Don't wait for the normal friendly welcome." He loaded the word *friendly*, as though recalling a previous time when it was far from that.

"Gavriel, be careful," she warned and got a stern look of disapproval from him.

"Loethar, ask your beautiful Davarigon escort to hurry."

She scowled at him now.

"I'd like to mount Elka," Janus grumbled from Ravan's back, but those were the last words anyone heard before each was hurrying, trying to beat the new threat.

No one noticed the lone figure on foot, arriving tired and dusty at the doors of the convent, her dull clothes blending all but perfectly into the landscape so she appeared nearly invisible from a distance.

Twenty-Nine

>>————————————————————<<

Jewd stared at Kilt, his expression thunderous. "You what?"

"You heard," Kilt said softly.

"And it worked."

He nodded. "Apparently."

"So what were all the years of running for if it comes down to your willingly allowing a Valisar to trammel you?"

"Well, the key word there, Jewd, is willingly."

"Don't condescend to me," Jewd snapped. "What the hell's going on?"

Kilt gave a helpless, uneven smile. "Duty is what's going on."

"Duty?" Jewd spat as though tasting something dirty.

"Foreign though it must seem, I am capable of it."

"Really? I must tell Lily that next time I see her," Jewd cut back at him.

Kilt felt the sharp wound. "All right, I deserved that."

"Yes, you did. What about Lily and the last ten anni she's given you, waiting for you to do the right thing?"

"What about Lily? The last time I saw her she was making doe-eyes at Felt the Vested," Kilt raged.

"Who was blind," Jewd said as though talking to a simpleton.

"What difference does that make?"

"Well, he couldn't see her making any sort of eyes at him," Jewd raged.

"Irrelevant! She was still making them. She was married

to him, let's not forget. But far more interesting was the reality that she was enamored with him, or are you so thick you couldn't tell that?"

"No, I'm not thick, I've just been deluded into believing I knew you well enough. But recent surprise after surprise should have taught me that the friend I'd give my life for is full of secrets and lies."

"Jewd—" Kilt began in soft exasperation.

The big man shook his head. "No. Not this time, Kilt. You're going to have to come up with something very convincing because I can't think of a single reason why you'd throw all that we've worked so hard to protect to the wind for this slip of a woman—a girl in fact, a total stranger."

Kilt looked down. He knew this would be hard but it was proving a lot more difficult than he'd imagined.

"Yes, she owns my magic now, Jewd, that's true. But she owns one part of me that I gave so freely I couldn't help myself. Even if there was no magic involved . . . even if she'd just stumbled into our camp or I'd run across her at Francham when I was dressed as a woman, I would still find myself helplessly handing her this part of me. I . . . I . . ." He hesitated.

"What?"

"Love her."

Jewd burst out laughing. "You're joking, right?"

Kilt scowled. "No joke."

Jewd continued laughing. "Oh that's rich. Poor Lily. She spends ten anni of her life waiting for you to feel like that enough to say it to her and a twenty-anni-old princess on whom you've never clapped eyes before snaps her fingers and you not only fuck her within a blink of an eye but now you're in love with her." He grabbed Kilt's shirtfront. "Kilt, you've never loved anyone but yourself!"

"I've loved you . . . and that's the truth. And now I have someone else to add to that list. I love Genevieve and I can't help that. I can't help that I never did feel about Lily perhaps the way you did. Isn't that what this is all about, Jewd? You love Lily?"

Jewd let go of Kilt as if burned. An awkward pause lengthened between them.

"Yes, I love her, you stupid bastard. But she's never going to love me as long as you're around."

They stared at each other, both lost for words at their respective admissions.

"I'm sorry, Jewd," Kilt said finally. "I'm sorry you've had to suffer around Lily and myself."

Jewd turned away. "Listening to you making her laugh, having to hug her better when you made her cry, reassuring her that you really did care. I picked up after you constantly where Lily was concerned and that's because I had more love for her in my thumb than your heart held."

Kilt nodded, deeply saddened. "Listen to me . . . please. I've never opened up my heart to any woman. You know that. Lily was . . . I don't know, Lily was . . ."

"Convenient. She's pretty and generous and she worshipped you, and she bound your wounds and cared for Leo in a way you never could. She raised him for you and she made all our lives so much brighter . . . but she was always simply convenient."

Kilt sighed deeply. "It's the truth when I say I didn't really know that. I asked Lily to marry me the very day of her disappearance with Kirin Felt."

"Well, I suppose it's a small consolation that perhaps Lily only thought you were the right one. Felt appears to have stolen her heart. I hate him for that but I'm glad she had his love."

Kilt rubbed his face, feeling helpless. "And she had to watch him butchered by that barbarian. I'll make him pay for that alone!"

Jewd leaned against the wall. They were in the same dry cellar in which they'd taken shelter from the first tendrils of Valisar magic. "What happens now?"

"That depends on you."

"Me?"

"I don't want to lose our friendship."

Jewd sighed, blew out his cheeks. "You don't even need me now, do you? I mean, aren't you all powerful?"

Kilt gave a sad smile. "No, she is, not me. I have no will of my own any more."

"Is that how you want it?"

He nodded. "I think that's what falling in love is all about—I've relinquished control." He laughed. "Yes, it's how I want it. I want to be her guardian, her champion . . . her husband. I want to put my life between danger and hers. The good luck is, we have a very powerful magic to aid that."

"And so might Loethar by now, or Leo."

"Doubtful but yes, it's possible. And there is the other Valisar out there, whomever he is. But, Jewd, this is about protecting Genevieve. She has no desire to take the crown. She proved that in desperately trying to give me my freedom."

"So we let them all slug it out, do we? All these Valisars?"

Kilt shrugged. "My only intention is to get us away from the battleground."

"I see. So we spend the last ten anni raising a king only to—"

They heard a yell in the distance.

"What the—?" Jewd said, stumbling out of the cellar. "It's de Vis."

"He was with Genevieve," Kilt said, instantly throwing up a shield around the princess. He and Jewd drew their swords in perfect tandem.

Corbel ran up. "Whatever magic you've got going on, Faris, you'd want to be wielding it right now."

"What's happening?" Kilt growled.

"Loethar! He's coming down the hill toward us with a giant."

Kilt and Jewd stared at him, dumbfounded. "The Davarigon," Kilt breathed. He was about to mention Gavriel but Corbel interrupted.

"Don't even bother to ask me if I'm sure, I don't forget faces. Especially his and even from a distance I know it's him! Sergius conjured a vision of him for me before I left, told me to remember it."

"How long have we got?"

"Half a bell perhaps. There are others with him—no barbarians that I could see—but his companions are too far away for me to make out. Loethar's leading, well in front, moving fast, riding the big Davarigon like a horse."

"Jewd, I'm going to get the princess. He mustn't know about her."

"He has to know about her already if he's here," Jewd said. "Why else would he come here?"

"Because his wife the empress is here," Corbel said, "and the daughter he doesn't know is alive."

Lily banged on the doors of the convent. She was happy to finally be here, to get some food and lodging but especially some quiet time to think through what was now ahead for her.

She sighed, lifting and dropping her shoulders. She was relieved that she was now a long way from danger but deeply saddened by the fate of her father. Perhaps the famed Qirin could offer her some insight about Greven.

The small viewing door shot back and she was shocked to be confronted by a man. She tried to smile but it failed her and he was quicker.

"Who are you?"

"I'm Lily Felt," she stammered, using her married name out of respect to Kirin.

"Lily Felt," she heard him yell out over his shoulder.

She blinked. Surely this wasn't the normal procedure. What was a man doing here? She was just about to say as much when the convent door swung open and she felt herself dragged inside. Gathering up her surprised indignation and straightening, Lily flashed an angry glance at the man who had manhandled her, but before she could say any more, she was marched from the gate.

"My name's Barro. I've been told to fetch you."

"To where?" she demanded. "The Mother?"

"Among others," he said and hurried her along, away from the main courtyard and into the cloisters where another man waited. There was something oddly familiar about him and she was just trying to place it when she heard a voice she recognized.

"Hello, Lily."

Her gaze snapped left to see Kilt emerging from the shadows.

"Kilt," she heard herself say unnecessarily.

It was Jewd, though, who laughed and was suddenly upon her, swinging her up into his arms. He twirled her around. "You're safe." He set her down and then paused as he looked at her, before he pulled her into a bear-hug. "Lo answered my prayers."

From beneath his huge arms she looked toward Kilt but as usual she couldn't fully read the look on his face. There was something hesitant in his gaze; a new secret, no doubt.

Jewd let her go after planting a kiss at each cheek. "Brave girl. Well done for coming here."

She smiled at Jewd, let it linger so he didn't feel she was ignoring his warm welcome. "I didn't know where else to go," she admitted. "Frankly I'm more surprised to find you here! I was worried you two wouldn't get out of the city."

"Only when we knew you were relatively safe in your swoon and that Stracker's sword had been sheathed," Jewd said.

She allowed herself to look at Kilt. "I had to marry him for my own safety as much as to keep an eye on him."

Kilt's expression crumpled into a soft despair. "It was too much, Lily. I asked far too much of you." He stepped forward and embraced her. It didn't feel the same. Was it her fault or his? They both stepped back. "Are you unhurt?" he inquired.

She nodded. "I escaped. I had help," was all she could think of to say.

"I'm deeply sorry about Kirin Felt. It was obvious that he had done his best to keep you safe and that you . . ." He cleared his throat. "That you were fond of him. He deserved that much." Before she could say what she wanted to, he continued, as though not wishing to hear her response. "Do you know who interrupted proceedings that day? We think perhaps—"

"I can tell you who it is. It's Piven."

"Piven! Don't be mad!" It was the familiar man she couldn't place, who railed at her.

"Who is this?" she demanded.

"Lily, this is Corbel de Vis."

She rocked back on her heels. "Gavriel's twin brother?" she said, unable to mask her confusion.

"It's a long story," Corbel said. "I'm sure Faris will familiarize you with it one day over a pot of dinch," he said acidly, "but right now with time at a premium, what do you know of Piven?"

"I have a better idea, given the time frame. Why don't you go to hell instead, Corbel de Vis?" Lily suggested. "I don't answer to you. In fact—" She paused to take a breath and Kilt laid a hand on her arm.

"Corbel's under some strain, Lily. No time to explain why fully."

"Really?" Corbel said. "This *is* the Lily you mentioned to me, Faris. I think she deserves your full explanation."

She watched Kilt turn and glance at de Vis with a look that spoke of pain. De Vis ground his jaw.

"There is no time! Was it truly Leo's invalid adopted brother?" Kilt asked.

She sighed, realizing there was not going to be a peaceful soak in a tub of warmed water, no much needed meal or quiet reflection.

"It was Piven. He is no invalid. His faculties are intact; in fact, he is frighteningly intelligent and eloquent. What's more, Piven is all Valisar. His adoption was a ruse by King Brennus that even the queen was part of." She enjoyed watching Corbel de Vis's face drain of its color, watched him struggle to find any words.

"There's more," she continued. "Piven has found an aegis."

She heard them groan as one, Kilt sucking in air as though struck, but he didn't look surprised.

"We wondered as much. But he knew to trammel the aegis?" he asked.

"He appears to know everything there is to know about the Valisar magic. He is very powerful in it."

"How do you know?" de Vis demanded.

"Because I was there! Because Piven took a fancy to me

and prevented Stracker murdering me as he hacked my husband to bits."

She choked back a sob. "And because I spoke with the aegis. He was the one who helped me to escape."

"Spoke to him?" Kilt said, frowning. "Why would he speak with you or help you?"

"Because the aegis is my father!" she hurled back, her glare defying them to deny it.

She was met with a stunned silence.

It was Jewd who came to her rescue. "Come on, Lily. You look exhausted. I hate to tell you but there's more danger coming."

"What?"

He nodded. "Loethar's on his way down to the convent."

She stared back, uncomprehending. "Why?"

"None of us know. But we don't plan on giving him much of a chance to discuss it." Jewd flexed the string of his bow. "Once he's in range, which is any moment, he's down."

"No killing," Kilt warned.

"How come?" she asked.

Again there was that slight hesitation. "Because we can handle Loethar."

She shook her head in amazement. "I can't be bothered with any of you at the moment, with your double-speak and what you're not saying. Get out of my way, de Vis. I can't say you've grown on me as your brother did so quickly," she sneered at him. "But welcome back from wherever the hell you've been hiding."

De Vis scowled at her but, at a shake of the head from Kilt, didn't respond. Lily stomped down the hall, running into a group of nuns waiting worriedly.

One of them, clearly senior, held out her hands. "I'm sorry you meet us under these difficult circumstances. I am the Abbess here, but clearly you know the gentlemen who seem to be overrunning our convent?" She said it so kindly Lily wanted to weep.

"Hello, Mother. Thank you for letting me in."

"My dear, wild horses wouldn't have stopped the big man, Jewd, when he heard your name."

"Strange isn't it?" Lily said, tiredly. "The man I was to marry greets me so formally and with such distance. Meanwhile his best friend hugs me as though we are long lost lovers."

The Abbess smiled. "This is the strange way of the world, my dear. Jewd is, er . . . clearly fond of you. Come, you'd better meet the princess."

"Princess?" Lily repeated. "Which princess?"

"The daughter of Brennus and Isadora," the Mother replied, shocking Lily once again.

"Tell her, or I will," Jewd said to Kilt, an edge to his voice that brooked no argument. "Loethar's your excuse, bless his savagely good timing. So you can make it quick. I'll keep an eye on things here. They've slowed down because it's so steep. He'll be in my sight the whole way."

Kilt nodded, knew there was no way out of this. And Jewd was right. It had to be done now. He followed after Lily, past the few chittering nuns who had ventured out of the rooms they and the Mother had suggested they confine themselves too. "Sisters," he said politely, walking on. He could see the Mother ahead, walking alongside Lily, and he could only imagine what was being discussed. He put a jog into his step and caught up.

"Excuse me, Mother. Might I steal Lily from you? It will only take a moment or two," he said.

"You see, Mother. That's just how much my absence and near death meant to him," Lily said archly. She clearly meant it as a joke for the Abbess but it was parched and scorching and full of fiery intent for Kilt.

"Of course." The Abbess looked at Kilt. "If you are sure about . . . ?"

"Jewd is watching Loethar's approach. You have nothing to fear. There will be no bloodshed in your convent, Mother."

"Or outside, Kilt Faris."

"I can't promise that, Mother," he said, firmly but amiably. "But I will do my best."

"I happen to like Loethar but this is your argument. Do not involve my convent in your troubles," she warned. "My dear," she said, turning to Lily. "This is not our usual hospitality toward women travelers."

Lily smiled sadly. "Thank you, Mother." She shrugged, palms open to Kilt. "Where would you like to go?"

He took her hand and led her to a quiet nook in one of the courtyards not far from where he and Barro had bathed. He sat her down at a stone bench and they both remained still and quiet for what felt like an interminable time.

"Tell me about Kirin Felt," he said. "The . . . er, the short version. In fact, I guess what I really want to know is, did you love him?"

She looked down at her hands. "I still do. I'm amazed at my depth of feeling for him and I'm ashamed that I could ever have believed you and I were for eternity."

He nodded. "Then I am truly sorry for his loss."

"Is that all you have to say?"

"I'm not sure what you want me to say."

"Perhaps display some shock, even mild surprise that I could be in love with another man."

"Yes, you're right, I should. But you have been candid and I should be too."

His gaze flashed up. "What surprise have you got for me now?"

"Firstly you should know I feel an intense relief that you found love elsewhere." It came out all wrong; he watched her eyes instantly fill with tears. "Oh, Lily, that sounds cruel but actually what I mean to say is that I was very bad for you. You deserved so much better than I was giving, than I was perhaps ever capable of giving you."

"Did you really ever try?"

"I thought I was in love but . . ."

"Don't. I think I know what you're trying to say."

"No, I don't think you do."

Her face grew grave and she sniffed away her tears. "What's wrong, Kilt?"

"I'm an aegis," he blurted out.

He could see that she wasn't shocked.

"I'm sorry," he added. "I know this must be hard to hear

after Kirin, and the revelation about your father whom I know you loved dearly."

"An aegis?" she whispered. He nodded.

"I've been running from the truth all of my life."

Her expression clouded. "So why are you admitting it to yourself, to me, to the world now?"

He swallowed. "Because I have met and been trammeled by a Valisar."

She gave a soft shriek of despair and then she grabbed for his hands, patting his arms, clearly looking for his wound.

"There is no injury," he said quietly but she took scant notice of him.

"Why? How?" she demanded, an edge of hysteria to her voice.

He took both her hands. "Lily, stop!" Her eyes, which were scanning his body, obeyed, coming to meet his. "Just stop. It required no wound."

"Which Valisar? Leo?"

He gave a sound of soft scorn. "No, but Leo would not have hesitated to chop my leg off. In your absence he changed, Lily. He murdered Freath, wanted to kill Loethar, would definitely have used me in the worst way."

"I leave you alone for a few days and look what happens," she said, trying so hard for the levity they could often share.

"Yes, indeed, you rush off and marry the first man you come across, fall in love with him, nearly get executed—"

She put her hand over his mouth. "Hush, Kilt. Don't. I can't bear for us to make light of it."

"I'm sorry. This is going to be a shock for you but the Valisar is Genevieve . . . the princess who apparently didn't die. Another of Brennus's cunning plots."

Dawning erupted across her face. "The Mother mentioned her. But she'd be . . . what? . . . ten anni or something. How could she possibly overwhelm you if you could resist Leo and . . ." Her voice trailed off as she searched his eyes. "She didn't overwhelm you, did she?"

He shook his head. "She desperately tried to let me escape."

"But you stayed. You let her trammel you. Why, Kilt?" she begged, hammering her fists into his chest with wretched despair. "Why?" she cried.

"Kilt?" came a voice.

And they both looked up. Kilt wasn't sure who was more surprised, Lily or Genevieve.

"Ah, your majesty. This is Lily. Lily, this is the Princess Genevieve."

Lily looked dumbfounded. She glanced at Kilt and then back to the beautiful young woman who stood before her. She swallowed hard. "You're meant to be ten. But then again, you're also meant to be dead."

Genevieve nodded. "What a long story I have to tell my children," she said, but there was no mirth in her voice. "Hello, Lily. Kilt has told me all about you."

Lily seemed to find her wits and actually curtseyed. "Your highness."

"Please don't. Call me Evie," she said but Lily was already turning to fix Kilt with a stare.

"You don't have to explain anything more, Kilt. I think I understand."

"I want to, I should and I owe you that explanation in length but Loethar is here and that is a problem that won't wait. And Jewd insists you know it all, so here it is, Lily."

Evie blanched. "Shall I—?"

"No," Kilt insisted. "You should stick close now." He returned his gaze to Lily. "I was trammeled today by Genevieve when we laid down together and she consumed a part of me that required no bloodshed, no wound, only my love."

The honesty hurt deeply. He watched it sink into her other wounds as though his words were salt being sprinkled onto them. He watched her catch her breath and her breathing change.

"I have no choice but to belong to Genevieve now . . . but I must add, as we are being honest, that even if I had the choice I would want it no other way."

"Please don't say any more," Lily asked, her voice quivering. "I think . . . I must leave now. Forgive me." She stood abruptly and ran from the room.

"Kilt, how could you do that? It was so harsh."

"Blame Jewd. Frankly, I wouldn't have said a thing. Lily was in love and struggling to work out how best to tell me. She was in enough despair over her losses to just add me to the list."

"It's Jewd's way of making you pay for deserting him, I think."

"I haven't," Kilt bleated.

"It's how it feels to him. He won't forgive easily what you've done for me and what's happened between us. You and he have been a close duo for most of your lives." She shrugged.

"Well, we've got much bigger problems now. Come on, your majesty. Affairs of the heart and even the grudges of lifelong friends must wait."

Thirty

The four men men and Evie were on the roof, watching Loethar approach.

"How did it go?" Jewd murmured.

Kilt's expression said enough. "I've told the women to remain behind doors."

"Then why bring Evie—" Corbel began, scowling.

"I need her magic here so I can shield us all . . . as best I can."

"Is that him?" Evie said quietly.

Corbel nodded. "That's your Uncle Loethar, barbarian warlord and self-proclaimed emperor, the man who butchered your father, pushed your mother into suicide and has been hunting Valisars ever since."

"He looks rather handsome," she remarked and won a stare of disdain from all of them. "And the tall woman?"

"Elka," Jewd breathed. "Very impressive. Davarigon. A race of near giant people who keep themselves to themselves in these mountains behind us."

"And the others?" she wondered.

Kilt raised an eyebrow. "I don't know the other trio but Corbel by now you should have recognized—"

"Gavriel," Corbel breathed. And then before anyone could stop him, he was on his feet, no longer hidden, yelling. "Gavriel!"

They watched in horror as the people approaching down

the hill froze. Loethar took two steps forward. He was close enough now for them to see his smile.

"Kilt Faris! I see you."

Kilt felt the first vague tendrils of magic waft around him like perfume. "Take him, Jewd," he snarled.

"With pleasure," Jewd replied. He stood and in a blink had taken his aim and let fly with an arrow that hurtled toward its mark in the middle of Loethar's chest.

"No!" Evie yelled.

They watched the arrow appear to strike its target but then it fell away uselessly to the ground. Loethar bent, picked it up and made a show of snapping it. Without saying anything else he hurried his group down the hills.

But Gavriel refused to move. He was just opening his mouth to yell something back when Kilt saw the Davarigon giant grab him and yell something in his face. Then meekly he followed, running along.

"He's got an aegis," Kilt growled.

"How?" Jewd thought aloud. "It's only been days."

"Well, you watched the aegis magic in action. There's no point in trying to finish Loethar now."

"Don't you think he would have taunted you if he really is this hideous tyrant you keep referring to?" Evie demanded. Kilt knew she was angry at him for breaking his promise to the Abbess.

Barro spoke up. "There is no way, if he's protected magically, he wouldn't have rubbed it in our faces. He's emperor; he would have wanted to reinforce that."

"Is that truly my brother?" Corbel said, wonder on his face, seemingly unconcerned by Loethar.

"That is certainly Gavriel de Vis," Kilt confirmed. "But something else is going on here, and I don't know what."

"Perhaps my uncle wants to talk?" Evie offered.

"To who? Me? He didn't know I was even here. You heard the surprise in his voice. No," Kilt said, frowning. "He's here for an entirely different reason. I think, Corbel, you could be right. Perhaps he's here for Valya."

Barro shrugged. "So what do we do?"

"Let him in."

"No!" Jewd growled.

"He can't hurt me, Jewd. In fact, his aegis and I cancel each other out. He will protect his people and I will protect mine. If it makes you feel any easier, you can train your arrows on whomever you wish in his party. None of them, other than Gavriel or the woman, look in any way dangerous. There's a lad in tow, for Lo's sake. But let's hear what he's got to say."

They clambered down from the low, flat roof. Everyone opted to wait in the courtyard, including Lily, who had stolen out to join them but stood well back as though she no longer felt part of Kilt's group. Jewd had his bowstring pulled taut, an arrow loaded and aimed on the gate, while Barro had his sword drawn.

Only Corbel refused to be still. Against their angry protests he had slammed open the gate and was running toward the newcomers.

"Gavriel!"

Gavriel de Vis's gaze locked onto the familiar figure. The man running toward him looked like his brother but surely this couldn't be him? "Corb?"

And he was dragged into the stranger's arms. "Yes, it's me. Don't be alarmed, brother."

Gavriel pushed back from the man, astonished; he could barely speak. "What . . . ? What's happened to you?"

"No time," Loethar said. "Greetings, de Vis," he said to Corbel, "but the family reunion must wait," he warned, his gaze firmly fixed on the gate. "Please, de Vis. It's not me I'm concerned for—but Elka, Janus . . . even you."

Gavriel hesitated and then grabbed his brother hard, fighting a swell of emotion. "We have to get inside, Corb. They're coming."

"Who?"

"Killers. Just move. Loethar's right, we must wait for our reunion."

He stepped back and looked at Corbel, entirely perplexed.

Corbel understood. "I have much to tell you, Gav, but I'm glad to see that I remain the good-looking one."

Gavriel actually scoffed as Loethar bundled them all through the gates and into the fragile safety of the compound.

At first everyone regarded each other in an awkward silence. It was Kilt who broke it at last.

"Well, well . . . look what the wind has blown in."

"Faris, you're looking at ease. Fortunate, isn't it, that I have my aegis so you need not sicken around me?"

"The stench of the blood staining your soul is enough to do that. Which one of you disloyal bastards lent your magic to the tyrant?"

"Me, sir," the lad admitted. "I am his aegis."

"A child? You trammeled a child?" Kilt hurled at him. "You truly are the lowest of the low."

"Faris, the boy gave his magic willingly," Gavriel said, already looking weary of the tension.

"What is your name?" Kilt said to him.

"Roddy."

"Why, Roddy?"

"I trust him. He is not all bad. And he tried to stop me from giving him my magic."

"So, Faris, you seem entirely untroubled by our presence which suggests you are not frightened of death," Loethar remarked.

"I would never have turned outlaw if I was frightened of death. Let's just say I am not frightened of you."

"So if I raised my sword?"

"I would shoot your Davarigon escort," Jewd answered casually.

"Over my dead body," Gavriel exclaimed.

The man Kilt didn't know stepped forward. "I'm tired and I could use some real food and a decent drink. If you'll all excuse me," he said and began walking away.

Kilt actually laughed. "Barro. Stop him please."

"Touch him and I'll kill whichever of you is Barro," Elka

said. "You know I can, Faris. This is a physic. He has no magic but the gift of his knowledge. He is tired, as he says. Let him be."

"Fine," Kilt said, and Janus disappeared deep into the convent. Kilt noticed him throw Elka a look of gratitude, which she returned with a tight sympathetic smile.

"Why are you here?" Kilt demanded.

"Would you believe me if I said we were trying to find somewhere safe . . . to think?" Loethar offered.

"No."

Elka sighed audibly. "Last time I was here I don't remember Kilt Faris being in charge of the convent. Where is the Abbess?" she demanded.

"Right here, Elka," said a new voice and the Mother swept into the courtyard.

"Mother," Loethar said and bowed politely.

"I'm glad they didn't kill you, my son," she said in her dry tone.

"They couldn't if they'd wanted to," he replied gently.

"Let's all, just for a moment, assume that I am in fact in charge here," she said. "I would be interested to know why you are here," she directed at Loethar.

"Mother, my army is approaching your convent at a steady march. My men are under the control of its general, who is pretending that he is answerable to me while in fact he answers to a far more sinister puppeteer."

Kilt frowned. "Piven," he murmured.

"That's right." Loethar briefly told them everything he knew, introducing Ravan and bringing both him and Roddy into the conversation to describe their first-hand experience with Piven.

"So why come here if Piven is hunting you here?" Jewd asked.

"I didn't know Piven was coming here."

"Why is he? Why would he leave the palace, the city, to come to a convent . . . an outpost far away from Penraven in the foothills of the mountains?" Kilt demanded with exasperation.

Lily stepped forward out of the shadows. "I think I can

answer that, Kilt. Perhaps my escape was not as clean as I thought. Hello, Gavriel," she added, embarrassed.

Gavriel stared at her, his mouth open. "Lily," was all he said but the emotion in his voice was naked to all.

Kilt sighed. "Right. Of course. You were followed." He quickly began to outline what he knew for the newcomers.

Lily chimed in and then ended up taking over, relaying all that she could recall from the time she'd spent in the company of Piven and Stracker.

"Stracker has willingly thrown his lot in with him," she said to Loethar. "But they likely have no idea that you or the princess is here."

"Princess?" Loethar and Gavriel said together, looking around.

Evie stepped up next to Kilt. "Corbel, it must be our turn to give an explanation," and a truly astonished audience listened in awe as their tale unfolded.

Roddy fell to his knees before Genevieve as she finished, "And Corbel brought me here."

"Your highness," he said. "Forgive me that I did not save myself for you."

Loethar glanced at Kilt and gave him a knowing nod. "I understand now."

Kilt smiled. "Genevieve has her aegis too, Loethar. I'll warn you now, she cannot be harmed."

"Brennus was surely the most conniving king of all the Valisars. He never fails to surprise me. First Piven, now Princess Genevieve." Loethar stepped forward and Kilt bristled but moved back at a warning look from Evie. "Your highness," Loethar said, taking her hand and kissing it. "I never imagined myself inviting any Valisar into my life, but welcome back, niece."

She smiled demurely. "Thank you, uncle. It's special to be meeting long lost family." And then she looked around at everyone. "It appears to me, as an outsider and an observer of these proceedings, that while you may have thought yourselves enemies, you should be united against this half-brother of Loethar's and my brother who controls him. Whatever has gone before, you must bury the hate and the pain. All this combined knowledge together with our aegis magic must allow us to find a way to protect the helpless, both here in our midst and those out there who should not share this fight for the crown. Let me say it now to all of you: I do not want the Valisar crown."

Loethar sighed. "And I relinquish my claim on the empire."

That brought a silence.

"He means it," Elka assured. "It's one of the reasons Roddy gave himself over. We came here to throw our lot in with you, your highness," she said to Evie. "We hoped to find you here. Ravan and Roddy believed you would be."

"Is this true?" Kilt demanded of Loethar. "You came here to offer yourself to the princess?"

Loethar nodded. "Without reservation. I do not wish to rule any longer. One day when we have more time I will explain it but right now we must work together, as my niece says, to protect these people who don't have a magical shield."

Surprising himself, Kilt reached out a hand. Loethar took it.

"This is for the innocents," Kilt said, "not the Valisars."

"For the innocents," Loethar echoed.

The three women actually clapped and the other men looked around at each other, bemused, as Kilt and Loethar shook hands, sealing their pledge.

Jewd shook his head. "Well, life is never boring around you, Kilt, that's for sure."

It was Gavriel who gave voice to a concern everyone seemed to have missed. "But if Piven is following Lily—and he has his aegis—why has he brought an army?"

Thirty-One

————◆————

Piven was becoming restless. "What an interminable journey. How much longer?"

"We are nearly there, your majesty," Vulpan said. "We just passed the marker stone."

"And we're sure she's headed for the convent?"

"So my men assure us," Stracker said. "There is nowhere else. She is hardly going to disappear into the mountains."

"Lily has survived in the forest most of her life. She's not scared of living rough," Greven warned. "I hope she does disappear into the Teeth, never to be heard from or seen again!"

"Be quiet, Greven," Piven said wearily. "Stracker, I've allowed you to bring one hundred of your men. You said you would explain as we neared the convent. Are you going to tell me why now that you have exasperatingly negated my ability to steal up on them?"

Stracker's tatua stretched as he grinned, his chains attached to his nose and ears, lips and eyebrows jangling lightly. He would normally not wear his "jewelry" into any sort of fray, Piven knew, so he was clearly feeling comfortable that whatever opposition was ahead, it would be minimal.

"I have given it a lot of thought and it's a precaution for Loethar. He's getting help and I don't know from whom or how many. But the person who gave me this," he said, pointing to the wound on his head, "was a Davarigon. If he has somehow won that people's support, then while you are hunting down Lily Felt for your own reasons, I want to ensure my brother is sent to the gods. And I want the men around me to bear witness."

"Oh believe me, Stracker, when I say that I want the same for your half-brother. But what makes you think your army will strike down their emperor?"

"These are the Greens only. And they will follow me—before anyone—to my death. I don't need them for the killing. That will be my pleasure. But I want them to see the leader of the Greens strike a blow, one that's been long overdue."

"They might have to kill, though, general, if the Davarigons are involved."

Stracker laughed. "The Davarigons are not aggressive. They will not take on the army. That's another reason I brought along the Greens: they will act as a deterrent. And they will show Loethar that he has lost control. If he's here and he sees the Greens arrive as one, the message between him and me is clear."

"Are you certain the Greens will follow you above the emperor?" Vulpan wondered and, at the glare from Piven, hurried to rephrase. "Er, I mean, if Loethar and you are kin, why wouldn't they want him spared?"

"Almost all of the tribal colors would refuse to move against Loethar but the Greens are different," Stracker acknowledged with a rare sigh. "The Greens have not forgiven him for not proudly tattooing his royal status to his face and body in their shared color. And what's more, he has shown no favor to the Greens since their generous help to make him emperor. Still, if it were anyone but their own leader asking it, they would not be a party to treachery," he said, grinning widely. "But I am a Green before I am anything and they know it and would kill for me. Through me they will enjoy the favor they want."

"And you think Loethar might be right here?" Piven asked.

"I last saw him in the north. I've had spies working hard. A Davarigon woman was asking for a physic's help in the

town of Francham not long ago, which is close to where
I was attacked. The physic she contacted has since disappeared and there are rumors that they were glimpsed heading east."

"And?"

"I know every step of this land," Stracker admitted. "There
is nothing near Francham this far north other than the convent. Besides, that's where Loethar sent Valya, so he is familiar with it, no doubt on friendly terms with its Abbess. It
would be a good place for Loethar to lie low unnoticed and
convalesce from his wounds."

"My, my, Stracker, your creativity has been working hard.
It all sounds thoroughly plausible and whether or not it comes
to fruition, I find your imagination most entertaining. Plus
it will be incredibly amusing to watch the nuns quake beneath your imposing gaze, not to mention your one hundred
Greens."

"Piven, this is madness," Greven counseled. "What can
you expect to gain from this?"

"Everything, if Loethar is here. And I have to tell you,
Greven—and don't deny that you aren't feeling it too—my
senses are twitching. Perhaps General Stracker has excelled
himself. I smell Valisar magic on the wind."

Greven looked away angrily and Piven knew he felt it too.
This was the moment he had been longing for. Which Valisar
would he slaughter first? Toying with that notion kept him
entertained for the last few dull miles of their journey. He
hoped it was Loethar.

Behind them lay a devastated compound on the outskirts
of Barronel. General Marth's mustering of the soldiers who
could still remember the old hate for the barbarians had
been a lynchpin of the attack but it had been Leo's inspired
idea to trial whether he could be used as a channel for magic
that had won the day. It was true that the Vested camp was
not the most heavily guarded of regions in the empire; they
were a community known to be non-aggressive, of almost
accepting their fate as imperial prisoners.

The Vested were so compliant in fact that their supervision

over the years had dwindled to what was essentially a skeleton guard. Loethar left the administration of the community mainly to former administrators of Barronel—civil servants who knew how to work as part of a group and keep good account of spending, provisioning the Vested, caring for them, providing the structure they needed, from accommodation to teaching to apothecaries. Barronel was now seen as an outpost, a place tribal soldiers were sent in their earliest years to do a "season" as it was known in their ranks, or somewhere those same soldiers—perhaps a bit older— might be sent as punishment for misdemeanors. It had evolved over the decade into a more casual, even sleepy hamlet where little excitement occurred and most of the men were keen to leave. They showed little interest in the Vested and as such there was all but nil interaction between Vested and imperial guard.

And so the uprising had not only caught the soldiers entirely "off guard" but Marth had planned the strike to occur during the night when it was left to locals of his ilk to keep an eye on the Vested's end of town. In the small hours the Vested were led as quietly as possible out of their compound while Leo and a small unit of Marth's most trusted patriots had moved silently on a killing rampage.

Marth knew there were exactly fifty-one soldiers in the city. Fate was smiling on them; that was the lowest number he could recall and he had deliberately and very generously greased the palm of the two innkeepers at the favored drinking spots to not water any wine or ale—in fact to be liberal with his servings. One final act of defiance that, while it didn't sit easily on Marth's conscience, was necessary to ensure their success was the drugging of the soldiers' liquor. Leo had insisted on every precaution being taken.

"Make no protest, Marth, this is war. Loethar used cunning for his overthrow. This is just a different form of fighting. Subterfuge is something my father was clearly adept at and would applaud if it meant it achieved our aim."

Marth had nodded, accepting that this was their one glittering opportunity to overthrow their captors.

And Leo had used the slackness in attitude by the barbarians to devastating effect, striking while the majority of the fifty-one men dozed in a drugged stupor. The rest he killed with startling efficiency with his own skills . . . a hefty dose of his new-found magic magnifying his abilities, Perl dragged alongside, her eyes wide with terror. But one man, found relatively sober in the arms of a whore, died awake. Tied naked to a chair, the whore's screams still echoing, he was conscious and entirely aware of the blade being drawn across his throat.

"Remember me, Welf?" Leo had said as blood burst forth and the young soldier had begun to gurgle and choke. "Let King Leonel's face—a Valisar—be the last face you remember on your way to hell."

Even Marth had chosen to look away when he'd seen the savagery in the eyes of the man in whom he'd placed his faith.

The Vested had emerged onto the main road between Barronel's easternmost point in either fast-moving family carts hitched to teams of horses or saddled up on horseback ready to ride hard.

Leo had consulted the runes for their best course.

"You cannot lie to me, Perl," he warned.

"I can withhold information, though," she said.

"Then I will make sure I ask all the right questions," he said as she spread her stones out by torchlight. "Now tell me what you see."

With a stormy look darkening her expression, Perl picked up her marked pebbles and gave consideration.

"I cannot predict the future," she snapped. "I can only get impressions of your life. East. Your destiny lies east."

You're sure now? Not south into Penraven, which makes a lot more sense."

Perl shrugged. "Ignore me if you choose. Follow your own instincts. The stones suggest east. But I'll tell you I sense darkness there. You would do well to take your chances elsewhere."

"Where is Tolt?" Leo called.

"Here," a sulky voice replied.

"What have you dreamed?"

"Killing."

"Who?"

"Many."

Leo gave a look of exasperation at Tolt's vague responses.

Suddenly Reuth shouldered her way forward. "I had a vision earlier this evening."

"And?" Leo said, standing from where he'd been crouching near Perl and her runes.

"Well, it was fast and made no sense. It was just a flash of a picture in my mind. I saw the convent at the foothills of Lo's Teeth, surrounded by the barbarian army—the Greens."

"The Greens are Stracker's," Leo hissed. "Did you see Loethar in your vision?"

"No, majesty. Only the walls of the convent surrounded by the soldiers."

"So, the convent," Leo repeated as though this would be the last place in the whole of the Empire he would imagine heading. "How do you know it's that one?"

"I recognize the landscape. I sought refuge there when we first escaped Loethar's clutch. It was the Qirin there who suggested I return to the south and into Medhaven; she said happiness would find me there. I thought she might have meant peace but I now realize she meant Clovis."

"Perl says east," he murmured.

"And the convent is east," Reuth said.

"Then east we go. By my reckoning if we ride hard, general, with scouts up ahead to make sure of no traps, we can make it by midday."

Marth nodded. "Let's get out of Barronel. We can regroup once we near the Teeth. I'm presuming you have a plan, majesty?" he said, an eyebrow lifting.

"I'm working on one," Leo said, with anger in his voice. "Let's ride. Come, Perl."

Soundlessly she stood, followed Leo and permitted him to help her up behind him on the fine stallion he'd stolen. With her arms around him they looked like lovers but that was where the comparison stopped. Their expressions showed there was no love between them . . . not even companionship. Marth suspected the young king had no time for friendship even though he'd permitted a Vested priest to say the words of marriage hurriedly for them.

Driving them hard through the night and sticking to the northernmost roads, Marth suspected they would encounter few, if any, of Loethar's people, and he was right. These were not densely populated areas anyway so there was scant reason for soldiers to be patrolling. But the handful of surprised barbarians they met along the way, who looked astonished to see a column of hard-riding, disheveled peasants on good horses, met a swift death. Leo had been well trained in the art of killing from horseback and with Perl's protection he won not a single scratch from the barbarian arrows. Galloping, howling with glee at the soldiers, he killed even those who ran from his swinging sword or begged mercy.

People ate, drank, even rested as they traveled and so the column never stopped moving. They were two hundred strong; most of the Vested had chosen to join Leo and Marth but some were too infirm or too young to make the journey, and a few simply refused to be drawn into what looked like dangerous times ahead. By dawn they had caught their first glimpse of Lo's towering Teeth in the distance. It was here, herding people into the nearby woods, that Leo called his first and only halt, and after watching that everyone was sufficiently hidden by the trees, he alighted his horse and called to Marth and Reuth.

They stood now on a rise talking about what was ahead.

"Do we have anyone among the Vested who is a specialist in the academic side of magic?"

Reuth nodded. "We have a scholar. He's Cremond and was formerly of the Academy."

"Could you fetch him, please?"

Reuth did so. He was a man getting close to moving into his seventh decade, tall with a head of thick silver hair and a neatly trimmed beard the same color. He looked tired but his pale, penetrating eyes were alert. "You wished to see me?" he asked.

It was obvious to Marth that no one was quite sure how to address Leo but the young king didn't seem to be worried about that for now.

"You are?"

"Trellon. Formerly Professor Trellon."

"Thank you. Professor, I need to learn some details of the Vested magic and I understand you are something of an authority."

Trellon seemed surprised. "I wouldn't call myself that. I suppose, though, I've been around the Academy long enough to have a solid grasp of the magics we find in the Vested."

Leo nodded thoughtfully. "I'm interested in how to harness magic."

"Oh, I see." At this Trellon gave a brief blink that turned into an uncertain shrug. "You mean wielding someone else's power? It has not been successful in the past."

"What has been attempted?"

"Oh, amazing concepts from trying to reflect it off mirrors, trying to concentrate it through glass . . . even water. I think the Academy tried to tap into it via the Vested's dreams even. And two Vested tried to pass on their powers to each other but look," he said, shaking his head, "none of this came to any avail. And I would be lying if I said any of us took it seriously."

"Did you ever try concentrating magic from many into one source?"

Trellon looked up to the graying dawn as he pondered the question. Then he returned his pale gaze to Leo. "No, I can't say I recall anything of that nature." He frowned. "We were just trying to get one Vested's magic wielded by or through another. We hadn't even thought beyond that challenge. What do you have in mind?"

Leo gave a tight mirthless smile. "I recently visited a soothsayer. He said nothing of any consequence for the most part—making no reference to my background, for example—but as I was leaving he told me that I should regard myself as the family chalice. That's all he said."

"What does it mean?" Reuth asked.

"You realize he guessed who you were," the professor said somberly, a silvered eyebrow lifting.

"That's what I'm hoping. But he didn't seem at all interested in that. Perhaps the gold sovereign I gave him helped.

But while he laughed off his 'tellings' as a bit of fun, there was something in the look he gave me when he described me as the family chalice."

"He wanted you to work it out."

Leo nodded. "And I think today I must."

Trellon smiled. "May I try?"

"Go ahead. Sit with me, professor."

"So," Trellon began once he was comfortable. "Chalice is a royal cup, used in the coronation of sovereigns." Leo gave a small grunt of agreement. "So that was him telling you that he believed you were of a royal family."

"Yes . . . and that's as far as I tend to get. The cup can have other significance, of course," he said frowning. "Full, empty . . ." He shrugged and grimaced. "Poisoned?"

"Or maybe you're looking at it too deeply," Trellon suggested. "Perhaps this man, though subtle in his method, meant something far more obvious."

Leo ran a frustrated hand through his hair. "Like what?"

"Simply that he acknowledged your royalty and was telling you that you are the receptacle."

"Receptacle?"

"The bearer, the holder . . . the . . . the . . ." It was Trellon's turn to search as he thought through the critical meaning. "The chalice is a royal cup," he repeated slowly, his eyes squinting into the distance as he reached for what he sought. And then he closed his eyes, a soft smile breaking across his face. "The vessel," he said as though arriving with a sigh after running a race. "Your majesty, I think your fortune teller was no charlatan and he was trying to tell you what he truly saw . . . that you are the Vessel of the Valisars."

Leo felt his gut twist with anticipation and a nervous energy he felt deep in his heart. "Vessel," he repeated softly. "So I carry something."

Trellon nodded excitedly. "Yes . . . yes of course. I think I understand now."

"What?" Leo urged and both Reuth and Marth had moved closer.

"You were on the right path. Your question about our trials to find a way to wield the Vested magic is so relevant."

Leo's face was eager, as flushed with anticipation as the dawn sky was luminous with soft pink lightening its previous gray. "Tell me I can harness the power of the Vested, professor, and I will build you your own Academy anywhere in Penraven. I've been told so many times I have no Valisar magic—tell me that's not true."

Trellon burst out laughing. "Well . . . perhaps. A chalice on its own and empty is powerless. But it can be filled with anything; in your case, perhaps power. I think, your majesty, your own Valisar magic was simply dormant because it has no power on its own. You must be filled with another's magic. We have witnessed the aegis magic working through you, keeping you safe. Now I suspect if we direct the magic of the Vested through you, your true magic will shine, and you will be able to carry the magic—harness it as you rightly guessed . . . and wield it."

Leo stood up and punched the air. "Not powerless at all! Just dormant!"

"What does this mean?" Marth demanded. "We can ask one of the Vested to use you as a device to magnify magic?"

"No, general," Leo said with a triumphant edge to his voice. "We ask all of the Vested here to channel all of their combined magical energy through me. With Perl's protection I can ride to that convent and slay that entire Green army." He stood. "Thank you, Trellon. I am in your debt."

"Majesty, it is a pleasure. My small talent is to be able to recall vast tracts of text. I have a memory that forgets nothing I see. May I be the first to lend you what little magic I have?"

"It would be an honor to accept it," Leo said. He turned to Perl. "Help me now, Perl, and I will keep my promise to you. Try it, Trellon."

The professor didn't seem to do anything particular except look at Leo but Leo smiled all the same. "I can feel it. Perl?"

Even she looked surprised, nodding with amazement, her face for once not pulled into a sour grimace.

Leo laughed. "Can you teach the others?"

"There's nothing to teach. I have tried to gift my magic

previously—there's nothing hard about the transfer—but it's in the acceptance of the gift. No one has ever been able to take it until now."

"Thank you, all," Leo said, looking around. "Now none of you need be in the maw of any danger. This will be my fight. Let's ride to the convent. How long, Marth?"

"We can arrive by the time the sun has barely fully risen, your majesty."

"Good. Position the Vested in a place of safety behind me. I don't want any of the soldiers' arrows to be within striking distance of them. The Greens are not to even guess what is happening or how it's happening. I want to have Loethar alone and on his knees before me before I slaughter him. We make history today . . . the Valisar crown will be returned to its rightful king."

sure they could survive, he shrugged. "At any rate, we have to speak to the elements. Which one way we look. Whatever enemy

Thirty-Two

————————————————

At the convent the immiment threat of Piven and Stracker's Greens overrode all the individual hostilities between the group now trapped behind its walls. A vague truce had laid itself softly around its visitors and Elka took a moment's pause to reflect with wonder how quickly sworn enemies had become allies. If they survived this new and terrible danger, there was potential for genuine healing. Even now she shook her head in a private but happy bewilderment to see Gavriel, Loethar, Kilt and Corbel talking animatedly without sneers on their faces.

She noticed with a pang of something that felt like sorrow that Gavriel was deferring to Loethar, nodding as her lover's natural leadership skills were coming to the fore. Kilt, she saw, had plenty to say too—he was a leader in his own right, used to having his orders followed.

Her heart soared. If this could happen there was hope for the empire, for former royalists finding a new way to live alongside the imperialists. Of course, it remained unclear who would lead this new imaginary union.

Her thoughts were interrupted as she heard Loethar call her name. She looked up and walked over to where the men had clustered. "Sorry, I was lost in my thoughts."

Loethar smiled. She knew that smile. It came rarely but he saved it for her. "Gavriel thinks we still have time to get the nuns out of here and away into the mountains."

She nodded. "Wise. But they would need to leave now."

"You're sure they could survive?"

Elka shrugged. "At most they'd have to spend a couple of nights in the elements. Whichever way we look at this I doubt very much our enemies are planning a siege. They're not going to hold off taking this place by force."

"Exactly," Kilt said. "We have to get the women out of here."

Elka blinked. "Well, not all the women but certainly the vulnerable ones. I, for instance don't—" She stopped and stared as the men exchanged awkward looks. "What?" she asked. "What?" she said more firmly, looking between Gavriel and Loethar. "Oh no," she added, finally grasping what had been decided without her permission.

"You are best placed, Elka. You know these mountains better than any."

"Not better than Gavriel!" she snapped. "And don't you dare add that it's also because I'm a woman."

"I definitely wouldn't dare," Kilt recommended to Loethar. "This woman is very scary."

She threw the outlaw a special glare. "You'll keep for another time, Faris."

"Elka, we can rely on you to get them out safely," Gavriel tried. "We're not trying to get *you* away to safety with the other women. We really do need someone we can trust, someone who can confront trouble if it raises its head and above all someone who knows how to survive out there for as long as it takes."

"Besides," Loethar added. "Of all of us here, it's you whom the Abbess trusts. She would entrust the lives of her nuns to you."

Elka gave a low growl of anguish.

"They must go immediately," Gavriel urged. "Come on, Elka, I'll help you round them up."

"Er . . . Elka, may I speak with you first?" Loethar said. "It will take only a moment."

He led her away from the others. She could feel Gavriel's gaze following them like a dagger, desperately wanting to plunge into Loethar's back.

"I wish you wouldn't make it quite so obvious," she said. "I don't want to hurt Gavriel any more than—"

"This is not about us or de Vis," he assured. And she noticed he suddenly looked uncertain.

"What is it?" she said, frowning.

"My wife," he began.

All the warmth in her belly fled, instantly replaced by her own jealous monster. She hated that he had a wife to come between them. Aware of the men watching them, she took a step away from him when he tried to take her hand. "No. Listen, don't touch me. Don't touch me again. In fact, thank you for reminding me that you are married. Perhaps my leaving with the nuns is the right thing for both of us. I won't come back from the mountains."

He sighed. "Then I will have to come and find you."

"Stop it," she warned. "Don't speak as if you are in a position to be with me."

His eyes met hers and they were soft and so filled with affection she actually hated him. She knew there would never be another man for her, and she hated that he would leave her alone forever.

"I am with you," he said calmly. "I never wish to see the woman I married for convenience ever again."

Elka blinked. "So what is . . . ?" she trailed off, unsure of what he meant.

"This is really not the time and place for this conversation but you need to know that I never once loved or spoke of love to or used the word love in connection with Valya. One day when there is time I will explain everything to you but for now you must search your heart and trust that I do not lie to you. I despise Valya . . . I think I always have."

She couldn't help but soften toward him.

"But what I was trying to say," he began—and again Elka's traitorous heart chilled—"is that Valya is still here. She was incarcerated by me when I realized she was responsible for my mother's death. She's been permitted to live because I can't prove it."

Elka stared at him, lost for words.

"She knows nothing about us. And she need never know but she is going to be among the women who leave with you.

I preferred you to hear that from me rather than the Abbess or even Valya herself."

"I see," was all she could murmur. She noticed Gavriel peel away from the group and knew he was heading off to round up the nuns.

"You have my permission to treat Valya in whichever way she needs to be treated. She is not special. She is a prisoner of the state and should be treated as such."

She nodded. "Then I will have as little to do with her as I can."

"Good. Now I do have to speak with her and I thought you should know that too so you would not get any strange ideas about why."

"Why must you?" she said, her voice hard.

"To tell her that our marriage will be denounced at the earliest opportunity. Before I left the palace, after my mother's murder, I never got a chance to tell her that she and I would be divorced."

Elka felt a blush creeping up her neck. "Right. Fair enough," she said matter of factly. "Then I will help Gavriel gather up the women. We will be gone very shortly."

He squeezed her hand. "You be careful. And, Elka?"

"Yes?"

"Don't you dare double back for any reason at all. Do you hear me? We all have our roles to play in this. I am safe, you know you don't have to worry about me. But you have no such protection and I cannot protect you over distance, so promise me that when you leave here, you leave for good. When it's safe to return will we find you and the nuns."

She nodded. "You'd better go talk to your wife."

As Elka, Gavriel and the Abbess gathered up all the women with cautions to take only warm clothing and some food, Loethar, with Roddy at his side, followed Barro to where Valya was being held. Barro had told him about Valya's attempt on the princess's life and Loethar had grimly remembered that Valya's resourcefulness and passion never failed to astonish him. If only she could channel those talents for

the good. But Valya's heart was dark, her soul black—he was
sure of it.

"I'll wait outside," Barro suggested. "Be warned, she's
like a snarling cat."

"Nothing I haven't witnessed before," he lamented and
Barro threw him an uncharacteristic look of sympathy.

Loethar watched him undo the lock and then he opened
the door and stepped inside the chamber. She had been dozing, he could tell, but she was instantly alert, casting away
any stupor of slumber as fast as one could shrug off a coat.

"You!" she accused. "That was fast. I suppose the Mother
just snaps her fingers and you are all but magicked out of
thin air. I don't suppose you're here to reinstate me."

"Hello, Valya, how are you?" he said brightly.

It was as though his sarcastic tone tipped her over the
edge—she launched herself at him, a sharp piece of metal in
her hand. He didn't have time to imagine where she'd got it
or what precisely it was but he did have a flashing moment to
understand that she intended to plunge it into his throat. Instinctively he raised his arms but he needn't have. Valya
bounced harmlessly off the guardian of air that Roddy had
presumably thrown around Loethar the moment they entered
the room.

She found herself on her backside, still clutching what
Loethar could now see was a crudely sharpened spoon, staring at it as though she'd forgotten what it was.

Loethar threw a look of gratitude at Roddy, who shrugged
a grin. "Let me help you up," Loethar said to Valya, not quite
masking his sarcasm as he offered her a hand.

She smacked it away. "What just happened?"

"I think you tried to kill yet again. This is quite a problem
for you, isn't it? But you picked on the wrong person this time."

Valya struggled to her feet. Her face was a riot of perplexity. She'd bitten her lip in her fall and blood oozed in a tiny
trickle from the swollen area. Her complexion was uncharacteristically white with high spots of red rage at the top of
her cheeks to match the blood at her mouth.

"Explain to me how this is not stuck in your throat," she
demanded.

"Well, Valya, I'm sure you've heard of the Valisar magic. I've talked about it often enough."

"The aegis magic. So you've finally eaten a Valisar, have you? And by some miracle you've acquired their magic!" she taunted.

"No, Valya. There's something I've been holding back from you all along. And while this is perhaps not the ideal time, there will never be a more important moment for you to understand who exactly I am."

She stared at him with an expression of deep incredulity. "Who exactly you are?" she repeated. "I know who you are!"

"You don't. You see, you actually did get your wish. You married a Valisar."

Now her expression clouded with all manner of emotion. He watched despair clash with rage and bump against horror, all while understanding began to smooth its way across her face. "You're a Valisar?" she finally uttered.

He nodded gravely before glancing toward Roddy. "By the way, Roddy here is my aegis. You cannot hurt me so you might as well put down your strange weapon."

Her gaze slid to Roddy. "Your aegis?"

"I am now magically protected." He shrugged and couldn't hide a smug smile for her benefit alone.

"Who is your father?"

"Darros. I'm his firstborn son. He slept with my mother during a trading mission that he was promoting into the Steppes."

She laughed helplessly; it sounded half sob, half genuine amusement. "Darros," she repeated, almost as a whisper. "It was revenge all along," she continued, as more and more made sense to her. "Your entire plan to conquer the Set . . . it was revenge for being denied your birthright."

He once again appreciated her agile mind and wished she had set out to put it to good use.

"Yes."

"Stracker has—?"

"No idea of the truth."

She laughed again. "Priceless."

"That's why I'm here to see you. Stracker is here too; his Greens are marching in force as we speak. I suspect we have the equivalent of a bell before they arrive at the gates of the convent. I'm giving you a choice. You can either use the escape we are providing for all the nuns into the mountains, led by an experienced guide, or you can take your chances with Stracker. Either way now, Valya, after your attempt on the princess, I wash my hands of you. If you go with the nuns you will remain a prisoner of the empire. What happens to you if you go to Stracker is up to my half-brother, though I will remind you that I cannot be killed, so Stracker's plan is flawed."

"He doesn't know that, though," she said, her eyes narrowing as her natural inclination to hatch a plan came to the fore.

"Not yet, no. You should also know he's traveling with another Valisar."

Her attention snapped back to him. "Who?"

He grinned. "Piven."

"The adopted retard?" she said, horror in her voice.

"Not adopted, it turns out. And far from the halfwit we lost ten anni ago. He's now a strong, eloquent and hugely intelligent youth with revenge in his heart—or so I'm assured by a most reliable source. Oh and he too has his aegis."

"So all the Valisars are safe!" she hissed.

"I cannot speak for Leonel. When I met him he was unprotected but that could have changed by now."

Her shock was complete, her face a picture of dismay. "Well, you have been busy. I suppose you know about the princess, too?"

"My niece. Yes, I have met her. She too has her aegis in place so you can stop plotting along those lines now, too. You should be cautioned that out of all of the Valisars I am probably the one who looks least unkindly upon you. Each of the others has good reason to see you suffer. I have no desire to do that." He sighed. "I'm sure you now regret killing my mother."

"She was a bitch! And now I discover she was a slut too, whoring for Darros!" she spat.

He kept his expression even. It was never hard for him to control his temper, which he knew infuriated her. "Does that mean you choose to throw your lot in with Stracker?"

"Lo strike you down, and all you scheming, heartless Valisars." Her chest was heaving with fury. "Tell me something, Loethar. Is the princess rich with her magic?"

"She is. You cannot hurt her. And while I'm sure you'll find it impossible to believe, Genevieve is precious to me. She is the only surviving Valisar princess."

Valya laughed and it sounded as though it had an edge of madness to it. "Is that so? I think I'll stay right here . . . I wouldn't want to miss the entertainment."

Loethar frowned. "I'd urge you to go with the nuns. Stracker holds no affection for you and he answers to Piven presumably."

"I'll take my chances. I might yet be able to bring him around," she said, cunning in her voice.

"You have nothing to offer him, Valya."

"I never run out of ideas, Loethar. You of all people should know that. No, turn me loose. It'll be the final act of kindness that I am owed as your wife. Whatever then happens, happens."

"As you wish. Gather up your belongings. You will be escorted to the gate shortly."

He turned and left without another glance.

It was Ravan who found her with the news that the nuns were leaving with the Davarigon woman soon. She'd discovered the apothecary and was marveling at all the medicines and salves on its shelves. It was a wonderful distraction from her sense of helplessness.

"They'll be safe?" Evie wondered.

He nodded confidently. "She is Davarigon. No one could know these mountains, or how to survive in them, better than her. She will keep them well protected."

"She's wonderful, isn't she?" Evie remarked. "I wish I'd had a chance to meet her."

He smiled. "I'm sure you will."

She returned his gesture. "Thanks for telling me. I feel so

useless with Kilt and Corbel so absorbed in their discussions with Loethar and everyone."

"Loethar's currently with his wife."

Her face clouded. "What's going to happen about her?"

"I don't know. But don't worry yourself. The first thing you should know about Loethar is that he is, despite what you've been told, very just. His days of random killing are long behind him. He will not harm Valya for her recent actions, though, knowing Loethar, he will find a subtle way to punish her."

She sighed. "There sounds to be a lot of activity out there," she said.

"Right now everyone's helping to get the nuns organized for their journey. Some are very old, most are understandably frightened."

"What about that one they call the Qirin? Corbel mentioned that she never leaves her room."

He shrugged. "I imagine she'll stay. She's blind and that is a burden Elka doesn't need. She'll already be trying to keep so many others safe."

"Then we must keep her protected."

"I am certain Loethar will see to it."

"You admire him," she said.

"I do. I always have. You don't know the story of Loethar and myself, do you?"

She shook her head. "But I'd love to hear it."

He told her briefly, and she shook her head in wonder when he had finished.

"That's . . ." She hesitated.

"Unbelievable?"

She laughed in relief. "Well, yes! I'm supposed to accept that you were a raven?" she said. "Though I suppose it's no more unbelievable than my story. You know, until quite recently I was someone who worked with facts."

"And yet our world denies you that logic. Perhaps it is you who should speak to the Qirin. She might answer your questions."

"It scares me."

He frowned.

She shivered. "All that hocus pocus."

Ravan frowned more deeply. "Hocus pocus?"

Evie grinned. "Stuff that's hard to understand. Fortune telling. Magic!"

He gave a soft look of surprise. "All she will do is understand you . . . and pass on that understanding."

"We'll see," she said.

"It will not be something you regret."

"Then you come with me."

"If she permits it, I'll be glad to accompany you."

They were interrupted by Corbel. "Evie, the nuns are leaving. You might want to say farewell to the Mother."

"I do," she said, putting down the jar of liniment she'd been smelling.

"Come on, then. The good news is the nuns will be out of harm's way in time. The bad news is that we have spotted the army. The barbarians are now in plain sight."

Thirty-Three

➤➤————————————◄◄

Kilt stared at Lily. Her still slightly swollen eyes and bruised expression told him how upset she remained. He drifted over to her as the nuns began their own teary farewells, not because of who they left behind but what.

"Lily, you should go with them," he urged.

"To ease your conscience?"

He sighed. "To ease my worry. Most of the people left behind here are either protected magically or have such an investment in this struggle that—"

"And I don't?" she said, looking even more wounded. "You don't think giving ten anni of my life to Leo . . . to your support of the Valisar Crown is an investment?"

"You know what I mean."

"No, Kilt. Nothing you say any more will ever sound sincere to me. You are like the Valisars—full of secrets. You and she are well matched," she said, throwing a glare toward Genevieve, who was hugging the Mother goodbye.

"She is so blameless in all of this," he tried.

"But still she ended up with the man she loves."

Kilt's patience was running out. "Lily, you got your man too!" he growled, ignoring the way she flinched. "I was there, remember. I risked my life, risked my magic, threw everything I had into chasing after you to get you away. Yes, I made an error in asking you to keep an eye on Felt. But that certainly should not have involved any danger to you. I don't know what drove you to your audacious and dangerous decision to pretend you were Felt's wife. But it was not because I asked it of you, or expected it of you."

She fought back tears. "I wanted to impress you."

"Well you did. You made a great impression upon me—of stupidity. After all I taught you about how careful we needed to be, you risked all of us in your actions. Forget me, what about Jewd? Did you consider his life? Or Tern, or any of the other men who look up to you and have kept you safe all these years? Did you consider Leo, who all of this was all about? You risked all those people because you wanted to be heroic and impress me? That's an outrageous claim and I refute it. You had no reason to impress me!"

"And you had no reason to love me!" she belted straight back. "Not even after I committed my life to yours. But you freely admit you fell in love with her in a heartbeat."

He hung his head. "Yes, yes I did. There's absolutely no accounting for love, I'm sure of that now. And I'm sure you didn't expect to fall in love with Kirin Felt . . . but you did. I watched that love between the two of you, Lily; it was real. Don't tarnish it by pretending losing me to Genevieve comes even close to how it feels to losing Kirin." He cleared his throat and looked around at all the people suddenly watching their heated exchange. "Forgive me, I don't wish to make you cry."

"But you do, Kilt. It's all you've ever done," she uttered through her tears.

He took her hands and kissed them. "And I am ashamed and sorry for that." He looked around. "And I'm sorry to all of you for having to witness this," he said, unable to meet Jewd's look of disappointment.

Lily sniffed. "The show's over. Kilt and I are over. We were just—"

"The best of friends," he finished and she nodded.

"But I'm not leaving. I led the danger here and I might yet be some use as bait."

"Bait?" Jewd boomed. "I don't think so."

But it was Gavriel who took her hand, not noticing the big man's scowl. "Come on, Lily. You've never been properly introduced to Elka but you should meet her before she leaves."

She looked grateful for his rescue and Kilt shared a guilty glance with Loethar as they watched the pair walk away to lick their wounds of unrequited love.

They were the last to leave the side gate, neither wishing to close it on the column of women and single man but knowing they must. Janus had gone with Elka; it seemed he couldn't bear to be parted from the Davarigon and as much as this amused everyone, Elka sourly admitted to Loethar that it made good sense to have a physic in tow. He was the only one who turned and gave a single wave farewell.

Gavriel shifted his gaze to Loethar. "I noticed no fond goodbyes. Too sentimental for you?" he said, nodding toward Elka's back as she led the nuns away.

"You had your chance, de Vis," Loethar cut back. "Friendship will only sustain a woman for so long."

"Says the all-knowledgeable barbarian," Gavriel snarled.

Loethar gave him a look of sympathy. "From what I hear it was your petulance that got you into trouble ten anni ago. You were still something of a youth then, so perhaps allowances can be made, but now you actually look like a man . . . so perhaps it's time to act like one."

Gavriel pursed his mouth, his teeth audibly grinding.

"You don't love her, de Vis."

"She is my closest friend."

"And she still can be. Don't be a fool and ruin that special bond you have with her." Gavriel's angry stance dissolved as though Loethar's advice hit its target. Then Loethar's tone changed. "Now what you did for that woman, Lily, a little while ago did impress me. She seems fond of you."

"There was a time . . ." Gavriel shrugged and shook his head, frowning. "She's been through a lot, I gather."

Loethar eyed him. "So have you," he said. "Come, de Vis, we have an army approaching."

"Let them come. I've been waiting for this opportunity for a long time."

Loethar grinned. "Vengeance knows no fear."

Gavriel's face was lacking in all humor but the tension in his body was gone. "I will never forgive you for my father's death."

"I know."

"If you weren't so magically protected I would attempt to kill you for it," he said casually. "But I'll settle for your brother."

"Half-brother," Loethar corrected with a dry tone. "But you see, de Vis, we've already found common ground on Stracker. Who knows where these first fragile bonds might lead us."

And Gavriel now smiled mirthlessly.

In much the same region that Corbel and Evie had been set upon by Barro and his companions, Leo now stood looking down at the convent with glee.

"Look at that, Marth! Exactly as predicted. The Greens are here."

"But why?"

"Why else but Loethar? I told you he was on the run from his own. He's here; I can all but feel his presence. This will be Stracker leading his men to finish him off. Though it's kind of Stracker to offer to do the job for us, we're going to finish Stracker first—and all of his tribal savages—because Loethar is going to be mine. I want him to look upon me and know who killed him."

Marth cleared his throat but before he could speak Reuth interrupted them both.

"Majesty. This is Raimon."

Leo turned, confronted by a slim, flaxed-haired youth with even, regular features made more memorable by his pair of bulging gray-blue eyes.

"Raimon is vested with eyesight that a hawk would be glad to have," Reuth explained. "He can see detail in the distance that we can only dream of."

"Very good. Can you brief us, Raimon? Give us a solid estimate of numbers, where the soldiers are all positioned. From here they look like a blur to the rest of us."

Raimon nodded. "My counting's not good, majesty. But I would reckon them a gate of sheep," he said, falling back into his farming upbringing.

"One hundred," Leo confirmed.

The boy blinked, glanced at Reuth and then back to Leo. He nodded. "No more than a gate of sheep."

Leo grinned. "Right. And what is their position?"

Raimon looked into the distance and then back again. "They've stopped moving. The column is spreading out." He made a circling motion. "They're surrounding those buildings."

"That makes sense," Leo agreed. "Are they carrying bows?"

"All weapons, majesty. I see bows, spears and swords."

"None to bother me," Leo admitted smugly. "Anything else?"

"Yes," Raimon said. "There is a carriage with them. An ornate one."

Leo swung back and tried desperately to see what Raimon had. "A carriage?" he repeated. "Whatever for? Describe it, Raimon."

The boy did. "Black. Shiny. Lots of gold on it. It—"

"That's one of the royal carriages, if it's trimmed with gilt, " Leo interrupted. "Surely Stracker wouldn't travel like that," he mused.

Marth grunted. "Absolutely not, from my experience. Stracker shuns any regal trappings."

"He's climbing out of the carriage," Raimon continued.

Leo exchanged an expression of surprise with Marth. "Are you sure?" he urged.

The lad nodded. "I know what Stracker looks like. That's him all right."

"Then he's traveling with others. I would stake my life that Stracker would not be in that carriage unless forced," Marth said. "He much prefers to ride proudly at the head of his Greens."

Leo looked out to the blur of men and horses around the cluster of buildings. "I agree. From what I know of him he'd sneer at the notion of being cooped up in a carriage all the way from Brighthelm. Raimon, can you describe the others?"

"There are three others. Ah, one is Vulpan, the blood taster. He's easy to recognize."

Reuth spat on the ground.

"Go on, Raimon," Marth pressed.

"I don't recognize the others. One is an older man."

"Describe him," Leo ordered.

"Tallish, slightly stooped, gray hair. He has only one hand."

"One hand. Wait! Is there a youth with him—someone of about your age?"

Leo held his breath in the pause as Raimon focused.

"Yes."

Leo smacked his fist into his palm. "We are too clever by half!" The others looked at him, bewildered. "The youth is my brother, Piven. The other man is called Greven. He originally helped me to escape into the forest in the north and then he, for reasons known only to him, headed southeast and made his way to Brighthelm. There he found Piven as a young child, just five. I heard this all only recently so my knowledge is sketchy and third hand but apparently he lured Piven away and raised him in secrecy. I'll never know why he did it or how because it turns out that Greven is an aegis. Piven, of course, as he grew out of whatever his ailment had been, recognized the magic and I heard that he trammeled Greven, cutting off one of the man's hands and devouring it."

Everyone listening winced, Perl especially.

"So your brother is here for Loethar as well?" Marth queried.

"Your guess is as good as mine, general, but as he and Stracker are traveling together, it would seem they have thrown their lot in together."

"If Piven has his aegis then he has probably claimed the crown," Perl commented. "Making your claim useless."

Leo rounded on her. "The crown is mine. I am the rightful heir," he hurled at her.

She shrugged, entirely unfazed by his attack. "Well, he can't be killed, you know that."

Leo ground his jaw. "We don't know anything. Until a few hours ago we didn't know that the Vested magic could be put together and channeled through one source. Until a few hours ago no one had heard of the Valisar Chalice. None of us really know what the magic is capable of." He took a steadying breath. "We have to trust in what we're attempting. And all of you have to believe in my claim to that throne."

"I do," Reuth nodded.

"I wouldn't be here if I didn't," Marth followed.

Perl shrugged. "All you Valisars are the same. What difference does it make and I have no choice anyway."

"It would be so much easier if you helped, Perl," Reuth scolded, "instead of sulking. His majesty's married you! You have an easy life ahead if you just help willingly."

Perl looked away as though disinterested in the conversation. Leo was already straightening, looking to Marth.

"We'll move forward now under the cover of the rocks. It's a good thing everyone's dressed so shabbily—that will help disguise us and aid our passage. We move in silence." He pointed. "See that rise?"

"I see it," Marth replied.

"There's where everyone can remain. It's high enough to have the vantage and if you warn everyone to remain low, they'll be safe. I'm leaving you in charge, general. Perl and I can move to lower ground. I look forward to feeling my sword kill a hundred barbarians." He glanced over at her. "You see, Perl, I'm not even expecting you to lift a finger. All you have to do is throw your shield around me."

She ignored him.

He sighed, frustrated, and turned to Marth and Reuth. "Do you two understand?"

They nodded.

"Where is Narine?"

"I'll get her," Reuth said, looking glad to have something to do.

She returned as Leo was giving final instructions to Marth; they were shaking hands.

"Good luck, general."

"I hope it works, majesty."

"We tested it to impressive results. Trellon's idea has more than earned him his own Academy! Now I'm going to unleash his weapon." He turned. "Narine," he said, nodding at her. "Are you ready?"

The stout, middle-aged woman with rounded features and rosy cheeks smiled self-consciously. "I've never actually had anyone encourage me to use my strange talent before. I was very surprised when Professor Trellon told me his idea."

Leo grinned. "And I can well understand why. But now, Narine, you have my royal permission to unleash that talent."

"Oh thank you, your highness," she said, helpless glee in her tone. "Just say the word."

Thirty-Four

➤➤————————————————◀◀

All the women remaining behind had been pressed into wearing the robes of the nuns.

"It's for your protection," Kilt insisted. "Frankly, I'm jealous!"

"He's right," Loethar warned. "And let's face it, he's the master of disguise. I never caught him in all the years I hunted him and he tells me now he moved freely around the towns and villages of the north."

And so Lily and Evie found themselves joining Valya dressed as sisters of the convent.

Everyone had gathered in the cloisters. No one had a plan, not even when they heard a loud banging on the gate.

"Sisters! This is General Stracker. Open up."

"Well none of us men can open the door," Jewd said. "It has to be one of the women."

Loethar frowned. "He knows Valya and Lily. It has to be Genevieve."

"Piven will sense her magic," Kilt said in a tone that brooked no argument.

"Don't make me get my soldiers to pull your gate off its hinges!" Stracker roared.

"Lily," Kilt said, "don't open the gate but can you hold him up while we think?"

She nodded and ran forward.

"Yes, general?" she said, disguising her voice.

"We are seeking a woman we believe is taking refuge with you."

"We have several women staying with us. What is her name?"

They heard Stracker say Lily Felt and Lily begin to give the general a very polite but nonetheless effective run-around.

"So?" Kilt said, looking to Loethar. "Ideas?"

"Come clean," Gavriel suggested. "It's not as though they can hurt Loethar or Genevieve. Kilt and Roddy can protect some of us; the rest could hide?"

No one seemed particularly impressed by this.

"I'd rather die swinging my sword," Barro remarked.

"I'll go," Valya suddenly said. She gave a cruel smile. "I'm not wanted here and my husband will be glad to see the back of me. Besides, they know I'm here and I want to join them. I can keep them occupied and buy you some time. I'll get my things."

No one could argue with her logic. Kilt ran ahead to whisper the change of proceedings to Lily. Loethar could hear Lily changing tack with the frustrated general, telling him that the Empress Valya wished to speak with him while Lily Felt was being found. That had brought a silence; Loethar guessed Stracker was conferring with Piven.

"You're not really letting her go out there, are you?" Corbel asked. "It's as good as signing her death warrant."

Loethar shrugged. "What choice do we have? She was given the opportunity to go with the nuns into safety. She is a grown woman. A former heir to Droste, an empress—fallen from grace, perhaps, but royal all the same. I respect her choice . . . flawed though it is."

"You really are a heartless bastard."

"Not entirely, de Vis, but I see you suffer from the same weaknesses as your twin when it comes to women. Be assured, Valya is not someone you should underestimate simply because of her sex. She is the equal of any man when it comes to cunning; it's probably one of the reasons I found her vaguely interesting for a while."

Corbel scoffed. "No matter how much you impress upon us that you are Valisar, Loethar, your upbringing as a barbarian is showing through. We might all fight for the same side right now, but we are not the same."

"Ah. You believe the other Valisars have some claim on female honor? Consider carefully all that Brennus allowed to happen to the women of his household. Do you think he really held his wife and daughter in such high esteem? Consider Leo, whom your brother would have given his life to protect—do you think he won't gladly kill his sister, or any woman who stands between him and what he believes is his throne? Don't preach to me, de Vis, about being Valisar, or your misguided code of honor." He looked away, showing his disdain.

Gavriel joined in. "We have to protect the women, Loethar."

He turned in disbelief. "Both of you now. Listen to me. The princess needs no other protection than what she has. No spears or arrows can touch her. Neither can Piven. Lily and Valya chose to stay. They knew exactly the situation."

"So you're just going to let your cur of a half-brother hack them to bits?" Gavriel snarled at him. "You don't care. You despise Valya. Stracker would be doing you a favor if he cut her down, let's be honest. And Lily just doesn't matter . . . she's expendable."

"What do you propose I do?" Loethar asked them.

"Nothing, Loethar," Corbel said, taking over from Gavriel. "I propose you do nothing, but I will." He held Loethar's gaze fiercely.

Loethar looked down first. "As you wish. What do you plan?"

"I will escort Valya out if she insists on going," Corbel said, watching her emerge from a chamber carrying a small bundle of belongings.

"Corb—" Gavriel began but then stopped, pushed his hands deep into his pockets, torn between duty and fear. He felt the familiar seeds he'd carried all of these years. His tiny touchstones, as he liked to think of them, his only link to a former life. He jangled them now, out of habit, feeling the comforting rattle in his palm that had sustained him through many a night of despair. "No, you're right. Father's bones would turn where they lie if he knew we could send out a woman unescorted."

Kilt arrived. "Make a decision," he whispered.

"We have," Corbel said.

"Send the empress out!" Stracker shouted.

"She is coming, general," Lily replied, stealing a glance over her shoulder. "My apologies, though, we cannot let any of your soldiers in."

"I will choose if we come in, sister, not you."

Lily looked back at Loethar, who shook his head. Next to him, Corbel gave her a nod.

"Er, general, here is the empress. She comes with an escort her husband sent with her. These are sanctified grounds, sir, not to be tainted with behavior that does not befit the convent."

"What of Lily Felt?" said a new voice, much younger. Loethar felt his heart jump. He knew it was Piven.

Lily sprang back from the gate as if burned. "She . . . er, we have sent messengers to find her. Who is this, please?"

"This is Piven talking to you, sister. But you may call me emperor."

Loethar's eyes narrowed. He felt his arm squeezed.

"Not yet," Kilt warned in a hushed tone "We don't know how this is going to play out. Keep your witchflame dry, as they say."

Loethar struggled but said no more. He watched as Valya very carefully walked to the gate where Corbel awaited, carrying her very modest bundle of belongings under her arm.

"General Stracker?"

"Yes?"

"It is Valya. I have some important news to share with you—news that might change how you regard me."

Loethar scowled. Next to him, Gavriel held out his hand to Kilt. "Remember these?" he said wistfully. "I never did work out why you gave them to me."

Kilt looked down and then at Gavriel with an expression

of pure wonder. He took one from Gavriel's hand and handed it to Corbel. "Suck this."

"What? What is that?"

"It's magic. Just do it! Hurry."

Corbel took the seed, threw it in his mouth.

"Suck hard. Like your life depends on it."

And Loethar watched in amazement as Corbel's face began to droop. He became unrecognizable, his features twisting and sagging until it was the face of a much older man, unrecognizable as a de Vis. Loethar felt his mouth drop; he saw that Gavriel was wearing an expression of shock that must mirror his own.

"What?" Corbel asked, looking at his twin.

Gavriel turned and stared at Kilt. "Why didn't you mention what those seeds could do?"

"How did I know you'd still have them, de Vis? They're not seeds but beads, given to me by a witch. She called them her 'disguises.' Here comes Valya. Good luck. Get back in here as quick as you can, de Vis. What you're doing is lunacy . . . but honorable lunacy."

"I thought you looked old enough but this is impressive," Gavriel said. "Just walk her out and step straight back, Corb. I've only just found you. I don't want to lose you."

Corbel nodded. "Tell Evie—"

"No, tell Evie yourself when you're back," Gavriel said, punching his shoulder. "I'm hoping we've thought up a plan by then."

"Right. Everyone ready?" Loethar murmured. "Faris, you know what to do. Genevieve, make yourself scarce; he can protect you over distance. Even if Valya tells Piven everything, we're not going to make this easy for him. And remember, he can't hurt you. Roddy, you know that you and Faris are throwing a ring of protection around everyone."

Roddy nodded, looked toward Kilt.

"Just take my lead, Roddy. We're few enough that if you take Loethar, Gavriel, Barro and Ravan, and I take Genevieve, Corbel, Jewd and Lily, I believe we can keep them safe," Kilt assured. "Go, Genevieve."

"I might take Ravan with me," she said. "He can tell you where I'm hiding."

"Good idea," Kilt said. "Right, de Vis," he hissed in a low voice. "Are you ready to escort out our not-so-esteemed empress?"

Barro suddenly leaped forward. "Let me go too. I can't stand waiting around and besides," he said, nodding with a smile at Corbel, "I can watch his back."

No one seemed to mind. They all knew they were moving on instinct now; there were no signposts guiding their path.

Evie and Corbel shared a glance that only Ravan saw and then he was hurrying her away.

"Your majesty, I thought you could hide in the—"

"No hiding. I want to see the Qirin as you suggested. What's happening here is ridiculous. Aren't I supposed to be the Valisar with all the power?"

Ravan blinked.

"Well, come on!" she demanded. "This farce of a legacy I'm supposed to wield. I haven't come all this way back for nothing. But for the life of me I've no idea what I'm supposed to do. I have questions for her."

Ravan nodded. "The Mother showed me where the Qirin stays; I promised we would not forget her. Come, majesty."

They were much closer now and their own eyesight provided all the information they needed. The Vested were all well concealed behind the rise of foothills that formed a small crescent around one part of the convent. They were holding hands, each Vested linked to the other physically, which had helped intensify the channeling during the test.

Among them sat Narine. Her power would be mixed with everyone else's but it was her particular gift alone that Leo planned to magnify once the magic arrived. He could feel the excitement building within him; it reminded him of the natural hot springs in Galinsea his mother had told him about.

It fizzes and bubbles against your skin, she'd told the young Leo as she'd tickled him, laughing at his shrieks of delight. That's how his anticipation was for him now, fizzing and bubbling against the walls of his skin. He felt almost light-headed with expectation and the ache of inactivity before battle.

"It's the empress," Marth hissed.

Leo dragged himself back to the present and watched as, right enough, Valya emerged from the gate, flanked by two minders. Her simple robes could not disguise the face he had loathed with a deep-seated passion since he was twelve.

"Well, well . . . it seems all my enemies are gathering in one place, general. Fate is conspiring to give me this opportunity to destroy them all in one fell swoop. Perl was right. My destiny is here." He held a hand up. "I am the Chalice, general. Cyrena visited me. No one has seen the width and breadth of my power yet. In just a few minutes they will all cower before me. I will kill all the pretenders who lay claim to my throne and then we will begin again, general. You and I, our Vested, all our people from all over the empire will return to their realms and Penraven will rule again."

Marth said nothing but Leo caught his glance at Perl . . . and behind her. Looking back, he saw that Reuth had disobeyed his orders and had followed closely behind, instead of staying higher up and safe.

"We'll give them just a little longer, general. Let's see what erupts before we unleash the Chalice of power on them. Reuth, you need to return to the group. It's not safe for you down here."

"Yes, your majesty. I'm sorry." Reuth turned to head back up the slope, and though Leo knew she thought she hid it well, he saw her throw a worried glance back at Marth.

Elka hated leaving the convent. Apart from the hollow feeling of what amounted to being sent away, behind her were the two people she cared most about in her life.

She knew that Loethar was invincible, but Gavriel was not. Loethar, sensing her anxiety, had promised that he would not permit any harm to come to her friend. "I will guard him as a brother," he had sworn to her. And she believed him. It was this promise alone that had convinced her to take the nuns to safety.

They'd left just in time it seemed. Elka's well-honed senses picked up the smells and sounds of the army, carried on the breeze: the sweat of beasts and men, the stale aroma of food, the low murmur of sound coming from a long way away. If she concentrated she could hear the rumble of hooves, rhythmic but daunting, the sigh of leather creaking and the clank of metal combining to form a special sound that spoke of war. The woman called Lily had certainly brought the most ill of winds with her; Elka could only just find it within herself to be mildly polite when Gavriel walked her over to say hello before the women left.

Elka had thought she would be one of the first to run from the danger so it was Lily's decision to remain and be used for "bait" if need be that had helped to restore some good opinion of her in Elka's mind. She didn't miss the way the petite and very pretty Lily seemed to fit so comfortably into the crook of Gavriel's elbow as he led her, or how easy and familiar with each other they were. Now that she knew the story of Gavriel's earlier days she could understand why he had formed such an instant bond with the herbal woman. They were of an age and even though it galled Elka to accept it, they looked good together. If not for Lily's attraction to Kilt Faris all those anni ago, perhaps Gavriel would have been with her.

But then Elka would not have met him, and he would not have led her down from the mountains; Loethar would not have crossed their path and she would not have realized that what she felt for Gavriel was not love but friendship . . . and perhaps pity.

She smelled a fresh waft of the approaching army and her sharp hearing could pick them out very easily now; Elka turned instinctively and her breath caught to see the dust in the distance. They were close—too close—and she had been dawdling, lost in her silly thoughts.

Elka trotted around from the front to hurry along the stragglers.

"Mother, you have to get them to move faster." She

pointed. "As soon as we get through that small pass and behind that row of rocks we are hidden and we can slow down
to a snail's pace. We can even stop there if you wish; I can
work out some shelter. But we need to get there. Urge them
forward, Mother; help me get them through."

The Abbess needed no further encouragement. She nodded and began shooshing and cajoling her women, young
and old, to find more pace. Elka noticed one of the eldest
being helped along by another nun and Janus; she could see
they were struggling.

"Here, let me," she said, and without waiting for a reply,
picked up the old woman, who felt light as a bird. She nodded to the younger nun. "You go on. I'll bring her."

"You could have picked me up," Janus jested, and she
grinned. He spoiled the moment by then starting to suggest
it would free his hands up to—

But she refused his problem its freedom. "Hurry!" she
encouraged. Janus gave a grateful look combined with con-
trition and sped ahead.

Elka began to run. After covering good ground she took
one longing look back at where the man who now owned her
heart was left behind and then set her mind firmly to the
task at hand. As she turned back to her charges, she glimpsed
a flutter of something—fabric perhaps—from the corner
of her eye. Her head whipped back, searching for it as she
moved. She couldn't find it again easily but was sure she had
not imagined it.

"Elka?" It was the Abbess again. "Is something wrong?"

"No. I'm coming, Mother." And as she lowered her eyes,
there it was again. "Actually, can you help her, please," she
said, setting down the aging nun. "You go ahead, I won't be
long."

This time she squinted, all her senses combining, and all
her harbored knowledge of the mountains coming into sharp
focus. She searched slowly, painstakingly, looking for the interruption, waiting for the snag in the landscape that shouldn't
be there. And there it was! She saw it: a hand pulling a length
of fabric around its owner. There was someone up there! And
as she concentrated she saw fresh movement: not someone

but several people. She drew a long silent breath as she
watched a quartet of figures break the cover of the rocky disguise and almost boldly walk down the incline.

She squinted harder, shutting out everything else—sights,
sounds, smells—and focused entirely on the figure at the
front, vaguely familiar. Elka blinked with a flutter of fright.
She threw a cautionary look behind her and noticed that all
the nuns were now safely hidden; they had not been seen,
perhaps had not even been noticed by this new group whose
collective attention was trained firmly on the convent itself.

Turning back, she concentrated once more. The leader
of the new group had been standing but now he crouched,
making himself as small and unnoticeable as possible
against the scrubby foothills, his plain dun colored clothing
the perfect choice to blend into that scenery. Now she recognized him. It was Leonel and he had brought people with
him.

Why?

Why was he here, if not to make trouble?

And why come here at all unless he was confident of the
trouble he could cause?

How would he know to come here of all places, given that
they had left him back in the high northern forests of Penraven?

And who were these people with him? They weren't soldiers. Now that she was looking with care she could see
more of them, hiding, yes, but they looked to be civilians.

Gavriel had briefly mentioned that he and Leo had
"crossed swords," as he put it. *He will try and kill me next
time he sees me*, Gavriel had murmured. She recalled how
he'd shrugged before he'd said sadly: *Valisars keep their
promises.* And then he had sighed. *So he'll try and I will be
forced to choose: my life or his, for I am the better swordsman, the better marksman.*

The better man, she had reassured.

Elka blinked again as a chill crept from her toes and began to find a dark form, like a blockage, in her throat.

Why was Leo here unless he was going to keep his
promise? And he would know Gavriel to be the superior

swordsman, so why make the attempt unless he was confident? Why walk into the lion's den of an enemy army he
could surely see from his vantage, unless he was confident
of cheating its blades too?

All these questions swirled in her mind and crystalized
down to one horribly clear, glittering fact: Leo had found an
aegis.

And Gavriel was mortal. And while Elka trusted Loethar's
promise to keep him safe, she trusted her own instincts more.

Elka hurried to find the Mother, and despite her protesta-
tions told her she had to leave but would be back. And then,
with little more than her slingshot and bow slung across her
body, she began a stealthy hunt for a Valisar royal with murder in his heart.

Thirty-Five

❯❯───────────────────────❮❮

Corbel made Valya remain behind him as they approached the quartet awaiting her.

"It might be wise for you to remember that I am risking my life to keep yours safe," he cautioned beneath his breath. "To reveal us now would be to welcome your own death. I will kill you myself if you betray the others."

He stepped ahead, recognizing Stracker from Sergius's vision. He didn't know either the one-handed man or the officious-looking civilian with the smirk on his face, but the fourth person he recognized despite the years and his heart skipped a beat, surprising him by the rush of emotion he felt to see Piven again. There was no mistaking the small sunny youngster of yesteryear, now a strapping youth. Though he was smiling, as he always had in Corbel's memory, the expression looked cynical now rather than open.

Corbel stopped himself from even murmuring his name as it sprang to his lips. As hard as it was to accept, Piven was the enemy now.

"Empress," Piven said. It sounded like a welcome but Corbel heard an icy undertone he did not trust.

To her credit, Valya hardly blinked an eyelash, not so much as a heartbeat passing before she was curtseying low before him. "I no longer consider myself that, your majesty. Through choice I return myself to a former royal of Droste and your willing servant." She did not rise, kept her head bowed. "But thank you all the same."

Corbel watched Piven's eyes narrow. As young as he was, it seemed the youth was not beguiled by Valya's servile attitude.

"And who are these fellows?" Piven wondered aloud, overly brightly.

"We are the men employed by Loethar to guard his wife," Corbel said, amazed that while the passing of time had surely changed his features, the beads had given him a cushion of security. There wasn't even a flash of recognition from Piven.

"I don't know you," Stracker growled.

"We are hired men, general. We were told she was not worthy of his soldiers."

Valya said nothing but, looking down, Corbel could see her trembling with rage.

"You are brave men to come out here," Piven remarked.

Corbel forced himself to give a soft but not insulting look of dismay. "I have no argument with you, my lord. Forgive me if I address you incorrectly. I am a simple man and have no interest in the politics of our empire. We have been paid to do a caretaking task, that is all. I mean no disrespect if you are now the authority."

"None taken," Piven replied. "Step back," he commanded.

Corbel lifted his gaze to Piven.

"I hope that's not a challenge I see in that look?"

"No, my lord. But my role is to guard the former empress."

"And now you have new orders from the new emperor. Step back."

Unhappily but disguising his trepidation, Corbel took one step back, keeping himself level with Valya.

Piven sniffed the air and suddenly laughed. "Do you feel it, Greven? Can't you just smell it?"

Corbel's gaze shifted to the one-handed man. This was Lily's father. He looked weary and disheveled but mostly he looked to be filled with despair. Corbel noticed he did not answer Piven and Piven didn't seem to care.

He was laughing again instead. "There is powerful magic in the air today," he said, rubbing his hands. "But whose,

I wonder?" He returned his attention to Valya, switching unpredictably to his former interest. "If you value your life, you'll tell me whether Lily Felt is behind those gates."

"I don't know a Lily Felt, majesty. Who is she?"

Corbel couldn't help but feel impressed. Valya was playing the most dangerous of games. What did she hope to achieve?

"Fair enough. I would imagine you have no reason to know her and perhaps would not be privy to all strangers crossing the convent threshold. So," he said, as if it mattered not, "to other things. Which Valisar is behind those doors?"

"Valisar?"

"Please don't ever take me for a fool, Valya, particularly as you seem to be standing before me hoping to find some favor. I have no reason in the world to extend a mote of sympathy toward you, so it would be wise to give me reason to at least be vaguely impressed by you. Is there a Valisar child hiding behind those walls . . . a daughter . . . because I want her."

And Corbel watched Valya smile; she'd painted her lips for this meeting and her mouth looked like a red gash as it stretched in cunning pleasure. His heart pounded. She was going to give Evie to them and though it mattered not— Evie was safe with Faris's aegis magic—he would personally despatch Valya for her treachery.

"Yes, majesty, there is a Valisar daughter," Valya confirmed.

Piven, who had been seated on the steps of the carriage, now stood, his eyes glittering in his still boyish face. "I knew it," he murmured.

"How did you know?" Valya asked.

Corbel noticed Stracker and Vulpan looked confused, while Greven looked at the ground, anger and despair all over his face. Corbel threw a glance Barro's way but his friend gave an almost indiscernible shake of his head to suggest he wasn't sure what was going on either.

"I have known about her for some time," he said and Corbel heard Valya give a soft gasp of shock. "Besides, I can feel her magic. I can feel the Valisar power too but this princess . . ." He smiled. "Her scent overlays it. She feels close enough to touch."

Corbel felt a wave of fresh tension grip him. Piven had always known? How? They'd only been back in the world for a matter of days.

"I would like you to give her to me now," Piven said.

Corbel bit the inside of his cheek to stop himself saying anything. He imagined drawing his sword and . . . and nothing; he would be bleeding out within moments.

"What will you do with her?" Valya asked, her voice trembling.

How well she acts, Corbel thought angrily.

"That's my business, Valya."

Corbel watched from the corner of his eye as Valya licked her blood red lips. "Your majesty, I am frightened. If I deliver her to you, then I have nothing left with which to bargain for my life."

"Valya," Piven replied reasonably. "You have nothing left anyway. If I really want to I can just take her. She is but a child. I have my aegis; I am in my full power. Let me ask: does she have an aegis?"

Valya shook her head, much to Corbel's surprise. He had no idea what she thought she was doing. She certainly wouldn't be safe with Piven and Stracker.

"So she has no aegis—that means she has no power to speak of. And what's more she is a child, frightened of her own shadow probably, crying when she is hungry." He said this so kindly that Valya fell for it, Corbel noted.

"Yes, oh yes, your majesty. She is just a child; simple affection and a soothing voice is all she needs. She will not challenge you."

"Cannot challenge me," he impressed.

She shook her head tearily. "No, she will not. So please, don't hurt her."

Corbel was stunned. Valya genuinely sounded as if she cared.

"Go and fetch her, Valya. At least this way you can cling to what little hope you have left of redeeming yourself."

Corbel heard the false note. Piven was toying with the

woman and while he had not an iota of fondness or care even for Valya, he would not see any woman humiliated. If Piven had killed Valya where she stood Corbel would have understood it—she deserved it, and it would be honest of Piven—but this sport he was making of her suffering turned Corbel's stomach.

"Can I redeem myself, majesty? Will you spare me, spare her?"

"We shall see," Piven said slyly. "But we have to start somewhere trusting each other. You first," he said, clearly enjoying himself. Corbel was disgusted. How had Piven come to this? If he was shocked to see the once invalid, sweet little boy so whole and alert, he was deeply saddened to see what a mockery he made of all that Corbel hoped the Valisar crown stood for . . . what his father had died for.

Valya hiccupped a soft sob, appearing torn. It seemed obvious to Corbel that she was going to attempt to hand Evie over to these men and he couldn't understand what her reluctance was. In fact he was spending more time worrying over Valya—a woman he hated—than Evie, the woman he loved, because Evie was safe . . . and Valya knew it. So what was the—?

The wheels of his mind suddenly stopped turning. His thoughts juddered to a loud and shattering halt as he realized that everyone, including him, but excepting Valya, had been talking about the wrong princess.

"You are right, she is close enough for you to touch, majesty," Valya tearily admitted.

And Corbel helplessly reacted as she reached to unwrap the bundle in her hands . . . the bundle that he'd thought was perhaps a change of clothes or a few precious items, but he now knew was her newly born child . . . the daughter that Loethar believed dead . . . the *other* Valisar princess.

Elka had crept up as silently as a rock mouse, her tread light despite her size, her balance perfect as she navigated the terrain, keen eyes scanning ahead for any spots of danger. And now she found herself at a perfect vantage to see exactly what was going on.

Leonel was smugly looking down at what was unfolding before the convent. Valya was bowing before the newly arrived strangers and this piece of theater fully held the attention of Leo's quartet. The biggest shock of all, however, was to see a crowd in the forest above them, sitting together in dread silence with their hands all linked. Elka couldn't tell if they were scared or simply full of anticipation but the atmosphere certainly felt tense and dangerous. What were they doing? Praying? Elka frowned. She didn't want to leave until she knew what Leo was up to.

One of the quartet—a middle-aged woman—peeled away from the others and moved back to the main group. Hidden but sharp of hearing, Elka listened.

"We await his signal," the woman said. She was talking to many and clearly was not afraid of being heard this high up. "General Marth and I are agreed that if the king uses our combined powers for anything other than what we believe is necessary force we will override him."

There was a murmuring among the folk who listened.

Elka watched the woman in charge shrug. "I don't like it much either but I know that for most of you this was never something you wanted to be involved with. Aggression is not the way of the Vested and perhaps I have always been more militant than the majority of you but I have lost more than my freedom to the barbarians. Perl as the king's aegis has no choice but to follow his command but the rest of us are not bound to him."

"What if he turns on us?" someone asked.

She shook her head. "I don't know what to say to that but I hope it won't come to it and frankly he has no reason to. We are his weapon, don't forget, and if we defy him you will have plenty of warning to scatter. I hope we don't have to stop giving him our powers. We only will if we feel he is getting out of control and killing innocents."

"No one is innocent down there," another remarked. "He can kill all the barbarians as far as I'm concerned."

"I know, Beltor, but not everyone feels like that. It is murder if no one fights back . . . and you forget that there are nuns down there in the convent, all of whom are innocent.

So, while I can't assure you of anything, at least we are trying to do something to help ourselves . . . that should be our comfort." She tried to smile. "The Vested finally fought back."

More murmurings moved through the people but Elka was no longer paying attention. Her mind was already running to Loethar and Gavriel down below. Leo wasn't just suffused with a new-found aegis magic but he was somehow in control of a different and clearly powerful way to kill. How he was going to do it, she couldn't tell but she had noticed that their spokesperson briefing them had looked at another middle-aged woman several times and the group had also glanced at the other woman. She seemed to be a focus of what might occur and yet she looked harmless enough with those rosy cheeks and her plump countenance.

Elka wanted to steal back down into the convent to warn Loethar and Gavriel, but her instincts told her to stay put, where if necessary she could either put the rosy-cheeked woman she was unsure about out of action or find a way to disrupt the Vested. Her hand twitched by her catapult. Though she knew Leo was protected by his aegis, all these people could not be as well. One way or another she would not allow them to hurt Gavriel . . . or Loethar.

Corbel shocked everyone, himself most of all, by leaping forward. "My lady, do not!" he warned, reaching out to stop Valya from handing over her helpless baby. Nothing, absolutely nothing—even if this cost him his life—would permit him to stand by and watch another innocent newborn lose its life over the accursed Valisar magic.

Horrific memories came rushing back as he recalled the sickening sensation of forcing the life out of that anonymous baby. It was his duty, his father had said gravely, but he'd seen the look of fear and loathing in Regor de Vis that day and could now almost believe that his father had happily ridden out, almost welcoming death from Loethar's blade as retribution for his part in Brennus's plan. Corbel had spent a lifetime trying to redeem himself by looking after Evie so fervently. He could not permit a child to die in his care again.

* * *

Genevieve walked through the door that Ravan held open and hesitated at the darkness inside.

Close the door, a voice sliced into her mind.

Ravan did so and Evie blinked, not sure it if was out of shock at the voice or the sudden plunge into the black.

You will need to use this link I have opened or I cannot hear you, child. Do not be scared. I believe I am in the presence of a Valisar princess. You have little to fear.

I . . . I have brought someone with me, Evie began tremulously.

Indeed. He is welcome too. Normally I do not permit two people at once but the man who calls himself Ravan is not entirely real, and you and he are linked so strongly that it would not have made sense to leave him outside.

Ravan and I? Evie echoed. *We are perfect strangers!*

Not through blood, the woman replied. *Come closer, child, let me touch you.*

Confused and a bit fearful, Evie gingerly moved through the dark. Her eyes were adjusting and she could just make out a small air vent through which tiny shafts of light penetrated high in the wall of the lofted ceiling. With each passing moment it became easier to make out shape and form. By the time she reached the woman, she could make her out with surprising clarity.

I am pleased to meet you, Qirin.

Genevieve. Well met, child. I never thought I'd hold the hand of a Valisar princess.

Or I the hands of a blind, mute seer who could speak to me in my mind. I am a woman of science, Qirin; this defies it.

Science? Hmmm, that word escapes me.

Evie tried again. *I trust only what I can understand.*

Do you misunderstand me . . . am I not speaking your language?

You are, but—

Am I real to your touch or am I a vision?

You are real.

Do your eyes deceive, do your ears lie, does your mind

not perceive my voice as easily as if I'd spoken the words aloud?

Evie sighed in the Qirin's mind.

Then we understand one another, do we not?

She smiled. *We do.*

You can trust me, Genevieve. I speak only truths.

Who is Ravan? Evie asked.

Ravan is a specter.

Of whom?

Of Cormoron, First of the Valisars. He is here to help the Valisars but particularly the female line.

How is he to help me?

He urged you to visit here. He was bringing Roddy to you when fate stepped in and Loethar crossed his path. Ravan has memories and knowledge that are vital to you and your magic.

People are about to die out there, Qirin. Can I stop it?

The old woman laughed in her mind.

Is that funny?

Amusing. You are the most powerful of the Valisars to have ever walked this land and you ask me the most simple of questions.

Please answer me.

Yes, Genevieve, you can stop the killing. But you can save more than lives, child. Individual lives are of no account. It is the greater good that matters most.

Evie felt frustrated and confused. *I am a healer, Qirin. I am interested in cutting away cancers, sewing wounds and making light in the darkness of people's lives. My focus is ordinarily so small. How can I help the greater good?*

You have spoken it, Genevieve. You do not need me. Consider who you are and what skills you possess and then consider the great legacy that was deemed yours by the goddess Cyrena.

Cyrena?

I am tired now. Ask Ravan. She made him.

No wait, Qirin, please.

Weariness comes and I am at the end of my life. Perhaps in meeting you my life has been made complete. Tell her,

*Ravan. Go now and remember, it is not your aegis magic
that is important but your own.*

Evie opened her mouth to ask more but there was no use.
The Qirin slumped forward, seemingly asleep.

"Come, your majesty," Ravan said. "Time is against us and
I have much to explain."

"Yes, of course," Evie said, dazed.

"Cyrena is a serpent, a very powerful goddess who watched
over the Valisars," he began as he led her to the door of the
chamber, "and she made an agreement with Cormoron, First
of the Valisars . . ."

In the courtyard, the men were watching what was unfolding through tiny peepholes they'd discovered in the walls. It
seemed the nuns had always had the ability to glimpse the
outside world from their closed one, but even with that unexpected help it was difficult to observe the action closely.

Gavriel had remained at the gate, his hand on Lily's arm,
startled by the grown Piven. He still echoed that bright
young child with the sweet nature and brilliant smile but
that's where the similarities ended. Everything else about
Piven, from his attitude to his strangely frightening presence, was a shock. And though it hurt him to believe it,
Gavriel suspected Piven was unpredictable and could not be
trusted.

Holding his breath, he had shared the tension in the courtyard with his new allies, witnessing the scene unfolding
outside. He had listened with escalating concern as the conversation had begun to turn less tolerant and a great deal
more threatening.

Gavriel had silently signaled to Loethar with a hand across
his throat that the situation had turned dire. The expression on
Loethar's face mirrored his own anxiety and the emperor had
arrived quietly at his side.

"I'll go out. It's the very best distraction we have."

Gavriel nodded. "We know you're safe. Buy us some time.
Pretend to negotiate."

Loethar clearly agreed. But just as he was beckoning Roddy
and Kilt from their peepholes to warn that they should inten-

sify the ring of protection, they heard a cry from outside and Gavriel just glimpsed Corbel making a sudden and unexpected lunge at Valya.

He was a heartbeat too slow.

"Valya, don't!" Corbel yelled.

But Valya had revealed enough of the infant to grab Piven's interest.

Barro, alarmed by Corbel's sudden lurch, instinctively drew his sword. Corbel yelled a warning to him but it came too late.

"Kill him, Greven," Piven said casually.

Greven's look of despair deepened. "You just had to draw your weapon, didn't you?" he growled at Barro, who had begun to back off.

Stracker began to laugh. "Your dog doesn't even have a weapon."

"Be careful, Stracker," Piven warned. "I might turn my dog on you one day."

Corbel couldn't bear to watch. He knew if he drew his sword he was committing himself to instant death too and while his life wasn't that important, Evie's was and the baby's was. He heard Barro uselessly swipe with his sword and soon enough the clang of the weapon being flung to the ground, then the terrible sound of Barro choking.

Hopelessly, Corbel doubled over, groaning. Piven was as twisted by his return to sanity and by the arrival of his magic as everyone had feared.

Stracker was laughing at him. Stracker couldn't know for a moment the anxiety that riddled Corbel's every waking moment, had been with him for ten long anni, since Brennus had put the newborn princes into his care. And so to the sound of Barro's death throes Corbel finally let his emotion bubble up. As Barro made his last struggled gasp beneath the suffocating and inhuman strength of Greven's hands, Corbel de Vis emptied his belly in a show of utter powerlessness.

Piven shifted his attention back to Valya. "Is this a jest?"

"I . . . I don't understand," Valya warbled.

Stracker drew his sword with relish as Piven advanced on her. "Do you really think me stupid? I know my princess sister is ten anni. Don't try and fob me off with some whore's brat!" He grabbed the bundle from her and Valya screamed as he carelessly handed it to his third companion, who looked the most shocked of all.

Corbel watched the man look around, unsure, and then place the child on the ground. At least the baby was unharmed for now. He snapped his attention back to Piven, who was standing over Valya as she crawled toward Stracker.

"Stracker! She's your niece!" she cried. "She's Loethar's child. Don't you see, she must have the—"

"You gambled and lost, Valya!" Piven hurled across her words.

Valya screamed and changed direction, throwing herself at Piven. Stracker wasted not a moment, hacking Valya's head from her body with one vicious cleave of his sword. Corbel groaned as her warm blood hit his face and her head rolled to where he was bent, stopping to stare sightlessly at him, her lips the perfect color for her bloodied end. Her headless corpse lay hunched over the sleeping child and he realized sadly she had not been lunging at Piven but was trying to reach her baby. She may have been a wicked woman but she had also been a mother who loved her child even when she knew their fate was hopeless.

Corbel, no longer able to contain his rage, straightened, his gaze scorching a path to Piven.

But there was a new look on Piven's face now, one of pure amazement.

"Corbel de Vis?" he murmured in a mixture of delight and alarm. "Is that really you? You look so old!"

Corbel realized the disguise was destroyed; in his anger he'd forgotten about the tiny spell-infused bead and it had come out when he had retched.

There was no point in denying it. "Yes, it's me, Piven, and it seems I'm not the only one who has changed."

"De Vis!" Stracker roared. In a flash of understanding Corbel realized that no matter how quickly he drew his own sword against Stracker's already drawn and bloodied one, only magic could save him now . . . and he had no aegis.

"Die like your pathetic father did," Stracker roared and brought his huge, heavy blade down toward Corbel's head.

Everything had happened so fast for the audience in the convent that there was a moment of silence so complete they could all hear the soft sound of a bird calling to its mate.

And then pandemonium ensued. Gavriel howled a sound of pure desolation and ripped open the door of the convent, drawing the sword at his side in a smooth movement as he ran out, yelling in rage.

"Stracker!" he howled.

Piven seemed to be staring in shock at Corbel, who was prone on the ground with a gaping wound in his side. It turned out that even in that moment of impending death, Corbel had twisted his body enough for Stracker's huge blow to miss its target. But it still had made enough mess of Corbel that Gavriel could tell in a glance that he was as good as dead, lying there in a pool of his own blood mixing with the already drying blood of Valya.

Suddenly Piven's head snapped up. "Gavriel!" he said.

But Gavriel was already advancing on Stracker, a sound of rage issuing from his throat.

It was Greven who moved though, raising his hand. Gavriel instantly found himself unable to shift a limb. Stracker too seemed to be suspended in the motion of realization, his bloodied sword halfway up to his shoulder again.

"Piven," Greven began and then he shrugged. "This is my magic. I can paralyze, usually for only a few moments but I believe the awakening of the aegis magic has intensified my abilities. I gave my word to my wife on her deathbed that I would never use them again and I have not until this moment. I realize all it takes is your word and I will have no choice but to release these two, but is this really what you want? You are happy for Stracker to fight Gavriel de Vis, your childhood friend?"

Piven looked at Gavriel. "I have no fight with Gavriel."

Gavriel tried desperately to speak or move but was unable to do either.

"But somehow I don't think Gavriel will rest until his brother's death is avenged." Corbel groaned from the ground, and Piven looked down at him. "I'm sorry, Corbel. Had I known that was you in disguise . . . if I had reacted faster . . ."

"Burn in hell, Piven," Corbel choked out and that seemed to sap his dwindling reserve of life. His head slumped back down.

Piven's expression became a grimace of cold fury. "Stracker, what you did to Valya is your business. I'm glad the woman is no longer so much as looking at me. As for the child, that already looks half dead. It's of no consequence to me but I see poor Corbel felt a duty of care toward it. Typical Corbel. He always did fight for the underdog, which is why he was always good to me. Both the de Vis twins were good to me and I'm struggling to find a reason to let you live, Stracker."

"He is not yours to kill! His head is mine!" said a new voice, almost softly spoken.

Piven's face changed from anger to delight. His accompanying clap of pleasure was drowned by the murmuring rippling through the Greens as their king and their new land's emperor walked out without a weapon, a boy following him.

"Loethar!" Piven exclaimed. "How many more surprises wait behind that gate? It's like the traveling show that Greven used to take me to as a lad. Every time the curtain was pulled back, another treat was in store. And there is no better treat than to see you."

"Greetings, Piven," Loethar said calmly. "Does Corbel live?"

"Just," he remarked, with what sounded like genuine sorrow. "But not for long."

"Release de Vis. You have no argument with him. Let him take his brother inside and have a moment with him. You can do that much, surely?"

"I could but why would I?"

"So you can watch my half-brother and I fight to the death. It's been a long time coming."

Piven blinked. "Answer me this, Loethar. I am puzzled. I feel Valisar magic radiating off you. I see a child standing behind you, not that much younger than me. Am I adding up correctly?"

"Your father not only hid your birth, nephew, but he hid mine as well. He and I share Darros as a father."

Piven erupted into gleeful laughter. "My uncle? *You are my uncle?*" His tone was laced with wonder.

Loethar's face showed no trace of amusement.

"Oh, this is precious!" Piven said, almost hugging himself with delight. "And the boy is your aegis, of course?"

"He is. This is Roddy. He is every fiber as powerful as Greven so we might as well accept that we cannot hurt each other."

Piven nodded. "A dilemma indeed for I want you dead, Loethar."

"I am not here to destroy you. But I will kill Stracker. He has killed my mother, my wife—"

"Oh, Lo! Don't tell me that was your child as well?" Piven exclaimed dryly. And then laughed.

Loethar's eyes turned to slits. "What?"

"The baby," Piven pointed. "She was bargaining with a baby."

Loethar felt suddenly unsteady. "What . . . ?" He couldn't finish his question.

"Beneath her body," Piven said, offhandedly.

First Loethar bent to Corbel. "Hold on, de Vis."

And then he reached for Valya, barely sparing her more than the time it took him to shove her corpse aside to reveal the baby Piven had spoken about. With a look of dismay, he lifted the child's limp, lifeless form; the baby looked dead too.

He gave a tight sob. "What is this?" he said, feeling as though he were unable to breathe.

"Your daughter," Corbel choked out, blood still oozing from the wound, his death clearly slow and painful.

And Loethar understood everything. Even in death Valya's

cunning didn't fail to make him catch his breath. It seemed his Ciara had been weak enough that everyone had assumed the worst, but she hadn't succumbed immediately. He raised his head to the skies and let out such a roar of anguish that Vulpan nearby stepped back into the carriage, while Jewd and Kilt hesitated at the doorway, obviously more concerned for Loethar than for their own presence being revealed.

Loethar buried his face into the tiny corpse for a few heart-breaking moments before he straightened and re-organized his expression to hide the naked emotion behind a mask of hate. When he spoke his voice, though raw, was even.

"Captain Gorin."

"Yes, emperor."

"Call me Loethar as you did on the Steppes."

"Yes, Loethar?"

"Have the Greens fall back."

"General Stracker—"

"Whatever General Stracker commanded is now of no weight or concern. General Stracker will be dead shortly. The Greens will bear witness to his demise and understand that this is what happens to any tribal man who challenges my authority. Is this clear?"

The captain licked his lips nervously but nodded. "Yes, Loethar."

And then in the Steppes language Loethar spoke only to his people: "I renounce my status as emperor but not as king of the Steppes," he roared, the magic swirling around him, magnifying the sound so that all the soldiers could hear him clearly. "Do the Greens acknowledge that?"

A roar of sound came back in a language only the Steppes-born could understand.

He continued. "Bear witness, Greens. And then return to your own. Take with you your families and your friends and head east. The tribes are returning to the Steppes. Those who wish to remain in the place they now call home may do so without threat of recrimination. But there will be no barbarian guard from today but an integrated Set and Steppes army to be known as the Imperial Fist. You may choose to belong to it or you may choose to go."

Now a huge roar went up; swords were shaken in the air and the very ground vibrated with their sound of appreciation.

Loethar looked back at Piven. "They should never have been brought here or involved."

"It wasn't my idea."

"I gathered as much."

"What did you just tell them?"

"Nothing important. They are no threat to anyone here, though. Will you release Gavriel?"

"Will you make the fight more fair? Vulpan and I are desperate for some entertainment."

"Certainly. Roddy, release all protective magic around me."

"No, Loethar!" came several voices.

Piven laughed. "Your friends over there disagree."

"Listen to me, all of you," Loethar called out. "When I fight Stracker it will be man to man, no magic involved. If anyone gets involved, I will kill him too." He swung back to Piven. "Now release de Vis so he can take his brother in to die."

Piven glanced at Greven and Gavriel could instantly move again. He let out a growl of despair and was on the ground next to Corbel in one leap.

"Corbel? . . . Corbel!"

"Too late, Gav," his brother croaked.

"Help him," Loethar called to his companions and Jewd ran quickly out to assist Gavriel, who was openly crying now.

"So help me—" Gavriel began, staring at Loethar.

"It will be done," Loethar said, nodding as he understood what Gavriel wanted. "Please hold my child; I will mourn her and bury her later. But take Corbel to the woman he loves. She will want to lay hands on him before it's too late to say farewell." Gavriel seemed to understand instantly the message and urged Jewd to hurry, taking the lifeless bundle with reverence and nodding at Loethar before he hurried after Jewd and Corbel.

"Before we proceed," Piven said, "I have some questions for you."

* * *

As they shuffled inside the compound under the horrified gaze of Lily and Kilt, standing with his arm protectively around her, they all saw Evie arrive with Ravan. She stifled part of her scream but no one outside seemed to care anyway. Her eyes widened with shock and distress.

"He's dying, Evie," Gavriel begged.

She rushed to where they laid him down. "I can save him. I can! I can!" she promised, her voice rising to a snarl. "Corbel, Corbel, it's Evie." She kissed his cheek and kissed his hand, which she then put against her own cheek. "I'm here. You're going to be fine. Just let go now. I can feel it. I can feel death coming but I'm going to chase it away. You just have to relax. Can you hear me, Reg? *Reg!*" she said through helpless tears, her expression distraught. "I can't help unless you let your life go. But I'll bring you back. You know I will."

Lily was weeping and had turned into Jewd's big arms for solace; Kilt was looking on helplessly, his face a mask; Gavriel was not winning the battle against his own tears and only Ravan stood by stoically, his expression concerned but even.

"He's slipping away," she said, her hands stained with his blood. "He's not letting go. I can't do it until he gives in."

"Do what she says, Corb!" Gavriel pleaded.

Corbel de Vis's eyes flickered open. "Evie," he said, his voice barely above a whisper. "I love you."

"I know, I know you do," she said, crying helplessly now. "And I love you."

"But not how I want," Corbel croaked.

"Oh, Reg, please, not now," she begged.

"We both know it," he said. She sobbed and he tried to smile in comfort but he failed; all he managed was a twitch at the corner of his mouth. He stroked her face. "I do not give you my permission to save me."

"No!" she said, shaking her head. "You will not die."

"It is my wish. And you have a responsibility as a doctor to follow my instructions."

"As a doctor I must preserve life!"

"Not with magic," he choked out and coughed as blood exploded from the wound.

She wept harder.

Corbel struggled to pull her close. She bent down to him. "I have had the best of your life and you mine. Let me go, Evie. I want to. I have been sad all my life . . . and I am tired of it."

She sat back and he nodded and she seemed to understand. He was already looking away, trying to find his brother. "Gav?"

"Corb—" But Gavriel couldn't finish. He dissolved into a heartbroken silence.

"Mend everything," Corbel sputtered. "Loethar's trying. Help him." Gavriel shook his head with anguish and bent his head low to his brother, who pulled him forward and whispered, "That Lily's got great tits."

Gavriel gave a teary, helpless laugh as he watched his brother finally let go. He shot a distraught look of disbelief at Evie.

"He's gone." She shook her head in anguish. Her lips were bloodless as she spoke. "He made me promise. But there is something I'm going to do," she said in a hard voice, wiping her eyes. "I just have to work out how to do it." And she stood up, helped by Ravan, letting the arm of Corbel de Vis slump dead to the ground as she stomped away, crying wretchedly.

Outside, Piven nodded. "Intriguing, but thank you for your candor," he said to Loethar. Stracker was nearby, still suspended and seething. "But you and I are at a stalemate. We are like kings on a chessboard. We could keep moving around each other forever."

"Something has to give?"

"Precisely."

"Why don't we let fate play her part?"

"All right and in the meantime you're going to give up your magic and give us all a show with Stracker . . . am I right?"

"Yes. But with the caveat that should you try anything, Piven, Roddy will secure me and our fragile truce is broken."

"I have no reason to break faith with you over this. Stracker is tiresome. He's like an angry ox blundering through a bed of violets. He has no finesse, little subtlety and he understands only what he can achieve with his fists. I thought he could be useful but he is the opposite. Killing Corbel de Vis was his final indiscretion."

"You don't see Valya's death as offensive?"

"Not at all. She was a rabid, obsessive liability and you are well rid of her. As for your child, I'm not sure what to say to that. I can't say I'm sorry. One less Valisar is a good outcome."

"You are yet to answer for that," Loethar said gravely.

"Your child was already dead even as she unwrapped the rags around it. Smothered probably. Perhaps Valya had already slipped into madness."

Loethar had to agree it did make sense. "Perhaps."

They eyed each other in a difficult pause. "Let us deal with Stracker," Loethar said. "The rest will take care of itself."

Piven nodded and looked at Greven.

Stracker slumped with a loud sigh as he was released from the magic.

Marth moved closer to Leo. "What are you thinking?"

"I'm perfectly happy for Stracker to die."

"But what if—"

"He won't, Marth. I can feel Loethar's anger. I can feel it fizzing through my own magic. Once this last little act has played out, we will announce ourselves and finish them all."

"As you wish."

"Make sure Narine is ready."

Thirty-Six

>>————————————————————<<

Nearby, not entirely displeased by Loethar's release from his marriage but hardly impressed by Valya's bloody end or what looked to be Loethar's dead child clutched in that bundle, Elka watched the older man talk quietly with Leo. She couldn't hear what was discussed but an educated guess suggested that Leo was still content to watch from a distance and not play his hand.

She crouched lower as Leo's advisor scrambled back to where the Vested sat. He was obviously a wily old campaigner; if anyone might spot her it would be him and she wasn't going to take any chances. He whispered to the woman who seemed to take charge of the others and then he murmured something to the rosy-cheeked woman, who smiled and nodded.

None of them seemed to be moving into action, so Elka returned her attention to below where Loethar was now circling his half-brother. She couldn't imagine how or why Stracker would take on Loethar if he knew he was protected by magic.

She checked again that Roddy was nearby and inwardly thanked her god for his blessing in keeping Loethar safe. Her heart was still bleeding for Gavriel, though, and she dearly wished she could see what was happening behind those walls in the convent. She focused her full attention on Loethar as someone threw him a sword.

* * *

Stracker sneered. He had never looked bigger or more ferocious. "Valisar?"

"That's right," Loethar said evenly, beginning to circle.
To one side Piven beamed and Vulpan watched from the
carriage like a spider in the shadows.

"Then our mother was raped!" Stracker spat on the ground
between them.

"Not so. She loved Darros. Never stopped all the while
she was with your father."

"Then my mother was a whore!" Stracker accused.

Loethar actually laughed. "Well, you're certainly cutting
yourself free of all your allies, Stracker. And now you have no
one. Not even your faithful Greens, who have seen through
your ruse and your treachery."

"They'll cringe before me when I kill you, Loethar."

"You've never bested me yet."

Stracker's face adopted a rictus of a grin. "There's a first
time for everything."

"Indeed. Including dying. Watch that open stance I've
warned you about so many times before, Stracker."

Stracker spat on the ground again. "You've gone soft,
brother. Too many years of playing emperor."

"That's half-brother, Stracker," Loethar said and danced
in to strike the first blow.

She let Kilt hold her but knew he could see her thoughts
were far away from this place and from him. And she
couldn't blame him for trying to console her, but his tenderness only made it worse.

"Genevieve, my heart hurts for you." He squeezed her gently. "I mean it really hurts. I am sharing your pain whether I
like it or not."

She dragged her gaze from the distance. "I can't believe
he's gone. He's been the most important person in my
life since I was old enough to make friends with an adult."
She held out her hands. "Look at these! They're useless.
They're meant to be healing hands—magical healing hands—
and I just let my closest friend die when I had the chance to
save him."

"If you had," he tried gently, "he might have hated you."

"He could never hate me."

"Genevieve, look at me." Reluctantly she turned her gaze to him. "Corbel was honest with you. He needed you to respect his pain and especially his sorrows. He said he'd been sad for most of his life."

"Oh, don't, Kilt," she said. Hearing those words again made her crumple.

"No, you have to hear this. Imagine why he's been sad all his life. It's because other than the tiny little ray of hope that you might notice him as something other than your big brother figure, he had nothing really to live for. He said as much. He'd lost his family, his home, his life . . . even his memories had been denied him in a way. He had to keep Brennus's secret. And then after years and years of being dutiful the opportunity arrives. He comes back and he brings his most precious of possessions—his only possession . . . you."

She began to cry again.

"He clings to the hope that now, back in his world, walking the landscape he knows, tearing off everything that smacked of his foreign life . . . clothes, pretenses . . ."

"Beard," she said, sniffing.

"Yes, all the disguise, all the lies fall away and he tells you the truth, believing after what is it? Twenty anni?" She nodded. "That you'd finally see him for the man he was."

"I did."

"But you saw him as Corbel de Vis."

"Every bit as wonderful as he was as Reg Dervis."

"But not the noble Corbel de Vis that he'd hoped would make you catch your breath and swoon at his feet. He was living a story in his head. He'd built up such a picture of how it was going to be when he brought you back—if he brought you back—and of course when you didn't react that way, it shattered his long-held dream."

"And then you," she said, putting her face in her hands.

"Yes, and then me. Do you regret it?"

"No, Kilt." She took his hand. "I'm grieving. Let me grieve."

"There's no time, my love. Loethar is fighting for his life out there and while I never thought I'd utter these words, something inside me will break if he dies. Right now he's fighting on our side . . . he's fighting for you and for the people of the Set. He's fighting for good."

"We have to do our bit," she said.

"Exactly. And the more I think about it, the more I believe that you are the solution."

"That's what the Qirin said."

"Then that's two of us who believe it and we won't be the only ones. It has to be your magic. It has to be the famed Valisar Enchantment . . . the Legacy, as it is known."

"But I don't know what it is."

"Well, it's within you. You must find it and you must use it. They say you can coerce people, make them do your bidding," he pressed.

"Force them, you mean," she said, frowning.

"Yes. I suppose that's the harsh way of looking at it. Do you know where that magic is?"

She shrugged. "I haven't had a chance to think about it."

"Then now is the moment. There probably won't be another chance, or a more fitting time."

"But if all the Valisars have their aegis, isn't it a stalemate? No one wins. Loethar can't keep fighting Piven, and if Leo has found his aegis, he can't keep fighting me, or Loethar. You've said we are invincible. I can't coerce them."

"I agree. Peace cannot be achieved until the Valisars reach an agreement. But that can't happen. We know Piven wants his siblings and Loethar dead. Leo will kill Loethar if he has just half a chance. Loethar . . ." He shrugged. "I'm going around in circles."

"The only solution then is to somehow rid all the Valisars of the aegis magic."

His gaze snapped to hers in bewilderment. "Are you mad? That's your only protection."

"But it's the aegis magic that is preventing harmony."

"There is no harmony any more."

Evie stood and paced, her mind roaming now. "Where is Ravan?" she asked.

"I'll find him," Kilt said.

"Hurry," she urged and then she was lost in her thoughts again. She felt a voice talking to her from the rim of her mind; she knew that voice. It was a familiar companion from her study days and perhaps even earlier than that, as she moved through her most awkward years and felt at her most isolated. The voice was an invisible friend who spoke to her, helped her to sort through problems to solutions. It was at times her conscience, her extra sense, a mirror that reflected back her negative feelings in an effort to turn them into a positive energy. And right now it was trying to make her see something, something that felt just out of her line of vision, just out of her reach. She stretched in her mind but still it evaded her.

And time was running out.

Loethar knew Stracker would get bored parrying with swords in the same way that Stracker got bored with intelligent conversation. And so Loethar knew that if he kept feinting and teasing Stracker—giving him small openings to tempt him but then shutting them down just as fast—sooner or later his half-brother was going to become wearied of the lack of action, the lack of blood. He simply had to stay out of that bludgeoning sword until Stracker was bored enough to be reckless.

"Stracker?" Piven called. "Can you listen and fight at the same time?"

The big man grunted.

"Can't you see what Loethar's doing?"

"Eh?"

Loethar gritted his teeth.

"Well, it's obvious. He's deliberately baiting you. He's just about inviting you to take a slash. Don't lose your temper. That last thrust was dangerous."

"Piven, I don't think explaining the rudiments of my strategy is altogether fair," Loethar commented, hiding his irritation as he jumped forward suddenly and slashed at Stracker, missing him by a whisker.

"Oh pay attention, Stracker, and at least make some sport of this, for Lo's sake."

"Stracker, you believe you'll kill me, don't you?" Loethar said, feinting left and hearing the whiz of Stracker's enormous blade cutting a little too close.

"I will kill you, Loethar, just for being Valisar."

"And you know Piven will kill you straight afterward? If not him, then Leo, who has probably found his aegis by now. Did Piven tell you that Leo is alive? I can assure you he is. I have seen him, met him even." He paused as Stracker went still. "Er, Stracker, you're not meant to stop attacking me in a fight to the death."

"You've met him?"

Loethar kept his guard up but sighed theatrically. "Thoroughly unpleasant, whinging sort of runt. The sort you'd personally like to chew up before your first meal of the day."

Stracker actually laughed. Loethar knew his half-brother had always found him amusing, especially when he bantered to Stracker across the battlefield or any sort of competitive activity.

"So we agree on Leonel?" Stracker asked, taking a monumental hack at Loethar's neck. Loethar blocked it but it left his arm near numb.

"That was good, Stracker. The closest you've got yet."

"I can get closer still," the big man warned.

"Can you see how he's wearing you down, you big oaf? You're going to be too tired to lift that wretched great sword soon and meanwhile his small frame is dancing around like a pillodillo." There was real venom in Piven's voice but the word made even Loethar laugh.

No one in this company had ever heard Stracker laugh with easy amusement. But hearing his half-brother described as an effeminate who was paid to dance for men who preferred the company of men seemed to tickle his fancy, and he erupted alongside his half-brother in genuine mirth. Loethar suspected they had the same sort of mental picture of Loethar draped in gauzy robes.

"Right, stop, both of you," Piven commanded. Stracker dropped his blade and Loethar did as well, more out of surprise than obedience. "This is not entertaining. There's no heat in this fight. There's no blood. You two seem to be treating this as a great jest. Loethar's right, Stracker, I will kill you if you're still standing at the end of this so you might as well die knowing you took your Valisar kin down with you."

Stracker's amusement died and his tatua stretched in the familiar grimace.

"And to ensure you fight hard, can I ask you both to look at that man over there. Captain Gorin, I think his name is." Loethar looked at Gorin, a feeling of dread unfurling in his belly. "Greven, kill Gorin, will you. Beat him with your only fist until his face is no longer recognizable and his green tatua have been obliterated."

Loethar felt his mouth fall open in astonishment. "Ah, Loethar, I see I shock you. Isn't this precisely the sort of thing you used to do to get what you wanted out of people? I seem to recall boys younger than me being slaughtered in numbers, I know you let Stracker loose on the Vested, that you roasted my father and ate him before my mother and I. Did you think I wouldn't remember those events? You taught me how to be evil, Loethar. You and Stracker. You're as bad as each other. You used Stracker, turned him loose whenever you needed a dark deed done. So now here's a taste of your own medicine. Watch the men you love fall. And by the way, use that strange guttural language to tell your men there is no point in fighting back. Greven cannot be harmed or wearied. He is relentless."

"A curse on you, Piven!" Loethar yelled.

Stracker immediately began bellowing to the Greens in Steppes language as the first cries went up from Gorin, who had tried to shake off Greven with a weapon to no avail. Others too were joining in but finding Greven impossible to hurt. Gorin's howls intensified.

"I'll tell you something else," Piven said. "Vulpan is going to count for us. And every time we reach the count of ooh, shall we say twenty-nine, Loethar? That's a number you should recognize. You killed twenty-nine boys before you were satisfied that Leo had been found. And now every time Vulpan reaches twenty-nine Greven will pick a new Green to murder. Start counting, Vulpan . . . aloud, so I can hear it."

"One . . . two . . . three . . ." Vulpan began.

"Wait!" Loethar said.

"No!" Piven denied. "Keep counting, Vulpan, or you'll be next to die. You two, you'd better keep fighting to the death as promised or the man closest to Greven will be next. And he's quite young, I see."

Gorin's cries had ceased. He was clearly dead, his face a pulp and unrecognizable as ordered. Greven looked sickened, staring at his only fist, a mass of blood and flesh clinging to it.

"Nine . . . ten," Vulpan continued, trying not to look at Greven.

"Gentlemen," Piven said. "It's up to you."

"Let's finish this," Stracker said, and instantly took a hack at Loethar. Loethar didn't move quite as fast as he hoped and took a nasty slash across his belly. The pain was sharp and he sucked in a painful breath but he managed to parry the next three furious blows.

"Ah, this is more like it," Piven said. "Now we have a fight on our hands, Vulpan. Greven, at the count of twenty-nine you kill that young Green next to Gorin's corpse."

"Any moment, now, Marth," Leo said. "I want Loethar weakened, not dead."

The general nodded and held a finger in the air to Reuth. When that finger dropped, it was the moment for Narine to turn on her best skills.

Elka couldn't believe it. Was that blood on Loethar's shirt? But Roddy was there! The aegis magic was in place. She'd seen it tested, knew it was sound.

She turned it over in her mind, her heart hammering with worry. And then it dawned on her. He had ordered Roddy to drop the protection so he could fight Stracker honorably.

She cursed silently and bit her knuckles: she was torn once again. Her good sense won out. Running down there would achieve little. She had no magical protection, and the truth was Loethar could turn his aegis back on with just a word to Roddy—a mere glance, in fact. He wasn't going to die, she told herself. He wouldn't let it happen. Not for Stracker. Not after Stracker had betrayed him.

She must trust Loethar. She had no choice. Besides, she couldn't help but admit that she despised Leo and she intended to put a stop to whatever little plot he was hatching.

They were both tired now. Each had struck blows and both their bodies had suffered cuts, some serious enough to be bleeding freely and hurting a great deal; both were wearing each other's blood on their clothes and in their hair. Certainly both swords glistened.

Loethar paused, swaying slightly, and took stock.

Four of the Greens had died the hideous death that Greven meted. Loethar had yelled an order for the Greens to scatter, which Stracker had reinforced, but the Greens had simply regrouped, too loyal to leave their most senior warriors, too dutiful to walk away from their king.

That they wouldn't save themselves even as he begged them to run brought tears to Loethar's eyes. There was only one thing for it, only one way to save another man's face being obliterated. He could hear one screaming defiantly now as Greven began to rain down the next set of blows to the sound of Piven's gleeful laughter.

And Vulpan counted monotonously on. Each time he reached twenty-nine, Piven would shout. "Next!" to Greven and then he would turn to Vulpan and order "Again!" before he returned his attention to the two bloodied fighters.

"Loethar can't last much longer. I won't begin to describe to you what's going on out there," Jewd whispered to Kilt.

Kilt, looked uncharacteristically tense. "She's trying to work her way through this. She and Ravan are together. I don't really know why she feels he is important but I think he keeps her calm."

Jewd shook his head. "I feel we are done for here."

"No, old friend. I will keep you safe."

"That's not good enough, Kilt. I'm worried about everyone else."

"What do you want me to do?"

"Kilt, you've always been able to dream up the most inspired ideas. We've never needed that to work for us more than now."

"Genevieve is the door that unlocks this. I feel it."

"Why isn't it Piven . . . or Loethar . . . or—?"

Kilt gave a look of exasperation. "I don't know. I don't know."

"Well why say it?"

"It's a feeling, that's all."

"What feeling?"

Kilt paced. "I think it's because we've all been drawn here. All the surviving Valisars—"

"Not Leo."

"We don't know where he is but we also don't know that he isn't here. There are four Valisars. We know three of them are here and it's very possible the fourth is too, hiding somewhere out there." He pointed to nowhere in particular. "My magic feels somehow complete as though it's sensing all of them. I could be wrong." He shook his head.

"Go on."

Kilt shrugged. "Genevieve arrived here first. No one bothers with this place. We've had our dealings with it over the years, and it's no more than a convent on the edge of mountains that very few people move through; home to the Davarigons, a quiet race we see little of."

"What's your point?"

"My point is that Genevieve finds herself here after ten anni away from Penraven . . . since leaving our world. And lo and behold, we all start arriving. Why did we come here?"

Jewd shrugged. "Any number of reasons."

"But no specific reason. And then one by one, the others begin arriving . . . all the major players in this game of chess: the Valisars, their individual champions, even Valya and Stracker."

"It is like a game."

"Well, the gods are having fun at our expense, if it is. But everything points to Genevieve, and the legendary Valisar Enchantment that a surviving female royal would possess. The most potent of all."

Jewd nodded and sighed. "The magic to cure all magics," he said and stood. "And while we've been here musing, Loethar's probably dead. I'd better check." He turned to leave, then paused. "I meant what I said, Kilt. If Genevieve is the door that opens the secret chamber, then you are the key that unlocks that door. Use that clever mind of yours and show us the way."

Thirty-Seven

The sword fight had taken on a grim countenance. There was
no more banter, no more baiting or taunting. The clash had
settled into a dour contest that was no longer about strength
or speed but about who wanted to live more. Gone were
Loethar's sparkling, crisp and inventive moves; he had re-
sorted to parrying more than thrusting. His stance was defen-
sive, his face a bleak mask of concentration.

His opponent meanwhile was tired enough that even his
grunts sounded weary. Stracker was moving his legs as little
as possible it seemed; he looked as though they had taken
permanent root in the spot where he stood and from there
alone he was hacking at his half-brother as though Loethar
were a tree to be felled.

But Stracker was the aggressor and it was clear from his
expression that he didn't understand Loethar's lack of attack. All provocation had fled and even his tatua couldn't
hide the frown that told anyone watching that he was sensing a ruse.

"Fight me, Loethar," he urged, the first words to be exchanged since the last Green had fallen. Vulpan was up to
nineteen and another man would be killed in ten counts.

Loethar couldn't listen to another one die. He flung down
his sword. "No more."

Stracker was just struggling to lift his heavy blade for another blow. He stopped midway, confusion deepening beneath the markings on his face. "What?"

"Kill me, Stracker. One last, clean, final blow."

"No!" Roddy said from the background, where he had silently watched the entire horrible contest.

"Quiet, Roddy. You may not defy me," Loethar growled. "Do it, Stracker."

"Why?"

Vulpan started again. "One . . ."

"I'm not going to let another Green die. I've taken long enough to reach this decision. I've let three die while I've pondered it! Now do it before another loses his life!"

"This is not the way it should be. You're just giving up?"

"I'm giving up," he echoed, exasperated.

"Then kill him, Stracker, and be done. I'm bored with you both," Piven said. "Shut up, Vulpan. Your reedy voice is giving me a headache and the smell of blood is spooking our horses. Greven," he called, "enough!" Vulpan had already fallen silent, and Greven stood like a broken man, unrecognizable from the blood and gore that covered him.

Stracker stared with disbelief at Loethar. "Fight me!"

"No. Kill me." Loethar sank to his knees. "Make it clean like a good barbarian."

"Rot in hell, Loethar. Get up and fight until you die. That's the barbarian way."

"But not my way. I was always the intelligent one, Stracker. I always knew when to retreat."

"Except your 'retreats' were usually tricks. Is this a trick?"

"No. I have no weapon, I have no magical protection, my neck is exposed. I'm making it very easy for you. Now just end it."

"End it, Stracker, and be quick about it or I'll start Greven killing again," Piven demanded.

"You do it!" Stracker said. "I've lost my appetite."

"But you love people on their knees cowering before you."

Stracker rounded on Piven. "He's not cowering. This is Loethar being defiant. Can't you see? He's defying both of us by making it so easy! Even in death he's going to make himself a hero to my Greens."

"Lo! Open your eyes, Stracker. They will no longer take

orders from you; he's seen to that. I can't kill him. That wretched aegis over there will sense any magic before it can touch him. And Loethar won't stand for me to kill him. But you can. Or do you still want him knocking around, making a mockery of you? Because that's what he does. He mocks you. You are nothing, Stracker, and he has seen to that."

Stracker had stiffened with rage as Piven spoke. He turned back to Loethar and spoke in Steppes. "Go join your whore of a mother, your jade of a wife and your slut of a daughter in hell. Tell Ciara her Uncle Stracker says hello and I've sent her daddy to meet her."

It was the mention of his precious child, the way her beautiful name rolled off Stracker's tongue as though it were filthy, something to spit on. Of all the insults Stracker could have hurled at Loethar, this one was ill-chosen. Nothing in Loethar's already seething and blood-drenched mind could permit him to allow the last pure image he possessed to be tarnished.

A heartbeat ago he had been prepared to die beneath Stracker's blade, but no longer. With a roar of anguish, fresh fury giving him a new-found strength and impetus, he launched himself forward, reaching and grabbing the dagger that was sheathed at his thigh in one smooth, upward motion. Stracker's arms were raised above his shoulders, his sword readying itself to swing down in a monstrous killing arc.

But Loethar's full body weight, powered with rage, met Stracker's wide-stance, well-exposed groin with a sickeningly dull thump. Not even Stracker's legendary might could withstand such impact on such a tender, vulnerable region. He crumpled, falling like a tree cut off at its base, his face twisted in agony as his stomach attempted to heave its contents. Snarling, Stracker tried to curl up but Loethar sat astride him.

He said nothing but without hesitation plunged his dagger into the throat of his enemy . . . and twisted once before lending his weight to drag his blade deeply and obscenely through Stracker's thick neck, cutting through flesh and ropelike tendons. Predictably and instantaneously blood spumed in a massively strong spurt, dissipating for the second spume as Stracker's choked death rattle began.

Loethar spoke in Steppe; as much as he despised the man he'd just killed, he was kin, and so he began to say the words of the prayer that sent a soul safely on its way. Stracker watched with steadily glazing eyes as Loethar prayed somberly, his breath no longer labored, death one last hearbeat away. And then the spark of life died in his eyes and Loethar knew his half-brother was gone.

He stood unsteadily, dragging his frame drunkenly from the corpse. Instantly he felt the aegis magic wrap itself around him like a comforting blanket of warmth, curing his ills. The wounds that could infect and take his life, the cuts that needed stitching were healed. Even the blood loss was stymied. Roddy was pouring strength into him and Loethar was shocked by how easily he straightened, stood proud again.

Loethar wiped the blood from his eyes and still without saying a word set about a grim task that had not been seen performed by a tribal man since his predecessor of two reigns previous deemed it unnecessarily savage. But scalping Stracker with his forehead intact—where the main tatua of his tribe and his status was displayed—was not about demeaning his kin's body. It was out of the love he knew his mother held for both of them. He would send part of Stracker—perhaps the most important part—back to the land it was from to be burned; offered up peacefully to the gods in the hope that Stracker would indeed find the peace that eluded him in his restless, empty and angry life.

A dread silence claimed the Greens, still no doubt chilled from the death of their own but mesmerized by Loethar's bladework. When it was done, he held up the slippery flesh and spoke to them in their own language.

"You will leave now. Take a part of each fallen warrior with you back to the Steppes and perform the ritual of Rok-ukk. They died badly today. They died sadly today. Their souls deserve peace."

Men began climbing down from their horses and setting themselves to the challenge of salvaging anything from the heads of the men Greven had battered and crushed.

And it was Greven who broke the trance-like atmosphere at last.

"Someone will make you pay for this atrocity, Piven," he threatened, a bloodied finger pointed at his jailer.

"Well, it's not going to be you, Greven. And no other Valisar is getting through my defenses and no other Valisar seems to have the stomach for—"

"Is that so?" said a new voice. "No stomach for what, Piven? For killing? Watch me, brother!"

Jewd whistled to him. "De Vis!"

Gavriel was still staring at the lifeless form of his brother; Lily was sitting nearby in a silence of her own private shock.

"Who's killed who? Frankly I don't care any more." He stood reluctantly and began approaching Jewd, who was beckoning him anxiously. Lily trailed behind.

"Loethar killed Stracker, which has some justice methinks. But that's not what I'm talking about. Look!"

And now Gavriel could hear all the yells and the roar of something—a sound he couldn't place. He bent his tall frame to peep through one of the holes in the wall and to his astonishment saw Leo hurling arcs of flame at the melee of Greens, who twisted and thrashed on horses as man and beast burned into an obscenely blended form.

It was the most horrific sight he had ever witnessed. Leo's mouth was a rictus of hate and Gavriel had no idea where this power was emanating from. Given everything Loethar and Kilt had said previously, Leo had almost no power to speak of.

"Get Kilt," he murmured, too shocked to drag his gaze from the inferno outside as the smell of burning flesh assaulted him, began to make him gag.

Loethar moved first. The sight of his precious men dying in this manner was too much for him to bear. In an instant he was running.

"Come to me, Loethar," Leo raged. "You can't save any of them and I will not stop until the last one lies dead and scorched in the way you roasted my father."

"It's me you want!" Loethar roared.

"But you have your aegis, so I'll take my kingly wrath out on them."

"You can have me," Loethar yelled above the screams of the dying.

Kilt, Evie and Ravan came running to the forecourt. Kilt couldn't take the restricted view of the peepholes any longer and wasted no time scaling his way to the top of the convent's flat roof. Ravan followed, helping the princess, who insisted she see as well.

What confronted them was too shocking to digest: men, horses, trees, grass, even the earth looked to be on fire. But the maelstrom left the magically protected untouched. It was so barbaric that Kilt began to yell.

"Genevieve, you have to stop this! It is within your power."

Up on her ledge, Elka's tolerance had dried up. If Loethar's body language was telling her anything, it was that he was offering himself to Leo: the savage anguish on his blood-streaked face, the way he was opening up his arms to his nephew, the look he threw back at Roddy.

No. No . . . no . . . no! She would not lose Loethar this way to a crazed Leonel.

Without giving herself another moment to reconsider, Elka raised her catapult, took aim and released the stone that she'd been weighting in her hand since she'd first clapped eyes on the Vested with their arms all linked and their glazed looks.

And with the practiced skill of an experienced hunter, Elka's aim was true, striking the temple of her prey with a crisp and savage force that first cracked and then splintered her skull. The woman was unconscious directly on being hit and died in that state not long later, her rosy cheeks burning as the firestorm had been.

Elka had already ducked back into the safety of cover, blending superbly with her rocky surrounds, but she could see that Leo was already beginning to turn, with a look of genuine savagery.

No more hiding, she decided. Crawling backward, away

from the Vested, who looked suddenly disoriented and weary as their power was disrupted, she was soon jogging down the incline and back in the direction of the convent. She would be at Loethar's side; even if he couldn't protect her, she would never leave him again while she still lived.

A deathly quiet blanketed the convent as everyone tried to take in the infernal scene outside. Bodies lay melted and entwined around each other in a deathly embrace, some still burning, others smoldering. The stench of crackled, bubbled and fried flesh and hair, leather and fabric blended into a revolting odor that had the unprotected gagging where they stood in their disbelief and horror.

Kilt knew that unless Genevieve acted now, the land—even the world as they knew it—might never recover. Not with madmen like Piven and Leo on the loose.

They had to be stopped. Their magic had to be quashed. It had to be possible or the Valisar Enchantment would not exist. Genevieve's whole point of being . . . her very existence had no meaning if not to be a weapon against this very situation.

He began murmuring while Leo and Piven swapped accusations and threats. He couldn't hear Loethar's voice in the fray.

"The serpent god and Cormoron made an agreement. In exchange for the Valisar powers of invincibility, she made a proviso that one alone would have the greatest of all powers," Kilt said.

Ravan picked up on his prattlings. "A female."

"That's right. But the magic was so great that no females survived."

"The females never survived because they were never needed," Ravan suddenly offered.

"What? Is that right?" Evie asked.

"Yes," Ravan said, blinking once, slowly.

"Until now," Kilt said, picking up that new thought and moving forward. "Ten anni ago providence played its unpredictable part."

"No, before then," Ravan counseled. "Darros stepped outside of the family and sowed a wild seed."

"He was the first?"

Ravan nodded. "Curiously, yes. Cyrena had won a promise from Cormoron that no Valisars would be born outside the family hierarchy."

"And everyone obeyed."

"The Valisars are dutiful, honorable. And seemed to beget single sons."

"Until Brennus."

Ravan smiled. "Yes. Fate dealt a terrible hand. Several Valisars were born, each of them strong in their magic. Strong in their convictions too. They were destined to clash, to challenge the crown, particularly with Loethar born outside of the normal hierarchy."

"And so Genevieve was born."

"Genevieve and then presumably the daughter that Loethar sired," Ravan reminded. "It appears Cyrena was taking no chances."

Kilt looked over to where the argument between Piven and Leo still raged. He saw Elka scrambling down the hill, and above her, a ragtag group peeked out from behind a well-protected ledge. An old man and an older woman had arrived near Leo. Who in Lo's name were they? His gaze was dragged away and down to where Jewd and Gavriel leaned against the wall, looking helpless.

His eyes rested on Jewd as he searched his mind for an answer. Jewd had said they needed to find a cure.

"A cure," he murmured.

"What?" Evie said, dragging her face from her hands.

"You have to find a cure."

She frowned at him.

"You're a healer, Genevieve. So heal them."

She stared at him and he could see the flickering of understanding catch alight in her formerly beaten expression and then a flame of dawning erupt in her eyes. She leaped up.

"Ravan, you said I have the power of coercement. Kilt, you said that too, right?"

"You could change the thinking of a whole realm, a whole empire, is my understanding." Ravan shrugged. "A world. This is a very dangerous magic."

"What if I wasn't interested in a world? What if all I wanted to do was heal just a few people: cure them of their ills . . . of their dark magic?"

He blinked at her.

"Do it!" Kilt demanded. "Do it for all of us!"

Thirty-Eight

>>————————————————<<

Evie fled within. The Qirin was right; she had the power inside, she'd just had to find what the secret was. And it was not something buried or hidden . . . it had been the most obvious of all answers. She was a doctor, a curer of ills. And in the same way that her finely honed surgical skills could slice away at damaged tissue, her magical skills set to work at slicing away at the very fabric of the Valisars to release the poison they collectively held.

She closed her eyes and went to work, reaching out not with her hands as she had done in her previous existence, but with her mind. And as she found each of them, each felt the touch of her immense power as it called to them, demanded they know her, forced them even against their will. Coerced them.

One by one they turned toward her.

Greven first. He turned to her with a look of gratitude, hoping she could tell that she should smite him magically, destroy him.

Perl next. She looked up, haggard and shocked, from where her head had been dropped between her knees and looked longingly at Evie.

Roddy turned with a big smile. He felt her presence so quickly and welcomed her so fast it felt like a ray of warmth through her.

Kilt could see it happening to the others and turned with wonder, his eyes searching, his mind open, waiting anxiously to be called. When she reached for him he gave himself to her willingly, with soft eyes and a smile that reached those eyes and made her heart pound.

She felt Loethar's mind filled with mystification but her touch soothed him and he swung around to stare open-mouthed at Evie. His magic all but leaped at her touch; he honestly no longer wanted it.

And now she called to Piven, who appeared confused. Greven was nodding at him, a look of wonder on his face. Piven turned, transfixed, and eyed Evie. *You!* Realization and understanding collided as he understood. She saw a terrible darkness in Piven but somewhere deep inside him she sensed the light might still shine.

Leonel, she called. *Come to me, my brother.* But Leo resisted her, physically retreating as he wrestled his mind away from her touch, his mouth taut in a silent yell of anguish. *You must not fight me. You cannot fight me.* But still he struggled and in his struggle she saw the void . . . the chasm of darkness that his heart held. He would not yield willingly. Evie pressed, calling upon her vast power, lashing it around his mind like mental ropes, dragging him screaming toward her where she could look fully upon the hatred that he embodied. *I am sad for you, Leo*, she told him. *But you must be cured. I will heal you.*

Gavriel, Jewd, Lily and Elka looked around at each other, baffled. It seemed all the Valisars and each aegis had focused their gazes on Genevieve. The strangers standing near Leo looked equally confused.

Gavriel seized the moment of confusion. "Who the hell are you?" he demanded.

"I am General Marth," the older one said indignantly, "although I don't expect you to—"

"General Marth of Barronel?" Gavriel asked, shocked.

"The same," the elder said, stomping down the hillside. "And you are?"

"Gavriel de Vis, sir."

"Regor's boy?"

"The same," Gavriel echoed the general.

"Well, well. What's happening here, does anyone know?"

"No, we're as confused as you. But standing up there on the roof is another Valisar, the Princess Genevieve."

"Princess?"

"It's a very long story, general."

"She survived?" the woman nearby said.

"This is Reuth. Er, she's with us," Marth said, pointing to the top of the hill. "Those are the Vested, from the Barronel camp."

"Is that what it was?" Gavriel said, filled with dismay.

"Long story, son. But Narine is dead, Reuth says."

"Was she the woman controlling the fire? I killed her," said Elka, arriving. "Someone had to stop the massacre."

Marth nodded. "It had spun out of our control. We had agreed to stop it ourselves if the killing stretched to anyone outside of the army. Can't say I mourn the Greens," he said, looking around with disgust at the corpses of men and their horses.

"Can they hear us?" Elka asked, moving toward Loethar, who appeared struck by some trick of mesmerization, staring with wonder at Genevieve.

"Search me," Gavriel said. "Nor do I care. I'm just grateful someone put an end to it."

"The princess is doing this?" Reuth wondered aloud.

"I would say so. It seems she's finally found her magic."

"Not before time," Marth replied softly.

Gavriel nodded. "Much too late for me," he murmured.

And one by one Evie began the healing process. With her surgical skill she began to strip away the aegis magic that bound each to his or her Valisar, cutting, as if with an invisible scalpel, at the strongly interwoven flesh-like bonds that magically roped each pair.

Roddy and Loethar were first. She worked fast and with a determined focus. She knew people were talking around her but they sounded like they were coming from a long way away. Sound was muffled whereas her mind was sharp and in focus. Though no words were exchanged, no sound issued, she felt Roddy and Loethar's support, sensed them both trying to pull apart. It hurt them, she knew, and she couldn't help that but they bore the pain and she knew she could heal the wounds once those tight ligatures had been severed.

It was working. Both were laughing in her mind even though she couldn't describe it as a sound. It was color and radiance. It was warmth and love. And finally they spiritually fell apart. It was a loss for each, she sensed. But quickly she moved to stem the flood of pain, staunch the wounds with her healing balm, soothe the agony.

She could see Gavriel and Lily rushing to the physical aid of Loethar and Roddy, who lay writhing on the ground, but she also knew there was nothing they could do. Not yet. First she healed Roddy of the palsy the Valisar magic had suppressed, pouring her magic into Roddy's small body, making it whole again. She watched his aegis magic begin to shrivel, like water that splashes from a simmering pot onto heated iron and simply bubbles away, evaporating to nothing. And then there was no magic left in Roddy.

Loethar's magic did not exist of its own volition; it had no source other than an inbuilt knowledge that it belonged to a Valisar. It was easy to find that knowledge and she cut it free and consumed it, burning it away so that it no longer existed.

She left Roddy and Loethar breathing fast and looking frightened but whole and cured.

Perl was easy. The young woman couldn't wait for Evie to cut away the aegis magic. The pain was immense but she pulled and fought, helping Evie tear through the fibers. Leo refused to assist. He waited, seemingly impotent, brooding and silent, giving nothing but hate back to her. Evie concentrated on Perl, gathering up her aegis magic and dissolving it, vanishing the markings on her head and allowing hair to sprout where before it had not been able to grow. Perl began to weep as she felt her prison melt away.

Leo had no magic of his own. Not an iota. Evie cut the knowledge of the Valisars from his mind as she had Loethar's. But unlike Loethar, who had welcomed the change, Leo was filled with hatred. She could not change that—it was the structure of who he was—but she could stymie that magic and she set to, weaving a cover over the receptacle that he had become, had opened himself up to being. He was angry. She could feel that. She couldn't change someone's feelings, or someone's character; their personality was theirs. And Leo had harbored a terrible sense of victimization and rage for so long that it was now part of the fabric of his makeup. Time alone—and perhaps the people who loved him—would heal that. Once he could no longer channel power she let him go, mentally releasing him. She noticed, briefly, that only Gavriel de Vis went to his aid.

Finally she turned to Greven and Piven. Greven was mentally begging her for release and he above all seemed to deserve it. She worked diligently and quickly, deftly cutting away bonds that had twisted and tied and re-tied themselves. These bonds felt stronger than the others had, more mature. She sighed in her mind, reminded herself that she had stood through long and tedious surgeries in the past . . . in a past life . . . and pressed on, unleashing the ties that bound poor Greven to Piven. Piven didn't fight her. She had expected him to treat her as Leo had but there was something simple and accepting about the way he acknowledged her presence.

Greven, like Perl, couldn't wait to be free of his Valisar, risking the agony, tearing at his mind as he fought to shake off whatever still clung between him and Piven. And then he too was free, rolling away. She cured Greven's dormant leprosy and then patched up a heart problem he had been carrying for a long time, perhaps his whole life. He would die of that heart problem but not yet . . . not for a long while yet. She could not give him back the hand he had lost but he looked so grateful to be freed from Piven she didn't think he cared. The woman called Lily was at his side, weeping and holding him and Greven looked like a new man.

Piven waited. She could feel his wonder; he was impressed by her. He was the first—the only—Valisar to express this and he waited patiently for her to heal him. She mentally stood back and looked at him. He showed no obvious signs of the pain he was bearing but she couldn't get past the notion that what Piven most needed was light. He carried shadows that were gobbling up his own light and the more he tried to let it shine, the harder they worked to obliterate it.

Evie gathered up her strength and courage for she sensed in those shadows was a cancer, a festering illness that consumed goodness. She'd heard about the Piven that Corbel and Gavriel had known. This Piven showed barely a trace of that character. But she sensed he existed; he could be found if only she could let the sun back into his mind. In a final push she dug deep into her well of power, found the sharp, blazing light that cut like one of her favorite laser scalpels and threshed the shadows, opening up slashes. The more they tried to regroup, the thinner and mistier they became. And Evie bent her will to it; her mind was strong, crusading with the power of healing until she had cut away the final ghosts of the dark in Piven's mind and what remained felt like sunlight that reached to her heart.

She let him go and watched him lower himself gently to the ground with a look of great amusement and joy. And to her surprise—the sort of surprise that reassured Evie that people were essentially good—she watched as Greven hauled himself to his shaking feet and walked toward Piven with his arms open.

Evie turned wearily. Kilt looked back at her, his expression loving and open.

She begged Cyrena if she was listening not to heal their love as she cut away the beautiful magic that bound them and released Kilt Faris from her thrall.

Gavriel nodded to Jewd who had joined him in checking that Leo was recovering. Whatever the princess was doing, it seemed to be working. One by one, the Valisars and their companions had fallen away from each other, apparently released from the spells that bound them.

All that mattered to Gavriel was getting his old friend back. As he'd approached Leo he had placed his bow on the ground. Leo looked helpless and confused.

"Just be still," Gavriel had suggested. "I don't really know what's happened but I think your sister is weaving

some incredible new magic to override all the aegis magic."
He had smiled at Leo. "Welcome back."

Leo had grimaced. "She is healing it."

"What?"

"Healing our magic. Curing us of our Valisar magical
bonds."

"Lo be thanked," Gavriel replied as Jewd arrived. "What
took her so long?"

"All right, Leo?" Jewd asked, but it was said dryly.

Leo's expression didn't change. "All right? What does that
mean, Jewd? I'm back to exactly where I was."

Jewd threw Gavriel a look of soft concern. "Oh, I wouldn't
say that. Come on. Let's get you down into the convent.
You're quite weak. Everyone is."

Gavriel had looked across at Elka and found a grin for
her. "Can you manage here, Jewd? I'll check on Elka and
Loethar."

"Sure," the big man said. He helped Leo to his feet as
Gavriel picked up his bow and the arrow he'd had previously
nocked, and strode down the hillside to where Elka was
helping Loethar walk back into the compound.

"De Vis," Loethar croaked. "How impressive is my niece?"
he said, nodding toward Genevieve, who looked to be working on Kilt Faris.

"Really impressive. She's even unlinking herself from Kilt."

"Very wise," Loethar said.

As they turned to enter the gates, they heard Leo's voice.
"Loethar!"

The three of them swung around. Leo was running toward
them, brandishing a blade Gavriel recognized as Jewd's. Loethar was unarmed; he simply let go of Elka and straightened,
seemingly prepared to meet Leo head on.

"You too, de Vis!" Leo roared.

Gavriel was aware of Elka fumbling on the ground for a
stone, but almost as though he could feel it happening at half
the speed it should, all other sounds and images falling
away, he saw only the bow that flashed up, nocked in an instant. He had a heartbeat to decide whether to wound or kill,
and then he let fly with his arrow.

Gasps and shrieks sounded around the killing field as Leonel was knocked off his feet as the arrow struck home . . . straight through his chest.

Before Gavriel could think about what he had done he sprinted to his oldest friend and crouched at his side.

"Call the princess," Jewd yelled.

"No! Leave it," Gavriel growled. "I shot to kill, or didn't you notice?" he snarled through his welling tears. "Leo . . . ?"

Leo tried to sit up, still fighting, perhaps not quite realizing that life was already fleeing from him. "Ah, Gav, you've put an arrow through me," he said, as blood began to bubble and froth at his mouth. And then a wry twist of a smile formed briefly before it turned to a grimace of pain. "Best you did."

Gavriel nodded, staring into Leo's dying eyes. "I know . . . because you never break a promise."

Leo managed to nod as he closed his eyes. "Never. I am Valisar."

Leonel of Penraven, who had always regarded himself as Ninth of the Valisars in a distinguished line of kings begotten from King Cormoron the First, sighed his last breath in the arms of Gavriel de Vis, who bent his head and wept.

Thirty-Nine

>>——————————————————————<<

While it was a somber mood that gripped those gathered around the convent's refectory table that night, there was no doubting that everyone was feeling a similar lightness . . . a true sense of hope for the future of the land formerly known as the Set.

The nuns had laid out a modest meal as a gesture of respect for those who had died this day. There would be no feasting while men lay dead outside the Abbess's convent. But the work of cleaning and cremating the bodies would keep until tomorrow, she had said. "Tonight we all heal properly. We eat and we sleep and we pray for deliverance from all that has troubled so many souls."

Quietly, a small party had broken away from the nuns and the Vested for a private discussion about the future.

"No one knows yet. That's the difficulty," Kilt had said, agreeing with General Marth's observation that there were still soldiers moving around the empire, oblivious that the chain of command had been broken, let alone that a change in authority was coming at them.

Gavriel had been silent, staring into space, and although he had joined the decision-makers as Lily had suggested, he seemed to show little interest. None blamed him. He looked hollow, a shell of the de Vis that they'd all got to know.

Loethar nodded at Elka, urging her to do something, get Gavriel involved.

"Or we'll lose him altogether," he murmured under his breath. "That's a man on the brink."

Elka touched Gavriel's wrist and he jumped like he'd been burned. "Sorry," she said softly. "I didn't mean to startle you."

He shook his head, said nothing.

"Any thoughts on all of this?" she tried.

"I'm not interested in any of it," he said and turned away. Elka glanced at Loethar with concern.

"Er, de Vis, before you leave, it would be helpful to have your take on this."

"Why? Since when has my opinion been important?"

"Since you were part of the old regime—an integral part," Kilt said.

"Leo is dead . . . or did everyone miss my arrow sticking out of his chest?"

"Gavriel," Lily said gently, taking his hand. "Be easy."

He pursed his lips and turned away from her.

Genevieve leaned across the table and offered her hand. "Take it," she said and reluctantly he did. "I wish I could heal the hurt for you, Gavriel, but I don't have that curative magic any more. It's gone too. But even if I could, I don't think I would. You have lost Corbel this day, but so have I. You had Corbel in your life for eighteen anni?" He didn't say anything but his eyes remained on hers; he was listening. "I had Corbel in mine for twenty and he was the person I loved most in the world. He was my rock, my best friend, my whole conscience. And though I am hurting very deeply over his loss I would never heal myself of it; to do so would be to lose the memory of him in my life. I'd rather bear the pain until it heals itself than bear the thought of not being able to recall why I should miss him or mourn him. So ache, Gavriel de Vis. Ache for Corbel because that way you know he's alive in your memory and will be with you always." She shrugged. "As for my brother, your instincts had to be right. You should know that in him I saw a terrible darkness—a tragic self-loathing. And that darkness was part of him . . . nothing to do with his magic."

"Why?" Gavriel demanded.

She gave a small shake of her head. "I sensed failure. He hated himself, he hated everything around him, he hated you for being true to your nobility and he hated Loethar for being able to rally the very people Leo had counted on. He hated Piven for his power and he hated me for existing. He hated our father for bringing this all upon us, and our mother for killing herself. He saved his greatest hate for himself, though—in this I'm sure. And he wouldn't have stopped. He would have kept trying to kill us. If he hadn't been stopped by your arrow, I suspect it would have been Kilt's, or Elka's stone, or Jewd's sword."

"Genevieve's right, Gavriel. It will take time but you must learn to forgive yourself or you'll end up with a twisted logic and loathing like Leo," Lily said. Then she sighed. "I think we all need time to mourn those we've lost." Her brave smile faltered. "If you'll exuse me," she said. "It's a full moon, I might take some air."

They watched her go.

"De Vis?" Loethar continued.

"There is only one solution as I see it," Gavriel replied, and Loethar realized the former noble had been paying attention. "*You* have to help the people through a time of transition."

"I want no part in ruling any more."

"Well, frankly, Loethar, I'm tired of that stance. You created this mess, you can damn well help clean it all up," Gavriel argued, surprising everyone with his sudden vehemence. "None of the tribal people are going to trust any of the old Set people and vice versa. So it begins with you. Whatever your past, the people do trust you right now. So whatever we want the empire to be, whatever it's going to become, you must at least begin by leading us there."

Loethar had no response; he could think of nothing to say.

"I'm serious," Gavriel said. "You must set the tone for the future. You must tell the Steppes people that they can leave or stay as they wish. You must tell the old Denovians what the new structure for rule is going to be. And you need to explain exactly why you no longer wish to be their emperor. You owe the people that much of an explanation."

"Hear, hear," Marth grunted.

Loethar looked around the table, astonished. "And you all agree with this?"

Heads nodded.

"De Vis is right," Kilt said. "Without your lead, we have nowhere to begin."

"Then this is how I see it," Loethar said. "It is no longer an empire but a union. I will reinstate the old boundaries, the old names even, and the new union will include Droste and the Steppes. And if the Davarigons wish to join the union, they too are welcome," he said with a nod to Elka. "There will no trade restrictions between the states. The Denovian union will be governed by someone I appoint but each state will have its own government to handle local issues."

"How can we trust the person you appoint?" Kilt said.

"Easy," Loethar said. "That person is you, Faris."

"Me?" Kilt laughed. So did Jewd. "I've got a price on my head in Penraven."

"That warrant was just torn up," Loethar said, miming the action. "There is no one better to administer than you, Faris. Yes, I know that you are a man of the forest and an outlaw and a renegade and all of those unsavory things, but I was also the least suitable emperor and I made a good fist of it. You will too. While you have an allegiance to Penraven—which is fair enough—I have found you to be a man of ethics. You have a moral take on the world, Faris. You and Genevieve, with her sense of community and social order, will make excellent heads of the union. If you won't agree to this, I won't agree to paving the way."

All eyes turned to Faris. "Why will the people agree to this?" he asked.

"Because I will persuade them and you will prove me right," Loethar said. "I'm not suggesting it's going to be easy but you'd be surprised how quickly a handsome couple with charm can work its way into people's hearts. And it wouldn't hurt to let everyone know that Genevieve is the Valisar daughter who escaped the barbarian invasion. Perhaps I could even give her away at your wedding—if I might be so bold," he added, looking at Genevieve. "That would be a brave and special statement about new bonds between old foes."

"Wedding?" everyone chorused.

"Yes, I'll even throw the feast."

All eyes turned again to Kilt. "Let me think on this."

"Ach, Kilt. Just say yes, damn it. You've always liked to be in charge. Now you get to be in charge of lots of people," Jewd said disdainfully.

"Well, Jewd, you'll be there right alongside me, if that's the case."

"Wasn't planning on being anywhere else," Jewd remarked.

Loethar turned to Marth. "General, how do you feel about what I've suggested?"

Marth sighed. "After today, I think anything that brings peace, unites people, and gives us all a chance to return our old cities to their respective people can only be a great achievement."

"Good, then you'll be head of the new Barronese consulate."

Marth nodded. "You trust me, then?"

"De Vis does. That's good enough for me."

It was Gavriel who turned to look at Piven, sitting at a table with a few of the younger Vested, grinning from ear to ear as they played a game of "knots," taking turns threading wool around their fingers in complex shapes.

"And what about the other Valisar in the room?"

Greven answered. "He's back to being the simple child and has been my son for the last ten anni and that hasn't changed. We will carry on together. I thought I hated him but the darkness has gone and he's healed, with the same easy smile and affectionate way that I remember about him when I found him."

"Bring him to Brighthelm, Greven. It's his home," Loethar said.

"Maybe," Greven said. "Maybe."

Gavriel stood. "I think I'll take some air too," he said, excusing himself.

* * *

Outside he inhaled the cooler air; it was the first sign that summer was giving way and he was glad of this, given what was strewn about outside the gate. He didn't want to think about the bodies, Corbel's and Leo's among them. The nuns had taken Valya and presumably her daughter to bury immediately. He wondered where Lily had disappeared to. She alone might understand his grief about Leo; she had practically raised him, after all. And she remained every bit as pretty and feisty as he remembered from ten anni ago.

He knew she'd spent years as Faris's lover and then promptly married the quiet fellow he'd seen about the castle with Freath just before he and Leo had escaped. He knew she must be grieving the loss of her husband and Faris's betrayal. But they were both hurting, both without anyone to hold or love. Why shouldn't they find solace in each other?

"Psst! Gav!" came the voice in a whisper.

"Lily?" he murmured, looking around.

"Ssh," she said, melting out of the shadows of the wall and pulling him toward her.

He thought for one marvelous, brilliant, impossible moment that she might kiss him but instead she pointed to a peephole. "Look."

He did. It was a full moon and everywhere was flooded with a silvery, ghostly light. "What am I looking at?" he asked, trying not to notice the twisted, burned bodies.

"The carriage," she breathed.

"Carriage." He squinted, and saw movement. "Is that a person? Who?"

"It's that snake, Vulpan. He's hidden in it all day and is still too terrified to get out. Watch him, he keeps checking to see if anyone's around."

"Why are you interested?"

"I have my reasons to want him dead."

"Dead?"

"Shh!" she said, pinching him. "He's not worth the air he breathes, Gav. He is one very evil little man. He brought misery to the lives of the Vested."

"Ah, the blood taster, is that him?"

"Yes. He's the reason Kirin is dead, and the reason I faced Stracker's blade. Frankly, if not for Piven's well-timed arrival my head would be rotting in a basket somewhere too."

He could hear the savagery even in her hissed whispers and looked out at the carriage again. "Well, your prey has found the courage to come out into the moonlight."

She pushed him aside to look. "What a snake he is. He's going to disappear and he doesn't deserve to, Gavriel. He doesn't deserve to not face justice."

"Your justice?"

She glared at him. "Not just mine."

He frowned. "Lily, you're not going after him."

"Watch me," she said, and pulled a blade from her skirt pocket. "Oh, don't worry, de Vis, I'm not going to kill him. I'm going to give him to the Vested. He's one of them, you know. They can be the ones who mete justice."

He grabbed her wrist. "It's night," he said.

She smiled. "Gavriel, I am a woman of the forest. The darkness holds far more fears for him than it does for me."

"What about the others?"

She shrugged. "What about them? They don't need me."

"Not even your father?"

"He'll be fine. He's been through a lot and he needs private time to put away his inner horrors for good. Right now I would put my life against the notion that he'll want to take care of Piven . . . almost like a penance. Together they'll form a new sort of bond and I suspect they'll be happy. He's told me where he'll head. I'll find him again." She turned to check the peephole. "Right, I'm going. I'm not going to lose him."

He grabbed her again. "Lily, you can not go out there into the night alone."

"Then, Gavriel de Vis," she said with daring and no little defiance in her voice, "why don't you come with me?"

He knew she wouldn't ask again. He thought of all the reasons to stay, and there were many. And then he thought of all the reasons to go with her . . . and there was only one.

But that one reason filled him with a sense of warmth and hope that he hadn't felt in a long time.

"Why not. I've got nothing better to do on a moonlit night," he replied and took her hand to lead her out of the convent.

Epilogue

> ➤➤━━━━━━━━━━━━━━━━━━━━━━━━━━━━━━━◄◄

Outside a hut on the western coast of Penraven, a man sat alone beneath the full moon, brooding.

He had said his goodbyes, and while there were many that he cared about there were only two that he truly loved; one was a man called Loethar, the other was a boy called Roddy. And it was his farewell to the boy that had been the hardest for Roddy hadn't understood why they were embracing for the last time . . . why wouldn't they see each other again, he had repeated, his face filled with perplexity.

Ravan hadn't been able to give him a reason. Somewhere within himself he just knew his time was close. His role for the goddess was done and he had acquitted himself well as a companion, a spy, a messenger. At the end it had been Cormoran's memories, after all, that had helped to solve the secret of the Valisar Legacy.

Secrets. He sighed. After all those secrets had been unravelled, he didn't think one little one would be missed. He had told a lie to Loethar, and though he had hated doing so it had been asked of him by a much higher power.

She had visited him through the Qirin, in whom he had entrusted the secret for the hours that he had needed it hidden.

Must I? he had asked.

You must, the Qirin had assured.

And so he had said his farewells to Roddy, to Loethar, to the others. Roddy had asked where he was going but Ravan had only shrugged. "I will only know when I get there, Roddy."

It had been painful to leave but he had, clutching his secret, running as fast as his legs could go, faster than he had ever run before. He was faster than the wind, and on this moonlit night, he had sat and waited for her.

The tufty, ragged grass around him began to shudder and the sounds of the night fell strangely quiet as the moon seemed to turn golden and loom much larger than it had just moments ago. She was coming. Even the grass stilled and the air seemed to thicken.

And then she was there. Not huge and towering this time but matching his height. She was even more beautiful than he recalled from their last meeting. Her serpent body glittered beneath the golden moonlight, her voice was soft and mesmerizing.

"Hello, Ravan."

"Goddess, you honor me with your presence."

"And you have honored me with your loyalty."

He bowed, moved by her praise.

"You have brought what I asked of you?"

"I have." He reached down to the basket and picked up his gift.

"Ah," she said as tenderly as a mother and sighed. "She is beautiful indeed," she said, taking the baby and cradling her.

As she held Loethar's infant daughter, the newborn squirmed, coming out of her stupor.

"I feared I was bringing you a corpse, goddess."

"No, dear one. This tiny girl is our secret . . . our Valisar secret. I gave her the protection of the shroud of death."

He frowned. "You were there?"

"I was. Piven felt me, when Valya was bargaining with him, but fortunately he just thought he was responding to one of his kin. I have never before intervened in the lives of the Valisars but this time we had two princesses and a set of circumstances we have never before encountered. I admit even I was taken by surprise to have a second princess survive. Whatever Valya was, she was worthy of the Valisars in secreting her child away. She drugged her, you know, for her confrontation with Piven. I have no doubt that she loved her and wanted to protect her."

"So you did when she could not?"

The serpent nodded. "I could not let a defenseless Valisar princess die on the ground like that." Cyrena smiled. "I kept her sleeping. It might have been wrong of me to weave the magic I did today but these were extraordinary circumstances. Whether I was right or wrong, it has been done."

Ravan smiled. "You are a goddess. You can do whatever you like."

Her laugh sounded like the tinkling of icicles and her breath on his face was like meadow flowers.

"What now for this child?" he wondered.

"She is Valisar—royal in every way. She must be permitted to grow and flourish in safety."

"Loethar—"

"Must not know. It would upset the balance of things. He believes his daughter dead and buried with her mother at the convent, and though he will grieve he will also move on. For now Ciara is best kept from all. She survived her birth without my help. And I would be lying to you now if I didn't admit that she possesses the Legacy."

He gave a sound of awe. "Another Genevieve."

"But right now this world doesn't need another Genevieve or indeed another Valisar princess."

"Where will she go?"

Cyrena reached a hand out and stroked the child's angelic face. "So like her father," she whispered. "She will go with you, Ravan."

"Me? I thought . . ."

"I know. But I have use for you yet, my loyal servant."

"I am going to raise a child?"

She nodded.

"Where?"

"Come down to the water's edge with me."

"Corbel de Vis did this once."

"Yes." She glided down toward the sea and he followed her, for he could not deny her.

"May I ask you a question, goddess?" he said as they arrived at the frothy waters. His head was spinning with possibility. The sea lapped at his feet but didn't wet her sinous body.

"Please," she said, gently.

"Why are we doing this?"

And now her smile was radiant. "Because one day, I don't know when, we may just need the magic of the Valisars once again."

"And so an aegis has been born for Ciara."

Cyrena nodded. "It is the way of the magic."

"What do I do?"

"Take this child," she said, kissing the baby's head tenderly, "and walk into the waters, to a magical place where the land and the water meet at full moon."

"She will not drown?" he asked anxiously.

"Trust me, Ravan, as you have before. And trust yourself. Take good care of her."

And Ravan, a man that was once a raven, now made in the image of a king, trusted the goddess. He walked into the waters to meet a new destiny with his land's most powerful sorceress squirming softly in his arms.

He whispered her name as the water claimed them, and as a great magic began to pulse around him, he knew that he loved her.

Glossary

➤➤————————————————————◀◀

CHARACTERS
THE VALISAR REALM
Royalty

King Cormoron: The first Valisar king.

King Brennus the 8th: 8th king of the Valisars.

King Darros the 7th: 7th Valisar king. Father of Brennus.

Queen Iselda: Wife of Brennus. She is the daughter of a Romean prince from Romea in Galinsea. Comes from the line of King Falza.

Prince Leonel (Leo): First-born son of Brennus and Iselda.

Prince Piven: Adopted son of Brennus and Iselda.

The De Vis Family

Legate Regor De Vis: Right-hand of the king. Father to Gavriel and Corbel.

Eril De Vis: Deceased wife of Legate De Vis.

Gavriel (Gav) De Vis: First-born twin brother of Corbel. He is the champion of the Cohort.

Corbel (Corb) De Vis: Twin brother of Gavriel.

Other

Cook Faisal: Male cook of the castle.
Father Briar: The priest of Brighthelm.
Freath: Queen Iselda's aide and right-hand man.
Genrie: Household servant.
Greven: Lily's father. Is a leper.
Hana: Queen Iselda's maid.
Jynes: The castle librarian (steward).
Lilyan (Lily): Daughter of Greven.
Morkom: Prince Leo's manservant.
Physic Maser: The queen's physic.
Sarah Flarty: A girlfriend of Gavriel.
Sesaro: Famous sculptor in Penraven.
Tashi: Sesaro's daughter.
Tatie: Kitchen hand.
Tilly: Palace servant.

The Penraven Army

Brek: A soldier.
Commander Jobe: Penraven's army commander.
Captain Drate: Penraven's army captain.
Del Faren: An archer and traitor.

From outside Penraven, but still in the Set

Alys Kenric: A resident of Vorgaven.
Claudeo: A famous Set painter.
Corin: Daughter of Clovis.
Danre: Second son of the Vorgaven Royals.
Delly Bartel: Resident of Vorgaven.
Elka: From Davarigon—a giantess.
Jed Roxburgh: Wealthy land owner of Vorgaven.
Leah: Wife of Clovis.
Princess Arrania: A Dregon princess.
Tomas Dole: A boy from Berch.

The Vested

Clovis: A master diviner from Vorgaven.

Eyla: A female healer.

Hedray: Talks to animals.

Jervyn of Medhaven: Vested.

Kes: A contortionist.

Kirin Felt: Can pry.

Perl: Reads the runes.

Reuth Maegren: Has visions.

Tolt: Dreams future events.

Torren: Makes things grow.

The Supernatural/Other

Abbess: The head nun of the convent at Lo's Teeth.

Algin: Giant of Set myth.

Aludane: A Steppes god.

Cyrena: Goddess. The serpent denoted on the Penraven family crest.

Deren: A baker from Green Herbery.

Qirin (Qirin Vervine): Deaf, blind and mute seer. Also referred to as the "Mother" of the convent in Lo's Teeth.

Ravan: Also known as Vyk, the Raven.

Roddy: A young boy, saved by and drawn to Piven.

Sergius: A minion of Cyrena.

Tod: One of Roddy's friends in Green Herbery.

Wikken Shorgan: The younger of only two wikken left alive in the Set. He can "smell" magic.

The Highwaymen

Jewd: Friend to Kilt Faris.

Kilt Faris: Highwayman, renegade.

Tern: One of Kilt's men.

Coder

Dorv

Outside the Sets

Emperor Luc: Emperor of Galinsea.
King Falza: Past king of Galinsea.
Zar Azal: Ruler of Percheron.

Loethar and his followers

Barc: A young soldier.
Belush: A Drevin soldier.
Bleuth: A soldier.
Brimen: A soldier at Woodingdene.
Dara Negev: Loethar's mother.
Darly: A soldier.
Farn: A Mear soldier.
Fren: A page who spies for Valya.
(Captain) Ison: A soldier.
Jib: A soldier.
Loethar: Tribal warlord.
Roland: A servant in Dara Negev's retinue.
Ronder: A soldier at Woodingdene; close to Stracker.
Shev: A soldier at Woodingdene.
Steppes (Plains) People: From the Likurian Steppes. Known as Barbarians.
(Lady) Valya of Droste: Loethar's wofe.
Vulpan: A Vested working for Loethar whose talent is "cataloguing" and tracking people by knowing the taste of their blood.
Stracker: Loethar's right-hand man and half-brother.
Vash: A soldier.
Vyk: Loethar's raven.

MAGIC

Aegis: Possesses the ability to champion with magic. Is bound to a person by the power of trammeling.

Binder or Binding: The person who binds himself to an Aegis.

Blood Diviner: A reader of blood.

Diviner: Gives impressions and foretells the future.

Dribbling: A small push of prying magic.

Prying: Entering another's mind.

Reading the Runes: Ability to foretell the future using stones.

The Valisar Enchantment: Powerful magic of coercion peculiar to the Valisar line.

Trammeling: Awakening an aegis's power.

Trickling: Low-level magic.

HEALING PRODUCTS

Willow sap, Comfrey balm (for pain)

Clirren leaves (powerful infection fighter)

Crushed peonies (for pain)

Henbane (for pain)

White lichen (used for dressing wounds)

Dock leaves (soothes itching skin)

Bermine: A painkiller

THE DENOVA SET

The seven realms are sovereign states, self-governed with a king as head.

Barronel

Cremond

Dregon

Gormand

Medhaven

Penraven

Vorgaven

The Hand: The continent that the Denova Set sits on.

Cities/towns within the Set

Berch: Close to Brighthelm. Home of the Dole family.
Brighthelm: The city stronghold (castle) and capital of Penraven.
Buckden Abbey: Religious place south of Brighthelm.
Camlet
Caralinga
Davarigon
Deloran Forest: The Great Forest.
Devden
Dragonsback Mountains: They separate Penraven from Barronel.
Droste: A realm not part of the Set.
Francham
Garun Cliffs: Where chalk is mined.
Green Herbery
Hell's Gate
Hurtle
Lo's Teeth: Mountain range in Droste.
Merrivale: Where shipbuilding is renowned.
Minton Woodlet
Overdene
Port Killen
Rhum Caves: Caves found in the hills outside of Brighthelm.
Skardlag: Where the famous Weaven timber comes from.
Tooley
Vegero Hills: In the realm of Barronel. Famed for the marble
  quarried in its hills.
Woodingdene

Places outside the Set

Briavel
Galinsea: A neighboring country.
Lindaran: The great southern land mass.
Likurian Steppes (or Steppes): Treeless plains. Home to
  Loethar and his tribes.

Morgravia
Percheron: A faraway country.
Romea: Capital of Galinsea.
Tallinor

MONEY

Throughout the Sets: Trents

MEASUREMENTS

Span: 1000 strides or 2000 double steps.
Half-span: 500 strides or 1000 double steps.

WORD GLOSSARY

Academy of Learning: At Cremond. It is the seat of learning for all of the Denova Set.
Anni: A year.
Aspenberry: Used to distil Kern liquor.
Asprey reeds: Used for support inside leather bladder balls.
Blossomtide/Blossom: Spring
Blow: Winter.
Branstone: A very special silver colored stone with sparkling silver flecks.
Chest: Coffin.
Cloudberries: Forest berries.
Cohort: A group of youngsters trained to be elite sword fighters.
Crabnuts: Grow wild in the forests. They are a sweet nut, purplish in color.
Dara: Word for "king's mother" in Steppe language.
Darrasha Bushes: Planted around the castle of Brighthelm.
dinch: A hot beverage.
Elleputian: A Davarigon mountain horse.
Faeroe: A handcrafted sword that belonged to King Cormoron.

Fan-tailed farla hen: A bright colored bird with a fan-tail.

ferago: A mountain herb.

flaxwood: A type of wood used for cooking.

Freeze: Late winter.

golasses vines: Grown in Penraven's South, its dense dark wine favored by the barbarians.

Harvest: Late autumn.

Ingress: Secret passages within the Brighthelm castle.

Kellet: A spicy fragrant herb that can be chewed.

Kern: The local and notorious fiery liquor of Penraven's North.

Lackmarin: Place where the Stone of truth lies.

Leaf-fall: Early autumn.

Leaf of the Cherrel: Chewed as a breath freshener.

leem: A mountain herb

Lo: Set god.

Lo's Fury: An alcoholic beverage

Oil of Miramel: Exotic essence.

osh: Slabs of roasted meat cooked a particular way.

peregum: A mountain herb.

Roeberries: Wild berries growing in forests. They are blood red.

Rough: A very strong alcoholic beverage.

saramac fungus: A woodland toadstool used in healing.

shakken: A wild Steppes animal.

Shaman: Spiritual healer.

Sheeca Shell: Found on the local beaches.

Shubo: In Steppes language it means second.

starren: A six-legged chameleon-like reptile.

Stone of Truth: This truth stone is at Lackmarin. All Valisar Kings must take the oath at this stone.

Strenic: A poisonous herb growing wild on the Steppes.

Summertide: Summer.

Tatua: Tattoos on the face, shoulders and arms.

Thaw: Spring.

The Masked: Magic users of the barbarian horde.

The Vested: Magics users of the Set.

Thaumaturges: Miracle weavers.
Thaumaturgy: The study of the craft of miracle weaving.
toka: A mountain herb.
Weaven Timber: From Skardlag. It is scarce.
Wikken: A tribal seer.
Wych Elder Tree: Used for woodworking.

Fiona McIntosh's internationally bestselling

The Percheron Saga

is

"First rate."
Publishers Weekly

"[A]n exciting, magical tale of forbidden love, treachery, betrayal, and possession. Fast and furious. A great read."
Sunday Herald Sun (Melbourne, Australia)

"Nothing short of astonishing. McIntosh weaves a captivating web."
Bookreporter.com

"Riveting . . . An ages-old battle for hearts and souls."
Adelaide Advertiser

"A tale of romance and sacrifice, mystery and magic that is redolent with lavish detail. Intriguing characters and an exotic setting make this series . . . a good choice."
Library Journal

It all begins in *Odalisque*. Turn the page for a sample.

The prisoners, chained together, shuffled awkwardly into the main square of the slave market of Percheron; six men, all strangers and all captives of a trader called Varanz, who had a reputation for securing the more intriguing product for sale. And this group on offer was no exception, although most onlookers' attention was helplessly drawn to the tall man whose searing, pale-eyed stare, at odds with his long dark hair, seemed to challenge anyone brave enough to lock gazes with him.

Varanz knew it too; knew this one was special, and he sensed a good price coming for the handsome foreigner well worth the effort it had cost six of his henchmen first to bring the man down and then to rope him securely. It puzzled him why the man had been traveling across the desert, of all places—that in itself a perilous journey—but also moving alone, which meant almost certain trouble, particularly from slavers renowned in the region.

But Varanz had a policy of not inquiring into the background of his captives; perhaps to ease his conscience he didn't want to know anything about them, save what was obvious to his own eye. And this one, who refused to name himself, or indeed mutter much more than curses, was clearly in good health. That was enough for the merchant.

Trading for this cluster of slaves opened at the sound of the gong. The Master of the Market called the milling crowd of buyers to order: "Brothers, we have here Varanz Set

Number Eight." His voice droned on, extolling the virtues of each on offer, but already the majority of potential buyers were in the thrall of the angry-eyed man, clearly the pick of the bunch and the only one of the six who held his head defiantly high. Sensing a lively auction, the Master of the Market decided to state more than the obvious healthy appearance, strong structure, and good teeth. "He was found emerging from the golden sands of our desert alone, not even a camel for company. Brothers, I'd hazard this one will make a fine bodyguard. If he's canny enough to travel our wasteland and remain as well as he looks, then I imagine he has excellent survival skills."

"Can he fight?" one buyer called out.

Varanz arched an eyebrow and looked toward the slave, wondering whether he'd finally get something out of the man. His instincts were right.

"I can fight," the man replied. "In fact," he challenged, "I demand to fight for my freedom."

A fresh murmuring rippled through the crowd. An oddity in Percheron's slave market was its ancient and somewhat quaint rule that a slave who was captured as a free person had one chance to buy his freedom—with a fight to the death. The Crown covered the cost of his loss, either way, to the trader. It was one of the market's oldest customs, set up by a Zar many centuries earlier who understood that such a contest from time to time would provide entertainment for the otherwise tedious business of trading in human cargo.

Such fights were rare, of course, as most prisoners took their chances with a new life as a slave. But now and then one would risk death in a bid to win back his independence.

Varanz strolled over to the man now that he knew his tongue was loosened. "You understand what you ask for?"

"I do. It was explained to us on the journey here by one of your aides. I wish to fight for my freedom. I also wish to speak with your Zar."

At this Varanz smirked. "I can't imagine he will want to speak with you."

"He might after he watches me best twelve of his strongest warriors."

Varanz was speechless at the man's arrogance. He shook his head and walked to the Master, briefly explaining in a quiet mutter what the slave was proposing. Now both of them returned to stand before the man.

"Don't try and talk me out of it. I want my freedom back. I will pay the price if I fail to win it," the slave warned them.

The Master had no intention of attempting to thwart the prospect of some sport after an already long and wearying day in the market. He could see that Varanz was unfazed, knowing that he would get a good price either way.

"What is your reserve, Varanz?" he asked.

"No less than two hundred karels for this one."

The Master nodded. "I will send a message to the palace for authorization," he said. Then, turning to the man, he insisted, "You must give us your name."

The slave knifed them with a cold gaze. "My name is Lazar."

The palace did more than give authorization. A runner returned swiftly with the news that Zar Joreb, his interest piqued, would be in attendance for the contest. "You understand how unusual it is for the Zar of Percheron to visit the slave traders," Varanz informed Lazar.

The foreigner was unmoved. "I wish to speak with him if I succeed."

Varanz nodded. "That is up to our Zar. We have told him you have offered to fight twelve of his men to the death. This is no doubt why he is coming to witness the contest."

"It is why I suggested so many."

Varanz shook his head, exasperated. "How can you best a dozen fighters, man? There's still time to change your mind and not waste your life. I will ensure a cozy position for you. A fellow like you will find himself in high demand by a rich man to escort his wives, families . . . take care of their security."

Lazar snorted. "I'm no nursery maid."

"All right." Varanz tried again. "I know I can sell you as a high-caliber bodyguard to a man who needs protection whilst he travels. I'll find you a good owner."

"I don't want to be owned," Lazar snarled. "I want my freedom."

The trader shrugged. "Well, you'll have it, my friend, but you'll be carried off in a sack."

"So be it. I slave for no one."

Their conversation was ended by the Master of the Market's hissing for silence—a troop of Percheron's guard had arrived, signifying that the Zar's karak was just moments away. Varanz nodded to one of his aides to escort the rest of the prisoners to the holding pen. Trading would resume once this piece of theater was done with.

"I wish you luck, brother," he said to Lazar, and moved away to stand with the Master, who was marshaling all the other traders into a formal line of welcome. The Zar finally arrived, flanked by several of the Percherese Guard, his karak carried by six of the red-shrouded Elim, the elite guardians of the Zar's harem who also performed bodyguard duties to royalty. The Zar's entry between the slave market's carved pillars of two griffins was heralded by the trumpeting of several of the curled Percherese horns, and everyone who was not attached to the royal retinue instantly humbled himself. No one dared raise his eyes to the Zar until given formal permission.

No one but Lazar, that is.

He was on his knees because he had been pushed down, but he brazenly watched the Zar being helped out of the karak; their gazes met and held momentarily across the dust of the slave market. Then Lazar dipped his head, just a fraction, but it was enough to tell the Zar that the brash young man had acknowledged the person who was the closest thing to the god Zarab that walked the earth.

The guard quickly set up the Zar's seat and the Elim unfurled a canopy over it. Zar Joreb settled himself. He had a wry smile as the Master of the Market made the official announcement that the prisoner, Lazar, captured by Trader Varanz, had opted to fight for his freedom against a dozen warriors from the Percherese Guard. No one watched the Master or even the Zar. All eyes were riveted on the dark foreigner, whose wrists and ankles were now unshackled and who was disrobing down to the once-white, now gray and dirty loose pants he wore. They watched his measured movements, but mostly they watched him study the twelve men taking practice swipes with their glinting swords, all bearing smirks, none prepared to take the ridiculously out-numbered contest seriously.

The gong sounded for silence and the Master outlined what was about to happen. It was a superfluous pronouncement but strict protocol was a way of life for Percheron's various mar-kets, especially in the hallowed presence of the Zar.

". . . or to the prisoner's death," he finished somberly. He looked to Zar Joreb, who, with an almost imperceptible nod, gave the signal for combat to begin.

Those who were present at the slave market that day would talk about the fight for years to come. Lazar accepted the weapon thrown toward him and without so much as a hurried prayer to his god of choice strode out to meet the first of the warriors. To prolong the sport, the guard had decided to send out one man at a time—presumably they intended to keep wounding the arrogant prisoner until he begged for mercy and the deathblow. However, by the time the first three men were groaning and bleeding on the ground, their most senior man hurriedly sent in four at once.

It didn't make much difference to Lazar, who appeared to the audience to be unintimidated by numbers. His face wore the grim countenance of utter focus; he made no sound, never once backed away, always threatening his enemy rather than the other way around. It was soon obvious that his sword skills could not be matched by any of the Percherese, not even fighting in tandem. His fighting arm became a blur of silver that weaved a path of wreckage through flesh, turning the dozen men, one after another, into writhing, crying heaps as they gripped torn shoulders, slashed legs, or profusely bleeding fighting arms. To their credit, the final two fought superbly, but neither could mark Lazar. He fought without fear, his speed only increasing as the battle wore on. Cutting one man down by the ankle, Lazar stomped on his sword wrist, breaking it, to ensure he did not return to the fray, and some moments later, fought the other into exhaustion until the man was on his knees. Lazar flicked the guard's sword away and gave a calculated slash across his chest. The man fell, almost grateful for the reprieve.

The slave market was uncharacteristically quiet, save for the cries of bleeding, paining men. Varanz looked around at the carnage, his nostrils flaring with the raw metallic smell of blood thick in the air, and he raised his eyebrows with surprise. No one was dead. Lazar had mercilessly and precisely disabled each of his rivals but claimed the life of none.

Throwing down his sword, Lazar stood in the circle of hurt warriors, a light sheen of perspiration on his body the only indication that he had exerted himself. His chest rose and sank steadily, calmly. He turned to the Zar and bowed long and deeply.

"Zar Joreb, will you now grant my freedom?" he said finally into the hush that had fallen.

"My men would surely rather seek death than live with the dishonor of losing this fight," was Joreb's response.

Varanz watched Lazar's curiously light eyes cloud with defiance. "They are innocent men. I will not take their lives for a piece of entertainment."

"They are soldiers! This was a fight to the death."

"Zar Joreb, this was a fight to *my* death, not theirs. It was made clear that I either win *my* freedom through death or through survival. I survived. No one impressed upon me the fact that anyone had to die as part of the rules of this custom."

"Arrogant pup," Joreb murmured into the silence. Then, impossibly, he laughed. "Stand before me, young man."

Lazar took two long strides and then went down on one knee, his head finally bowed.

"What is it you want, stranger?" the Zar demanded.

"I want to live in Percheron as a free man," Lazar replied, not lifting his head.

"Look at me." Lazar did so. "You've humiliated my guard. You will need to rectify that before I grant you anything."

"How can I do that, Zar Joreb?"

"By teaching them."

Lazar stared at the Zar, a quizzical look taking over his heretofore impassive face, but he said nothing.

"Become my Spur," Zar Joreb offered. "Our present Spur must retire soon. We need to inject a fresh approach. A young approach. You fight like you're chasing away demons, man. I want you to teach my army how to do that."

Lazar's gaze narrowed. His tone sounded guarded. "You're offering to pay me to live as a free man in Percheron?"

"Be my Spur," Zar Joreb urged. This time there was no humor in his voice, only passion.

The crowd collectively held its breath as Lazar paused. Finally, he nodded once, decisively. "I accept, but first you owe Varanz over there two hundred karels apparently."

Joreb laughed loudly in genuine amusement. "I like you, Lazar. Follow me back to the palace. We have much to speak of. I must say, I'm impressed by your audacity. You put your life in danger to get what you want."

"It was never in danger," Lazar replied, and the semblance of a smile twitched briefly at his mouth.

Turn the page for a sample of *Myrren's Gift*, the first installment in

Fiona McIntosh's internationally bestselling trilogy

THE QUICKENING

"Vibrant and engaging . . . An intricately plotted tale of love and politics, set against the backdrop of a rich fantasy realm with interesting magic, and peopled with characters whom the reader grows to care about. A fast-paced and enchanting page-turner."
Kirkus Reviews (*Starred Review*)

"A just one more chapter sort of book. Don't start reading *Myrren's Gift* in the evening if you have to get up early the next morning."
Robin Hobb

"[A] winner."
Publishers Weekly

"Fiona McIntosh is a seductress. I have not moved from my sofa for three days, beguiled by her new fantasy novel, *Myrren's Gift.*"
Sydney Morning Herald (Australia)

"Fiona McIntosh scores."
The Guardian (London)

"[A] rich, satisfying confection of vivid detail, engrossing characters, and their dark doings. I was enthralled."
Lynn Flewelling, author of *The Hidden Warrior*

Gueryn looked to his left at the solemn profile of the lad who rode quietly next to him and felt another pang of concern for Wyl Thirsk, Morgravia's new General of the Legion. His father's death was as untimely as it was unexpected. Why had they all believed Fergys Thirsk would die of old age? His son was too young to take such a title and responsibility onto his shoulders. And yet he must; custom demanded it. Gueryn thanked the stars for giving the King wisdom enough to appoint a temporary commander until Wyl was of an age where men would respect him. The name of Thirsk carried much weight but no soldier would follow a near-fourteen-year-old into battle.

Hopefully, there would be no war for many years now. According to the news filtering back from the capital, Morgravia had inflicted a terrible price on Briavel's young men this time. No, Gueryn decided, there would be no fighting for a while ... long enough for Wyl to turn into the fine young man he promised to be.

Gueryn regarded the boy, with his distinctive flame-colored hair and squat frame. He so badly needed his father's guidance, the older man thought regretfully.

Wyl had taken the news of his father's death stoically in front of the household, making Gueryn proud of the boy as he watched him comfort his younger sister. But later, behind closed doors, he had held the trembling shoulders of the lad and offered what comfort he could. The youngster had worshiped his father, and who could blame him—most of Morgravia's men had as well. It was especially sad that the boy had lost his father having not seen him in so many moons.

Ylena, at nine, was still young enough to be distracted by her loving nursemaid as well as her dolls and the new kitten Gueryn had had the foresight to grab at the local market as soon as he was delivered the news. Wyl would not be so easily diverted and Gueryn could already sense the numbing grief hardening within the boy. Wyl was a serious, complex child, and this would push him further into himself. Gueryn wondered whether being forced to the capital was such a good idea right now.

The Thirsk home in Argorn had been a happy one despite the head of the household having been absent so often. Gueryn had agreed several years back to take on what seemed the ridiculously light task of watching over the raising of the young Thirsk. But he had known from the steely gaze of the old warrior that this was a role the General considered precious and he would entrust this job only to his accomplished captain, whose mind was as sharp as the blade he wielded with such skill. Gueryn understood and with a quiet regret at leaving his beloved Legion, he had moved to live among the rolling hills of Argorn, among the lush southern counties of Morgravia.

He became Wyl's companion, military teacher, academic tutor, and close friend. As much as the boy adored his father, the General spent most of his year in the capital, and it was Gueryn who filled the gap of Fergys Thirsk's absence. It was of little wonder then that student and mentor had become so close.

"Don't watch me like that, Gueryn. I can almost smell your anxiety."

"How are you feeling about this?" the soldier asked, ignoring the boy's rebuke.

Wyl turned in his saddle to look at his friend, regarding the handsome former captain. A flush of color to his pale, freckled face betrayed his next words. "I'm feeling fine."

"Be honest with me of all people, Wyl."

The lad looked away and they continued their steady progress toward the famed city of Pearlis. Gueryn waited, knowing his patience would win out. It had been just days since Wyl's father had died. The wound was still raw and seeping. Wyl could hide nothing from him.

"I wish I didn't have to go," Wyl finally said, and the soldier felt the tension in his body release somewhat. They could talk about it now and he could do what he could to make Wyl feel easier about his arrival in the strange, sprawling, often overwhelming capital. "But I know this was my father's dying wish," Wyl added, trying to cover his sigh.

"The King promised he would bring you to Pearlis. And he had good reason to do so. Magnus accepts that you are not ready for the role in anything but title yet but Pearlis is the only place you can learn your job and make an impression on the men you will one day command." Gueryn's tone was gentle, but the words implacable. Wyl grimaced. "You can't stamp your mark from sleepy Argorn," Gueryn added, wishing they could have had a few months—weeks even—just to get the boy used to the idea of having no parents.

Gueryn thought of the mother. Fragile and pretty, she had loved Fergys Thirsk and his gruff ways with a ferocity that belied her sweet, gentle nature. She had succumbed, seven years previous and after a determined fight, to the virulent coughing disease that had swept through Morgravia's south. If she had not been weakened from Ylena's long and painful birth she might have pulled through. The disease killed many in the household, mercifully sparing the children.

Although he rarely showed it outwardly, Wyl seemed to miss her in his own reserved way. For all his rough-and-tumble boyishness, Gueryn thought, Wyl obviously adored women. The ladies of the household loved him back, spoiling him with their affections but often whispering pitying words about his looks.

There was no escaping the fact that Wyl Thirsk was not a handsome boy. The crown of thick orange hair did nothing to help an otherwise plain, square face, and those who remembered the boy's grandfather said that Wyl resembled the old man in uncanny fashion—his ugliness was almost as legendary as his soldiering ability. The red-headed Fergys Thirsk had been no oil painting either, which is why he had lived with constant surprise that his beautiful wife had chosen to marry him. Many would understand if the betrothal had been arranged but Helyna of Ramon had loved him well and had brooked no argument to her being joined to this high-ranking, plainspoken, even plainer-looking man who walked side by side with a King.

Vicious whispers at the court, of course, accused her of choosing Thirsk for his connections but she had relentlessly proved that the colorful court of Morgravia held little interest for her. Helyna Thirsk had had no desire for political intrigues or social climbing. Her only vanity had been her love of fine clothes, which Fergys had lavished on his young wife, claiming he had nothing else to spend his money on.

Wyl interrupted his thoughts. "Gueryn, what do we know about this Celimus?"

He had been waiting for just this question. "I don't know him at all but he's a year or two older than you, and from what I hear he is fairly impressed with being the heir," he answered tactfully.

"I see," Wyl replied. "What else do you *hear* of him? Tell me honestly."

Gueryn nodded. Wyl should not be thrown into this arena without knowing as much as he could. "The King, I gather, continues to hope Celimus might be molded into the stuff Morgravia can be proud of, although I would add that Magnus has not been an exceptional father. There is little affection between them."

"Why?"

"I can tell you only what your father has shared. King Magnus married Princess Adana. It was an arranged marriage. According to Fergys, they disliked each other within days of the ceremony and it never got any easier between them. I saw her on two occasions and it is no exaggeration that Adana was a woman whose looks could take any man's breath away. But she was cold. Your father said she was not just unhappy but angry at the choice of husband and despairing of the land she had come to. She had never wanted to come to Morgravia, believing it to be filled with peasants."

The boy's eyes widened. "She said that?"

"And plenty more apparently."

"Where was she from?"

"Parrgamyn—I hope you can dredge up its location from all those geography lessons?"

Wyl made a face at Gueryn's disapproving tutorly tone. He knew exactly where Parrgamyn was situated, to the far northwest of Morgravia, in balmy waters about two hundred nautical miles west of the famed Isle of Cipres. "Exotic then?"

"Very. Hence Celimus's dark looks."

"So she would have been of Zerque faith?" he wondered aloud, and Gueryn nodded. "Go on," Wyl encouraged, glad to be thinking about something other than the pain of his father's death.

Gueryn sighed. "A long tale really, but essentially she hated the King, blamed her father for his avarice in marrying her off to what she considered an old man, and poisoned the young Celimus's mind against his father."

"She died quite young, though, didn't she?"

The soldier nodded. "Yes, but it was the how that caused the ultimate rift between father and son. Your father was with the King when the hunting accident happened and could attest to the randomness of the event. Adana lost her life with an arrow through her throat."

"The King's?" Wyl asked, shifting in his saddle. "My father never said anything about this to me."

"The arrow was fletched in the King's very own colors. There was no doubt whose quiver it had come from."

"How could it have happened?"

Gueryn shrugged. "Who knows? Fergys said the Queen was out riding where she should not have been and Magnus shot badly. Others whispered, of course, that his aim was perfect, as always." He arched a single eyebrow. It spoke plenty.

"So Celimus has never forgiven his father?"

"You could say. Celimus worshiped Adana as much as his father despised her. But in losing his mother very early there's something you and Celimus have in common and this might be helpful to you," he offered. "The lad, I'm told, is already highly accomplished in the arts of soldiering too. He has no equal in the fighting ring amongst his peers. Sword or fists, on horseback or foot, he is genuinely talented."

"Better than me?"

Gueryn grinned. "We'll see. I know of no one of your tender years who is as skilled in combat—excluding myself at your age, of course." He won a smile from the boy at this. "But, Wyl, a word of caution. It would not do to whip the backside of the young Prince. You may find it politic to play second fiddle to a king-in-waiting."

Wyl's gaze rested firmly on Gueryn. "I understand."

"Good. Your sensibility in this will protect you."

"Do I need protection?" Wyl asked, surprised.

Gueryn wished he could take back the warning. It was ill-timed but he was always honest with his charge. "I don't know yet. You are being brought to Pearlis to learn your craft and follow in your father's proud footsteps. You must consider the city your home now. You understand this? Argorn must rest in your mind as a country property you may return to from time to time. Home is Stoneheart now." He watched the sorrow as those last words took a firm hold on the boy. It was said now. Had to be aired, best out in the open and accepted. "The other reason the King is keen to have you in the capital is, I suspect, because he is concerned at his son's wayward manner."

"Oh?"

"Celimus needs someone to temper his ways. The King has been told you possess a similar countenance to your father and I gather this pleases him greatly. He has hopes that you and his son will become as close friends as he and Fergys were." Gueryn waited for Wyl to comment but the boy said nothing. "Anyway, friendship can never be forced, so let's just keep an open mind and see how it all pans out. I shall be with you the whole time."

Wyl bit his lip and nodded. "Let's not tarry then, Gueryn."

The soldier nodded in return and dug his heels into the side of his horse as the boy kicked into a gallop.

FIONA MCINTOSH'S

MASTERFUL EPIC FANTASY
THE PERCHERON SAGA

* * * ❧ * * *

ODALISQUE   978-0-06-089911-0

In the exotic land of Percheron, the fifteen-year-old heir to the throne, Boaz, must assume the mantle of leadership, guided by his trusted warrior adviser, Lazar. In the midst of roiling covert intrigue, a headstrong young woman is brought to Boaz's harem, inflaming unexpectedly strong feelings in both Boaz and Lazar. And, unbeknownst to all, the gods themselves are rising in a cyclical battle.

EMISSARY   978-0-06-089912-7

Lazar offered up his life to protect Ana, a prisoner in the forbidden harem of the great Stone Palace of Percheron, accepting punishment intended for the bewitching odalisque. Now, with Lazar's guiding hand absent from the city, Percheron has become a darker, more treacherous place, as the young Zar Boaz has to battle the machinations of his mother Herezah.

GODDESS   978-0-06-089913-4

While enemy ships threaten Percheron's harbor, heroic Lazar lies afflicted with the drezden illness. And Zaradine Ana has been taken prisoner by the mysterious Arafanz and his warriors, and is believed to be with child—carrying the heir to the throne, the unborn son of Zar Boaz.